Come Fly with Me

BOOKS BY CAMILLE DI MAIO

The Memory of Us
Before the Rain Falls
The Way of Beauty
The Beautiful Strangers
The First Emma
Until We Meet
A Parade of Wishes
Come Fly with Me

COME FLY WITH ME

A Novel

CAMILLE DI MAIO

LAKE UNION
PUBLISHING

This is a work of fiction. Names, characters, organizations, places, events, and incidents are either products of the author's imagination or are used fictitiously.

Published by Lake Union Publishing, Seattle

www.apub.com

EU Product Safety contact:
Amazon Publishing, Amazon Media EU S.à r.l.
38, avenue John F. Kennedy, L-1855 Luxembourg
amazonpublishing-gpsr@amazon.com

ISBN-13: 9781662523946 (paperback)
ISBN-13: 9781662523939 (digital)

Cover design by Shasti O'Leary Soudant
Cover image: © Stocktrek Images, Inc / Alamy; © Leonardo Baldini / ArcAngel; © Iris Sokolovskaya, © Watch The World / Shutterstock

Printed in the United States of America

To the World Wings family, particularly Nancy Gillespie, without whose untiring, unwavering, unparalleled help, this book would not exist. The women and men of Pan Am have made an impact of global proportions. They serve as models of bravery, class, and accomplishment, and I am honored to make this small contribution toward keeping the legacy alive.

Mass air travel—made possible in the jet age—may prove to be more significant to world destiny than the atom bomb. For there can be no atom bomb potentially more powerful than the air tourist, charged with curiosity, enthusiasm, and goodwill, who can roam the four corners of the world, meeting in friendship and understanding the people of other nations and races.

—*Juan Trippe, founder of Pan American World Airways*

PROLOGUE

Mo'orea, French Polynesia
Today

I didn't think it would take this long to get back here. To the claw-shaped island that has worked its way into my dreams for all these years. These decades. Little has changed since we sat here. Coconuts still wash up to the shore, bobbing in the shallow waves, their wispy strands fanning out like your hair did when you floated gleefully in these turquoise waters. Chestnuts still rest on the ground, waiting to be picked up and boiled and enjoyed. Children still swim in nothing more than their underwear, diving into the deepest, darkest spots of the reef.

I've forgotten how much I loved watching the children. There are four in front of me now, giggling as the breeze tickles them. Their ages are similar to my great-grandchildren, but what different lives they lead.

Oh, to be a child again. To have minds and skin unblemished by life's inevitable burns. Where every path holds possibility.

Unstained. Unclaimed. Unjaded.

I have seen much in my life. Traveled to remote countries. Met fascinating people. Eaten exceptional food. And yet I've learned that while those moments are enviable, a life of simplicity surrounded by the ones I love is the greatest luxury imaginable.

I open my straw tote, purchased so many years ago at the two-story open market in Papeete, just across the water from where I sit now. It is brittle from age and its weave has loosened.

My bones, too, are brittle and my skin loose.

But at the time of its green newness, and our own carefree beginnings, we filled it with freshly picked avocados and ripe papayas and hired a fisherman to take us here to Ōpūnohu Bay. We shared our secrets and spilled our tears and promised that someday we would come back here together.

Here we are, then, dear one. You and me. Not quite the ending to the story we imagined.

But I will smell the jasmine-scented air for you, and I will delight in the children, and I will marvel as the fish and the birds come together at the water's surface to vie for the same morsels. A kiss where water and sky meet.

And I will spread your ashes across these shores. You said it was the most beautiful place you'd ever seen, and I agreed. I'll ensure that you get to stay here forever.

CHAPTER ONE

Judy

1962
New York
Pan American Office Building

It takes everything in me to keep my leg from twitching. The soles of my only pair of dress shoes will echo down the vast, near-empty hall if I am not still. Such a change from this morning, when the acoustics had been muffled by rows and rows of chairs filled with hundreds of perfect, eager girls who know the same thing I do: that most of us will be turned down from this thing we want so desperately.

Or in my case, need.

One in fifty will be awarded the signature blue uniform. One in fifty will be deemed the best of the best of the best.

Only fashion models and movie stars garner more notoriety than a Pan American stewardess. Raquel and Brigitte and Sophia—they are the undisputed darlings of the screen, but you can't get up close and personal with them. They are relegated to the flatness of glossy magazine paper and celluloid filmstrips, at least for the average admirer.

For the price of a seat across the ocean, however, you can enjoy the rapt and enthusiastic attention of a stewardess as you shoot across the sky in a metal tube fitted with wings and engines before landing in the exotic destination of your choice.

I sound like an advertisement. Maybe I'm pursuing the wrong side of things, but I suspect the women who work on Madison Avenue are more often the secretaries, not the copywriters.

I reach into my purse and pull out my good-luck charm. A bottle of English Leather cologne. Nearly empty, but forever stained with the amber-colored remnants of what once was. I don't have to open it to know that its initial citrus scent mellows into something warm and evokes the season of fall when it settles onto skin. One of the things that reminds me most of my dad. I used to dive into the piles of leaves he raked and giggle with the innocence of one who doesn't know what is to come. Always smelling the English Leather that he wore every day.

I imagine him cheering me on. Proud that I'd come here to rectify the horrible mistake I'd made.

My dad gave me a copy of Frank Sinatra's album *Come Fly with Me* when I was nineteen. It wasn't even my birthday or a special occasion—just something he'd seen in a record-store window and knew I'd like. He often did things like that. He put a big pink bow on it and laid it on my bed so I'd see it when I came home from school. I listened to that thing until the grooves formed deep canyons in the vinyl and rendered it unplayable. I'd stare at Frank's big blue eyes on the cover as he stuck his thumb out and pointed to the TWA stairs behind him and invited me to escape with him to all the places he'd sung about.

Capri. Mandalay. Paris.

London. Brazil. Hawaii.

And yet here I am at Pan American headquarters—it almost feels like a betrayal to that faded, well-loved album cover. If things don't go well here, I'll indeed apply at Trans World Airlines. But there is one very important difference between the two companies: Pan American only flies international routes, and I need to get as far, far away as possible.

Even an ocean may not be enough.

I take a deep breath, telling myself that I have nothing to worry about. I've done my homework, and I'm ready for any questions they can throw at me. I borrowed aviation books from the library and hid them in the cellar behind the Christmas decorations, reading them only in the daytime when I was alone. I can tell them that the Wright brothers first flew their airship composed of sticks and canvas sixty years ago. Or that it had been only five years since Boeing unveiled the 707—a jet clipper that could fly straight across the Atlantic Ocean with only one stop to refuel in Newfoundland.

If it comes down to a history quiz, I will ace it. I always was a good student. But it's not a history lesson that passengers want, is it? They want to cross the miles in as much comfort as possible. Pampered by the starlets of the sky.

The young woman across from me is called into one of the interview rooms. Upon first glance, she is beautiful in a girl-next-door, Donna Reed sort of way, a trick of cosmetics enhancing her simple appearance.

The hardness of life has dulled my own features prematurely, and I hope I've mustered one half of this girl's talent to revive them. I borrowed mascara and rouge from my neighbor Ronelle for today's interview, determined to paint on some of my prior verve. The lipstick was a gift from her—brand new in glossy red Elizabeth Arden packaging.

It's not all that Ronelle has given—she's risked much to make sure I could get here without anyone finding out.

I am counting on our plan working.

My legs are itching again, as I feel my stockings compress my skin. But more than likely, it's due to an excess of nerves.

What if someone here learns what I've taken great pains to conceal?

The girl to my right pulls a compact out of a handbag embellished with embroidered flowers. Expensive, if I had to guess. The kind I couldn't even dream of affording.

The kind I might have been able to buy if I'd made different choices. If I'd listened to my mother's advice. But that is a topic still so delicate that I can't let myself think on it.

She pulls a red pencil from the bag and lines her lips, just outside their natural boundary, making them appear to be plumper than they naturally are. Then she takes a matching shade of lipstick and fills it all in, and I have to admit that the effect is extraordinary. Already graced with matinee-idol beauty, the enhancements serve to elevate her to goddess status.

I am clearly not the only one who thinks so.

"Beverly Caldwell." A man steps out of one of the interview rooms and looks at his clipboard. And when Beverly stands—grace and elegance and sultriness all in one unbelievable package—it is as if it is the first time he has seen the dawn, its magnificent light rising until the full comprehension of its brilliance reaches his eyes. He quickly moves the clipboard down to waist level, and, as man's predilections are not unknown to me, I can see that she has turned him into a teenage boy once again, with her a pinup of his youth live and in the flesh. I watch, engrossed, as the silent exchange unfolds, and I have no doubt that she is fully aware of the power she wields. Aware and adept at using it to her advantage. She walks toward him with a look of innocence on her face and a sashay in her high-heeled step that could make an onlooker seasick. Oh yes. She is clearly well practiced in the art of femininity, and I doubt there is a man alive who would not be conquered if she set her sights upon him.

She reminds me of Marilyn Monroe, who recently made headlines for singing to Kennedy on national television. Happy birthday, indeed, Mr. President.

Whatever will the male passengers do if she is hired?

I am not envious. Such a presence has a lifespan of one, maybe two decades before the inevitable peak of perfection starts to diminish. Like the lilac bushes my mother used to tend outside my childhood home. In May, their purple blossoms would burst with fragrance, but by June, they'd withered and dried before falling to the ground.

Beauty is fleeting.

But in this moment, in this one-in-fifty endeavor, such advantages make all the difference.

As the door closes behind them, I try to put all thoughts of competition out of my head because it will only deject me. I know nothing of her circumstances nor the situations of any of the hundreds of girls who have fidgeted alongside me during this long, long wait today. I know only my own, and it is laced with this truth: *I have to get* this job.

It may, quite literally, be a matter of life and death.

CHAPTER TWO

Judy

"Judy Goodman."

I steel my nerves and walk into my interview room—the one at the end of the hall. Three people sit at a table across from me, and I have the unsettling sensation that I am the defendant in a Perry Mason courtroom drama. I push the thought aside. I must remain strong. I cannot make mistakes.

I imagine a stack of books atop my head, just as Ronelle rehearsed with me. And when I sit in the chair they offer, I cross my ankles and sweep them to the side and fold my hands in my lap. The picture of effortless poise. I recall my application. The truths. The exaggerations. I read over my paperwork seven times before sending it in. I have to pretend to be confident even if I am far from it.

Smile. Show my teeth, but not my gums. Smooth down the flyaways. Speak in a clear and calm manner. Strategically place my delicately manicured hands so that they'll be seen. Nail biters are disqualified—a nervous stewardess makes for an anxious passenger.

In my purse, I have my birth certificate as the proof of citizenship they will require, as well as the transcript from the two years of college I completed before dropping out. My grades were top tier, my scholarship secured. I hope it's enough to impress them.

I wonder how many of the girls completed their diplomas.

I feel the two women scrutinize me, though I cannot say that it is with unkindness. I know it's their job to be meticulous. The good name of Pan American rests squarely on the slender shoulders of its stewardesses, and they need to determine if I am worthy and able to carry such a mantle.

One woman has hair so black it could only come out of a bottle, wrinkles on her skin revealing the age she's trying to mask. The other is just a little older than myself and has the weary look of someone who is relieved that this is the last interview of the day.

I understand.

The third person is a man, different from the one I saw earlier. He is standing with his back leaned against the painted brick wall. Brown hair, light-brown shirt, dark-brown pants and shoes. I don't need to look at his left hand to determine that he's not married—if he is, his wife has no imagination when she purchases his clothes. But his uninspired attire does not hide the fact that he is quite nice looking. Square jaw, striking blue eyes. Like Sinatra.

I shouldn't think these things. I shouldn't notice those things.

I take a deep but imperceptible breath and remind myself that I am here for one reason and can't give in to distractions.

The woman with the jet-black hair seems to be in charge.

"Name," she says.

"Judy Goodman."

True.

"Age."

"Twenty-three, last week."

True.

"Height."

"Five foot five."

True.

"Weight."

"One hundred seventeen pounds."

True.

"What language do you speak other than English?"

"French."

True.

I am breathing with a little more ease. I can answer all these questions with honesty.

I have my father to thank for the French. He hailed from Montreal, a veteran of the First Canadian Army that went to Brest. He insisted on speaking his native language to me before I was even old enough to go to school. My mother encouraged it, ignoring admonitions from the women at church that we were no better than them. She'd lived under the shadow of their suspicion ever since she'd married an *outsider*. The gossips saw no use for French in Red Lion, Pennsylvania.

Corn would forever be *corn*. Not *maïs*. A *cow* would forever be a *cow*. Not a *vache*.

Foreigner would forever bear a black mark, as étrangers were seldom embraced in the superstitious town. Locals didn't even cross the Susquehanna River into the next county if they could avoid it.

But my father's gift is now my salvation—Pan Am requires fluency in something besides English.

If only that was all they wanted.

"Marital status," the woman continues, drawing me out from my memories.

A rock forms in my stomach, and I feel the acidity of bile well up. I don't know if I can do this.

I was taught that lying is wrong.

I am careful to keep my voice steady. "Single."

False.

I cover my left hand with my right, keeping my blush-pink nails visible. Although the wedding band with its splinter of a diamond grows cold in my coin purse, the indentation on my skin is noticeable to one looking for it. My heart beats faster, faster. It is my first deception, and I hope there won't be the need for more.

"Have you ever flown before?"

My smile widens, stretching to the capacity of the muscles. "Yes. Several times out of Harrisburg."

False. I don't think this is a required experience, but I'm afraid to admit that I am such a novice. What would they say if I told them that the only airplanes I'd ever seen up close were the crop dusters on my cousin's farm in Reading?

I don't like this person I've had to become.

The man speaks up, looking at me for the first time. His Sinatra eyes are soft. Kind.

"Why do you want to be a Pan American stewardess?"

It's the first question that isn't merely a collection of facts that make up the biography of Judy Goodman. It's one that seeks to know *me.*

I keep smiling, confident that weeks of rinsing with hydrogen peroxide have turned my teeth dazzlingly white.

"To see the world and to represent the good name of Pan American Airlines."

True.

My heart slows down a bit. I think of the map I've had since childhood and all the pins I put in it as I learned about new places to explore. Blue for those of highest priority. Yellow for those of moderate interest. And white for those I'd rather skip.

There were very few white pins. I wanted to see it all.

I think of Frank Sinatra's words that suggest that exotic adventures are within my reach. Far beyond the banks of the Susquehanna. Far beyond the box in the attic where that map is folded, hidden from sight.

I don't know what the other girls before me have said, but I am certain that it is a variation on a theme. We are still caught in the shackles of a culture that limits our choices to teachers, nurses, or mothers, though there are cracks in that thinking that widen every day.

But the lure of being something else altogether is intoxicating. To do it in tropical locations and world capitals is positively heady.

I look at the faces across from me and see that my answer pleases the panel but does not surprise them.

What I do not tell them is this: if I don't escape living under my husband's roof, I fear that he will kill me.

◆ ◆ ◆

The train ride home is nerve racking. Already, I have gotten up three times to use the lavatory, as if all the emotions that I held at bay liquefied at the first opportunity. I chose poorly in selecting a window seat—I'd looked forward to watching the scenery go by. But I'd clearly irritated my seatmate, and I promised that this would be the last time.

I hope it will not be my third lie of the day. I wouldn't want to form a habit of it.

I look at my watch and pray that everything is on schedule.

Three and a half hours from Grand Central to Lancaster, then half an hour in a taxi back to Red Lion.

I'd been naive to think that the interviewers would make a decision on the spot. They said they'd notify applicants by letter within two weeks, which might as well be two centuries to me. It consumes me with a new anxiety: I will have to be vigilant in getting to the mailbox before Henry does.

Even if they do not accept me, the mere discovery that I'd applied will land me in heaps of trouble.

I shiver at the thought. I am exhausted by the end of each day, spent from having to consider every move, every thought, hoping that I don't do or say something that angers him.

What will I be coming home to today?

If all goes as planned, Henry will not be back until several hours after my arrival, and I'll have time to whip up the shepherd's pie that he likes so much. The one with ground beef, plenty of carrots, no peas, chunky potatoes. He's always in a better mood after that. I would make it every day if that was all it took to appease him, but he is not so easily tricked.

Ronelle cajoled her husband, Richard, into introducing himself to Henry and inviting him to his parents' hunting cabin in the Poconos for a couple of nights. *Cabin* being a loose word for the elegant mountain house that she showed me in photographs. They boast an impressive whiskey collection and a trophy room lined with souvenirs from their shoots. Though I know little of such things, I've been told that their rifle collection alone is insured for twenty thousand dollars.

Guns and alcohol sound like an ill-advised combination, but Ronelle knew it was my only hope to keep Henry from discovering that I'd gone to New York for the day. He'd never resist an offer like that, no matter his feelings about the Rorbaughs. The scandal of their mixed marriage permeated the community despite it being perfectly legal in Pennsylvania. But a chance to pretend, even for a weekend, that he was more than the supervisor of a small-time concrete company in a small-time town was catnip to his big-time ego.

I don't know what I'd do without Ronelle. We met four months ago when I was up early shoveling snow from the driveway so that Henry could leave for work on time. She invited me to her place for coffee, and I wanted nothing more than to say yes. A hot drink and the hope of making a friend. But I declined. My husband believed that other women would be bad influences on me, so until he met them and gave them the Henry Goodman Stamp of Approval, I was not allowed to visit beyond the outward pleasantries that were the basics of human interaction. Hellos at the mailbox and such trifles.

And under no circumstances would he condone my friendship with a woman who had dark-brown skin and the audacity to marry a *good local boy*. *Local* being a euphemism for a color he found acceptable. Not that he'd come out and say it that way. And not taking into consideration that being from the adjacent town of Shrewsbury, Ronelle was certainly *local* by any reasonable definition.

But Ronelle, I came to learn, was not made of convention or passivity or demureness, and her searing sense of justice had bolstered me ever since that day when I took the first step toward thinking for myself.

The last time I'd acted on my own accord was when I spoke those vows—*I do.*

I was hopeful that the merits of this time would undo the mistakes of the last.

It had to.

Maybe it was the full moon or the bone-deep cold of that Pennsylvania morning, but something snapped in me that snowy day. Once the taillights of Henry's Chevy had disappeared, I trudged over to Ronelle's house through the knee-high drifts and rang her doorbell with gusto. I didn't take the normal precautions to hide the bruises on my arms as I removed my jacket. And when Ronelle saw them, I didn't make up a story about where they'd come from. If she was meant to be a friend, she would have to see my life for what it was. And if she was one of those women who would defend the husband come hell or high water, then that wasn't a relationship I wanted.

She turned out to be the former.

Oh, God, did she ever.

It was a lot to reveal on the first day of knowing someone, but it also sped us past the do-you-have-children-are-you-from-here-what-are-your-hobbies stage and thrust us into the kind of meaningful friendship that usually takes years to cultivate.

Ronelle Rorbaugh loves a cause, and I became her newest one.

By lunchtime, it felt as if we'd known each other forever, and she'd talked me into something I would have never had the courage to do on my own: leave my lamentable marriage.

CHAPTER THREE

Judy

The letter from Pan Am arrives precisely two weeks after the interview, and I'd spent every one of those impossibly long days fashioning myself into the perfect, perfect wife. I cooked all Henry's favorite dishes. Ironed his shirts with extra care and optimal starch. Curled my hair the way he liked it even though the pins poked my scalp when I tried in vain to sleep on them. I wore the satin nightgowns that he preferred and let him do the things to me in it that he liked. If he noticed all the effort, he didn't say anything.

But his moodiness stayed at bay. So I must have done everything right.

I began to wonder if I had been the problem all the time. Had I not been putting in *enough* effort? Had I incurred his wrath because I hadn't tried my best?

Ronelle told me such thoughts were weeds in the garden of my mind and to pluck them right out before they took root. But it was tempting to believe when they were all I heard from my husband.

Henry's criticisms had seeped into my thoughts like a slow poison whose effects only show themselves after a duration. Like the seemingly harmless erosion of water over a rock whose damage is revealed in crevices and canyons only after much time.

The peace was short lived.

On the twelfth day, Henry's boss turned down his request for a raise. The cashier at the cigarette shop shorted him by seventy-five cents. And the Phillies were shut out by the Pirates, creating some razzing at work toward those who'd bet on the losing Pennsylvania team. All of these riled him out of the quiet I'd been tentatively enjoying, and I paid the price. My skin was going to be a rainbow of yellow, green, purple.

But not my face. Henry never touched me anywhere that couldn't be covered up. It was the *one thing* that convinced me that these were not just bursts of emotion that he couldn't control. They were actions that had *just* enough precision behind them as to keep me from being able to believe that they were anything but intentional.

Because I had a long history of making excuses for the man who had so enthralled me when we first met.

The man who had caused an irreversible rift between me and my mother. A division that was never healed before she went to be with the angels, just a few years after my father.

Ronelle snapped me out of my doubts when she came over the next morning. In fact, she sat in my kitchen, holding my hands, crying as if the pain was her own. Pleading with me. To come to her house. Or go to her in-laws'.

But Henry would find me at either of them. And then Pan Am wouldn't find me at all.

I had to remain here until I got their letter.

Ronelle ran home to grab her Polaroid Land Camera, taking pictures of my skin until the package of film was spent and we were left with a mosaic of images spread across the table. They could not portray the colors, but even the gray tones revealed the truth. Insurance in case . . . well, I don't know. Henry likes to go to the horse races with his buddy since grade school—the chief of police in Red Lion. So I would have no recourse through local law enforcement. But Ronelle was right to insist that we have evidence.

If the Pan Am letter is a rejection, I will find some other way to leave. I have to.

Today, the green shoots of spring have given way to the blossoms that suggest that summer is upon us. New life heralded by my small flower garden and, I hope, a sign of good things to come. I see Ronelle step out of her house and make her way toward mine. Of course, she'd waited a good half hour after Henry had left for work just to be safe.

I fling the door open before she gets a chance to knock. As excited as I am to open the envelope that arrived with the mail this morning, I wait until she finishes the careful routine we'd put in place.

She removes her boots outside the front door so as not to leave any tracks, and she has no trace of perfume or lotion or anything whose scent would linger. Henry still knows nothing of our friendship, let alone the mornings that we spend planning my departure.

My escape.

I hold up the envelope, waving it in the air.

"It came?" she asks as she pulls me into a hug. I cling to her like the life preserver that she is, her heart beating against mine in a unified rhythm that makes me feel the kind of love that I haven't known since that of my mother's.

She sways, still holding me as she speaks. I can smell maple syrup on her breath. "Wow—fourteen days on the nose. That speaks well of their punctuality."

I stand back, my chest constricting in anticipation of what the letter will say. My skin feels clammy and my head is light. I grip one of the decorative spindles by the front door to steady myself.

"Am I really doing this?" I ask her.

She nods, and her dark curls bounce. She threads her fingers through my hair, and I bite my lip to keep from crying. I'm going to miss her. Because I'm leaving whether it's with Pan Am or not. "You're really doing this. You have to, Judy."

"What if he finds me?" I manage to admit the fear that has been gnawing at me. Just the thought sends a chill through my lungs. I can hear the quiver in my voice.

She puts her hands on either side of my arms and looks at me with her familiar intensity.

"How will he? I'm not going to tell him. Richard's not going to tell him. And you'll open a post office box wherever you end up so he can't find an address."

"I'm just afraid that half a world away isn't enough."

"Then you'll apply to the space program and hope they take you on as an astronaut. You can wave to John Glenn as you pass him in orbit. They'd do well to shoot that pretty face of yours up to the moon instead of that damn test monkey."

I grin. Ronelle does that to me. She makes me smile no matter what.

"I wish you could come with me," I say under my breath.

She shakes her head. "I am happy here making my mark with Richard Rorbaugh at my side in this funny little corner of the world. Besides—they don't let women like me apply." And then she grins as she waves a finger in the air. "At least, not *yet*."

She always believes that tomorrow will be better, and not for the first time, I am swept up in her unrelenting optimism.

She supports me by the elbow as we walk toward the kitchen. The letter rattles as my unsteady hand tries and fails to hold on to it. It falls onto the green linoleum tiles, covering a patch that has been worn from a chair rubbing against it over time.

I pick it up.

"Do you want me to open it?" she asks. She takes it from my hand, pulling it with some force because I don't even realize that I'm gripping it.

She takes a knife from the drawer and slides it through the top. I think, *What does it matter if it's jagged; just rip it open,* but I realize that her methodical way of operating is exactly why I've gotten as far as I have with all this. Without Ronelle, I might not have the courage to leave. Without Ronelle, it might have been too late.

I close my eyes. I hear her take some papers out and then she *shuffles* them, and I wonder if that is a good sign or a bad sign that there are several, but she doesn't keep me waiting long because she lets out a gasp.

I look up, and her hand is covering her mouth. Her eyes are wet, and her mascara is melting off her lashes.

"Judy. *You're in!*"

CHAPTER FOUR

Beverly

Bernice brings my mail in on the new bone-inlay tray that my mother found in an antique store on Park Avenue. That gaudy shop with the jewel-encrusted cheetahs guarding the way as you walk in. I talked her out of buying those, at least. Lordy, this apartment doesn't need any more ostentation than it already has.

There are six letters today in as many colors. Five of them are invitations—I can tell by the size and the carefully written script. I recognize two of them and can guess what they contain. Pamela's handwriting slants to the left, just like her politics, and she's surely including me in her twenty-first-birthday party that will no doubt be held at the Plaza. A brunch in the atrium, the same place she had her twentieth birthday and her nineteenth and her eighteenth. Pamela has an abundance of money and a dearth of originality.

Suzanne's handwriting slants right, just like *her* politics. Perhaps there is a psychological meaning to be found there, but that is for me to ponder and someone else to analyze. Her printing is so precise that it seems as if it was produced by a machine. No doubt it's an announcement for her annual gala raising money for the cause du jour and landing her a spot in the society pages pretending that she is deeply concerned about clean water in countries she's never heard of. Because

God forbid she set foot in a place that doesn't have a five-star hotel and chilled mimosas at breakfast.

All of the invitations are jarringly alike, rote copies of those that arrive at our penthouse apartment regularly. But if the sixth envelope contains what I hope it does, I'll be able to send my regrets to all of the above because I will be leaving all this opulence behind—with few actual regrets at all.

New York City is the only home I've ever known, and for better or worse, I am one of these girls that I am casually disparaging. But my soul is restless for something else. It always has been. And I don't know why.

I slip the last envelope out from under the others. The address is typewritten, and the blue Pan American logo sits in the top left corner. The *blue meatball*, as I've heard it called. A pedestrian nickname for such an illustrious company.

The envelope is thick.

Does that mean what I think it does?

What I hope it does?

I am nervous despite all evidence that I am everything they say they are looking for in a stewardess. Check the boxes: education bought and paid for at Marymount School of New York, housed, unsurprisingly, in a mansion built by the Vanderbilts. Cosmetics purchased at the Bergdorf counter. Figure carved during daily laps in our rooftop swimming pool. French taught by private tutors.

Raised to be the perfect society wife.

Except that's not what I want to be.

I don't know what I want. I just know that I won't find it here.

I'm twenty-two years old, and my whole life has been charted out for me since that disappointing moment in which they learned I wasn't the boy Mr. Wall Street expected. (After the *New York Times* ran a feature piece about my father, giving him that moniker, it's what I call him behind his back because, jeepers, *Daddy* doesn't exactly roll off the tongue.)

If the gossip pages are to be believed, and Mr. Wall Street is to be mollified, I'll have a *ring by spring* courtesy of Frederick Bahr, and though his name bears a close resemblance to the romantic professor of Louisa May Alcott's tales, this one is a junior version of my father through and through. Down to sporting tailored wool suits from Brooks Brothers. Pinstripes, of course.

If my father took to wearing purple clown shoes, his illustrious protégé would no doubt follow in his comically large footprints.

They say imitation is the highest form of flattery, don't they?

I do have one thing to thank young Mr. Bahr for, however. It is because of him that I've learned my own power. A walk, a glance, a pout, a smile. The mere *possibility* of what might be ahead should the match go forward transforms him, especially in the few moments we find ourselves alone.

Frederick *is* a handsome one, I'll give him that. And there are a dozen girls at every party who are green with envy that I'm the one on his arm. Don't think that doesn't give me a small thrill, or that I am some kind of villain for thinking so. Whether we admit it or not, we women are so used to being underestimated and overlooked that we welcome any chance to win approval.

We all think it. I'm just honest enough to say it.

I know there are worse things than getting engaged to a tall, attractive man whose pulse shoots to *full speed ahead* every time he sees me. If he were some kind of weasel or troll or reprobate, some would understand. The fact that Frederick Bahr is considered *such* a very, very good catch will make it even more shocking that I plan to refuse him if he asks.

Oh, I'll do it kindly. I'm not cruel, and I'll get no thrill from turning him down. I'm just not made of the stuff that would give us a happily ever after. It's for his own good. He'll see that someday.

Marrying him—or anyone here in New York for that matter—would only perpetuate the *sameness* that has slowly wilted me for years.

I will have the *same* friends that I do now. I will shop in the *same* fine stores. Summer in the *same* idyllic Hamptons playgrounds.

Carve the *same* path for the daughters we might have.

Wish that they were sons so that they might have a better chance at something *different*.

I don't presume at all to compare my woes to the many who have to worry about where their next meal will come from instead of *who* will prepare it and *what* they will place on the china plate before me. So I'm not seeking sympathy where it's not warranted.

And yet, once the hunger of the belly is satisfied, a new hunger rears its head—the bone-deep ache to find out what you're capable of.

I yearn to discover who I am on my own instead of settling into a definition that I've inherited by the lottery of my birth.

No matter the cost.

And it may cost me everything.

Father has threatened to cut me off if I turn Freddie Boy down once he gets around to asking. His father's in shipping and mine's in trading, and somewhere in there is a strategic partnership that I care nothing about. If it were simply about the money, I could learn to get over that. But I know that Mr. Wall Street merely has to say the word, and every door in New York will close in my face.

And as much as I want to leave, as scant regard I have for the people in his circle, it is the only life I've ever known. To walk away is not to say that I wish to discard it forever.

I worry, though, that his considerable influence may extend beyond the confines of Manhattan. Christmas cards arrive every year from Juan Trippe—the founder of Pan American, having met my father when they were aboard the *Hindenburg* on what was hailed as the Millionaires Flight twenty-six years ago. Yale alum both, and though my father was seven years behind Mr. Trippe, it was nevertheless enough to spur the annual correspondence.

If I cross my father, will he retaliate by making the call that could derail my career before it gets a chance to start?

It's why I've kept my interview secret thus far.

I look up in the mirror and pull my hair back to tie it into a bun, imagining myself in the fitted uniform, the pert hat. Thinking about the adventures that await. I purse my lips in an attempt to convince myself of my determination.

It works.

I will not be stopped.

Inside, my blue blood runs red.

CHAPTER FIVE

Beverly

The day after the Pan Am letter comes (*Congratulations,* it read. *You've been accepted . . .*), my mother invites me to join her at the hairdresser's. It is one of my favorite things we do together, and one of the few places we never run into anyone we know. The day always follows the same course. She has our driver drop us off on 36th near Herald Square and we eat lunch at Keens Steakhouse. Though it's been over fifty years since actress Lillie Langtry waltzed through these doors in her feather boa and sued the gentleman-only establishment to allow for her entry, my mother feels like it's an act of rebellion to eat there.

It's like she's a different woman on these days. When she steps away from her role as the perfectly put-together society woman of Park Avenue, she can actually be a bit of fun.

Dare I say, she can seem—maybe just a bit—*happy*?

I've even known her to jump onto a chalk-drawn hopscotch game and wave goodbye to the children as she leaves it behind. It was just the one time, but still.

After our filets mignons, mine medium rare and hers charred to a crisp—what a waste, in my opinion—we walk a few blocks to the cathedral-like marbled halls of Penn Station. Very soon, we'll have to plan a new route, as it was just announced that the once-magnificent train station has fallen victim to modernization and a desire for a flashy new sports arena. Train travel has given way to the jet age, and although I am wholly enthusiastic about getting up in the air, I cannot help but be saddened by the impending loss to the city's glorious past.

I'm feeling rather nostalgic today. It's not the norm for me. But then, that's the point.

By the time the train station is gone, I will have leveled my own history as well.

I will be many miles away, rebuilding myself.

I dare not glance at my mother. She will ask why my eyes are glossy. I've waited until the last minute to tell her, fearing that Mr. Wall Street will make that call to Mr. Trippe and my offer will be rescinded. Perhaps it's paranoia, but I can't take any chances.

We take the C train to Spring Street and then a shortcut through an alley to Sami's Salon in SoHo. It smells of flowers and hair spray, a concoction that formulates one of my fondest and earliest childhood memories. I asked my mother years ago why we come here and why we take such a circuitous route rather than having the driver bring us directly to the door front. She replied that Sami cuts hair better than anyone on Park Avenue and that she doesn't want to appear showy in front of the ladies who work there by arriving by chauffeur. It also explains why she leaves her jewelry at home and insists that I wear my simplest dress.

As usual, my mother has called ahead for an appointment, and Sami has a steaming plate of lumpia ready for us. Thin, crispy egg rolls that taste like I imagine heaven would. The texture of the flaky exterior and the softness of the ground beef and rice noodles.

She also has rambutan-flavored hard candies for me, as always. My favorite.

"What is a rambutan?" I once asked her when I was around nine years old. She showed me a photograph. It was a red, spiky fruit the size of a golf ball. When cut open, the top pops off like a hat and an egg-shaped jelly is revealed.

"May I have a real one?" I'd said, using my manners. I usually got anything I wanted if I asked politely and flashed a smile.

"No, no," Sami had said. "You won't find rambutans in New York. They come from the Philippines, where my family lives. My auntie sends me the candies to remind me of home."

I never asked her why she lives here and her family lives across the world because it didn't seem like something she wanted to talk about. But I did go home and look up the *Philippines* on the globe in my father's office.

So far away. Across the Pacific.

Today, my mother kisses Sami on the cheek, which I'd never seen her do to anyone on the Upper East Side. Sami has been an old woman for my whole life, and she could be sixty as easily as eighty. She is just shy of five feet tall and cuts hair standing on a rusted metal stool.

"Anything new? Or just a trim?"

My mother pulls a magazine cutout of Elizabeth Taylor from her purse, the movie star's hair full and alluring, but she sets it down and sighs.

"Just the usual," she says in resignation. And I know that she'll have her beautiful brown hair cut conservatively and close to her face. Just like always. Mrs. Wall Street isn't supposed to look like a bombshell. She's supposed to look respectable. To blend into the background in quiet elegance along with the brocade curtains and crystal sconces.

She hands me the picture. "Maybe for you, Beverly. This would look quite attractive with your high cheekbones."

I hold it up to the mirror and imagine Elizabeth Taylor's hair on my head, agreeing that it would suit me. And I am tempted to say yes. But I don't yet know what Pan Am will require. They hired me with this hairstyle—straight down my back to the halfway point, bangs straight across my forehead. Neat. Easy to pin up. Or easily changed if they so choose.

"No, thank you. Just a trim for me. Two inches."

I wonder again why we always come down here to SoHo for such humdrum choices, but I'm not complaining. The afternoons at Sami's with my mother every two months is nearly the only chance I get to fly outside the gilded cage we live in. A glimpse at that *different* that I so desperately crave.

Today, Mother takes a seat on the burgundy vinyl salon chair, not seeming to mind the tufts of cotton poking through the rips in its seams. This from the woman who goes berserk if an errant speck of dust dares to reveal itself on one of the fireplace mantels.

I wait to speak until Sami has begun work on my mother's hair. I already feel myself losing the courage. But I have to say what I have to say, and this may be my best chance. Even though I wish I could just disappear into the night and not have to tell my mother I've left New York. Left the life she's built for me.

I owe her this face-to-face confession.

At least here, I'll have Sami as a buffer. Instinctively, I know that Mother will not cause a scene in front of her.

"I can't make it to Mrs. Bahr's tea next week," I say, testing the waters.

My mother doesn't move, even as she speaks. Sami's scissors hover at the nape of her neck.

"Why ever not? She called me yesterday and asked if you were available on that date specifically. She wants you to meet some of her friends."

"I'm not engaged to Frederick, and everyone acts like I am."

Her head remains as still as one of the antique marble busts in our parlor while Sami works her magic. But her eyes search for mine in the mirror.

"Not *yet*," she says as she finds them.

I shudder. I need to get myself out of this entanglement.

"Not *ever*," I announce. I turn away. I can't meet her gaze.

Even Sami stops. She lowers her elbows to her hips. I get the sense that she knows more than she's letting on. My mother turns her chair to face me, and I finally look up. I'm not sure how to read her expression. Her jaw is firm, like she's upset. But her eyes are—*understanding?*

I have never seen this expression on her.

Mother doesn't like to have family conversations in front of *the help*, but she's not even trying to delay this until we're behind closed doors.

And then she says something I never, ever expected her to say.

"I'm so glad to hear it."

I jump out of my chair as if I've had an electric shock.

"What?"

So much for those classes in deportment. They didn't prepare me for *this*.

My mother's jaw spreads into a thin smile. "I'm so glad to hear it. Frederick is a nice enough boy, but he's not the one for you."

I plop back down, the puffy sound of the vinyl seat sighing out, and my skin tingles as confusion courses through my body.

She continues. "You got the job at Pan American, didn't you?"

"How—how did you know about that?"

Pulse. Pulse. Pulse. It feels like drums. My heart zipping to fight or flight.

Her smile widens, but her voice is sad. "Bernice knows who signs her paychecks."

I don't even have to ask how Bernice knows. There is nothing that gets past her. The Central Intelligence Agency would do well to steal her away from us.

"You're not angry?"

Sami gives up trying to work in this situation and rests her rail-thin body in the third salon chair. I don't blame her. This is going to be a conversation worth watching. Better than any show up on Broadway. And this one with a front-row seat.

My mother shakes her head, and little wisps of already-trimmed hair flutter to the ground. "Angry? No. Perhaps a little hurt. I wish you had confided in me."

Yes, this is why I love these days at Sami's. My mother becomes unrecognizable from the buttoned-up grande dame I otherwise know her to be.

"I wasn't sure if you or M—" I almost slip and say *Mr. Wall Street*, but I know she doesn't like that moniker, and I need her on my side. "I wasn't sure if you and Daddy would even notice."

She reaches across to my chair and takes my hands in hers. The warmth of the maternal gesture overwhelms me. It is not the norm for us, and I'm taken aback even as I'm starved for it. "I always thought there would be more time. But there's not. Whether you marry Frederick or fly to every corner of the globe, you're not mine anymore. And I'm not sure you ever have been, despite my efforts to the contrary."

I see Sami dab a tissue to her eyes.

"I'll always be yours," I begin. But the words feel like dialogue on a movie screen. She's playing the role of the caring mother, and I'm playing the role of the devoted daughter. Not that we aren't speaking with sincerity—but these sentiments are not a regular part of our vernacular. What if we have felt these things all along but just never said them aloud?

Could we have been wasting time all these years giving the performances that we were expected to? The roles we were cast to play? This is the seed of my doubt—that I've missed something that was right under my nose. Just as I'm about to leave it behind.

She leans back in her chair, and the vinyl again makes a sound like a sigh. Like it's expressing the emotion we're all feeling. "I got everything I ever wanted when I married your father. Stability, security, social standing."

I notice that she doesn't say *love*.

She continues. "And maybe it's a luxury to say this now that I have them. But they don't satisfy. Not really. They only feed one kind of hunger. But they suppress a truer one—the hunger of your heart."

I hold my breath. That's exactly what I'd been thinking this morning. How did she know? Or are we more alike than I'd ever considered?

A hint of regret sinks into my heart as the loss of time is imminent. And more apparent than ever.

"Then why—" I start.

And I realize that maybe my mother knows me better than I thought she did. Because she finishes my sentence for me. "Then why did I raise you to think that all of that is important?"

I nod. The debutante festivities. The elite schools. The positioning to get into the best parties.

The things that suffocated the woman I ached to be.

Her shoulders fold in, and in that gesture, she looks as small as Sami. "Because security is a siren. Once you have it, it takes a particular kind of courage to detach from its golden leash. And I'm afraid that I haven't been courageous enough for myself. Or for you."

She stands and walks over to my chair, turning it toward the mirror. She picks up a comb and works the end of my hair, just like she used to do when I was a little girl. But this time it's gentle. Not perfunctory. We're not in a hurry to be anywhere.

I have her eyes—dark and intense, flecked with green, as if embedded with shards of emeralds. I have my father's facial features, though—strong and determined. Stubborn.

"Anak na babae," she says in words that I have never heard and which come with no explanation.

"What will I say to Daddy?"

Her chest swells, and she holds a breath. "I will handle him."

"But he said—"

"I will handle him," she repeats.

Sami rises and walks over to us, and as the three of us stand, we are reflected in the mirror like a portrait. I look between them and at myself and am stunned to see something I'd never noticed.

Sami's eyes, too, are dark. Intense. Flecked with emerald tones.

We *all* have the same eyes.

Mo'orea, French Polynesia
Today

I'd originally planned to come here on the twentieth anniversary of your death. It seemed like a nice round number. But it took me that long to just to come to grips with what happened. Today, kids think nothing of visiting a psychologist. It's almost become a badge of honor. "My therapist said . . ."

My oldest granddaughter is in that line of work. I'm proud of her for that, and I picture her days spent sitting on a chair with a notebook in hand as a patient reclines on a leather chaise and talks. Or maybe that's just how it's done in the movies. I've never asked.

I'll bet she doesn't know that back in our day it was almost a scandalous word. That something must be wrong with you if you needed to ask for help. That it could—hush, hush—go on your permanent record. We didn't have phrases like post-traumatic stress disorder *to make sense of the traumatic things that we witnessed.*

We just covered up our unhealed wounds and lived life as people fraught with invisible scars.

Even when America's boys came home from Vietnam—bitter, bewildered, battered—we expected them to buck up and carry on as if they hadn't witnessed and done the most appalling things.

So, yes, it took me all of those twenty years to feel like I could do this. Like I was ready to put you to rest.

But I can't deny the guttural relief that swept over me when a cyclone named Veena struck the islands with her ninety-five-mile-per-hour wrath, destroying the roads and leaving tens of thousands of Tahitians homeless. Of course, my heart broke for those poor people. Especially since I could still picture so vividly their generous smiles and happy ways. The images on the news showed majestic palm trees that were felled like matchsticks, and I imagined all the feral roosters and chickens and dogs that roam the dirt streets being trapped beneath their fronds.

Flights were canceled—including mine—adding additional devastation to a country where no one could visit and bring their tourism dollars.

Veena saved me from having to face this moment, though.

After that, there were too many children, too many bills, too many excuses, and I did not return as I'd promised.

I hope, now, you can be at peace. That your soul has not wandered restlessly all this time because I failed to bring you back to these aqua-blue waters you so loved. But I'm here at last.

CHAPTER SIX

Judy

I almost miss my flight to Miami.

The day I'm supposed to leave, Henry comes down with a wretched cold and stays home from work. I'd planned to call a cab, get to the train station, and make my way to the airport in Philadelphia. But now that he's here, it's thrown a wrench in my ability to get away.

My suitcase is packed, and hidden in the attic. Every day for the past month, I'd taken one thing from our closet and put it away. I'd spread out the remaining clothes on their hangers, hoping that my husband didn't notice how sparse it was becoming. If he asked, I'd tell him that I was donating them to charity, though I'm sure his response would be that he didn't work long hours just so that I could give my things away. But it was better than the alternative—telling him I was leaving.

Additionally, I'd put aside some of the cash he gives me for groceries and gasoline, skimping where I can on dented cans, lesser cuts of meat, and anything that will add a few more dollars to my pocket.

I've never had an infant, but I've heard it said that men act like babies when they are sick. And I can attest to my husband's incessant neediness. Ever since I woke up this morning, I've been frantic attending to his every wish.

He wanted chicken broth—the homemade kind where I'd boil a carcass in water and vinegar. He wanted lemonade with honey in it. Fresh lemons, of course. Not the powdered mix. His pillows had to be fluffed just right.

I did it all.

I am spent.

But if I don't leave now, the plane will take off without me.

My salvation comes from a phone call. The pharmacist rings and says that Henry's medicine is ready, and I am quick on my feet to tell my husband that we'll save the dollar-fifty delivery fee if I pick it up myself.

He agrees and gives me the car keys and tells me to get a bottle of Coke while I'm there. Ice cold. None of that stuff sitting on a shelf *like a goddamn freeloader*. Whatever that is supposed to mean.

This is my chance. The flight is in three hours, and the drive to Philadelphia will take up two of them. I've already missed the train. So it's now or never.

I close the bedroom door behind me and lean against it to gather strength. My palm is sweaty as it rests against the chipped brass door-knob. My heart is beating as if it will leap out of my chest, but I have to keep my wits about me if I am to pull this off.

I look up at the attic and wish I'd chosen a different spot to hide my things. It would be a noisy endeavor to pull the ladder in from the garage and climb up to the ceiling. I'd been doing it while he was at work, worried that my suitcase would be found if it wasn't well hidden. But now he is home. Should I risk it? Will Henry come running from the bedroom when he hears the clatter and catch me pulling my luggage down?

And how long would it take?

I decide to abandon it. All the sentimental items I'd stashed away—a photograph of my parents on their honeymoon to Niagara Falls, the Frank Sinatra album from my father, the map, the copy of

James Michener's *Hawaii* that I intended to start reading, plus all my essentials. These things will have to be left behind.

Because all that matters is leaving. Now.

Determined, I grab a macramé market bag from a hook in the pantry and stuff it with whatever I can grab in a hurry, hoping that nothing falls through its holes. I take my purse from the hook near the front door and feel around for the envelope of money I've stashed there. Relieved when I find it. I would be lost without that.

My hand is shaking, a palsy conspiring to try to stop me. I grasp the handrail and struggle to breathe, panic tearing through my lungs like serrated knives. I set the bag on the sidewalk and bend over, trying to pull together the courage to take the steps to walk to the car, turn on the ignition, and drive away. My body feels like lead as I stand up again and force my feet forward.

The wind flows from the west, carrying with it the distinct and putrid odor of the paper mill in Spring Grove. It smells like death, and in a way, it is. Tall trees reduced to pulp. There is something that feels symbolic about it.

This marriage almost killed me.

When Henry and I met, I was two years into taking classes at Franklin and Marshall College in Lancaster. Pursuing a major in English. Hoping to save enough money to finish up in a bigger city. Philadelphia. Or Boston. Or New York. I always had dreams that spanned beyond the limitations of my geography.

I worked as a cashier at the historic Central Market on weekends, the coppery brick edifice of it and its origins dating to its charter by King George II in the early eighteenth century. Being there made me feel connected to something old, something bigger than myself, and it always put me in a good mood. So I was in a romantic frame of mind when a handsome man not much older than myself came up to the counter and bought a package of Amish noodles and baked apples. And asked if he could make dinner for me the following evening.

Henry was funny and charming and claimed that he wanted to travel as much as I did. In all the time we dated, he never had more than an occasional beer. Never said a cross word. Told me he loved me on a daily basis. Brought me flowers as soon as the last batch he'd brought had browned.

All my dreams had not particularly figured a man into them, but how could I say no when such a gift had been placed in front of me?

My mother had been hesitant. She told me that she had a bad feeling about him, though there was no evidence to justify her usually reliable intuition. She even thought he might be rushing a wedding to avoid getting drafted. Though nothing imminent was on the horizon, there were stirrings that the conflicts in Vietnam might involve the United States in the future.

I made the mistake of telling Henry about her concerns, and he used what I later learned was his cunning way with words to convince me that she was jealous. My father had died only a year before, so wasn't it possible that she wanted me to be as alone as she was? To stay single so as to be hers for as long as possible?

Love is blind may be a well-worn phrase, but only because women often look into the dazzling brilliance of infatuation and allow it to eclipse the wisdom of the women who came before them.

I told my mother not to come to the wedding, parroting the sentiments that Henry had fed to me. I didn't want her there if she didn't embrace my choice of husband. So like any other conscientious objector, she fled to Canada. My father's country. Where she'd spent happier days.

It was only after we were married that a different Henry was revealed—the *true* Henry that she'd warned me about. The one who'd captured me and didn't need to try anymore.

It wasn't immediate. His approach was subtle. A comment about how my hair looked better when I didn't wear it back. How my cooking needed improvement. How my dresses were too revealing. How we couldn't afford for me to continue college.

How we couldn't afford to travel. Even to Rehoboth Beach for a weekend.

A thorough, incremental, strategic dismantling of the independent woman I'd once been and a fashioning of what he wanted me to be: a helpless girl who needed his approval at every turn.

And then he took up drinking. Or maybe resumed it.

I was too embarrassed to return my mother's calls. And then she stopped calling. Because an icy car accident after a late-night shift at the hospital took her from me forever.

My tears over not being able to afford to go to Toronto for her funeral prompted the first time that Henry squeezed my arm hard enough to leave a bruise. At first, I thought it was an accident.

The first time he hit me, he made me believe that I deserved it. I don't even remember the cause. It became too commonplace an occurrence to recall.

But no longer, thanks to Ronelle. A maternal stand-in, though she is not much older than me.

Ronelle has shown me a way out.

I wipe tears from my eyes with the itchy wool sleeve of my sweater and place the key into the car's keyhole. The pink sweater with yellow flowers is the last one my mother crocheted for me before she left Red Lion, and if I'd put it in the attic with my suitcase, I would have had to leave it behind. It will be my only memento from my previous life. I wear it like it's a hug.

I look up toward Ronelle's house and see the curtains to her living room pulled back. She is standing there, silhouetted by the two lamps on either side of her, but I can imagine that her face is filled with relief and maybe tears that match my own. She waves and I wave back.

I don't know when we'll see each other again.

CHAPTER SEVEN

Beverly

The humiliation of my last day in New York still rankles me as I lean my head against the city bus that will take us all to the training offices in Miami. But I've learned that sometimes fire needs to scorch the old land before it can be reborn into something new and better.

"Let's go to the Plaza for one last tea," my friend Eve had suggested. She'd been a boarder at Marymount, a cattle heiress from New Zealand whom we affectionately called "Kiwi."

It had been our Saturday tradition, Eve being my closest friend when I usually kept them at arm's length. But here she was, a literal world away from her home, and I'd always been fascinated—envious—by how she managed to live her life on her terms.

I pulled off my gloves one finger at a time and folded them into my handbag as we entered the Plaza's tearoom. One last hurrah before I left for Pan Am training.

"I'm sorry, Miss Caldwell, but we don't have a table for you today."

The maître d' would not meet my eyes as he choked out the words. There were at least twelve tables available.

"But we have a standing reservation." *And I always tip you generously,* I thought to myself.

"I'm sorry, but we will not be able to accommodate you at this time."

Confused, Eve suggested manicures at Kenneth Salon instead, but again, we were met with rejection.

"My deepest apologies, Miss Caldwell, but your account has been closed."

"Closed?" My chest tightened and my face burned with embarrassment. I should have seen this coming.

"I'll pay," offered Eve, pulling out cash as she spoke.

But the salon owner squirmed and shook her head. "We cannot accommodate you anymore."

That was the same word that the maître d' had used.

If I'd had any illusion that this was all an anomaly, it was shattered when I went to pick up a hat I'd ordered weeks ago at my favorite milliner's.

"Beverly. Dearest," the Frenchman said in words dripping with honey. He took my regloved hands into his own and kissed each of them, squeezing as he let go. "Your account is paid in full and your hat is ready. But"—his face darkened as he continued—"I am so sorry to deliver the news that this will be the last one I can make for you."

"What do you mean, Marcel?" My words came out as ice.

Because I knew. I *knew*, even before he said it. My father had made good on his threat. My hands were shaking at the realization that I'd called his bluff. And he hadn't been bluffing.

Marcel leaned in, elbows resting on the glass counter. "I'm not supposed to be telling you this, but your father has rung up all the places where you have accounts and permanently closed them."

Eve gasped. "He didn't!"

But I wasn't surprised. My anger bloomed until I could feel the blood vessels in my cheeks blossom.

"He *did*, darling. You don't get to be a lion in New York without having a roar, and my girl, he used it today."

Something that he said lingered in me. "Did you say he called himself? Not his secretary?"

"Not his secretary."

He really meant business, then, and my mother hadn't been able to stop him. My own father was shutting down the only life I'd ever known, one vendor at a time. It was his way of forcing what he wanted. But while I had my mother's eyes, his stubbornness was my greatest inheritance.

Two could play at that game.

"What are you going to do, Beverly?" asked Eve. Who, despite her distance of thousands of miles from her family, was still irrevocably tied to her allowance from them. This news must be even more inconceivable to her than it was to me.

I curled my hands into fists and stuffed them into my pockets before coming up with an answer.

"As one last favor, Marcel, may I use your phone?"

He lifted the mint-green telephone over the counter and handed the receiver to me. I dialed the number I knew by heart but rarely used.

"Richard Caldwell, please," I said, tempering my ire for the sake of the innocent secretary. "Tell him his daughter's on the line."

One minute passed. Sixty long seconds that I'm certain were a ploy on his part meant to give him the upper hand.

"Beverly," my father said when he came on the line. A triumphant tenor to his voice, no doubt convinced that I'd called to concede in the face of his drastic actions.

But I was not going to give him that satisfaction.

I said only one thing before hanging up: "I'm going to be the best damned Pan Am stewardess that anyone has ever seen."

If I'd known how blisteringly hot Miami would be, I might have welcomed Mr. Wall Street derailing this venture with one phone call to Mr. Trippe. But that never happened—maybe my mother successfully intervened at last. And the result is that I am positively *boiling* here in the southernmost tip of the country.

Jeez Louise, how does anyone live here and endure it? I'm afraid I'll barely survive the day, and yet we have *six whole weeks* of training ahead of us before we get assigned to our bases. Well, I can tell you this. If we get any say in the matter, Miami will not be at the top of my list. Nor will New York, for obvious reasons. That leaves London and San Francisco and a smattering of others. But it's probably going to be luck of the draw, so I can only hope.

The training room is rather dull, belying the glamorous life we're supposed to be embarking upon. White walls, blue carpet, green chalkboard. We could be anywhere, save for posters illustrating all the exotic places that are within Pan American's vast purview. But even their corners are curling in protest of the humidity. Ceiling fans are roaring at full speed, accompanied by four box fans placed around the floor. Both are so loud that I fear it will be difficult to hear the instructor.

I pull a compact from my purse and powder my nose and chin, adjusting the mirror ever so slightly with the subtle purpose of taking a peek at the other girls who've made the cut.

My competitive side begins to stir. Even though we've all made it this far, there is a precedent that thirty percent of us won't finish training for one reason or another. I am not going to be one of them.

I can't be.

I will not go back to Manhattan a failure. I will not give my father the satisfaction.

I recognize a few girls from the interview in New York. Three or four in this class of forty. The others have come from all over the world—from thirteen countries, I'd heard. Recruited from interview posts established in major cities, mostly on college campuses. The Texas delegation—there are a disproportionate five of them—look positively unaffected even as the rest of us wither in the heat.

But maybe that's part of the test. They throw you into the most distemperate climate possible and see who survives.

I. Will. Survive.

The nervous chitchat dies down as the classroom door opens and a man enters with an armful of paperwork. He's a good-looking one, I must say, but doesn't seem to know it. That's the best kind. He's young—maybe five years older than me. Blue, Sinatra-like eyes. But unfortunately, he doesn't smile. This one is all business.

"Good morning, ladies. If you can all have a seat, we are ready to get started."

He turns toward the chalkboard and writes his name on it as if we are back in first grade.

Joe Clayton

I'd whistle, Joe Clayton, if I hadn't been taught to act like a lady. And looking around the room, so would every other girl.

Eyes back in your heads, lassies. We're here to do a job. The fun will come later.

He faces us again. "Welcome to Pan American Airways. You've been selected from a highly qualified group of women. So congratulations on being here. I'm Mr. Clayton, and I'll be on hand for most of the six weeks assisting with the classes."

He sounds like he's given this talk one too many times. Smile, Mr. Clayton, won't you? Let's see those teeth. I'll bet they're as pearly white as that shirt you're wearing.

"There is more than meets the eye to being a Pan American stewardess," he continues. "To the passengers, you are ambassadors of the airline, of the United States, and of the countries you are visiting. At all times, you are expected to be professional and pleasant. Making them comfortable and relaxed from takeoff to landing. We want them to have only the best things to say about their experience."

I traveled with my mother several times growing up. Paris for shopping. Denver for skiing. Maine for cooling off in the summer. And so on. We flew many different airlines (not to mention the occasional private charter), but there was something about the Pan American stewardesses that was a cut above. They were the *best.* To pilfer a Marine Corps advertisement, "The Elite of the Elite."

Exactly.

Joe Clayton pauses and looks around the room. All eyes are on him, but maybe not for the reason he thinks. When his glance lands on me, I see none of the flush that I usually encounter from the men in my circles. Yep, all business this one. Maybe he's married. If I were his wife, I'd be worried about him spending so much time with those *elite of the elite*, but I don't see a wedding ring. So who knows?

He continues talking as he hands out thick binders row by row. They're the size of a New York phone book and they make a thump as they hit the desks. I think he's doing it intentionally.

"My associates will be lecturing you on the finer points of customer service throughout our time together. But there is another side to training that is more technical. You will be expected to learn how airplanes operate. What terms like *aft* and *starboard* and *thrust* and *turbine* and *yaw* mean. For all you Scrabble fans, yes, *y-a-w* is a legitimate word and will get you a good score if you can get that *Y* or *W* on a bonus square."

He looks up as he takes a breath, and I stifle a yawn. I'm not sure a Scrabble reference was the most in-touch point he could have made, but I'll give him some of those bonus points for trying.

"Keep your passports and vaccinations up to date," he drones. "You will need to understand weather and its impact on flights and turbulence. You will need to be skilled in first aid and emergency situations and how to perform in those situations without breaking a sweat. You will need to memorize the three-letter codes of all the airports to which Pan American flies, which are, I warn you, substantial. Plus the routes between them, the alternative landing sites, and the types of aircraft we employ to each of them."

He stops again, maybe for effect, and he gives the faintest of smiles. "Have I frightened anyone yet?"

I look around the room. These girls are pros. Not a flicker in their eyelids or any telltale signs of regret, but I guarantee you that they are each thinking the same thing I am.

What the hell have we gotten ourselves into?

Sister Mary Clare at Marymount wouldn't approve of such language, but Sister Mary Clare didn't hear all that I just heard. And it seems like even her most arduous tests would be left in the dust by all we are expected to learn here.

No one admits *out loud* to Mr. Clayton that she feels completely overwhelmed, so he nods in satisfaction and returns to the front of the classroom.

"Brains and beauty. That's what a Pan American stewardess is, in that order. You have to be clever. Resourceful. Knowledgeable. Friendly. Classy. And perhaps most importantly, calm under pressure. Because while our goal is that every Pan American flight is flawless, I can tell you that not one of them is."

The room is still as the girls all sit at attention.

"But there is one thing to remember above all else." His tone grows serious, and I feel in my stomach the gravity of whatever he is about to say. "We're not too many years off the days when this country fought battles across either ocean that we sit between. Some of you lost fathers and uncles, and you will be flying with the daughters of people who were considered enemies at that time. This makes *you* part of the future. Part of the mission of permanent peace. This blending of cultures makes Pan American more effective than any United Nations gathering. And *you* will be on the mission's front lines."

His words reverberate with importance. I can see the other girls flush with pride. Of all the things that he's said, this more than most gives a hint at that *purpose* that I've been hungry for.

I don't look down at the manual he's placed on my desk, but my fingers slide along its edge, and the scope of what lies ahead of us daunts me. Not for the first time, I wonder if I can do this.

But I've never fallen short of anything I've gone after, and I'm not going to start now.

I'm going to make my words to my father come true.

CHAPTER EIGHT

Judy

Three days. Three whole days that I haven't woken up next to Henry and had to worry about what lay ahead when the sun rose. There is a lightness to this feeling, as if I have been buried under sandbags and suddenly, they've been removed.

I've forgotten how to breathe. My lungs struggle to gulp the thick, salty Florida air. But I am also suffocated by the fear that Henry will discover where I am, fly to Miami, and insist I come back to Pennsylvania with him.

And what choice would I have? If Pan American finds out that I'm married, I will be fired on the spot. No married girls. No women with children at home. No daughters with elderly parents who depend on her. No exceptions.

A stewardess must be completely unattached, a point that was drilled into us on the second day of training when our instructor reviewed the basic guidelines of working for the company. Of course, these had been covered in the interview, but were repeated so as to leave no doubt in our minds.

I will have to stay alert.

Pan Am has put us up in the Miami Airways Motel, a two-story square building surrounding a swimming pool lined with palm trees that tower over it all. A black-and-white-striped awning welcomes us to our home for the next few weeks. The rooms all face each other, bordered by outdoor walkways. And there is a *housemother* whose room has a particularly good view of all the others. No overnight guests allowed. No shenanigans.

We are all adults. But we are all plebes to Pan American.

"If I'd wanted to go to boot camp, I'd have joined the army," one of the girls commented upon check-in, aptly making the same military comparison I had.

And yet, it is paradise in my eyes.

It is freedom.

There are two sets of bunk beds per room. I have an upper one. The girl underneath me is from Arkansas, a town called Fordyce, which she pronounces *for dice.* Jean has red hair and freckles, but they disappear under the thick paste she puts on her face in the morning. She left school when she received the Pan Am envelope, but keeps a Boll Weevils banner pinned to the wall. I haven't talked to her much—she's spent an inordinate amount of time and money on the telephone with her boyfriend.

The girl in the other upper bunk is the one I saw in New York. Beverly something. The bewitching one. Like me, Beverly has no mementos of home to adorn the room, and I wonder why that is.

What does that say about us? That we have everything ahead of us?

Or nothing to go back to?

I hope I'll get to find out. Other than Ronelle, it's been a very, very long time since I've had a friend.

The bunk below Beverly's remains empty. A girl dropped out before classes even began when the routine physical exam revealed that she had the beginnings of varicose veins, a detriment for someone who would have to spend a great deal of their time standing.

But we'd heard that she wasn't too broken up about it. Her boyfriend had proposed to her upon her arrival home.

I am delighted for her, whoever she is. And I'm pleased at my reaction—it means that I am not as thoroughly jaded by love as I feared. Perhaps there is hope for me.

Beverly is in the shower right now. I can hear her singing something I don't recognize, muffled by the impressive water pressure of the showerhead. And though her bed is void of personal mementos, her many clothes are splayed across the empty bed, which she claimed early on through de facto squatter's rights when neither Jean nor I objected. Silks and linens and all kinds of fabrics that must be specially cared for rather than washed in a bucket and dried on a line. I don't know where she expects to wear them—our outfits for class must be practical. And after graduation, we've already been encouraged to pack wash-and-wear clothing for our downtime so as to maximize the precious hours we have to explore on a layover.

But to each her own. I am not going to mimic my husband and demand that all people see things my way.

I look at my own rack in the wardrobe—it is sparse in comparison to Beverly's substantial array. Not by design, but because I took so little with me when I was hurrying out of the house. I smile at the sight of the pink-and-yellow sweater. My mom would be proud of me for being here. I wish she could have seen me.

I feel bone tired, the kind where if you don't get moving, the ground might just swallow you up and it would be a welcome thing. My hands are numb from taking notes. My head is stuffed and cannot contain one more fact. I want to sink into the softness of my mattress and never wake, but I have to either get up and wash the clothes I'm wearing or buy new ones before tomorrow. I try not to think of my suitcase back in the attic in Red Lion and all that it holds. None of which I ever expect to see again.

When Henry finds it—because he will, undoubtedly searching every corner of the house for me—he will discover that I didn't have an accident somewhere on the way to the pharmacy. He'll figure out that I am gone. That I've left him.

Did I leave any clues as to where I was heading? I've done inventory in my head like an unending carousel going round and round and round. But I think I am safe on that front.

I slip out of the motel room and put a cardigan over my shoulders because I've found that the evenings here mercifully cool off after dark.

There is a Sears, Roebuck on Biscayne Boulevard, a short bus ride from our lodgings, and I'm sure they will have what I need for not too much money.

An hour later, I have bought two skirts and two blouses, which will have to do until I receive my first paycheck. Polyester, easy to wash in the hotel sink.

I hear the lap of waves, and my head swivels east. It is only a bay, not a beach. But it is more water than I have ever stood in front of, and I know that the Atlantic Ocean lies beyond the strip of land on the horizon. The Atlantic Ocean. On the other side sits many of the places that were mere pinpoints on my childhood map. London. Paris. Rome. Athens. I feel myself glowing with possibilities in spite of my exhaustion.

I walk to the bay's edge and am mesmerized by its gentle kiss to the thin shoreline. And even more by the tiny crabs that skitter along it. They creep into dark, fingerlike holes in the sand and disappear.

That is a sentiment I can understand.

The sky is unremarkable—the sun is setting behind me, and I remind myself that one of these mornings, I should get up early enough to see it rise in the east. That must be a spectacular sight.

I hear music coming from a nearby café. I turn and see four men with leathery skin wearing wide-brimmed straw hats and playing drums and guitars. I believe they're singing in Spanish, and it is unlike anything I've ever heard. I close my eyes and begin to sway. I have not yet left the country, but I already feel as if I'm transported to a new land, one where Henry will never find me. I smell rum and sweat and rain in the air, and it is an enchanting, heady combination. It is the melody of starting over.

"Miss Goodman?"

I am jolted from this trance, and I open my eyes to see one of our instructors in front of us. Joe Clayton, the name still emblazoned on the chalkboard. He looks different—he is not wearing a tie and has a relaxed look about him that has not yet made an appearance in our classroom. It's hard to believe that this is the same man who wore drab brown in New York and a plain button-down shirt during the first days of training. This loose cotton one becomes him. Even if it is still basic white.

"Yes—I'm Judy Goodman."

I smile and hang my head before looking up at him again. He has this effect on me—I feel shy and I don't know why. "That's quite a talent," I say. "How do you know my name after such a short time?"

He grins, and it is a nice look on him. Sheepish. I know the definition, but can't recall seeing it so precisely on someone before.

"A hazard of the trade, I suppose. When you spend a few years memorizing the manifests on each of your flights, you pick up a few tricks for recalling names. The *Pan Am International Standard of Service.*" He chuckles. "Don't worry. You'll get that phrase so stuck in your head soon that you'll get sick of it."

"You were a steward?" I ask. I don't know why this surprises me. He certainly knows his stuff.

"Yes. Didn't I mention that in my introduction?"

"No. You haven't told us anything about yourself."

There's that look again, as if he's a little embarrassed by it. "I guess you're right. I tend to skip all the pleasantries. There's so much to cover."

"That doesn't sound like a very good trait for a steward."

I regret it as soon as I say it. I didn't mean it to sound like a criticism.

He shrugs and rubs his hand across his chin before crossing his arms across his chest. "It wouldn't seem so, but in a way it is. Time is limited, the passengers are plentiful, so you can't waste time on unimportant words. Although what you do say, you have to say with a smile."

He smiles as if to underscore his point.

I like his smile.

I clear my throat. "Got it, Mr. Clayton. I'll add that to my notes."

The volume of the music increases, and the pace becomes frenetic, drowning out our words. I am about to say goodbye when a waiter approaches us.

"A table for two?" he shouts.

I feel my stomach growl, and I'm glad that it can't be heard. I haven't eaten anything since lunch, and whatever is coming from that kitchen smells delicious. But I don't have much money. A candy bar from the Sears counter sits in my bag and will serve as my dinner.

Mr. Clayton looks at me and maybe he reads that in my eyes. "Yes. If you have something in a quieter spot."

"Right this way, sir."

We follow him to a room at the other end of the café, and I realize that it is much more extensive than I'd first assumed. In this back area, the band is muffled, but I'm glad we can still hear it. It's completely new to me, and I love it.

The waiter heads toward a window. I can see the lights from boats sparkle on the distant water and the palm trees sway in a gentle dance. Mr. Clayton holds out the chair with the better view and motions for me to sit down.

As he takes his own seat, I am struck by how very different this moment is from my life just seventy-two hours ago.

I need to put aside such thoughts. If I am to have a new beginning, I cannot keep comparisons to the things of the past. And yet—I also can't make the same mistakes. I learned the hard way that men are not always what they seem, at first, to be. The past is a necessary reminder to have caution.

The table is small and the proximity intimate. My feet brush Mr. Clayton's unintentionally. I am mortified and pull them away.

But the electric feeling that ran through me remains. What could that mean?

I'm grateful again for the music in the background, which offers a good excuse to sit in silence. What should we even talk about? This is not a date. He is my instructor, and I am his student, and even though we're both adults, I don't know if this is allowed.

Not to mention that *I'm married.*

But too much quiet makes me uncomfortable.

"So how long were you a steward?" I ask.

A safe, simple question. I'd rather he talk about himself than have the spotlight on me.

Mr. Clayton leans in and folds his hands together on the table. "Just two years. It was a good life, but at some point, I wanted to settle in one place and build a life. So when they offered me the stability of this training job, I took it."

"You live here in Miami, then?"

"Yes—the Magic City, as they call her."

I don't ask him why that is, though its magic is certainly working on me. I'm more curious about why he's here. "I thought I'd seen you as one of the interviewers in New York. So I assumed you lived there."

"Ah, you remember me?" That seems to please him. I notice him fidget with the stem of his water glass, and if I didn't know better, I'd guess that he is nervous.

"Probably better than you remember me," I answer. "You all must have seen hundreds of girls that day."

He shuffles in his chair. "I recall you very well, Miss Goodman. In fact, I fought for the approval of your application."

This takes me by surprise. And my next words catch in my throat. "You did?"

He presses his lips together and nods.

A million things race through my mind. Not the least of which is the realization that if someone had to fight for me—that means I almost didn't get the job. I shudder to think of that possibility. "Maybe you can't tell me," I begin. "But you bring up something I've wondered ever since then."

"What's that?" he asks. I am probably right in thinking that he regrets having said too much, but now that he's opened that door, I have to walk through it.

"Why did I get picked? There were so many qualified girls. And so few spots."

He takes a deep breath, clearly deliberating, and now I'm sorry that I've inadvertently put him in this position. But I see a decision come over his face, and his words are spoken with a resolute tone.

"I could tell you wanted it more than any of them. And in my experience, those are the women who work out the best."

My heart beats faster. Maybe from knowing what the alternative could have been. Had it shown that much? Or is he just particularly perceptive?

I nod. "Yes. I needed this—wanted this—very badly."

I see him relax a bit, leaning in, just as I start fiddling with the stem of my own water glass. They certainly are convenient distractions.

"You see, Miss Goodman, a Pan American stewardess is more than just the sum of what is on paper. Like most of the young women, you met all the qualifications. And there were some who checked more boxes than you did. Three languages. Or a completed degree. But I guess one side effect in this trade is a knack for sizing people up. Thousands of people coming through your flights will do that."

I'm dying to know what those conversations were like in New York. Debating the merits of one girl over another. But I won't press further. He already told me enough. I do him the favor of changing the subject even though I find myself burning to know more about what he thinks of me.

"And are you liking Miami so far?" I ask.

"I am." A smile spreads that reaches all the way to his eyes, rendering them even more brilliant. "All six days that I've been here."

"Six days! So you're not quite accustomed to this heat either?"

He laughs and shakes his head. "Let's just say that if I ever flirted with doing things I shouldn't, this heat is a reminder that I want to avoid hell at all costs."

It's probably best that we don't see this side of him in the classroom. I, for one, would be too distracted to pay attention.

The waiter interrupts and asks for our drink orders before we can continue.

"We should try their mojitos," Mr. Clayton says. "I've heard it's their specialty."

"Am I allowed to?"

Can I afford it, is what I think to myself.

"You're not in uniform, so yes." He sits back in his chair and hands his menu to the waiter.

I don't drink. *Ever.* I lived through what it did to Henry—and then what he did to me. It was frightening.

But then an idea strikes me. The decisions I'd made before had been disastrous. Maybe the way to embrace this new life is to do everything opposite of what I've done in the past. Then the result will, logically, be flipped.

At least, that's what I tell myself.

"I'll have one as well," I say to the waiter in a low voice, holding up a finger to emphasize *one.* A shiver runs through me.

Am I really doing this? I am really doing this.

I feel victorious. I feel *daring*. Goodness, I don't know when the last time was that I could have said that. But I like it.

The drinks arrive in minutes. Condensation drips down ice-cold glasses and pools on the table. A yellow paper umbrella sticks out, and a swirl of fresh mint laces through ice cubes. I take a sip and lose myself in the way it makes my mouth and throat feel warm and cool all at the same time. Then another sip, and the sensation travels down to my empty stomach, burning and relaxing me.

One drink full of contradictions. I am lightheaded, and it is absolutely glorious.

"They're good, right?" asks Mr. Clayton. "The menu says that the rum is from the Dominican Republic. The owner imports it from his nephew."

My words are slow. "If I were you, I would have left New York just for this!"

He grins. I'm enjoying this relaxed version of him and I feel like I have this secret knowledge about what he's like outside the classroom. Something that belongs just to me. At least in this moment. "You can get just about anything in New York," he answers. "There is a pretty big Dominican community in the north part of Manhattan called Washington Heights, and I'm sure they could have made a great mojito if I'd wanted one. But it just feels more fitting here in the tropics. I rarely drink, but if I do, it has to feel like a special occasion."

I feel my cheeks flush, and whether it's from the drink or the notion that sitting here with me might be considered a *special occasion*, I don't know.

I motion to the waiter to bring another after all, and in minutes, I've started on my second. I'm beginning to get really, really comfortable. I forget, briefly, about anything outside of this moment. That I have a husband. That I'm from Pennsylvania. That I have class tomorrow. That Joe Clayton is our instructor instead of a handsome man that I met outside a bar by the water in Miami.

Isn't that the point?

If only Ronelle could see me! She'd be so thrilled. I will have to send her a postcard.

We grow comfortable in our conversation and the hesitancy I felt at first has vanished. I slur a word—*bacon*. But I say *bacom*. Why were we even talking about breakfast meat? I don't remember, but I find it *hilarious* that I said it this way.

Mr. Clayton laughs when I laugh but insists that I need food and should start drinking some water. He's on his second mojito as well, and though I can see that it has mellowed him, too, he seems far more put together than I feel.

Somehow, I don't care.

We're halfway through dinner—arroz con pollo for me and something called boliche for him—when he tells me that it feels silly for me to call him Mr. Clayton, at least in this setting, and so I start to call him Joe.

Joe. Joe. Rhymes with snow. *Crow. Row. Glow. Toe.*

Toe! Ha, that's funny.

Did I say that all out loud? I don't think I did.

I *do* feel like a new person.

Maybe that's why Henry drinks. To make all your troubles go away. It certainly has done the trick for me. I won't make a habit of it. But for tonight, I'll make an exception.

Our banter turns more jovial in nature, though I notice that neither of us says anything revealingly personal.

It's better that way.

"And then the plane hit an air pocket, and the man who had been *so* rude to me spilled whiskey all over his pants. It hadn't dried by the time we landed, so he tried to adjust his bag to hold it in front of him, but the zipper caught on the back of a seat, and all his items fell out."

I giggle. It is the fourth funny story that he's told me about his career in the air. By the time our dessert arrives—flan—I am feeling much less nervous about this job. There is a camaraderie that seems to exist among the crew. And I've always wanted to feel like I was a part of something.

I might have joined a sorority at Franklin and Marshall if I hadn't had to work during every hour of my free time.

And if I hadn't dropped out to get married.

But I think the Pan Am family might be the very best one of all. Maybe some things work out as they should.

The waiter presents the check and Joe takes it, refusing any contribution from me. "Remember that I know what they're paying you," he insists. Though he seems like the sort of man who would never let a woman pick up the tab anyway.

The night sky is pitch black through the windows, and the band has started up again. Joe pulls my chair out, and I shiver at the light touch of his hand on my back as we weave through the tight spaces between the revelers who have filled up the place since we arrived.

"Where do you live?" I ask as we return to the waterfront.

"A few blocks that way." He points to the left. For about two seconds, I imagine what it might be like to go home with him. But I have not drunk so much as to lose all my wits and I dismiss the thought as soon as it comes to me.

"Ah, our motel is near the airport. I have to catch the bus."

My head swivels back and forth. Where was that bus stop?

"I'll take you there," Joe offers.

"You don't need to. I can find my way." But I stumble on a crack in the sidewalk as I say it. Perhaps the lingering effects of the drinks. Though as I look down, it was rather uneven. Anyone might have done the same.

"I think I have to insist." Joe steadies me by holding my elbow and I am not sorry for an excuse to make contact again. "I wouldn't have suggested the mojitos if—"

He lets the sentence drift unfinished. What would he have said?

If I'd known you were a lightweight? A cheap date?

There is no flattering end to that statement, and I fear that I have ruined something before it's even begun.

All I can say is, "It's not your fault."

The bay glistens under the streetlights, and it conjures memories of every romantic movie I've ever seen. Except that this isn't romantic—it can't be. I must keep reminding myself of that.

It turns out that the bus stop is right across the street, and we ride in silence for the couple of miles back to the Miami Airways Motel. My head feels heavy, but I dig my nails into my skin to keep myself awake.

To keep myself from leaning into him for support.

That would not be a good idea.

When we arrive, I expect him to hop off and wait for the return ride, but instead he walks me up to the front door of the building.

I turn to thank Joe. Joe, dear Joe, the uptight instructor of the past few days who let down his hair a bit and gave me a chance to see another side of him. Tomorrow he will resume being Mr. Clayton, but tonight, he is Joe.

Then I do something I've never done. I raise myself up on my toes, close my eyes, and kiss him. On. The. Lips. I've never kissed another man besides Henry. Henry's face was always perfectly shaven, and Joe's is stubbly from a day of growth. It tickles my mouth, but I like it. It's new, like everything else right now.

I am instantly sobered when I realize that he's not kissing me back. And take a step back in stunned embarrassment.

I turn and don't open my eyes until I'm facing the door of the motel office. I don't thank him, I don't look back at him.

Instead, I run inside and race up the stairs to our second-floor room. I press my forehead against the bedroom door and worry that I have made a disaster of everything.

What if the housemother saw us?

What have I just done?

CHAPTER NINE

Beverly

Oh, today should be prime entertainment indeed. Only day three, and there is already some intrigue. One of my roommates—the girl from Pennsylvania—came back late in the evening. I was sitting at a desk by the window that faces the street. I was reading a novel when I saw her come up the sidewalk *with none other than our straightlaced instructor, Mr. Joe Clayton.*

And as if that wasn't enough, the girl kissed him. *Smack-a-roo.* Right on the lips.

Then she ran away.

I wouldn't have guessed she had it in her. She doesn't seem the type.

If she'd looked back at him, she'd have seen what I saw—the streetlight illuminated his face, and there is no doubt that he was surprised by her action. He reached out to her and called her name. But I don't think she heard him.

That, though, was the face of an infatuated man.

I should know. I've seen enough of them with their droopy puppy-dog eyes waiting for any bone you can throw them. She threw him a bone and didn't hang around to see how eager he was to pick it up.

Poor girl. There is something about her that I haven't been able to dissect. Inexperience? Shyness? Maybe, but I don't think so. She's hiding something. I'd bet my fortune on it if I had one left to lose. She's not the wide-eyed innocent that she first seems to be. But I can't decipher it.

I set my book down and hopped under the covers, pretending to be asleep when she slipped into the room.

She tossed a shopping bag on the floor and climbed up the ladder to her bed without changing into nightclothes. I heard the muffled sound of tears as she buried her face in her pillow.

I've cried, too, when I thought no one could hear me.

So we have that, at least, in common.

Initially, we were spoon-fed days and days of Pan American rules and culture and etiquette, and I have so much information in my head that I feel like an overstuffed sausage. I know . . . glamorous analogy, but it's the most apt one I can come up with.

For the listening pleasure of anyone interested, I am now able to rattle off a myriad of details like:

- Our vision must be 20/40 or better. No glasses or contact lenses allowed.
- We'll be compensated for costs when we're away from our base station, averaging thirty dollars per month. But oddly, we will *not* be compensated for our uniforms, which will cost as much as three hundred dollars! To include all required accessories and branded luggage.
- We'll be on probation for six months, subject to being terminated without notice. Yikes.
- No chewing gum, no drinking, and no smoking while in uniform. Better to let the passengers think we're some kind of otherworldly paragons who are above such trifles as halitosis and other vices of commoners.
- Don't apply lipstick in public. It's in poor taste. (I've been

guilty of that one!) But when you are in uniform, you *must* wear lipstick. And only one color. Revlon Persian Melon. For everyone. No matter if the hue complements your skin tone or not.

And so, so much more.

It occurs to me that having been reeled in by this lure of newfound freedom, we are, in fact, incredibly restricted.

But I understand it. A company like Pan Am must have standards. High ones.

And I will meet them all. I must. I have to show Mr. Wall Street that as a woman, I have more value than a stationary accessory on some business colleague's arm.

In that vein, the television sets in our motel rooms were removed before we even arrived, with the thought that the lack of distraction would keep us cracking those books these six sweltering weeks. So no *Beverly Hillbillies* on Wednesday nights. It was my secret indulgence at home in New York. And not just because we shared a name.

Today, though, the monotony ends, not only because Miss Pennsylvania and Mr. Clayton gave me the promise of a real-life soap opera. Today, we start the adventure.

Instead of the desks and chalkboards, clock conversions and system timetables, we're assembling in a hangar near the Miami International Airport, and the enthusiasm among us is palpable. But if we'd thought the classroom was hot, we were not prepared for this special variety of inferno. Walking on the tarmac could almost melt your shoes. Good thing I'd left my Bergdorf-bought ones at home in favor of a sensible pair from Macy's. Heeled, of course, per requirements. Flats were not becoming on a Pan American stewardess. Even one in training. Not that these thick wedges are exactly sexy, but I suppose that's better than wobbling on a stiletto while trying to navigate stick-thin aisles while also balancing trays of untold delights.

Or pretend ones, today.

The humidity on the nearby runway creates a rippled look in the air, a phenomenon I've seen only a few times on the sidewalks of New York. Usually in August. I'm beginning to think that training is intentionally Darwinian in design. Survival of the most desperate, or something like that.

But my inward complaining is short lived. Inside the hangar sits a sparkling new plane. A Boeing 707, the workhorse of the Pan American fleet. She's a beauty, this gateway to the jet age. Gleaming white sides with the trademark blue stripe painted right across her rounded midsection. Wide cockpit windows for maximum viewing of the world from above. But with one distinct difference—she is sliced in half from nose to tail. Specially made for us. This remarkable lady's wingtips will never touch the clouds—her life will be spent right here in this building, sacrificed for the purpose of our learning.

Still, she's magnificent.

A man might make an argument that an airplane should be spoken of in masculine terms, and they would not be wrong if you consider that it is rather phallic in design. (Intentional or a necessity of engineering? Discuss, everyone. Discuss.) But she's more than that. She's all curves and grace and poise. Majestic.

I hereby claim her for womankind.

I have to admit that I'm a little starstruck. Sure, I've been on plenty of planes before, but up until a few years ago, they had propellers. Clunky ships in the sky. And now, I will be more than a passenger. I will be a part of her very sleek being. Lifeblood running through her upholstered veins.

Looking around, I'm not alone in this reverence. Silence descends among the forty of us, a collective awe stealing our voices. The heat is forgiven and forgotten, and we are renewed in our elation that *we are the ones chosen to be here.*

I search for Miss Pennsylvania—I really should start calling her Judy—and I find her underneath the port-side wing. She's rubbing her hand along the underbelly of the fuselage—*I've studied the anatomy!*—marveling, no doubt, at how this giant fortress can be thrust into the sky. And stay there.

"It's all a little surreal, isn't it?" I say to break the ice.

She's not startled by my appearance here, but turns toward me slowly, as if waking from a dream. I can understand the sentiment. Maybe our kinship is to be founded in our mutual admiration of this vessel.

"I don't even have words for it."

"Have you flown much?" I ask.

She shakes her head. "Never before the trip here. Philadelphia to London and London to Miami."

Then she lowers her voice and leans in. "I was terrified."

Poor thing. The first time *is* frightening if you don't know the science behind it and it seems as if it flies by pixie dust.

And on top of that, they went and catapulted her across the ocean from the start. I had a similar route—New York to London to Miami. A confusing choice until you understand that Pan American has no domestic routes, so they wait for a flight you can deadhead—taking an unsold seat—rather than pay the money to fly you direct on a competing airline. Rough start for a newcomer, if you ask me. Especially if they don't have an available first-class seat. I'd gotten lucky on my second leg and drowned my exhaustion in the free Dom Perignon.

I hope to reassure her. "It took me at least six flights before I remember feeling comfortable with it."

"What were we thinking?" she asks. I see sweat form along her hairline, and I don't know if it's from the heat or the nerves. "We're going to do this over and over and over, trusting that the engineers got it right."

I employ the tactic that had worked for me. "I figure that thousands and thousands of flights have flown successfully in the last few decades, so they must know what they're doing. Besides, you're more likely to get killed on a highway than in an airplane. But that doesn't stop you from getting in a car."

I see a little of her hesitation fade away, so I continue. "And I suppose anything worth having merits some degree of risk. Just think of the upside. We will meet fascinating people. Travel to interesting destinations. Learn something of the world. More than we would from the comfort of our homes."

She looks away at the word *home*, and I see that shadow come over her that I'd noticed before. My heart fills with sympathy, and I don't even know the reason. It's too early to ask. But I do know how to lighten the mood. A party trick learned early on in etiquette training—distract from the unpleasant.

"What place are you most excited to see?"

Her shoulders relax, and she turns back toward me. It worked. It always does. "I haven't given it too much thought yet. Everything?"

I lean against the round frame of the turbine and nearly burn myself at the touch. *Lordy, it's hot in here!* And the metal is absorbing it all.

"I know exactly where I want to go," I say, standing back and folding my arms. "Hawaii. Polynesia. The Orient."

She cocks her head. "Not Europe? I figured that seeing places like London and Paris would be a good place to start."

How do I tell her that I've been to both, several times? I am often uncomfortable talking about the things I've been able to do. I mean, who takes lessons in dressage at a stable in the Hamptons every summer? Me, that's who. But it's not as if I asked for those opportunities. Nor did I earn them. We are subject to the circumstances of our birth, for better or worse. Mine happened to be more posh than most.

I knew I'd face this when I emerged from my own circle. And I had decided to be honest because sidestepping is so much more work and can trip you up. But now that I'm actually in the situation I envisioned, I hesitate.

Maybe there is a middle road. The truth, but not all of it. I don't know this girl or what trouble lies behind her eyes. Besides, now that I've been cut off, discarded, dismissed, I suppose we are starting on even ground. My past matters less than my future.

"London and Paris," I answer affably. "Of course those are some top picks. Who *wouldn't* want to visit Buckingham Palace and eat crepes in front of the Eiffel Tower? But there is something in me that wants to do what's unexpected. I want to walk on beaches that are uninhabited. I want to drink water from coconuts that were hacked open with a machete. I want to eat papayas that were not purchased in season at the corner bodega."

A dreamy look comes over her face and the corners of her lips widen. I have hit the mark.

"Frank Sinatra sang about Hawaii on his album *Come Fly with Me*," she muses.

"Yes! *Blue Hawaii.* Where the lovers meet on the sand under the moon."

She sighs. "Isn't he the best? I could listen to him forever. It's like drinking honey and rum. Or what I imagine that would be like."

"Agreed." I nod. "Hey—here's an idea! What if we each pledge to see every place he sings about on the album?"

Judy is smiling fully now, and I feel a sense of accomplishment. Whatever is troubling her is forgotten for the moment. "I'd love that!"

I pull my notebook from my purse and tear out two pieces of paper. "Good. It's a pact. Wherever we end up, we'll have to keep in touch and let the other know when we've checked one off the list."

I start to write.

Hawaii. New York. Paris. Capri. London.

I know I'm missing some. I put my pen in my mouth and look up at the fuselage.

Judy finishes them out, though, without hesitation. "Vermont, Brazil, Mandalay, Chicago."

I add them to the list. Then I duplicate it and hand one page to her.

"You're well versed in your Sinatra," I say.

"I listened to the album until I wore it out," she admits.

"Does Pan Am even fly to Vermont since it's domestic? I don't think it does."

She laughs. "You mean you don't have *all* the airport codes that our illustrious employer flies to memorized yet?" I know she's teasing me.

"Guilty as charged. It's not on the test until next week."

We hear Joe Clayton clap his hands to get everyone's attention and the echoes in the hangar quiet to nothingness as all the girls pay attention. "Ladies, let's gather on the port side so we can get started." I sneak a glimpse at Judy and find exactly what I expect to see.

She's blushing.

Isn't this going to be fun?

CHAPTER TEN

Judy

I'm never going to make it. One girl quit yesterday, cracking in the mock galley when she kept burning the meat for her coq au vin. It wasn't the moment itself that did it. It was the culmination of the busiest week I can ever remember living. Ten-hour training days followed by hours of study back in the motel.

Rules. Cosmetics. Cooking. Service. Routes. Customs. Protocols. Medical terminology. Currency conversion. Uniforms.

And safety. The most important one.

What if I fail that one when it counts? The thought leaves me shaking in my no-nonsense heels.

I've started dreaming in airport codes, perhaps the most mind-boggling bit of all of it.

Some are intuitive:

Lisbon: LIS

Athens: ATH

Havana: HAV

Some make no sense upon first impression:

Montreal: YMQ

Rome: FCO

Jakarta: HLP

HLP sounds like *help*, a word that definitely races through my brain as I struggle to rest.

On top of that, you have cities that share a name. Barcelona, Spain is BCN, not to be confused with Barcelona, Venezuela, which is BLA. Or cities that have multiple airports. London LHR or London LGW. Though at least in the latter case, Pan Am only flies to one of them. Still, you have to know which one is which.

To my surprise, I have memorized them all in time for the test. Or I think I have.

Keep cool and keep calm during all circumstances.

It is written on every chalkboard. Recited every morning like a prayer, and I try to take it to heart.

I wonder if the pace of training is purposefully intense so as to weed out those who can't keep up with that expectation.

It might break me if I were not already so broken.

Today is a day off so that we can recover from the first batch of vaccines we received earlier. Typhoid and cholera with more to come through the next few weeks and even after graduation for boosters.

For the more intrepid of stewardess trainees, Joe and the other trainers have offered to be available at the hangar for anyone who wants additional practice in lieu of the break.

I won't be going. I have managed to avoid all eye contact with Joe ever since I drunkenly kissed him under the motel awning. There's no way I plan to see him more than I have to. And my arm is terribly sore from where we got the injections. I never handled them well as a child either.

No, today, I will catch up on some sleep and maybe start reading a novel.

"Mail!"

Jean enters the room, her red hair peeking through pink foam rollers, a cigarette stub dangling from her lips like the permanent appendage that it seems to be. She is flipping through a small set of envelopes and flings one up to my bunk.

I catch it, and my heart races.

Please don't be from Henry, I think. *Please don't let him find me.* Relief floods me when I see Ronelle's scroll-like handwriting. I rip it open, not having her patience to slice it neatly with a knife. It's dated three days ago.

Dear Judy,

I hope all is well for you in Miami. I'm enclosing a Saint Christopher medal from the gift shop near Saint Joseph's in York since they told me that he's the patron saint of travelers. And forty dollars. Don't you dare send it back. Richard got a bonus at work and we both agreed that you deserved a bit of it. Promise me you'll spend it on something utterly unnecessary.

But I'll skip right to what I know you most want to hear. Henry came over to our house the day after you left, demanding information that I did not acknowledge having. In fact, I denied knowing you at all other than occasionally seeing you walk to the mailbox at the end of the drive. I think he believes me—my mom always told me I was a good little actress.

We told him to let us know if we could help. When really, we want to be in the loop on anything he discovers. So that we can warn you if necessary.

He returned the next day. The police found your car at the Philadelphia airport. I knew that was just a matter of time, but it had happened more quickly than I would have hoped. I suggested that maybe someone had kidnapped you and you were lying hurt somewhere while they stole away with your car. I don't think he bought it, but if the suggestion delays him for even a few days, I'll consider that a victory.

By the time you receive this, you should have almost four weeks of training left. That's a long time,

Judy. I'm not sure how many stories I can feed him before he insists that authorities turn over the manifests of every flight leaving from the airport. We had no time to get a new identification for you, nor would I even know how to go about faking such a thing. But I have some hope that he won't look past your flight to London.

Anything to keep him from tracing you to Miami.

Still, I'd be careful if I were you.

Sending all my love. Hopefully, I'll mail a cheerier letter in the future.

Ronelle

I press the letter to my face, and the paper soaks up some scant tears. I can smell her lavender-scented lotion, her homemade concoction that is nicer than anything you could buy at Peoples Drug. Though maybe I'm just imagining it, wishing for it, as I ache for the friendship that became my sole lifeline. I've been so alone for so long, cutting ties with everyone I knew. All at Henry's insistence.

Fear makes you do things you never would have thought possible.

I read her note again. It is exactly what I needed. I cannot quit, I cannot take a break no matter how hard this is. Because I know what I'd have to return to. And that's even worse.

I slip on my stockings and heels and head toward the hangar.

Joe is sitting in a metal folding chair under the wing reading the *Miami Herald*. My heart flutters every time I see him, and I wish I knew how to make it stop.

He looks up when the click-clack sound of my heels is magnified in the near-empty space. I pretend I don't see him, looking for the other trainers, but those two women are already occupied with a couple of my classmates who also came for extra help.

I'm too late. I have no choice but to work with him.

I flex my hands back and forth before walking over. I can do this.

"Miss Goodman." He stands up when he sees me and I hope he can't hear how fast my heart is beating. It is deafening to me.

"Mr. Clayton." I know I sound stiff. I intend it that way.

"How can I help you?"

I swallow. "I'm not very comfortable in the galley yet and needed to get some help with that."

He folds his newspaper and sets it on the chair before approaching me.

"Of course. That's why I'm here today. Any particular aspect you want to work on?"

I'm relieved. He's the Joe Clayton of the classroom and not the one I sat with in the restaurant on Biscayne Bay. I can almost pretend that nothing happened between us.

I can almost pretend that I merely imagined the kiss.

"I feel pretty good about the rules of service. Window to aisle. Plating the meat at the two o'clock position. Six drinks to a tray. But the galley itself is, to be honest, a little intimidating."

He smiles and his sharp blue eyes take on a softer look that is reassuring.

"That's the hardest part for almost everyone. We can certainly practice. But don't worry about it too much. You'll make mistakes up in the air. We all did. But you'll have your purser and your crew to ask for help. You're not alone up there."

"But they'll be busy with their own duties, won't they?"

He shakes his head. "We're a family up there. And our first duty is to make sure that the customer is happy. So if you burn a few eggs or turn them green, they'll help you make more."

"Green?" I ask.

"A unique quirk to the Pan American ovens. If you cook the eggs too long, it turns them green. And creates a smell that you will never forget." He shrugs like it's something they're all used to.

"I still want to learn how to do it correctly," I say.

"Then you've come to the right place."

I follow Joe up the metal staircase, shoes echoing as they land upon the steps, and enter the half-open 707. It's like being in a *Twilight Zone* episode, seeing this giant airplane split in two, with only a thin iron railing to keep us from falling. And I feel wobbly enough around him as it is.

I turn back toward the cabin, determined to get to work. My hand brushes against the turquoise-and-green upholstery of a nearby seat, and I find its tactile feel to be oddly soothing.

"Was it the first-class galley or the tourist-compartment galley giving you the most trouble?" Joe asks.

"First class."

"I figured. We all feel extra pressure there. The higher the ticket price, the higher the expectations."

I follow him to the forward galley and start opening drawers and compartments. There are so many, like an old-time desk that has drawer upon drawer hiding even more secret compartments. There is a place for everything, I know. Even chopsticks and kosher food trays. I just need to study them.

It's an efficient system once you get to know it, but until I memorize the purpose of each nook and cubby, the trial and error will waste precious time. It wouldn't do to have the sole au vermouth get cold or the lobster thermidor coagulate while I search for the square-shaped salt and pepper shakers and the etched crystal wineglasses.

Joe slides in behind me. The space barely fits two people, and I feel his closeness acutely. It's already hot in here, but his presence raises the temperature even more.

Every nerve in my body is on alert.

I try to shake it off. I am here to do a job.

Why is it so difficult to do so?

He seems as unaffected as I am affected, so I resolve to let this inaudible rejection ground me and ignore the disappointment it causes.

"Let's see what they left us to work with today. With any luck, Maxim's de Paris sent over something simple." He opens a steel warming cabinet and pulls out a sliding tray. He lifts the foil covering and smiles. "Jackpot. Veal à l'estragon. And I think I spy some flan in the back."

Flan. It reminds me of our dinner, but if it stirs the same memory for him, he doesn't show it.

"Any guesses as to where our fictional flight is going?" he asks.

I look at him with a blank expression. Was there a clue that I missed?

"South America. Or Mexico," he says. "Here's a little secret. The dessert offering is reflective of the country you're flying to. So—the flan is a tip-off that we'd be heading south."

"How marvelous," I say with genuine wonderment. Is there nothing that Pan American doesn't think of?

Joe pulls a stopwatch from his pocket and sits in a passenger seat, one leg crossed over the other. An acceptable position for a man. As a stewardess, we can only cross our ankles. More feminine that way.

"Okay, Miss Goodman. I'm a first-class customer. I'll have the Waldorf salad, the veal, the cheese plate with extra Camembert, the flan, Café Sanka, and a shot of Drambuie."

He clicks the button on the watch, and that is my cue to begin.

I smile. "Hungry, are we?"

"That's two seconds gone, Miss Goodman. You have three minutes total."

I snap to attention. Three minutes! To do so much! I take a deep breath and look at the puzzle of compartments in front of me. Salads—refrigerator. No, wait. I have to heat the oven first to make the veal hot enough to serve. Three hundred fifty degrees. I slide the platter into it and close the door. Now the refrigerator. I open it up and see two salad choices. I think the Waldorf is the one with grapes. I set one on the counter, unwrapping it from its cover with my right hand as I open cabinets with my left. It takes me three tries before I find the one with the white china. I pull out a plate, but it slips from my hands and shatters on the floor. I look for a broom.

"Forget the plate, Miss Goodman," Joe calls. "The passenger doesn't care if the galley is tidy. He just wants his food."

Got it. I'll clean the mess later. I pull out another plate and spoon the salad onto it, taking time to arrange the grapes neatly.

Cheese. I open another refrigerator and remove two platters, each full of a variety of cheeses. Which one is the Camembert again? I know it's white. One of the soft ones? I make a selection of six pieces. I think six was the standard number. But he wants extra. So I place three more white pieces, hoping they are the right kind, and find a small plate on which to serve them.

Nine is an odd number. Should I make it ten? But the nine fit into a perfect circle and presentation probably counts almost as much as speed.

I leave it as it is.

The coffee! I should have started that first. I switch the pot on and pour in some water.

I can smell the veal through the oven door but am not sure if it's ready yet. It seems so early.

"Ten seconds left."

Joe taps his stopwatch, and I think I see a glimmer of amusement in his eyes.

I pull the veal out and tip the contents of the container onto the plate just as he stops the watch.

"How do you think you did?"

I look down at the plate, mortified. The juices from the veal have pooled across everything, saturating the salad. I never got the plate onto the service tray. I forgot the Drambuie. And although he didn't ask for it, we're supposed to give water to every customer.

Then I look at my cheese plate. Camembert! I suddenly realize I put on cubes of Swiss.

And the coffee. It's burning.

My shoulders slump. This is impossible.

But Joe is grinning. He stands up and walks over and pats me on the shoulder. "Congratulations. You've just completed the Clayton School of Plating, as taught to me by my own trainer years ago."

"What do you mean? It's a disaster." I wipe my forehead with my uniform sleeve, certainly a forbidden gesture, but I feel so defeated that I just don't care. My pulse is racing from the stress of it. How did I ever think I could do this?

Joe looks down at my sad excuse for a presentation, and his voice softens. "Of course it is. Everyone's first try is a disaster. And their second try, and their third. So you're in excellent company, and believe it or not, you did better than most. See, the curriculum in the book focuses on precision. Which I don't mean to diminish. But when you're in the air and you have multiple hungry passengers, each with a different request, you *have* to learn how to do it quickly. I find that if you start to train yourself by the clock, the details will work themselves out. A book can't teach you that. And what happens in the air is more important than what happens on paper."

The uncertainty I feel must show on my face. His eyes take on a gentle expression, and for a moment, he resembles the Joe from the restaurant. I'm grateful for it.

"You would have learned this on the job, eventually," Joe encourages. "But if I can teach it to you now, I'll be saving you a world of hassle. Trust me. And—here's the twist. First-class passengers get a seven-course meal. But it's not served up all at once. So you won't have to worry about mixing the juices with the salad. You can relax. There is more time than you think."

I want to be angry. Until I realize the sense of his tactic. Make it as hard as possible on me now so that the real thing will be easy.

He patiently walks me through the most efficient way to do each step, even down to memorizing the shapes of the various liquor bottles so that I can grab them by touch instead of sight.

I notice that he is careful not to let his hands touch mine.

When we've slowly mimicked the process several times, he asks if I'm ready to be timed again.

I say yes. And just for kicks—he grins—he'll change up the requests.

Green salad with blue-cheese dressing. Veal again, but only because that's what Maxim's de Paris delivered for training purposes. A plate of cheddar only. And a slice of chocolate cake. Café Americano and a dry martini with olives.

It takes me almost four minutes. But I already feel more comfortable with it. The plating is neater. The coffee didn't get scorched. All I've forgotten are the olives.

"Wonderful!" he says, and I beam under his praise. "How did you feel about that?"

"I feel like I made some progress." And I do. My spirits have lifted a bit, and I believe that I can do this after all. I am out of breath but feeling quite proud of my performance.

"You did! You're a quick study. Totally proving my faith in you. This will smooth out with practice, I promise. Having the pressure of the stopwatch makes every move more deliberate. Every second is useful because you'll be serving many people at once. You are definitely going to have a leg up on your classmates after this."

I don't know what to do with such encouragement, and it paralyzes me. I never received this kind of praise from Henry after we were married. He always pointed out my shortcomings. The ways I'd failed.

I know that isn't the way to live. My parents had modeled something much better, much more loving. I never saw my dad belittle my mom.

I have more rebuilding to do than I realized. But this is a start.

Joe starts to slip by me in the galley again, but he pauses, and we are face to face. So close because the cabinets in the tiny space corral us together. I can feel his breath on me as he whispers.

"We shouldn't let this food go to waste," he suggests.

"We shouldn't," I whisper back. I hope my words are steadier than my body feels. My heart is still racing. The stress. The hurry. The jubilation.

The *proximity.*

"Would you like to join me in the first-class section?" Joe asks. "You pick—Waldorf or green salad."

Every bit of me wants to say yes. I *almost* say yes. But I am keenly aware of the two students and the two trainers who are still in the hangar, and I cannot risk being tarnished by even the smallest bit of impropriety or gossip. I have to keep my position here, and although I believe that Joe would not suggest anything that isn't acceptable, I am too afraid to take the chance.

I thank him and leave in a hurry.

CHAPTER ELEVEN

Beverly

I've just stepped out of the shower when there is a knock on the motel door. Noxzema covers my skin, and a glance in the mirror makes me feel like I've seen a ghost.

Judy sits up on her bunk and stretches, the straps of the thin chemise she borrowed from me slipping from her shoulders. The girl had been sleeping in a T-shirt because she hadn't brought anything nicer. And I'm a firm believer that satin is a requirement for a restful night. Lord knows she can use it.

Jean answers the door, untangling herself from the telephone cord that is wrapped around her wrist. She tells her boyfriend to hold the line.

An embarrassed-looking desk clerk stands in the doorframe, staring down at his shoes, and I tie the sash of my robe around my waist before he can see me in my delicates.

Maybe he'd get a kick out of that, but I wasn't going to let some stranger be the first man to see me in my nightgown.

"There's—there's a telephone call for Beverly Caldwell in the lobby," he sputters.

My breath stops. Only my mother knows the name of the motel, and she wouldn't call this early in the morning if it wasn't important. If it wasn't bad news.

Could it be my father? Just the possibility that something is wrong with him makes it feel crass to think *Mr. Wall Street*.

I find my voice. "I'll be down in a minute. Let me get dressed."

I slip into my thick pink housecoat and button it up in the bathroom, rinsing my face with one wide swipe of a hand towel. As I step outside, the sun rests on my skin, bare of cosmetics. I can only imagine the sight I am! But that's inconsequential at the moment.

There are a few people milling about in the lobby in various states of pouring themselves free stale coffee and turning in their keys. I see a phone on a side table near the registration desk, the receiver resting on its side.

"Beverly Caldwell," I answer. I have to remember to breathe.

"Beverly." It's my mother's voice, but it's altered. Like she can barely speak.

"Mom, what's wrong? Are you hurt? Is it Dad?"

She sniffles. "Oh, God. No. It's Sami."

I switch the receiver to my other ear, tugging it out of habit to remove a clip-on earring that I haven't yet put on today. Sami's sweet face comes to mind, and I instinctively run my hand through my hair, remembering that she had trimmed it just a few short weeks ago.

"What happened?"

Mom exhales and slows her speech. "She was walking down Mercer Street when someone snatched her purse. She tried to hold on to it, but he pushed her away. She fell and hit her head on a fire hydrant."

"Jeez Louise, will she be okay?"

She sniffles again, and this time it is clear that she is really holding back the floodgates. I've never known my mother to become unhinged, and even the hint of it is an indication of how wrenching this is for her. I have an urge to reach out through the telephone lines and hug her.

Not our typical dynamic, but—but something had changed that day at Sami's.

"We don't know yet, darling. We don't know. It's pretty bad. She's in a coma at Beekman Hospital."

I look for a chair, but there is none, so I slide down the wall until I'm sitting on the floor. I don't care if I look like a vagrant.

How the mighty have fallen.

She continues. "Beverly, I never told you. I *should* have told you. I don't know why I didn't."

"Told me what?" But I already know. I feel it in my soul. I saw it in our eyes when we all looked in the mirror at Sami's salon. In the weeks since then, though, I hadn't broached the topic. Bonding with my mother was still in its infancy.

"Sami is my aunt. Your great-aunt. My mother's sister."

I feel my blood all rush to my head. I don't know how to answer, so I'm silent. There is a whole swath of family history that has remained a mystery. It seems like half of me has been smothered my whole life.

She takes a deep breath. "But first, how are you doing in Miami?"

The woman has class, I'll give her that. Even in a crisis, she remembers her manners.

"I'm fine, Mom. I'm fine. Nothing much to report. Tell me more about Sami."

It's the only invitation she needs to keep talking. To keep telling me the things that must have weighed on her heart all these years. She sounds like a dam that has broken, all its information pouring out in tumbling, turbulent waves.

"My parents met just after the Philippine-American War. My father was a college professor from New Jersey who volunteered to go over there as part of a new program to instruct Filipino teachers in American methods. He'd always wanted to see another part of the world."

I feel my face flush. My father's parents lived in New York, and while they were both very busy in all the same society-saturated ways my parents were, at least I knew them. So I hadn't missed having maternal grandparents. And whenever I asked for family stories as a little girl, my mother changed the topic. So I stopped asking.

My mother's words settle in my heart in a way that make me feel like I'm just getting to know myself. It explains the restlessness in my blood: a piece of me is connected to the other side of the world. It feels like a magnet that has been pulling me, but I didn't know to where.

And now I do. I can hardly comprehend it.

"Tell me more," I encourage. Of course I want to learn everything I can. But above all, I am relishing how it feels to talk with my mother like this. Real conversation. The kind we only ever had on our outings to Sami's.

How sad that it took me leaving, took Sami's accident, to bring us together.

"There's not much to it, really," she continues. "They fell in love and got married. But eventually, he needed to return home since his sabbatical from the college was almost up. My mother refused to leave unless her sister Sami came with them."

"Why was that?"

"As much as my mother loved him and as much as she idolized the notion of a life in America, it also terrified her. The idea of having Sami by her side was reassuring."

And there it is again. A precedent of crossing an ocean to create a new life. I feel like I *belong* somewhere for the first time. In New York, I had everything a person could ever want. But I wanted something *different*. So, apparently, did my grandmother.

I feel like I make sense to myself now. It's a dizzying realization.

"Thank you, Mom, for telling me this. But I—I have to ask. Why haven't we talked about this before? Why did you always put me off when I asked questions?"

She sighs, so deeply that I might have heard it from a thousand miles away even without the assistance of a telephone line.

"Because I was embarrassed, Beverly. We didn't have much growing up. Sami and my mother cut hair to make ends meet, and my father's hours were reduced after the university found out that he brought home a Filipino bride. The wives of the other professors excluded her from their gatherings, and it made her miserable. As soon as I was old enough, I moved out, crossed the Hudson River, and made sure that every step I took brought me closer to being the ideal New York woman, as I imagined that to be. I didn't want to live on the periphery."

"Oh, Mom." I look at the clock on the lobby wall. We're supposed to gather at the swimming pool in fifteen minutes to begin our ditch exercises. I don't want to hang up. But I can't make excuses to my trainers. One tardy can lead to dismissal. "Will you be home this evening? May I call you back?"

I have so many questions. Did my father know about my mom's heritage? Did she ever see Sami outside of our salon days? Had my mother sworn Sami to secrecy—even from me? What happened to my grandparents?

"I'm sorry, darling. I'm detaining you. But I wanted you to know about Sami. I'll keep you apprised of her condition. And I want to tell you one other thing—"

"Yes?" I want to stay on the line almost as much as I've ever wanted anything.

"If any of your routes take you through Honolulu, you have several cousins who live there. I've never met them, but I think it's time that you know that part of your family. And to deliver our apologies."

"Apologies for what?"

"After my mother and Sami left Manila, their mother died. The family said it was from a broken heart. And none of them have spoken since."

I feel a shock roll through me as if I'd touched an electrical outlet. Family! The world has just opened up for me a little more, and I feel more dimension to my purpose here.

But will they even want to meet me?

CHAPTER TWELVE

Judy

We've each been given a swimsuit. Pan American blue, of course, today's sky matching it like it was planned that way. On our heads, we wear a bathing cap for our planned exercises. Piped in white, just like the pillbox hats we'll receive upon graduation.

Lined up, the thirty-six of us who are remaining look like a jagged mountain range crested with snow. The swimsuits are all the same size. Easy enough since we all fit the narrow weight requirement for the airline. But in height, we vary from five feet three to five feet eight. So for some—like myself—the suits bunch a bit. On the taller girls, like Beverly, it looks as if it was tailor-made for them.

No matter. We'll be spending most of the time submerged in the water of the motel pool.

The lead instructor today is Delores, who has largely stayed in the background while Joe Clayton drilled the rules and memorization parts of our training into us. Delores was not only a Pan Am stewardess but was a member of Vassar's swim team, so she seems the ideal woman for the job. Joe is here, though, as is our other instructor, Patsy. All tasked with molding us into Pan American perfection.

Joe is not wearing swim trunks, and I am embarrassed by my disappointment in that fact. His personal uniform seems to be a white linen shirt and brown slacks. Sometimes changing it up with a white *cotton* shirt. At least his sandals seem to be appropriate for poolside work, a departure from his typical penny loafers.

I wonder if his eyes are really that blue or if they stand out because he doesn't otherwise wear color?

I need to get my mind off such things. Especially today. Ditch exercises are legendarily challenging.

"Ladies," begins Delores, pacing the deck with her hands behind her back. "You will probably loathe me by the end of the afternoon. But of all the time we'll spend together, the emergency-training week is the most essential. Our excellent customer service will mean nothing if our passengers are not safe. They *must* feel confident that we know exactly what to do in every situation. And considering that much of our flight time is spent over oceans, the water training is of particular importance. So pay attention."

My pulse races. I'm not the strongest swimmer. I can manage to keep my head above the water line—I certainly spent enough time splashing in the Susquehanna River growing up. But I never took the kind of lessons that would differentiate a breaststroke from a butterfly. I want to peek at my classmates' reactions, but there is something militaristic about Delores that dares you to look at anyone but her.

"If you're inclined to complain," she continues, "remember this. Until recently, this part of training was handled in New York. Their water exercises took place in the Atlantic Ocean in nearly all kinds of weather short of a hurricane. You ladies get to bask in the Miami sun and dive into a shark-free swimming pool. A luxury in comparison."

Joe and Patsy walk down the line handing out deflated life vests. He pauses in front of me and our fingers brush as I take it from him. He lingers, which I notice he didn't do for anyone else. And he smiles, causing me to do the same. It seems to be a reflex when I'm around him. But then I doubt myself. Henry used to elicit the same response from me. And I was so wrong about him.

How can I truly move on with my life if I don't know who to trust? Or how?

All too soon, Joe continues on, and Delores directs us to bring our toes to the edge of the pool. I close my eyes and remind myself why I'm here. This is about the job. Not about matters of the heart. I'm almost grateful for the need to focus on this today.

At Delores's command, we jump in, and I'm happy to learn that the water comes to my shoulders rather than engulfing me. It's warm, but it's still a good deal cooler than the thick, humid air surrounding us. We're told to breathe air into the vests through a tube on our left and discover that doing so while in the water is a comical feat worthy of Lucille Ball. As air fills its cavities, it increases our buoyancy, challenging the reassured grip I'd had when placing my feet flat on the bottom of the pool. I already felt whalelike beneath its bulk, and I struggle with the awkward dance of filling it up while trying to stay upright.

At least I'm not alone. All around me are capped rubber heads bobbing in the water like apples in a barrel at Halloween, so there is some comfort in knowing that we all look rather ridiculous. It's hard to distinguish one girl from another, but I hear a familiar voice behind me and turn—slowly—to see Beverly.

"If only my father could see me." She laughs. It is the most personal thing she's said up until now, and it strikes me that we know so little of each other even after weeks of sharing a room. "This is not exactly what he envisioned for his daughter."

Then, a sad look that she doesn't elaborate on. "Though none of this is, I suppose."

A pang shoots through me as my own father's face comes to mind. In it he's smiling. "You can do anything, Judy," he'd always told me. I think he'd be pleased to see me here. A blessing Beverly doesn't seem to possess.

Maybe I shouldn't envy her still having a father when I'd at least had such a wonderful one.

I open my mouth to respond, but a loud crashing sound comes from behind me, and I am knocked unsteady as a wave pushes me into Beverly. The force of it launches us against the pool's wall, and my arm scrapes against its rough cement edge. I wipe the water from my eyes and through the blur, I can tell that Beverly is doing the same.

Turning around, I see that an enormous orange raft has been hoisted into the pool, nearly taking up the entire space. We've all been pushed to the perimeter.

I hear a laugh. An older couple—presumably other guests of the motel—are outstretched on beach towels behind the diving board, chuckling at the absurd sight.

I think again that Lucille Ball could do wonders with a scene like this. I'm sure from the vantage point of the cement deck it looks like a physical-comedy routine par excellence. Almost worthy of her chocolate-factory antics.

Joe and Patsy are opposite us, towering over the pool and smirking as they put their hands on their hips and watch us. They've been through this, I presume. And so they've earned the right to be amused by it. This is necessary hazing, if there is such a thing. Maybe I don't need to regret not staying to pledge a sorority at Franklin and Marshall. I'm getting my fill of it now.

Delores isn't wasting time on ruminations, though.

"Get on the raft," she barks. "And get serious, girls. What if you have to ditch into the ocean? Your toes will not be able to touch the ground. You'll be battling waves. Watching out for sharks. Trying to grab supplies from the sinking plane. Praying that you won't be stranded before food runs out. And most of all—*you'll be getting terrified passengers to safety.* With a Pan American smile plastered on your face."

It is a sobering demand, and any disposition we have toward the comedy of the situation disappears. She's right. This isn't fun and games. If we don't take this seriously, we might miss what we need to know if this rehearsal ever becomes reality. And it could have life-and-death consequences. This is the kind of sobering thought that I am well used to. I lived it every day in my own home.

Duly chastised, we struggle to follow her orders, but there is no easy way to manage this.

All at once, all thirty-six of us attempt to hoist ourselves onto the giant floating Frisbee. It is the most inelegant thing I've ever done. Limbs grasp and flail and struggle, and at last, and after much consternation, we have all managed to wrestle ourselves up there. I hope that by some miracle Joe wasn't watching—any shred of poise or modesty I might imagine myself to possess left in the first few seconds.

I purposely avoid looking in his direction. Ignorance is bliss, they say. At the same time, I'm counting my blessings that we're not attempting this in the Atlantic. I can tolerate the heat of Miami if it means not having to endure the ocean in New York.

The sun hits its highest point in the sky as Delores begins the fourth hour on the dreaded lesson, instructing that in a true emergency, we will have to use filters from the plane to make the seawater drinkable and that we may have to survive for days on nothing but chewing gum.

Possibly in the dark.

Possibly in a storm.

Always with a smile, she reminds us.

"To smiling." Beverly grins. It's Friday night, and we have the whole weekend ahead of us. We should be studying, but when Beverly finds out that I have never seen a beach, she dismisses my protestations and whisks me off to a waterfront bar for the evening.

"To smiling," I respond. I raise my glass—a gimlet—and clink it against Beverly's sidecar. I take a sip and let the tart lime flavor tickle my mouth. I understand better now how to pace myself after that embarrassing display of insobriety in front of Joe when I first arrived. Though I'm safe in the knowledge that despite her being movie-star beautiful, I have no inclination to kiss tonight's companion. I'll have only this one drink. Better for my budget. Better overall.

That thought somehow makes it taste better too. I'll savor it rather than rush to the next one.

"And to never having to make a water landing." Beverly shudders.

I grin, raising my glass again. "Yes. May we always be preserved from that."

"Cigarette?" Beverly empties her glass and sets it on the table. She slips a gold filigree case out of her purse and the top springs open at her touch.

"No, thank you," I say. I lost all interest in smoking after I married Henry. He went through a pack a day. It saturated our clothing and our upholstery, and I spent too many hours trying in vain to wash out the smell.

Beverly shrugs and puts one to her lips, her mouth gripping it like a vise. In a flash, the waiter is at her side and offers to light it. "You're a cat," she tells him, showing off her sparkling-white teeth. I'm amused by how red his cheeks get as he relishes her praise.

"I'll tell you what, handsome. Tequila shots for both of us. Bottom shelf for her, top shelf for me. And keep them coming." She opens her wallet and takes out a twenty-dollar bill, one of many that are visible. She must notice my wide-eyed expression and seems to feel the need to explain.

"Daddy Dearest cut me off for running away to join Pan Am, so I sold some of my things before coming here, and I plan to live it up until the paychecks start coming in."

It's more money than I've ever seen in one place, but I'm also keenly aware that it can only last so long. And that our paychecks will not exactly replace them in full. I wonder if Beverly has ever had to live within a budget, and I suspect not.

Running away, though, is something I can certainly relate to. I'd assumed that Beverly had every advantage over me, but I'm learning that people present a facade to conceal the wounds they are not yet ready to share. I find myself even more drawn to her because of it, a desire to know the Beverly Caldwell who lies behind the confidence and the cosmetics.

But it feels too early in our new friendship to pry.

She turns back to me as she taps the cigarette on the glass ashtray, swirling the ashes around into the shape of a diamond.

"I've never tried tequila," I say, swerving the conversation back into territory in which she has control. She seems to be most comfortable in that position.

"You're in Miami, darling. There's no excuse for not trying it."

"But—"

"But nothing. What are you, a schoolgirl or a woman? A mouse or a tiger? When you're a Pan Am stewardess, men in hotel lobby bars are going to be wining and dining you right and left, and you'd better build up a tolerance if you don't have one already. Believe me. I'm doing you a favor."

Beverly speaks with the kind of formidability that doesn't allow for dissension. Not that I intend to argue. I remind myself that if I want my life to be different from what it was, I have to make different choices.

Having a drink does not make me a drunk like Henry.

"Here you go, ladies." The waiter returns with two small glasses on a wicker tray. The drinks look identical to me, clear like water, but he is deliberate about which one he gives to me and which he gives to Beverly.

"What's the difference between them?" I ask. *Bottom shelf, top shelf,* she'd said. But Beverly waves him away and answers before he gets a chance.

"Nothing, Judy. Raise your glass."

I follow her lead.

"To Pan Am," she says.

"To Pan Am," I repeat.

Down the hatch. It burns.

"Carlos!" she calls. He hasn't gone far. "Another round, just the same."

He brings two more.

"To freedom," she says.

"To freedom," I repeat.

Down the hatch again. It burns again, but somehow less so. My head feels light. Good Lord, this is good. The breeze feels like little kisses on my skin.

"One more, Carlos! I think we're almost there!"

What does she mean by that?

The waiter brings a third round of drinks, and this time I raise my glass before she tells me to.

But now her look is less jovial and she stares at me with a penetrating glance.

"To truth," she says resolutely. She doesn't blink.

"To—truth?" My hand shakes as I send the last one down my throat. It's a familiar feeling now. The one I felt after several mojitos with Joe, but this one came on faster. Harder.

Beverly sips at hers and then sets it down. She leans in, all business, fully in control of herself. She points to our empty glasses one at a time.

"Here's the difference between the drinks. Bottom shelf is the cheap stuff. It will hit your system quickly and become a truth serum. Top shelf is the pricey stuff. It goes down smoother, and you can have several without feeling a thing."

"Truth serum," I manage to say. But it comes out slurred.

"Yes. But first—a word to the wise. If a man ever tries to order a tequila shot for you, insist that it be top shelf and watch the bartender as he pours it to make sure you're not getting shafted. Or worse."

I nod. I can barely keep my head up. It feels like bricks, my tongue feels like a sponge.

"So. The time has come. You're holding something back, Judy Goodman, and it's not that crush you have on Joe Clayton that you think you're hiding. Because that shadow in your eyes was there before our first day of training. Spill the beans. I'm just looking out for you."

Joe. Show. Mow. Grow. Fro. Toe.

I'm doing it again. I've heard of happy drunks. And Henry was an angry drunk.

But I'm—a *rhyming* drunk?

I'm just sober enough to be embarrassed by this discovery. But at least I didn't say any of it out loud.

"Okay," I begin, acquiescing. I don't get the impression that Beverly is mining for gossip. I take her at her word that she is looking out for me. I need a friend. Desperately. And she seems to be offering to be one.

Besides, if I don't tell someone my secret, I might explode. It's too much to bear alone.

"I'm married."

Beverly sits back in what seems like slow motion, a whistle escaping her lips.

"You do beat all, Judy Goodman. You do beat all. I have a pretty vivid imagination, but I didn't see *that* one coming."

I hang my head and nod.

"I don't want to get fired. I need this job at Pan Am."

She taps another cigarette out of its pack, and our ever-attentive waiter appears out of nowhere to light it up again. She folds her arms after taking a puff and considers this.

"We're not going to let that happen."

It's exactly what I needed someone to say to me. Only then do my words spill easily. I tell her about meeting Henry at the Lancaster market. About him hitting me. About how Ronelle helped me. The tequila has not made me lose control, as I might have feared. But it has loosened my lips, and I'm glad for it.

Beverly finishes her cigarette as I finish my story. She puts her elbows on the table and considers all I have said.

Then she makes a pronouncement. "What you need is a Mexican divorce."

"What is a Mexican divorce?" It almost sounds like the name of another drink. I don't want another drink.

Drink. Sink. Blink. Clink.

Oh, please.

"Simple. You go to Mexico. Or you send a lawyer on your behalf. Or better yet—you hire a local lawyer, and then you don't have to pay his travel expenses. Quick, easy, cheap. And you won't have to face your husband at all. It's just what's done. Katharine Hepburn did it. And Charlie Chaplin. Lots of stars."

She lights a third cigarette, taking a matchbook out of her purse since the waiter is attending to another table. She takes a long puff, blowing the smoke out the side of her mouth. "And Marilyn Monroe," she adds. "How's that for some fine company?" She folds one arm across her belly and leans her head back. Effortless sex appeal. I look around and see numerous men at tables around us stealing glances when they think the women they're with aren't looking. It's rather funny.

But our discussion isn't. I wish Ronelle was here to chime in. Not that I don't want to be permanently, irrevocably separated from Henry. Or that I take the vows I made lightly. But I wonder if such an action would provoke him. I am already living in daily terror that he will show up at the motel demanding to see me.

Is it too much to hope that his search didn't get any further than my flight to London? I wish I could telephone Ronelle for an update, but it would be too dangerous, since her line, like most in Red Lion, is a party line. We could not risk having someone listening in.

"I wouldn't know where to start," I tell Beverly. "But I can't rule it out."

"Easy." She shrugs. "I read about it in *Harper's Bazaar*. If you don't want to hire a lawyer, you fly to San Diego. Drive across the border to Tijuana. Look for offices that say *abogados y divorcios*. I guarantee they'll have someone who speaks English and can get your paperwork in order for fifty dollars."

She makes it sound so simple and appealing. But there are a lot of things to consider regarding it. And I don't want to dwell on Henry right now. I am *in Florida*, looking out over a marina that must have a hundred boats bobbing in its waters. Beyond that is the Atlantic Ocean. Henry cannot take this from me right now unless I let him.

I will give it some serious thought. Later. Tonight is for tequila. And friendship. And new beginnings.

Carlos brings our appetizers, six jumbo shrimp balanced on the rim of a bowl with cocktail sauce. As he walks away, the band begins a familiar tune.

Come Fly with Me.

The lyrics wash over me, and I close my eyes and bask in them. Line by line, invitations to see the world.

"You too?" Beverly smiles at my reaction.

"This song. It's my favorite." The effects of the drinks have mellowed into a dreamy haze. No more rhymes.

"Oh, don't I know it," she agrees. "I was in the audience a few years ago for a *Kraft Music Hall* airing. Frank was the main act."

"You saw him *in person*?" There's a thought that sobers me. Goose bumps form on my arm at the very idea of it.

"Of course." She takes another puff of her cigarette and tries—but fails—to blow the smoke out in a ring. So she's not *all* perfect and I find that oddly reassuring.

"Are his eyes as blue as in the pictures?"

"You mean, are they as blue as Joe Clayton's?" She leans forward, and her own eyes narrow as they wait for an answer I'm not prepared to give.

"No," I insist. "I didn't say that."

She hesitates, clearly debating whether or not to push the Joe angle. Thankfully, she decides against it. For now. I have a feeling she won't let it go forever, though. "They're *bluer* in person, if you can imagine. And I had front row seats. But I have to tell you. And don't hate me for saying this. He's not as good performing live as he is on the records. It dimmed the whole fantasy for me a bit."

"What do you mean?"

In the distance, I hear the bass-tone horn of a ship passing by. It sounds like the mating call of a whale.

Beverly shrugs. "His performance was just a little—off. Think of it this way. In a studio, you can sing and sing and sing and put the best version on the album. But in person, that's it. That's your one shot. Sometimes, it's not going to be that great. And that night, it wasn't."

She makes a point. But it's *Frank*. "I'd still die to see him," I counter.

"Maybe you'll have your chance. I heard he flies Pan Am *exclusively* when he goes overseas."

"Despite TWA being on his album cover?"

She shrugs. "Who knows. Maybe that was a paid promotion. Or maybe my information is incorrect. But there are plenty of accounts of him flying in the old blue meatball. Although I hear he hates doing it. Scares him to death."

That comes as a surprise to me. Frank Sinatra is the very face of aviation. The popularity of that particular album was probably the best favor the airline industry had ever been granted.

A wistful look comes over Beverly's face as the song continues. She closes her eyes and then opens them again as she leans toward me.

"Okay. Don't think. Just answer. We're going to revisit that first conversation we had and make some real plans. Where's the first destination you want to go when training is done? And you don't get to say *everywhere* this time."

My answer is immediate. "As far away from Pennsylvania as an airplane will take me."

She wrinkles her mouth. "Hmm. Considering all you told me about your husband, I'll give you a pass on that glaring lack of specificity. But seriously. There is a whole world waiting to meet the new, improved Judy Goodman."

I take a sip of the gimlet that I never got to finish, and then another. Each one feels like it takes me back one year and then another. When this night is done, I'll feel like I'm in high school again. Before I met Henry. A restart of myself.

"Won't it be neat," I muse, "to learn all the secret spots around the world that stewardesses can discover?"

"I hope you brought a camera."

My camera was in my suitcase in my attic. Along with everything else I hold dear. "I'll buy one before we graduate." I hadn't spent any of Ronelle's generous gift. Maybe that's what I'd do with it. Then I could send pictures to her.

"Me?" Beverly says, answering her own question. "I'm going to go to Hong Kong at the first possible opportunity. Get this." She sits up and shifts in her seat. "You can buy custom-made clothes and jewelry for a pittance there. Silk and pearls. There's a man who meets the girls at the airport. You'll know him by the measuring tape hanging around his neck. He takes you on a bus to his studio and jots down your numbers. You pick the fabric, the design, the works."

She flicks an ash with a red manicured fingernail and continues.

"Then, a few weeks later, you're in Hong Kong on another layover. It's almost finished. You go back to his shop to try it on, and he pins it where it needs adjustments. Quick as lightning, you're in the city a third time and voilà, a fabulous, one-of-a-kind dress is all yours for just a few dollars. Whole thing takes about a month from what they say."

I sigh. That indeed sounds grand. I could buy myself one new outfit a month and in no time, I'd have more dresses than I could wear in a week! And the jewelry—pearls were my mother's favorite. Maybe I'll find a strand in remembrance of her.

That part of my life, I don't plan to talk about with Beverly. Not yet. I have not yet forgiven myself for cutting my mother out of my life. I don't know if I ever will.

Brushing off this thought, I return to the conversation and realize that Beverly is not the only one who keeps an ear open for little-known secrets of Pan Am stewardesses. I'm pleased to be able to offer one of my own.

"I heard that in Paris, there are miles of tunnels underground where you can see the bones of millions of people laid out decoratively."

Beverly nods, and I can see that she has already heard of this one. Maybe she's even been. But she has the manners to refrain from telling me so. "That sounds rather macabre, but it could be a lark to go to. We'll add it to the list."

She pauses and gives me an enigmatic smile that warns me that she is not going to let me off the hook for the earlier part of our conversation, though. Despite my attempt to distract her.

"So," she says, leaning in with a conspiratorial tone. "Back to Joe Clayton. Specifically *you* and Joe Clayton. It's time to tell me everything."

CHAPTER THIRTEEN

Beverly

No one wants to admit that her mother was right. But five weeks into training, I can tell that I've gained a few pounds. Mother always warned me that my sweet tooth would catch up with me, but I dismissed the idea the way we all do when we're young enough to believe we're immortal. In New York, walking was as natural as breathing. In Miami, I have been largely indoors and stationary at a desk. With candy bowls splayed on a table in the back for that quick energy fix.

My favorite is Big Hunk nougat, but don't read anything Freudian into that.

One Friday evening, some of us let off steam laughing about all the euphemistic opportunities that candy-bar names offer, a girl from Texas even managing to turn Swedish Fish into something to make you blush. Although what that is, I can't remember. It was that kind of night. There was alcohol involved.

The weight is not a casual worry. At the beginning of training, we were measured—bust, waist, hips, height, for the uniforms that would be custom made for us and delivered right before graduation. Uniforms that we were personally paying *three hundred dollars* for and that now may not fit once they arrive.

I'm not the only one with this challenge. Looking around as we laze on the sands of Miami's South Beach on the weekend, miniature hamburgers and birch beers from Royal Castle in hand, I can see that most of the remaining twenty-nine of us have grown a little pudgy. It hasn't been helped by the cocktails and the flan and the rich Cuban food that saturates this city. But, *criminy*, they've all been worth it.

Judy is one of the few to have escaped this affliction. I suspect anxiety is as effective as a diet pill, and if that's the case, our Pennsylvania girl has that prescription in abundance. And she's barely spent a penny on our frivolity.

She remains trim and lithe, the perfect specimen of a good Pan American stewardess, causing some of the girls to comment unkindly behind her back, even as they give in to the indulgences from which she refrains. I've even heard her called *unsociable* when she is out of earshot. She's clearly here with a job to do even as the rest of us are indulging in a certain freedom, and I resent the moniker on her behalf. I've said so. Never being one to keep my mouth shut when there's something I want to say.

As far as I know, I'm the only one Judy's told about her frightful marriage. I'm the only one who understands why she approaches the training with such determination. For most of us, it's an adventure. For me, it's like my first breath of fresh air after a life of stagnation.

But for Judy Goodman, it's a lifesaver.

If only she would loosen up enough to realize how much life there is for her to live. And to see how Joe Clayton looks at her. Yes, I notice. And so does everyone else at this point. But in just one week, our base assignments will be cast, and unless she's stationed here in Miami, her chance with him will have disappeared.

I am enjoying a rare break in the lounge chair by the motel's pool, even as Judy is upstairs in the room surgically attaching herself to our Pan

Am binder. Well, that *would* be a sight. But truly, she is all kinds of nervous with our final exams coming up.

Me? I never was one to cram for a test, and I'm not about to start. I figure I'll let all the little facts swim around in my head while I enjoy the sunshine. Under an umbrella, of course. Pan American doesn't want its stewardesses to tan beyond recognition.

"Hi, Beverly." A slender shadow falls in front of my chaise, and I slip my sunglasses down my nose to see sweet, blond Bobbie Wisnoski standing there. Our sole Polish import in this training class, she came in convinced that she was only hired to fill a language need, but proved to be among the most naturally gifted stewardesses of all of us.

"I bought some diaries for everyone," she says with a gentle accent. "I'm sure we'll all want to keep notes of our adventures."

She hands me one of several leather-bound books in a shade of blue remarkably similar to the Pan American brand. I take it from her, and my hands almost burn with the weight of possibility that the empty pages contain.

"Dziękuję," I say, certain that I have mispronounced my *thank you*, but pleased that I have at least tried to learn basic phrases in the six languages represented in our class.

She smiles with amusement and has the class not to correct me.

Like I said. She's a natural.

Bobbie leaves to go share the rest of her stash. I adjust the umbrella to move with the changing sun and pull a pen out of my bag as I consider how I might like to begin. A few weeks ago, my mind was squarely fixed on escape, on exotic notions. But lately, the siren of family has been calling, and it has colored my original purpose for being here.

I'd called my mother this week to check in on Sami, happy to learn that she was out of the hospital. The coma was thankfully short lived, and in a grand display of how tragedy can turn to triumph, the incident had brought the two of them together for more than the occasional salon visit. Mother was apparently paying for Sami's recovery and had put her up at the Waldorf Astoria, right there on Park Avenue.

How she worked that out with Mr. Wall Street, I don't yet know. But I do know that the floodgates have opened. My mother has become uncharacteristically forthcoming about her family, and I am the happy recipient of all she is sharing.

She told me that after my grandmother and Sami left Manila and after their parents died, there were two remaining siblings in the Philippines—Diwa and Tala. They'd been small children when their older sisters moved—unexpected twins when my great-grandmother was thought to be past childbearing years. Diwa ultimately left Manila, too, for New York, but for reasons that Sami didn't know, she never made it there. She'd heard through other relatives that Diwa had settled in Honolulu, married, and had children.

So that means I have cousins. That's an experience that is common to most people. But Mr. Wall Street had only one sibling—an older sister who was institutionalized as a teenager. And so the possession of cousins was never mine to know.

I'm thrilled, nervous, dizzied by the knowledge of what this will change for me.

I close my eyes and let words cover me. I lay my hand on the pristine, virginal diary.

And then I open its pages and begin to write.

I've seen fog roll across the ocean. It isn't immediately noticeable until you look up and suddenly an island in the distance that you can always see is no longer visible. It reminds me of the angel of death in the movie The Ten Commandments, its wily tendrils gliding so stealthily that you don't recognize its danger until it is upon you. Then—you are suddenly cold, as if you have passed through a ghost. And maybe that is what fog is. Not the consequence of a particular concoction of precipitation, but a collection of spirits and memories passing through, searching over the years for an escape from their limbo.

If you believe that our past is woven into our present, this would explain the restlessness that has wearied my soul in all the years of my young life. I have played my part to perfection. Pleasing my parents. Representing our name. Living impeccably and irreproachably. But a fog has always pervaded my notion of happiness.

I now believe that it is the spirits of my ancestors who have resided in the fog. Oh, not the kinds one might try conjure in a séance from the spiritualist days of Conan Doyle. But I do believe that history has a dimension to it that can linger and haunt you. Until recently, I thought that the melancholy I concealed meant that there was something wrong with me.

I learned only a few weeks ago startling things about my mother's family that I could never have imagined. And as much as it awakened a natural curiosity to learn all I can, more so it has given me an answer to the why.

I hope it is not overly optimistic to think that when I find my cousins, they will embrace me as one of their own and I will sink into their arms and feel that at last, I am in a place where I belong. Because as much as the Atlantic waters have been the playground of my youth, I have always had the sense that it was not quite right. And even before seeing it, I have a feeling that when the Pacific Ocean first comes into view, I will know that I am home.

And that journey will begin in Honolulu.

CHAPTER FOURTEEN

Judy

I have been avoiding Joe.

Well, as much as I've been able to, considering that we spend five days a week in the classroom and have done so for nearly six weeks. But after that kiss, and after the surge of emotions I felt when we were squeezed together in the galley of that sliced-up 707, I didn't trust myself to be alone with him.

So I am startled when I arrive at the steps of the Villa Vizcaya and hear a man call my name. I look up and there is Joe, holding a fedora in his hand and waving to me from underneath one of three elaborate stone arches. He puts his hat on and hurries down, taking almost two steps at a time, and sidestepping a full-plumed peacock that seemed to appear out of nowhere. I see the metaphor that this display from the exotic bird is its mating ritual, and I try to put the comparison out of my mind.

Joe is out of breath when he approaches.

"There you are," he says.

I'm not unhappy to see him. Not *at all,* I'm afraid to admit. But I was not expecting it.

"Where is Beverly?" I ask, immediately sorry that I wasn't kinder in my response. Whatever the source of the confusion, this does not seem to be his fault.

"What do you mean?" Joe put a hand up to his face to shield himself from the unrelenting sun. He is wearing a pale-yellow shirt today. Not much of a departure from white, but enough that I notice.

"I'm supposed to meet Beverly here. She said that we had to see these gardens before we leave Miami. She said that they're ro—"

And then I realize what had happened. Romantic. Beverly had said that the gardens are romantic. She'd planned for Joe to be here all along. To take her place.

"She said they're what?"

"They're . . . *robust* examples of a Floridian version of Italy."

It sounds ridiculous coming out of my mouth. But I sure as heck was not going to say that other *R* word.

Oh, she's good. She's really good.

I can't say that I'm sorry about it.

Joe looks a little confused. "Yes. I suppose that's one word for it. But Judy—you look like you're surprised to see me. Beverly told me that you'd been dying to come here. Her words. And that you wanted me to meet you here."

I smile thinly. I am so happy to see him. This casual version that I've been able to see when he is not restrained by the classroom. I don't want to hurt his feelings. But before I can assure him, he takes a step back and answers. His eyes grow wide.

"Ooooh. I see what happened here. Judy, I'm sorry. I don't know why you've been avoiding me. But I can leave if you want me to."

"No!" I say. A little too quickly, too emphatically. And then I cover it with softer tones, pressing my hand against his arm to reassure him. "No—please stay. I'm—I'm glad that she did this. She took care of what I was too afraid to."

He leans in, concern growing in his expression and his voice mellowing into a tender whisper.

"Why would you be afraid of me?"

"I'm not afraid *of* you. I'm—"

I don't really know how to finish that sentence.

He takes my hand in a gesture that feels more friendly than intimate, and I try to dismiss the rush of heat that goes through me as he does so. The dizziness I feel can't be attributed to weather, though I wish I could cast the blame there. "I'll tell you what," he suggests. "I've never been to Villa Vizcaya, either, but it looks incredible. Shall we walk around for a bit? I mean, we're already here."

"Yes." I don't try to hide the delight I feel at this invitation.

Joe grins and holds up two tickets. "I was hoping you'd say that."

I pull my ticket from his hand, the most delicate way to separate from him. But immediately, my skin feels the unmistakable prickle of loss. How long had it been since contact with a man had made me feel appreciated?

Already, I am parched for his touch again.

But that lifts as soon as we pass through the entrance of the beautiful Villa Vizcaya.

"My God!" I exclaim. I look at Joe, and his expression matches my enchantment.

It is a wonderland.

We stand in the presence of an enormous white Italianate mansion, ornate with columns and scrolls and arches. Its red-tile roof is adorned with a weather vane that reveals that the scant breeze is coming in from the east. Mangrove trees surround it, thick to the point of appearing like a forest and swaying like they know a mysterious tribal dance belonging to long-ago natives.

Elaborate scrollwork adorns marble arches, and koi fish swim in the waters of a fountain, their bright scales an orange shade that rivals the sun. Rounded balcony upon rounded balcony line the gardens, every one of them reminiscent of where Juliet might have stood as she longed for her Romeo. We hear the tropical-sounding calls of birds that we cannot see, and we see multicolored lizards that scatter in silence.

I will have to write to Ronelle about this, though it might sound garish because words fail my ability to adequately describe it. It would surely miss the mark.

I hope that they will have a gift shop, and I can send her a postcard. Without a signature, of course, and with disguised handwriting. In case, for some reason, Henry were ever to see it.

Joe slides his hand into mine, and everything else is forgotten. I sense that his gesture is less about the growing rapport between us than the need to simply connect with another human being in the face of something so transcendent.

I don't mind. And I don't pull away.

"Look at the stones, Judy," he says as he points to the path in front of us. "They're *fossilized*. Fossilized!"

And, indeed, before us lays a carpet of large, flat stones that were embedded with all sorts of ancient impressions—shells, ferns, and other flora and fauna that I cannot name but certainly marvel at.

"Can you even imagine where they found them, let alone how much they paid for them?" Joe asks.

"Or how they got them there. They didn't have Pan Am Cargo services to help out back when this was built."

Joe throws his head back and laughs, which breaks the spell of the place for both of us. And I am thankful because it is this Joe—this casual, lighthearted, dear Joe—that I had fallen for that early evening in Miami.

The one whom I have resisted ever since.

Or tried to.

"You sound like an advertisement, Judy. Maybe you should be writing in our offices rather than flying off to the other side of the world," he suggests.

For one heartbeat, I want to take him seriously. If I could work in Miami—if I could stay near Joe—what might happen?

Maybe when I am free. And once I've had my chance to explore the world. This venture started as a way to protect myself from my husband.

But the last six weeks have tantalized me with dreams that I had never thought could come true. The real possibility that those colored pins I'd stuck on that childhood map might become flesh-and-blood experiences for me. I've already let love derail that once before. I owe it to myself to see this through.

"How about this, Clayton?" I ask with just a tinge of flirt in my voice. Perhaps Beverly has rubbed off on me, and for that I'm grateful. "You save an office spot for me here in Miami, and I'll think about coming back after I've checked off every place I've been longing to see."

"I might hold you to that." Joe has my attention, and I can't look away.

My pulse quickens, and I don't know how to answer, but something in the background catches my eye and gives me the perfect escape.

"See that statue?" I ask. The part of the gardens we've walked to now is an outdoor gallery of crisp white figures that look like they belong in the Louvre. Or so I believe from the photographs I've seen.

Joe follows my gaze as I look at one that depicts a bearded middle-aged man strumming a lyre.

"The nymph?"

"No—the one to the right."

He nods.

"That one reminds me of my father."

Joe cocks his head. "In what way? Is he a Greek god of music?"

"Was."

He looks confused, and then he realizes my use of the past tense.

"I'm sorry. I didn't mean to make light."

"It's okay," I say as I shrug. And I find myself feeling happy as I say it. Like I can speak about Dad to Joe in a way I haven't done before. Henry would shut me down whenever I mentioned him. He probably didn't like that I'd ever loved another man, even if it was my own *father*.

I have always wondered, if my dad hadn't contracted the pneumonia that turned fatal, if he would have joined Mom's soliloquy of concern over my chosen spouse and given me more pause to consider their instincts.

Maybe the united voice of my parents would have raised the concern in me that my mother's alone didn't.

"It's okay," I say again, retreating from those well-worn ponderings. "I feel—I feel like that statue is him giving me his blessing. He's the one who gave me the *Come Fly with Me* album in the first place. And my map to mark the places I'd want to visit. He had a beard like that, and a jawline almost as square. And played the violin for the Philadelphia Orchestra."

"I'd love to hear more about him."

That is the very, very best thing he could have said to me. But between that and the peace I feel from the statue—as if it is a little hello from Heaven—I don't necessarily want to revisit nostalgic moments that will only dampen this time.

"Thank you, Joe. Let's do that. But another time. Today is about—" I almost said *us*. "Today is about this beautiful place."

And the goodbye ahead of us.

I look up, and the hands of the clock on Villa Vizcaya read 12:05 p.m. Just an hour ago, I was looking forward to spending the afternoon with Beverly. We don't know where we'll each be assigned, so this week could very well be our goodbye as well.

Instead—and not unhappily—I'm here with Joe.

"Judy—look at that!" I turn around, and Joe is pointing to a magnificent white crane, its wings outstretched as it glides over the lake waters in front of the mansion. Its image is reflected on the ripples, and as it gets nearer, the bird and its twin become one. With its large stature, it frightens away a number of geese that were gathered, and they emit angry squawks at the disruption to their peace.

Joe grins. "Speaking of family, I was thinking that my sisters would love this place. There are four of them. All older than me. Then I came along and invaded their little nest."

"Four! How did you survive that?" Though, in truth, I am envious. I have always wanted siblings and the built-in friendships they might provide.

"Well despite the times when they put curlers in my hair and gave me the enduring nickname of *Noelle* on account of my Christmas birthday, I think I've done pretty well for myself!"

I can't help but grin at the image, but I don't want to outright laugh. "Christmas?" I manage to say. "What a day to be born."

He shrugs. "Mom went into labor just before midnight Mass. If my dad hadn't gotten her to the hospital when he did, I might have had a starring role as baby Jesus."

This image, too, makes me smile.

Joe makes me smile.

It's easy to feel disarmed around him. Even though I've grown such armor around myself.

We arrive at the edge of the lake and find a spot of grass to sit on. In front of us large poles rise out of the water, like what I'd seen in pictures of Venice. On the dock sits an enormous iguana, easily three feet long, and I'm stunned by the presence of the prehistoric-looking creature. This place is indeed Florida and Italy combined, the intention of the builder of Vizcaya on full display.

"Tell me about your sisters," I say, remaining in territory that deflects all that I am feeling right now. "Surely you have lots of stories."

Joe picks at a blade of grass, tearing it in half, and then looks at me with those water-like eyes. "Well, they are all fans of *Pride and Prejudice*, and since I was not the girl they wanted, the fifth sister, they recruited me into playing the part anyway whenever they'd get the notion to stage a production in our basement."

"I'll bet you looked cute in a pinafore."

"Perish the thought."

I grin and nudge his shoulder with mine. "This is very, very valuable information, Joe Clayton. The sort of thing that could be quite useful in case I ever have the need to blackmail you."

"It would be. Good thing there's nothing else to blackmail me over. Call me boring, but I've lived a pretty basic life."

I look at him as if I don't buy that for a minute. "Says the man who was a steward for Pan Am, has lived in New York City, and just moved to Miami."

I wonder if Joe misses being a steward. For the foreseeable future, Pan Am is only hiring women for that role—the days of male stewards have all but passed. I am about to ask him, but am interrupted.

A goose waddles over to us and tilts her head before wandering off. Her honk echoes across the vast space, making her sound like there are dozens of her, though she's the only one I see.

"I guess *boring* isn't the right word," Joe continues. "But I never got myself into trouble. I worked my way up to Eagle Scout by the time I was a senior."

I bite my bottom lip as I consider this. The man is literally a Boy Scout. Either I am phenomenally gullible or I've been given the second chance of a lifetime.

I look at him slyly, goading him to reveal a misstep. "No dalliances with a Girl in Blue?" Surely, being surrounded by so many beautiful women donning the Pan Am uniform has been a temptation, at least.

He scoots closer to me and raises his eyebrows in an exaggerated way. "Not. *Yet.*"

I feel my cheeks redden. And my heart beats faster. I want to believe him. And something tells me I can.

Then he grows serious and pulls back a bit. Maybe my initial reaction to seeing him today makes him hesitate. "Actually, this is never something we directly covered in training, but Pan American insists on a certain *classiness* for its employees despite the culture's prevailing theory that a job in the air somehow equates to a looseness of behavior. I'm not going to say that there is never an occasional affair or that some passengers don't try to push their luck. But it's not the—pardon me here—mattress romp that people imagine our career to be."

I'm thoroughly blushing now. I can feel it. I hope he doesn't notice.

But I'm glad to hear it. I think on some level, I'd known it to be true. Other airlines featured drawings of the stewardesses in their advertisements. Short skirts. And even men looking out from their seat as she walks past, the roundness of her rear end emphasized by the artist. Some of the more innocuous posters are produced by Air France and United, but even they still emphasize the stewardess over the travel.

Pan Am is different. Their magazine advertisements are about the *destination*. They promise exotic locales. Palm trees. World-class cities.

Joe stands up and helps me to my feet, letting go more quickly than I would have liked. I smooth my skirt as he brushes some grass off his pants.

"There's a sign for a maze over there. Want to walk through it?"

It looks like it's got an abundance of shade and would be a welcome change from the sun that is now directly overhead. I feel sweat bead along my hairline, and I see it doing the same to him.

"Yes. Let's go."

Joe takes one of my hands again. And I let him, relishing the newness of this feeling. Or maybe not newness. *Dormancy.* Awakening something that has been slumbering. I never dared to hope that I could feel this blush, this anticipation again. We walk side by side toward the maze grown out of shrubbery twice our height.

My pulse quickens at his nearness. What did Beverly tell him that made him think that I would welcome this . . . this . . . advance? She must have led him to believe that I wanted this.

And maybe I do. Because I don't pull away. It's sweet. There is even a shyness about him as we walk along.

I take a deep breath. I need to say something, anything, to break the silence because I'm overwhelmed by the romanticism hanging in the air around us. The statues. The koi fish. The exotic birds. Even the stepping stones that are cut from fossils. Impressions that are millions of years old tell me that they were here long before I was and will be long after I am gone.

They give me permission to give myself over to this moment. It's a drop in the eternal waters of time.

But I'm afraid to let my emotions run away with me. I don't know what's right and what's wrong. I no longer wear my wedding ring, and I do plan to pursue a Mexican divorce, but I've never imagined myself to be a girl who would cheat on her husband.

And yet, if Ronelle or Beverly were here, I know they'd tell me this: that it was *Henry* who broke our vow. The first time he laid a hand on me. And every time since.

How long were women supposed to sit quietly and withstand that kind of treatment? Or would this relatively new decade be the chance for us to have an equal voice in what happens in our lives?

Joe speaks before I can think of what to say. Certainly these worries of mine are a little too intense for a conversation so early into our—friendship.

"To get back to the culture at Pan American," he begins, "there is one rumor that is founded in a lot of truth. Many of our regular clients have gone on to marry stewardesses."

I'd love to avoid the topic of marriage. But I never seem to be able to escape it.

"Is that why Delores told us that the average career for a Pan Am stewardess is only eighteen months?"

"Exactly. There's a good chance in that time that the stewardess will meet some dashing character in first class. Champagne in Paris and before you know it, he's bought her a huge diamond on the Via Veneto in Rome."

I stop as we consider which way to turn in the maze. I pull Joe to the right.

"Well, that won't be *me*," I say decidedly. I realize as the words come out of my mouth that I probably sound like the kind of woman who has no interest in being tied down. But that isn't the case for me. I *liked* being married. I *wanted* to be married. The reality of it, however, had been debilitating.

I knew that they weren't all like that. Look at my parents. Happy until the end. It was possible.

"Why not?" Joe asks, reacting to how declarative I must have sounded. "You're not the marrying type?"

I don't know if this is casual conversation, or if he is already imagining a future for us right here on our first—accidental—date. I decide on the former.

"I *am* the marrying type. I am. It's just not something I can think about in my life right now."

Joe is looking at me. We're still holding hands. Time seems to pause and even the breeze stills.

He decides not to press it. And I find him all the more endearing because of his discretion.

He steps back, saving me from making a mistake.

But he still hasn't let go of my hand.

And I still haven't pulled away.

We take a left, and then another. Then a right, and before I know it, there are no more people around, and it is as if we are the only two people in the world. The trees cast their shadows across us, enveloping us in privacy.

"Judy," he whispers with a pressing urgency. He lets go of my hand and turns toward me. We are only inches apart, and I can feel the heat of his breath on my neck. I am engulfed in the scent of flowers wafting from somewhere within the maze, and I think that if these were different circumstances, it might feel like a movie.

"Yes, Joe?" I answer. I feel my heartbeat in every part of my body, and I purse my lips to keep control of myself.

I want him to kiss me. To make a declaration that will assure me that all I am feeling is not merely my imagination.

But his words are not the ones I expect, and his voice is laced with sadness.

"The base assignments were posted at the training center before I left. Your friends should all know where they're being sent by now."

I am conflicted. All I've wanted all this time is to be far away. As far away as possible. And now when he says these words, I find myself wanting to be right here. It is a strange thing that a decision made by someone else will have an impact—a big impact—on me for the rest of my life.

"Do you want to know where you're going?" he asks. He brushes a strand of hair behind my ear.

I nod. I want him to say Miami. I *want* him to say Miami. I want to stay and see what could happen between us. Come what may.

Joe pulls me close, encircling me in his arms. My skin tingles where we touch, and I feel overwhelmed. I stand, hands to my sides, but I lean into him because I fear that I will fall with the magnitude of all that is about to happen.

I feel the heat of his breath again, this time on my ear as he whispers, "San Francisco."

A reel passes through my mind with every image I've ever seen of it. The Golden Gate Bridge. The fog. The vineyards. The Pacific. It is everything I wanted. Right up until this moment when I would have given anything for him to tell me that I didn't have to leave Florida at all.

That I wouldn't have to leave him.

"San Francisco," I repeat, my face pressed against his shoulder.

We stand there, swaying just a little, consoling one another. And although I am struck by how little sense it makes considering that we hardly know each other outside these weeks of training, I feel a sense of loss and can tell that he feels it too.

The loss not of what had been. But the loss of the opportunity for what *might have been.*

Mo'orea, French Polynesia
Today

The sun casts its rays over the Pacific waters through a lone cloud, dispersing them in a fan-shaped pattern that reminds me of old paintings where God was depicted in such a scene. The trade winds have picked up early, creating rolling waves of whitecaps far into the horizon, contrasting with waters that variegate between turquoise and deep blue depending on the depth of the ocean floor.

I stretch my legs—my skin wrinkled and spotted—across the sand and let the warmth wash over me. It is an elixir. Like many my age, I live in Florida to escape winters farther north. But unlike those my age, who sink into the ease of golf carts and bridge games, I enjoy the bustling city of Miami.

It is a setting more suited to the young, but once upon a time, it was the beginning of my new life. So it's the place where I want to spend my remaining years, holding off the reaper by daily walks on the beach and abundant doses of sunshine.

It is where I trained with Pan Am and my life changed for the better and taught me to look ahead, not back.

Once the obituaries of friends became regular occurrences in the newspaper, when my grandchildren became occupied with their own children, when death robbed me of my spouse, I returned to the city where it all began.

You and I had met earlier, of course, in New York. But I don't count that. It was brief and impersonal.

A long, lean shadow falls across me, and I look up expecting to see a figure equal to its size. Instead, I discover a small girl, maybe six years old, standing in just the right spot for the sun to hint at the woman she will become.

"Qu'est-ce que c'est?" she asks.

What is that, *it means. I understand her perfectly.*

How do I condense my thoughts into an answer that a child will understand?

I respond to her in the language of the once-French island, though I have been out of practice in its use for a very long time.

"C'est un vase," I respond. The word vase *is thankfully similar to its counterpart when spoken.*

"The ashes of my friend are in here." I continue in French. It is mostly the truth, but my rusty words limit me from telling the entirety of the story.

I wonder if she will understand, but a look beyond her years comes over her face, as if this is not an unfamiliar custom to her.

"Someone you loved?" she asks.

"Someone I loved very much."

"How did it happen?" I am surprised that she asks this. It would be natural to assume, looking at my wrinkles and the many liver spots that my great-grandchildren love to connect with marker pens, that my friend was similarly old. I do not explain that you were taken in your prime. That this delay in the return to Mo'orea falls entirely on my shoulders.

"It was an accident," I begin. "In the sky."

"In an airplane?"

I have underestimated the child. The primitive surroundings do not mean that she is unfamiliar with the world.

Tears form in my eyes, fresh as the day I heard the news.

I can only nod.

CHAPTER FIFTEEN

Beverly

I am sealing the envelope of a letter to my mother when someone begins to pound on the motel door.

"I know you're in there," shouts an angry male voice.

For the life of me, I can't figure who I've crossed. Only Frederick would have been justified in such ire, but it's been six weeks since the news of my departure, and already I've heard that he's taken up with Suzanne of the Perfect Handwriting. And as I know that word of my father cutting me off has spread like measles around my old set, I would no longer be quite the catch Mr. Bahr would have once thought.

I slip some scissors into my skirt pocket, the closest thing I have to a weapon. Perhaps it is a lunatic who has stumbled into the wrong place.

I crack open the door, holding it in place with my foot.

A man I do not recognize towers over me, and though he looks harmless, his breath reeks of tobacco and gin as he speaks. His manners become suddenly genteel when he realizes that I am not who he was expecting.

"Please excuse me," he says as he tucks a wayward corner of his shirt into his trousers. "I'm looking for Judy Goodman. Do I have the right place?"

My heart tightens. I know who this must be.

Judy's husband, Henry.

I know his type. A model of docility to those he encounters. A villain behind closed doors. He will be on perfect, perfect behavior in front of me, so I know I have nothing to fear. Because in the event that I know Judy, he'll want to discredit anything untoward that she says by merit of his irreproachable deportment.

I am not fooled. But I do know how to play the game.

I open the door wider so that he does not suspect my seething hostility.

"Hello," I say. "I'm her friend—Sami."

There's no need for him to know my real name. I borrow the one that belongs to my great-aunt. It's the first one I thought of.

I slip outside before he can try to come in. "How can I help you?"

"I'm here to surprise my wife. Judy Goodman. Do you know her?" He smiles, charisma on full display. A trick that Judy fell for once upon a time.

I look at my watch. Three o'clock. Judy and Joe met at Vizcaya at eleven. I hope this means that they're having a good time together. But our graduation starts in two hours. She could be back any minute.

Whatever happens, I need to make it happen fast. He can't be here when Judy returns. It would ruin everything.

"Yes. Judy. What a gal. But I'm sorry—you've just missed her."

"Well, now, what a shame. I can wait, though. Do you know when she'll be back?"

"She won't be. At least, not here."

A look of anger passes over his eyes, and I see his fists tighten at his sides. But in a flash, he's controlled both. No doubt hoping that I didn't notice.

But I did notice. I'm going to protect her with everything I've got, and God may strike me down, but I feel no shame in lying.

"And where is she?" he asks with measured breathing.

"She went home."

This surprises him.

"Home?"

"Yes," I fabricate, the excuses coming with alarming ease. "Home to Pennsylvania. To you."

He scratches his head. "Well, how do you figure that?"

"She said that she wanted to come talk to you before she got her assignment."

Good. I've thoroughly confused him. But if he's made it all the way here, he's discovered what she'd been up to for the past few weeks. The most plausible lies are the ones that acknowledge some truth.

"Her assignment?"

"Yes. Judy graduated from the program a few days ago. They loved her. They picked her for a prime location—Paris."

I do know that Judy got San Francisco. Just like me.

But also like me, Judy's second language is French. So he might buy the deceit.

"Paris?"

A wild look takes over him. But again, he controls it.

Poor Judy. How did she ever endure a day with this man, let alone years?

"Yes," I answer sweetly. I lean against the doorframe, softening my voice. Disarming him with the coyness I know how to conjure when it's needed. "What a wonderful husband you must be. Supporting a swell girl like Judy in this dream of hers. And how proud I can imagine you are. She's top of her class. You are going to love exploring the City of Lights with her. How romantic it will be for the two of you."

I can tell he cares about the City of Lights about as much as he cares about sobriety.

"In fact," I continue, "her flight to Paris from Philadelphia leaves tomorrow morning, so I know she was going to try to catch you tonight. You'd better get right on back! Which airline did you come in on?"

"Delta."

"Perfect! I'm quite sure Delta has an evening flight from Miami to Baltimore, and I'm certain they'll let you exchange your return ticket. Baltimore's not so far from where you live, right?"

Good thing Judy and I had stayed up talking so many nights. And that I'd gotten her to open up as much as she did. Those kinds of details were making this so much easier, so much more believable than it could have been.

But the seconds were ticking. I had to get him out of here.

"You'd better hurry. I think that flight's at five," I improvised. But surely there was one this evening. "That's just enough time if you leave now. The front desk can call for a taxi."

I put my hands on his shoulders and point him toward the stairs. Touching him disgusts me.

"So she's really not here?" he asks over his shoulder. But he's already taken a few steps forward.

"No! She was due in Paris immediately. Top of her class, remember? They don't want to waste a minute getting her up in the air. Now, go on! If you catch this flight, you can have a beautiful night at home with your wife before she leaves tomorrow."

That does it. Without a goodbye, Henry Goodman (what a waste of a last name, if you ask me) scurries toward the front office. I lean over the second-floor railing and watch until a yellow cab pulls up and whisks him away. I put my hand to my heart, and as I suspected, it's racing. I take a few deep breaths until it slows. I think we're out of the woods.

Just then, the city bus pulls up to its stop and Judy steps off.

I want to retch from how close they came to seeing each other, and I grip the door handle for support as I step back into our room.

It's then that I see Judy's pink sweater with yellow flowers hanging from the top bedpost.

I try to remember—did she bring that from home? Or did she buy it here?

And more importantly—is there any chance that he saw it?

◆ ◆ ◆

Tonight's the night. Our tailor-made wool uniforms and cotton blouses have arrived in zipped cloth bags. My name is embroidered in Pan American blue thread.

Beverly Caldwell

I run my hand along it, my newly manicured nails stroking the soft lines of the letters, and it is all I can do to keep from revealing how emotional this makes me feel.

I did it. *We* did it. This was the hardest thing I've ever done in my life. Fourteen girls went home because they couldn't hack it, or didn't want to, which somehow makes this feel like even more of an achievement.

And I did it without my father's help. Outside of the occasional splurge with the cash I'd come with, I washed my laundry by hand, drank cocktails only at happy hours since they're half price, and headed to the sale racks at department stores for any wardrobe updates. Judy was helpful with tips like that.

I'm no Madame Curie, but I still feel a sense of accomplishment.

And the adventure has only begun.

Jean unzips her bag with careless gusto and yanks the clothes from it when the zipper gets stuck midway.

"Here we go, ladies. The world's most coveted uniform. Ya think any of us are going to even fit into them? I don't know about you, but I enjoyed more than a few empanadas over in Little Havana."

I have seen more of Jean than I ever need to, as she has spent our little downtime these past six weeks lounging in our room in only her brassiere and panties, sometimes accessorizing with a light robe left unbelted. Always on the phone with her boyfriend. If she's gained an ounce, you can push me over with a feather. She slips the fitted skirt over her slim hips and turns around. "Zip me up?" she asks. And I have no choice but to oblige.

She's being sent to Berlin, which is a far cry from Arkansas. I wonder how long she'll make it before she decides that she can't live without Erwin and moves back to marry him.

Jean struts over to the lone mirror that hangs on our bathroom wall and smooths her hands over her waist, turning left and right. Her lips form a pout. "I'm going to have to starve myself if I want to be able to move in this thing."

We hear a knock at the door, and Bobbie from Poland peeks her head in. Bobbie will be heading to London tomorrow and covering European routes. No surprise there. "We have ice cream sundaes in our room to celebrate! Please come join us!"

"Coming!" shouts Jean. And she races out the door to the room next to us, not even bothering to put on the accompanying blouse.

I hear Judy giggle. And as much as I try to keep my composure, I can't help but join in. Which gets worse as I try to slip into my own skirt. It fits over my hips, but I can't zip it up.

I throw myself onto my bed and laugh until my rib cage aches.

"Oh my goodness. Do you think laughing burns any calories? Because unlike our skinny friend from Arkansas who apparently can chomp empanadas and not get bloated, I have drunk my way through every martini and chardonnay and mojito joint in this city, and I think it shows."

In a far more ladylike fashion than what I've just displayed, Judy comes to lie beside me, and we both stare at the bottom of the upper bunk as if it holds the answers to the meaning of life.

I hear her breath and the faintest sound of a hum.

"I presume things went well at Vizcaya?" Meaning, *Did my plan work?*

"Yes." She sighs. "What a beautiful place. It even has a swimming pool that looks like a cave bedecked with shells."

"Bedecked? I think Sister Mary Clare put that on a spelling test once upon a time."

I can feel Judy smile as she relaxes into the mattress. But she remains silent.

"I think you know that I wasn't asking about the *property*, Judy. How were things—?"

"With Joe?" she finishes.

"Mm-hmm."

"It was—perfect." She is silent for a moment, and I have enough sense not to press it.

"But what does that matter when I'm moving to San Francisco tomorrow? And that—I can't be with him anyway?"

I'd spent the last hour debating whether or not I should tell her that Henry had been here looking for her. And that I'd sent him away. She is so happy right now. She has so much to look forward to. How can I tell her something that will make her look backward?

Maybe another day. But not tonight. Ignorance is bliss, they say. And he should be boarding his flight any moment.

"Perfect is good."

She runs her hands through her hair. "Oh my word, Beverly. It was even more than that. I don't think the right word exists. There was just a *rightness* about it. Do you know what I mean?"

I pat her hand. "I've read my share of romance novels. I can *imagine* what you mean."

She knows that despite my flirtatious personality, I have scant *actual* experience with men, so they're more lore to me than reality. I do hope the real thing lives up to what I've built in my mind, or goodness, what will centuries of all that hype have come to?

She turns over on her side and props herself up on her elbow. With Jean in the room down the hall, this is like a sleepover of two girls who are fast becoming best friends. I've never had a lot of good friends outside of Eve the Kiwi. The ones who sent those myriads of invitations were never the ones I could have a heart to heart with. This is like having a sister, or what I imagine that to be like. And as my ties to family are thin as it is, it is a more welcome thing that I would have expected.

"Yes," Judy says. "I read a bunch of romance novels before—before I was married. And then I realized that they were all fiction. Stories to fill us up where only emptiness stood. But now—"

"Now?" I encourage.

"Now that I've met Joe, even for so short a time, I can almost believe that they aren't necessarily fiction at all."

"I think that's the very best thing you could say about it."

Judy turns onto her back and looks again at the upper bunk. "I'm not saying that Joe Clayton is my happily-ever-after. I hardly know him, and we'll be a continent away as of tomorrow. But I think it gives me hope for—for the *possibility* of a happy ending. With someone. And it's been several years since I believed that could be the case."

"Then my little Vizcaya setup was worth it." I feel as smug as it surely sounds.

Judy arches her back and laughs. "That was your onetime pass. No more surprises like that, Beverly. Promise me. Just because I had my first taste of that kind of feeling in a very long time doesn't mean I can be rushed. Or that I approve of meddling. Besides, if my marriage taught me anything, it's that a woman can't hang her happiness on a man. A bad one or a good one. She has to make her own happiness."

"Here, here," I say, lifting an imaginary glass of champagne.

"Speaking of happiness," Judy says. "Have you heard from your father? I would have hoped he'd be in touch now that you've seen this through."

I shake my head. "Mother says he sends his regards, but I think she made that up. Mostly, we avoid talking about him."

"I'm glad you and she are talking, though."

"Yes. Small blessings."

"How is your aunt? Sami?"

I smile. Judy has been a patient audience as I've talked through this new frontier of having family. I know she misses her parents and is eager that I nurture for myself what she has lost and buried in regret.

"Better. She should be able to start up at the salon again in a few weeks. She and my mother want me to come up to New York before San Francisco. But there's just no time. I've promised postcards for the time being."

I hop up, pulling Judy with me.

"And if we don't get to graduation, there won't be a San Francisco for either of us. It's almost five!"

Judy pulls me toward her and gives me a tight squeeze.

"You're right. Let's get going."

Our graduation is simple. It's held in a conference room at the Taj Mahal, the brand-new headquarters for Pan Am's Latin American division.

The name bears no resemblance to pictures I've seen of its illustrious namesake in Agra, India. Though I hope to bid a route that will take me to see that for myself someday.

Rather, the reference is merely because the architect was the same one who built the US embassy in New Delhi. Still, it is impressive in its own way. Space-age cinder blocks set in repeating horizontal patterns give it a thoroughly modern look that I adore. Mr. Wall Street and Mother like to collect ornate, onerous antiques, and whether out of rebellion or actual aesthetic preference, I find myself quite drawn to the minimalism that has swept the imagination of my generation.

So this is why I am dazzled by this paragon of new architecture in front of me. I'd even go so far as to say that it looks magical this evening. We walk parallel to the reflecting pool under an umbrella of palm trees and flags representing every country to which Pan Am flies. Which are many. Hidden lights illuminate both our path and the building, and its glow reflects the excitement I know we're all feeling.

Jeez, what an intense six weeks it's been. Time to reap the rewards.

Deportment be damned, I reach my hand out and find Judy's as we walk two by two into the building. I feel her squeeze it back. Maybe if we'd been friends for years instead of weeks, we could convey our thoughts through such a medium. But I think we're getting there. Tomorrow, we'll both fly to San Francisco. Pan Am will put us up at a hotel near the airport until we can find an apartment to rent.

A light wind blows past us, and I feel it on my neck. We've both just had our hair cut—collar-length, as required. And I'm not yet used to it being so short.

The ceremony itself is brief. Delores gives a speech that neither bores nor motivates us. Or maybe it was sensational, but we are all too stuffed with information to retain any more.

After we award Delores with some polite applause, Joe Clayton, who'd been standing a few feet behind her, clears his throat as a means of asking permission to approach the podium. She steps away, and he steps forward, gripping each side and looking almost as nervous as we all are.

It's something I'd noticed about him. When Joe is teaching, he is in full command of his subject. He wears confidence as comfortably as his well-fitting chinos. But when anything off-the-cuff is called for? The man seems to lose a couple of inches from his height. Not so much as to diminish him. But we all have our lesser points. And extemporaneous public speaking is his. It's kind of cute, that vulnerability. I can see why he and Judy are so well matched. Maybe the thousands of miles of distance don't have to be the end of things.

One can hope.

Joe clears his throat again.

"Ladies," he says. "This is the first class I've ever seen through start to finish in our new Miami location. And I have to say that you've certainly set the bar high for future ones."

He looks down, as if searching for notes that are most certainly not there. He takes a deep breath and then returns his eyes to the group, some of that classroom confidence returning now that he's gotten started.

You can do this, Joe, I think. As if either of us is telepathic.

"Tomorrow, you will be sent across the world. New members of the Pan American family. You will see places you've only read about. Eat food you've never heard of. Shop in stores unlike any you've been in. You'll meet the rudest people you've ever encountered and the kindest ones. You'll fly higher than man ever imagined possible, and you'll be profoundly and irrevocably changed in ways that you cannot imagine."

He straightens up to his full height. Our boy Joe is on a roll. Good for you, Joe. I'm rooting for you.

"The funny thing is that while this particular group is spreading out to Paris, New Delhi, Mexico City, New York, Berlin, London, and San Francisco, this is not goodbye. Inevitably, you'll end up on some route at some future date where you will be scheduled with someone you haven't seen since your time in this room. You'll grab a drink at the hotel's bar—out of uniform, of course—and swap stories of where you've both been since this moment. And whether it is this time next month or this time next year, you will already be full of more experiences than the average person will ever encounter in their lifetimes."

He glances at Judy, but it's brief enough that someone less attuned to it would not take notice. He looks nervous. "So I leave you with this," he continues. His eyes find Judy again, and this time, he doesn't look away. "No matter how far you travel, no matter where life takes you, I very much hope that our paths will cross again. Don't forget those of us in Miami. We won't forget you."

He steps away, and I sneak a peek at Judy, who is seated catty-corner to me. Her eyes are glistening. I wonder just what had happened between them in those beautiful gardens of Villa Vizcaya.

CHAPTER SIXTEEN

Judy

Condensation drips down the glass, the result of the chilly air tens of thousands of feet above the ground and the manufactured warmth of the inside of the cabin. I trace my finger from top to bottom, following what looks like a raindrop. Or a tear.

If it is a tear, I hope it's a happy one. Mine certainly would be.

On this, the fourth flight I have ever taken in my life, I am seated by a window. Previously, on my New-York-to-London, London-to-Miami flights, I'd been squeezed into a middle seat. A gaseous businessman on one side, a chatty dental student on the other. Even then, in the most claustrophobic situation I'd ever found myself in, the Pan Am stewardesses went out of their way to make me feel comfortable. And they didn't even know that I was on my way to training to become one of them.

Now, I am luxuriating in first class, this prime window seat generously offered to me by Beverly. We'd flown together from Miami to Mexico City and would be landing soon in San Francisco. Just six weeks ago, I'd barely traveled beyond a small radius around my home in Pennsylvania. And now, I'd crossed the Atlantic Ocean—twice—the Gulf of Mexico, the Gulf of California, and I am eager beyond words to see the Pacific.

The Pacific Ocean. Just the thought of it brings to mind all sorts of exotic images. Palm trees, hula skirts, islands. It's a mythical place in my imagination. Granted, that's not what I will find on the California side. But it is just a matter of time.

I am going to see it all.

Tipping my hat to you, Mr. Sinatra.

My fantastical thoughts are sobered, though, by the headlines that plastered the newspapers today, announcing the tragic death of Marilyn Monroe. I hadn't thought it was possible for me to be any more appreciative of this opportunity, but now I am. Life is short, as her untimely passing reminds me. I've made the right choice in seizing the chance to live it.

I lay my aqua-colored ticket inside a book and slip them into my purse. I'm going to frame this someday.

The stewardess comes by to refill our coffee. Bone-china cups and saucers, quite an upgrade from the Styrofoam ones I'd relied on in college for the caffeine I needed to stay up studying. And served on a crisp linen tablecloth that covers my pullout tray. With a bud vase holding a fresh white rose. All through this flight, I've paid attention to the details. From walking to the blue carpet to how the stewardess moves. Or more aptly, how she *glides* through the aisle. The phrases she uses. The order in which she serves the food. The eagerness to please. I'd learned that her name is Miss Mendoza, and Mexico City is her home base.

But she leans down and tells us to call her Rosamaria. At least while we're off-duty passengers. I decide that Rosamaria will be the model for how I will carry myself in the job. I'm eager to get started.

Beverly leans over. "Are you going to eat those olives?" She points to my tray. Her breath smells of the spearmint candy that had been served in a little wrapper along with hot, lemon-scented towels at the conclusion of the meal.

"I don't care for the green ones," I say. "Have at it."

Dinner had been a seven-course extravaganza, and I'd eaten every morsel of the filet mignon with peas and roasted potatoes, the chocolate cheesecake with raspberry drizzle, the garden salad with bits of blue cheese, and everything else except for those olives. I was glad that they would not be wasted.

I was relieved that they hadn't served Camembert. Already the growing geography between Joe and myself was tearing me up, mile by mile, six hundred miles per hour on this 707. And that cheese that I'd served him—incorrectly—in that sliced-up galley during training would have felt like the deepening of a knife wound.

"Good thing we won't be fed like this every day. I'd never be able to fit into my uniform after a couple of them." Beverly sits back in the extra-wide cushioned seat and exhales. She runs her thumb along the inside of her skirt's waistband. "You're going to have to teach me to grocery shop on a budget, Judy."

"Poor little ex–rich girl," I tease with exaggeration. "You know I will. Eggs and bananas. Your reliable and inexpensive doses of protein and potassium." I sink my head back into the cushioned headrest and place my hands on my belly. I don't want to think about budgets at a moment like this. "That. Was. Amazing. Easily the best meal I've ever had."

I feel the now familiar shift in the plane that tells me we're going to prepare for descent and know that the pilots will soon lift the spoilers. I've grown used to the thunder of the engine, the red lights at the tips of the wings, the vapor emanating from the air-conditioning. These things no longer frighten me.

"Who would have thought that food as grand as this could be prepared in such a tiny galley?" I ask rhetorically.

"Well, it *was* from Maxim's de Paris."

I turn my head to my right, looking at her with lazy eyes. I feel the same relaxed bliss that she's exhibiting.

"I know *that*," I say. "But I can't imagine that it tastes any better in the restaurant than it does here, reheated and all."

"Mother and I went there once. To Maxim's. I had the same thing—the filet. So I can say unequivocally that there is no difference."

Throughout our newfound friendship, Beverly had made several references like this, wistful comments about the life she left behind. But she has a way of making such comments with an air of detachment that never makes me feel like my own more limited experiences are any less significant. Or that she has any regrets.

I'd learned something else in this time of knowing her. Despite her father cutting her off—or maybe because of it—Beverly wants to be independent, and her eagerness to learn to live within her means is as enthusiastic as one in my financial state might be if I discovered a winning lottery ticket.

Beverly has schooled me on some of the finer parts of life. And I am prepared to return the favor in San Francisco by teaching her about matinee-movie prices, late-evening bakery purchases for half off, and dented-can discounts at the grocery store.

We will need some seniority before our Pan Am paychecks reflect our glamorous appearances. Although a truly independent woman needs to be smart about her money, no matter what she is paid.

Rosamaria glides toward us again, her feather-like presence catching us by surprise.

"Is there anything else I can do for you before we land?" she asks in a sincere but singsong voice.

"Pour me into a luggage cart and wheel me to our hotel." Beverly laughs.

Rosamaria grins. "Well, that's a bit beyond the scope of my abilities, but I think this might help." She bends her knees so as to not have to lean over the passengers—the famed clipper dip pose—and looks behind her. She hands us a large Pan Am–branded cotton bag. "I put together a few things to make your transition to the Bay Area a little easier. I sincerely hope our paths cross again."

After she walks away, Beverly peeks in and gasps. She hands it to me, and I'm equally as delighted.

Inside is a new bottle of the Dom Perignon we'd enjoyed at takeoff, four elegantly wrapped chocolate bars, and handfuls of the Hermès soaps and lotions that are available in the first-class lavatories.

I see the corner of something else and pull it out. "It's a note card," I say.

I open the envelope and whisper its contents to Beverly.

Welcome to the Pan Am family. It will be the best time of your life.

Beverly crosses herself—forehead, heart, shoulder, shoulder. "Amen to that."

We have a few days off before we are set to take our inaugural flights, each to Honolulu, but on different schedules. Beverly's will be round trip, and mine will continue on as a portion of Pan Am's legendary around-the-world jaunt. As time progresses and we earn seniority, we'll get to bid on our routes, but at the very beginning, we will be scheduled strategically with more senior staff until we get our air legs. We'd been chosen for this base because our abilities to speak French will come in handy on the Polynesian legs.

The other reason for the planned delay is the myriad of inoculation boosters we are required to get before we can fly, compounding the shots we got during training. Polio, diphtheria, smallpox, tetanus, and pertussis. I'm certain that I've already received the combined DPT one when I was nine years old. But all my paperwork is back in Pennsylvania along with everything else I've left behind.

And I am not about to call Henry to find it.

So my second day in the Bay Area, in which I'd planned to help Beverly look for an apartment, is spent languishing in our hotel room in San Mateo, woozy from all those chemicals being shot into my body at once.

Depending on the countries we'll fly to, there might be more shots ahead. I can't say I'm looking forward to *that.* Though I think the girls getting the African routes have the most rigorous inoculation schedule.

Beverly was not at all chagrined by my setback, and is, in fact, seeming to thrive in this new circumstance in which she has total independence. This is evidenced by the chicken soup she had delivered from a local Jewish deli and the flowers she'd had the hotel gift shop arrange for me.

I'm going to have to teach her that fresh flowers are an extravagance that she may have to forgo. But how can I dismiss the kindness the gift reveals?

Hours into the afternoon, I've watched my fill of *The Lucy Show*, *The Match Game*, *Benny Hill*, and *The Jetsons*.

I had high hopes for the new *Lucy Show*, having always been a fan of its predecessor, *I Love Lucy*, but I find it to be a lacking substitute to her earlier, funnier, *married* years. She and Desi Arnaz divorced a couple of years ago, and though, as a soon-to-be-divorcée myself, I champion her break for freedom, I can't help but feel deflated that on screen, she seems to be a shadow of her former, larger-than-life self.

I hope the same fate won't befall me. I plan to take Beverly's suggestion and fly south to get my Mexican divorce and never look back on those years with Henry again. Just as soon as there is a break in my schedule to do so.

I can only hope that Pan Am doesn't find out beforehand.

"Knock, knock!" Beverly chimes as she opens our hotel-room door. And just in time. With the setting of the sun, *Alfred Hitchcock Presents* is beginning, and I'm not sure I'm up for its dark storyline. I'm tired of the television being my only view.

She breezes in, shopping bags dangling from her arms like the accessories they likely contain, and falls like a board onto her bed, even making the pillows jump. "What a day!" she exclaims.

To her credit, the bags came from a five-and-dime.

I lift myself up on my elbows, which causes me to feel lightheaded. But a quick mental assessment of the rest of me reveals that I am already doing much better than I was this morning.

"How did it go?" I ask.

"Splendid. Just splendid." She rolls over onto her side to face me and curls her legs up to her chest.

"Okay," she continues, "so here's what I learned. I telephoned the local chapter of World Wings, which is a group of former Pan Am stewardesses who now get together monthly for lunch, gossip, and philanthropy. I read about them in the in-flight magazine, and sure enough, they have a chapter here. Lucky thing for us. Rentals are at a premium right now, but they're like one big, happy sorority, and they gave me an in."

Relief washes over my exhausted body. I'd looked up rentals in the classifieds, and it wasn't pretty. When we got this assignment, I had not given any thought to the difference in cost of living between Red Lion and, well, just about anywhere in the world that Pan Am might station me.

The rents here are shocking—two hundred sixty dollars for a two-bedroom downtown! A fortune compared to the eighty-dollar mortgage that I know Henry paid every month.

Some girls resort to renting the same *bed* and changing sheets between their flights. I hope we won't have to do that.

"Put me out of my misery," I plead. "The classifieds made me want to cry. What did you find?"

Beverly sits straight up. She is clearly bursting with news, and her smile spans ear to ear. "Here's the scoop. There's a four-bedroom stew zoo house just one town over in Burlingame that is regularly rented to rotating Pan Am stewardesses. It's owned by one of the World Wings members. It's a win-win! She gets steady, responsible tenants and the girls get a great property for a fantastic price. One of the girls just got transferred to Miami, so a room came up."

I know the phrase *stew zoo*, a term for housing rented by multiple stewardesses to save money. But it was one other comment that makes me take notice.

"Only one room?" I feel the bitterness of panic rise in my throat at the possibility that she might have already taken it for herself and I will have to keep looking.

I'm ready for independence too. But ironically, I don't want to do it alone.

Beverly leans over and rubs my knee before holding up two fingers. "One room. Two beds. You don't think I would leave you high and dry, do you?"

I shake my head, ashamed that the thought had crossed my mind at all.

"Anyway, I took it. I'm sorry I didn't wait to discuss it with you. She already had other calls from interested girls, but I was the only one with the pluck to hang up the phone and scurry right up to their luncheon at the Presidio Officers' Club in San Francisco to introduce myself as they mingled. I hope you don't mind."

I leap out of my bed, suddenly full of energy, and throw my arms around her. Beverly laughs and puts her hands on my arms, gently pushing me back.

"Hold your horses, Zorro. It's not as if I just announced the cure for cancer."

I walk over to the desk chair and plop down on it, grateful to not be prone for the first time today. I stretch my arms over my head and my legs out in front of me. Such a simple thing, yet so effective.

"I'm sorry. I've had nothing to do but watch television and worry today. That sounds great. And I appreciate it, Beverly. I really do."

She waves a hand. "Worrying will give you wrinkles. It was nothing, really. All those years of tricking the nuns at Marymount got me into the habit of thinking up all sorts of schemes."

"Habit? Nuns? I see what you did there."

It takes her a second to catch it, and then she crosses her arms over her stomach and folds down in laughter. "You do beat all, Judy Goodman. Nice to have you back in the land of the living."

"Nice to be back. But, Bev—"

"Hmm?" She's already preoccupied taking her purchases out of their wrapping. Chewing gum, cigarettes, and a beach towel. Nothing extravagant. Good for her.

"This place is in Burlingame? Not in San Francisco?"

"Righto. And that's the other scoop." She folds her arms across her chest. "Even though it would be very exciting to live up in the city, the ladies warned me that the traffic can be terrible getting to the airport since it's so much farther down the peninsula. And we both know if we're late for a flight, we're canned. No questions asked. Especially during our probation. In Burlingame, we'll practically be close enough to walk."

I nod, mulling over this disappointment. I'd been so excited to leave the semirural town of Red Lion, and the prospect of living in a big city is more important to me than I'd realized.

And it seems like it would be much harder for Henry to find me if I'm in the heart of a metropolis. But maybe that's just fear taking over.

"You're right. That sounds much smarter. How much is it?"

"I'm glad you asked." She grins. "It's the final cherry on an already delicious sundae. It will only be forty dollars a month for each of us."

"Forty dollars?" My heart almost stops in astonishment. "Are you sure?"

"Yeah! Four bedrooms, eighty dollars per bedroom. Three hundred sixty per month. But we're splitting a room. So—forty dollars. Plus our share of the utilities."

"That will leave us enough to buy a few pineapples in Honolulu."

Beverly giggles. I love her in this mood. "We can save up for a whole plantation of pineapples, my friend."

CHAPTER SEVENTEEN

Beverly

I am out of my league.

It's the first time I have ever had that thought. Even when the nuns of Marymount advanced me to an upper-grade literature class, I aced it. I am used to things coming without a tremendous amount of effort.

Maybe that's why I feel so out of sorts.

All the training that I'd thought had been so difficult paled in comparison to the dozens of expectant paying customers looking at me with utter confidence that I was going to show them a remarkable time as we jetted over the dark-blue waters of the Pacific Ocean.

I have twice slipped into the tiny lavatory, afraid that with all these nerves I would lose my lunch. My belly rumbled like the roar of the engine. But thankfully, I was spared that embarrassment.

Instead, each time, I'd unzipped my tight skirt and splashed water on my face. And soldiered on.

That's what being the daughter of Mr. Wall Street does. It trains you before you can even walk to carry yourself with unimpeachable conduct no matter how much your insides are swirling. Don't let them see you struggle. That, I can do.

My primary station is the tourist compartment galley, which gives me the least interaction with the passengers. A typical assignment for someone their first time around. But occasionally, I step out, flash my whitened grin as I steel my nerves, and ask them if they'd like a refill of water or coffee.

I haven't spilled any yet, so I'm going to consider that a win. Despite the fact that the carafes—made of real silver and etched with the Pan American logo, of course—feel like they weigh fifteen pounds each. And that's *before* filling them up. I am like a tightrope walker holding one in each hand, serving coffee while somehow managing not to lean over two people to reach the one in the window seat.

It is a precarious ballet that will take time to master.

I've always been inclined toward being exceedingly pleasant to waitstaff at restaurants—perhaps as a counterbalance to Mr. Wall Street's dismissive ways—but now that I am among their ranks, I am even more appreciative of what I feel may be the most challenging job on earth.

Or in this case, in the skies.

The chief stewardess, Miss Kessling, steps into the galley. Her demeanor is as severe as her features. At least here, where no passengers can see us.

"I just put the buttered string beans into the warmer," I answer to a question she didn't ask. As if I need to justify why I'm here.

She raises an eyebrow. "We use the French here. Les haricots verts au beurre. That's what is printed on the menu. And that is what you will say, no matter which compartment you're in."

I swallow hard and nod. Sister Mary Clare has nothing on this woman.

"And we're running low on the La roulade de veau aux rognons up in first class. So I'm taking some of yours."

Miss Kessling proceeds to pull the entrée drawer out and sets six platters on a tray. In first class, they have a choice of meals. In tourist, they have a choice among what's left.

As first class apparently has an appetite for roast loin of veal today, the tourist compartment will have to be satisfied with the breast of chicken.

Excuse me. Le suprême de volaille au Muscadet.

It could take months before I get an assignment in first class. With their wide seats. Two and two, versus the three and three here. Complete with a lounge area and a lavatory just for them. I always flew first class when Mr. Wall Street was paying. Now I'll have to earn a place there.

"And," Miss Kessling turns to say as she steps back toward the aisle, "Mrs. Harrison wants a pillow and Mr. Oakley would like for you to bring him a *LIFE* magazine." Her Norwegian accent is beguiling and I know I'm not the only one to think so. She keeps a tally in a small leather journal of the number of marriage proposals she's received from passengers in her four years at the airline. I spied an impressive number of marks on its pages.

"I'm on it." And I step out into the aisle. She takes my place in the galley to finish pilfering what she needs for the first-class passengers.

I don't know who Mrs. Harrison and Mr. Oakley are. In training, they encouraged us to memorize the manifests and know our passengers' names, but I'm afraid that's one parlor trick that I will have to master at another time. For now, I run my finger down the list hanging in the galley and look for their names.

Harrison—10B

Oakley—15A

I shake off an encroaching feeling of intimidation and assure myself that Miss Kessling was probably as nervous on her first trips as I am now. Maybe I'll ask her if I have the chance.

Maybe I won't.

I flip through our stacks of periodicals until I find the latest issue of *LIFE* and turn sideways to get past her, and then open a slim closet and pull out a freshly cleaned pillow.

I've already forgotten the names. But at least I remember the seat assignments.

Seat 10B looks familiar to me. Mint-green dress, belted with a caramel-colored belt. When she boarded, a man whom I presumed to be her husband said goodbye to her. His right hand held on to a pigtailed little girl, and in his left arm, he held a toddler. He kissed the woman and told her to have a good time.

In the few quiet moments I've had since we took off, I have busied myself with imagining what might be bringing each passenger on this flight, on this date, to the island of Oahu. Adventure? Love? Business? Each must have a fascinating story to tell.

I particularly would like to know 10B's story, and I get goose bumps at the notion that this decade might be showing signs that women—mothers, even—could have a chance to take a break and fly off to *Hawaii* on their own. Whatever their situation, it was an unusual occurrence, but maybe a good sign of things to come.

Mrs. Harrison looks relaxed, and murmurs a gentle "thank you" when I tuck the pillow behind her head.

My high hopes are curbed at my next stop. The man sitting in 15A is wearing a tailored pin-striped suit, the standard uniform of my old stomping grounds, and even in this sitting position, he exudes the confidence of Mr. Wall Street's set. Though his hair and skin wear the respective sun-bleached and sun-kissed hues that are incongruous with those who sit behind desks all day.

And he's younger than those executives. Not much older than me, if I had to guess.

He's not smoking, which is a relief. I can't enjoy a cigarette while in uniform, and the smell of it all around me is giving me a withdrawal headache. The gentlemen in both 25 and 27 have small clouds of smoke swirling around their heads, and the odor from these and others in this close proximity of the plane have already permeated the wool in my uniform. The first thing I'll do at the hotel is send it off to the laundry.

The ashtray in the armrest belonging to 15A is blessedly clean and unused. One point for him on that front, at least.

"You requested a copy of *LIFE*?" I ask sweetly as I hold it out. There is no one sitting in the seats next to him, a circumstance I'm sorry for because it makes it more difficult to deliver it and leave. Something about him draws me in. Which makes me want to resist it all the more.

"That's the one," 15A says with a grin. He shifts himself closer to the window and pats the seat next to him, clearly inviting me to join him.

There aren't any specific protocols about this. Though Delores *had* touched on it in training, saying that it was our duty to keep the passengers comfortable and entertained. So if sitting for conversation was convenient, I was *allowed* to do so. But not required.

I look left and right in the aisle as one might crossing a busy street in New York City, but it appears that everything is under control and no one needs me. Unfortunately. Dinner isn't quite ready to be served in this class, so I'm going to summon all the skills I learned growing up as a proper New York socialite and apply them to the here and now.

I sit in the aisle seat, pressing my lower back against the armrest and leaving as much space as I can. I am used to having the upper hand, especially in the company of men. But up here, there is no way to make a polite exit and leave a party. I'm like a caged bird. Or a marionette. Tired old metaphors, but they're apt. In a way, the passengers control the stewardesses—we are there to accommodate their whims. Within the boundaries of our job description, of course.

"I don't bite," he offers, flashing a white smile and seeming to see right into my nerves. If he knew it was my *maiden voyage* as a stewardess, he might—if he were of the ilk of some New York men I knew—find that to be an apt and welcome metaphor.

I am not going to be anyone's *maiden.*

But I'm being unfair. The man is guilty of nothing except reminding me of the life I just left. I should give him the same chance I would want someone to give me.

Seat 15A—Mr. Oakley, I remember now—unbuttons his suit jacket and slides it off his arms. Pretty smoothly, I'd say, given the confines of space. And despite the intimacy of our proximity, he doesn't brush against me as he maneuvers. Or even pretend to accidentally do so.

Good for him.

"Do you have proof of that? That you don't bite?" I mean it to be witty, conversational, but I realize how very flirty it sounds as soon as it leaves my lips.

If he thinks so, too, he's polite enough to not exploit it.

"Page twelve."

"What?" I say as I tilt my head in confusion.

"Page twelve," he repeats. He flips the magazine open and turns to the page. He smiles, folds it back, and hands it to me. "That's my proof."

I hold my hand out, considering the unusualness of the conversation. But I'd better buckle my seat belt—another metaphor here—because the very life of a Pan Am stewardess is unusual by definition.

The paper crinkles in my hands, and I smooth it out before looking down.

My eyes widen. There, in bold black-and-white splendor, is the glossy face of the man sitting just inches away from me. He is not in a pin-striped suit, though, but in long swimming trunks. And his physique—well, I think it's best to avert my eyes if I intend to maintain a modicum of professionalism here. *That's* what's covered up underneath that suit? I resist the urge to loosen the collar of my blouse and breathe a little.

Of additional interest, though, is that he's surrounded by four boys. Ranging, I'd guess, from ages six through sixteen. It was difficult to tell, though. Because what they have in common is that each has a handicap of some kind. Two with crutches, one in a wheelchair. One missing an arm.

Gold-Medal Swimmer Has Heart of Gold to Match

"This is you?" I ask, though the answer is obvious. A gold-medal swimmer?

Oakley hangs his head a bit before turning back, and I can see a faint blush on his cheeks.

"Yeah. I'm sorry. I didn't know it would be so—blatant."

"You mean you haven't seen this yet?"

Mr. Oakley—Mark Oakley, as a quick glance at the article shows—shrugs. "That's why I asked for a copy. The airport tobacco shop was out of *LIFE*. And it just came out today, so I didn't have a chance to get it anywhere else."

"Then how did you know which page the article would be on?" I try to read his face for conceit, but I see none. Maybe I've rushed too quick to judgment.

"My coach told me. Page twelve. Just like my lucky number."

"You have a lucky number?"

"Mm-hmm. I was born on the twelfth day of the twelfth month at twelve noon on the dot. And the number has followed me ever since."

There is something midwestern about his voice, even though his look is Fifth Avenue. I can't figure him out. But I am intrigued. And I haven't even read yet what *LIFE* has to say about the man.

But a picture tells a thousand words, right?

And the laudatory nature of the headline is a pretty good recommendation.

I look up and see Miss Kessling trying to catch my eye. I begin to stand, but with more reluctance than I'd had sitting down in the first place. "My chief stewardess needs me. It was—it was nice talking to you."

"Wait," he says, placing his hand on my arm. But he pulls it back just as quickly and seems embarrassed to have done so at all. "I—I have never been to Honolulu. Do you have a long layover there? I could use a tour guide."

It is on the tip of my tongue to tell him that it will be my first time as well, but it might reveal my very novice position here when I am eager to come across as the consummate professional. I did not join Pan Am to get involved with its passengers. Mark Oakley is just one of many fascinating people I am likely to meet in this new career of mine, and it will do no good to make a mistake so early on.

"I'm afraid we have too quick a turnaround. I'm sorry I can't help you. But for the remainder of the flight, please let me know if there is anything else I can get for you."

I wince at the abruptness in my voice, but it is necessary to conceal the waver I feel hovering in my throat.

I've not had such an immediate reaction to a man before.

I walk back toward the galley and check my wristwatch. Five hours behind us, two hours to go. I can do this.

The Royal Hawaiian Hotel is everything I've been told it would be. It is a pink palace that appears to rise from the sand like a stuccoed phoenix. As I exit the taxi that I shared with two of the other stewardesses, I am momentarily stunned by the pineapple-scented air and the smallness that I feel as building-high palm trees sway above me. Chipped into their trunks are loads of nicks, and I think at first glance that they grow this way. But then I see a man hooked to the top of it, metal cleats on his shoes as he grips the trunk and whacks coconuts and fronds from their tops. As they fall to the ground with a thunk, I realize how dangerous it would be for those to fall on an unsuspecting passerby. But I'd never considered that such a thing would be someone's *job*.

It's just one of the many sights I'm taking in as I stroll toward the lobby of these historic grounds. I'd read in the in-flight *Clipper* magazine on the way over that this hotel was built on the site of the coconut groves that were the vacation grounds of King Kamehameha and Queen Ka'ahumanu over a hundred fifty years ago.

The history permeates the air as much as the pineapple does.

Indeed, I feel like royalty myself as a lei of purple-and-white plumeria is placed around my neck while a group of men play simple tunes on ukuleles to welcome us. And in front of them, a woman clad only in a coconut bra and grass skirt gently sways her hips and raises her arms in the air, all moving with the fluidity of the water.

I am transfixed.

Until my roommate for the layover—Rachel—slips her arm through mine and whispers, "Just so you know, it never gets old. I must have been here forty or fifty times by now, and it still takes my breath away. Even then, there's nothing like your first experience. Inhale it all while I go get our room key."

She runs ahead, not giving me a chance to try to help. But I'm grateful for her consideration because I can't begin to think about anything except taking in the myriad of sights around me. I know that people come to Hawaii to relax, but to me, it is a circus of color and wonder that leaves me feeling energized. Up until today, I thought I was well traveled, having been to all the cities of the world that my set considers fashionable. But these tropics—this hemisphere—goes largely unmentioned in New York.

I have shopped for couture in Paris, but none is so splendid as the boastful bird-of-paradise flower that parades its orange splendor around the perimeter of the walkway to the hotel. I have toured the ruins of Rome, but the porous black lava stones that frame those flowers surely predate any human endeavor, having their birthplace in the very belly of the earth itself. And I saw Carol Channing onstage on the opening night of *Show Girl* on Broadway just a year ago, but even the plumage of her costume was not of the caliber of the fan-shaped palms that flank each side of the entryway into the hotel or the beds of plumeria blossoms that look like a bridal convention on the rug.

All this, and I have not even stepped one foot inside.

"Your bag, miss?" I am roused from my stupor by an eager bellhop who wishes to help me with the small rolling suitcase that is the staple piece for a stewardess. I am about to dismiss him so that he can go seek larger tips from more prestigious clients, but I see four other Pan Am–labeled suitcases already on his cart, including Rachel's, and I am not going to be the one to buck the tide so early on.

"Thank you," I say, handing him a dollar, wondering if it's too much or too little. He tips his hat and walks off, pushing the wheeled cart and whistling the same melody that the ukulele players are strumming.

I step inside and am again wide eyed at the Moorish archways that frame the view. Beyond the hubbub of the familiar noises of a hotel—telephones, chatty concierges, elevator bells—I see the cake-like layers of blue sky, turquoise water, white sand, green grass. It reminds me of a petit four—the little cakes my mother always ordered from the Plaza. Bright colors that entice the senses.

But I turn away when I hear the brisk clip-clip walk that I already recognize as Rachel's.

She gestures for me to hold my hand out, and I comply.

"Key. Map of the island. Cigarettes." She places each one down firmly. "I'd stay and show you around, but I have a date."

I raise an eyebrow, and she gives me a conspiratorial grin.

"Oscar in Oahu. Harry in Hong Kong. Ted in Tahiti."

I must have registered some surprise, though I don't know why. Despite being educated by nuns, I consider myself a worldly woman.

"I'm pulling your leg, Caldwell. That might fly on other airlines, but we Pan Am girls are supposed to be *classy*. No one will want to marry you if you get a rep for having a man in every port. My one steady is plenty for me."

She looks around the vast hallway of the hotel, and I notice her eyes stop when the captain of our flight comes in. Looking admittedly knee melting in his crisp uniform.

"Landing lips?" she asks me, puckering up. It's the phrase the stewardesses use to make sure their lipstick is in good shape.

"Looks great," I assure her.

"Thanks! Got to run," she says, slinging a large tote bag over her shoulder. "I'll be back late. Get yourself a good night's sleep. And whatever else you do tomorrow, meet the crew in the hallway at three o'clock sharp. You can't be late for your flight. And we will not wait for you."

She hurries off—clip, clip—and I try to remember if I'd seen a wedding ring on Captain Paul's finger when I'd brought him coffee in the cockpit. But I don't think I did. Which makes sense. He is on the young end of the pilot core, as most of them are veterans of the war. Married and settled now with a light dusting of gray in their hair.

I look at the room key: 1212. I remember what Mark Oakley said, and a shiver runs down to my toes. I'm not one for signs and symbols, so surely that's no more than a coincidence. I shrug it off and head toward the bank of elevators to my right. When I arrive, my bag is already placed on the bed nearest the window, Rachel's on the other, and I'm glad I had the foresight to tip the bellman upon arrival since he is nowhere to be found. I toss the cigarettes on my bed, and they make a crispy sound as the cellophane meets the leather trim on top of my suitcase.

It's a lonely sound. It reflects how I feel at the moment, a sensation that surprises me. This is my first solitary adventure. Everything I've wanted. Everything I've been dreaming of. In arguably the most beautiful setting in the world. But I am struck, suddenly, that there is no one to share it with. I look across the room and find a telephone. I could call my mother, and I almost do. Then I see a portfolio of exquisite stationery embossed with the image of the hotel and decide that writing a letter will suffice. After all, I'm counting my pennies now. Maybe later, I'll call collect.

But first, I'm going to shower to get the feeling of sweat, tobacco, and travel off my skin and out of my hair.

When I'm finished, feeling exquisitely rejuvenated, I wrap one of the hotel's plush white robes around my body and run my fingers through my short, wet hair.

I hear music wafting from outside, muted by the thick glass doors that separate me from the balcony. I pull back the curtains and open the doors to reveal a spectacular sight—the Pacific Ocean stretches before me like a majestic carpet that blankets the earth. I step out, and the warm sun kisses my cheek. I breathe the salty air deeply into my lungs, and I am instantly happy. The intimidation I felt at being the new girl on board washes away, all but forgotten, and I realize that this, at last, is what I'd pined for. That something different that had been so elusive in New York.

I can't believe that I have family that lives here. That gets to experience this every day. I can't wait to learn more about them. My mother has promised to find out more from Sami so that I can reach out to visit them on a future visit. If they want to see me.

I look to my left, and I see the unmistakable jagged shape of Diamond Head. Almost no advertisements of the island are printed without portraying it. Below, more ukulele music surfs on the breeze and makes its way to my ear. But not from the group of men greeting visitors at the front of the Royal Hawaiian. Instead, I see a man who has a small gathering of people surrounding him. I hear the words *We're going to a hukilau, a huki huki huki huki hukilau*, and with all my soul I want to know what a hukilau is.

I run inside, throw open my suitcase, and pull out the two outfits I brought for this trip. Each is more appropriate for a luncheon at Bergdorf's than a stroll on the beach. A pink-tweed pencil skirt with matching bolero and a belted number with a gingham pattern. I should have known better—we'd been advised during training to pack what was simple, free of wrinkles, and easy to wash. I wish I'd listened.

Then I look again at Rachel's suitcase. She did say that she wouldn't be here until late. Did that mean that everything she needed was in the bag she held on to? My hands shake as I approach it. I was not raised to be a thief, but I feel like I've fallen under the spell of the island, and I don't consider myself fully responsible for my actions.

Two layers in, I see a bright-yellow dress, loose fitting and embellished with matching fabric buttons and a wide belt. It looks like the sunshine just outside my window, and I thank the airline gods who require the stewardesses to be nearly the same size. This dress will surely fit me, and with any luck, I'll be able to have it laundered and returned before she notices it missing.

On second thought, I'll leave her a note. Apologizing and promising to have it cleaned and returned before our flight.

I put it on and take a quick look in the mirror, pinching my cheeks, applying gloss to my lips, and strapping on the sandals that, at least, I'd had the foresight to pack.

The soundtrack of *West Side Story* enters my head. *I feel pretty,* Maria had sung. But not out of conceit, as I understand now. Out of the sheer exhilaration that her life was about to begin.

I share her glee. But hopefully not her fate.

I skip to the elevator, and before long, I find myself among that small crowd of people that I'd seen from my balcony, swaying and smiling and swooning as the singer looks at each woman as if she's the only woman in the world. Even my heart skips faster when his eyes lock with mine.

But that is eclipsed when I feel the heat of a man whispering in my ear.

"His name is Don Ho. I think he's going places."

I turn around and my heart jumps.

"Seat 15A." I say it more breathlessly than I would have liked.

"Beverly. My favorite Pan Am stewardess."

"Only Pan Am?" Oh, this island magic is reawakening my confidence, my flirtatious spirit. I am feeling like myself again.

Or maybe it's him.

Mark Oakley—yes, I remember his name—places his hand on his heart. "Have dinner with me, and I'll forsake all other airlines. Unless you still don't have enough time on your layover."

I feel heat rise to my cheeks, and I know it's not the glare of the sun because we're standing under the shade of a palm tree. He is referring to my dismissal when he'd suggested a tour of the island.

"One drink," I respond, not wanting to commit to more just yet. "And on one condition."

"Anything you ask."

"It must have a little paper umbrella in it."

He tilts his head back and laughs, and it is as beautiful a sound as the waning laps of the waves as they ebb back into the ocean.

"I think that won't be a problem in Honolulu."

CHAPTER EIGHTEEN

Judy

It takes me only a day to recover from the vaccinations, and on my third day in the Bay Area, I am ready to move into the house in Burlingame. I drop a postcard at the front desk, addressed to Ronelle and telling her of my whereabouts. Unsigned with disguised handwriting, as usual. But she'll know.

Beverly is still away on her first assignment to Honolulu. Grateful for all she did to find us a place to live, I want to return the favor. So I gather her things as well as mine and leave the airport hotel in a taxi. Having left almost all my belongings in Pennsylvania, my whole life now fits into a moderate-size suitcase. But Beverly has boxes and boxes that take up the entire trunk of the cab and most of the back seat. She hadn't had this much stuff with her in Miami, but her mother had shipped all of this ahead to the hotel in San Francisco.

Whether her father is aware of that is unknown. I hope that someday, he can see Beverly for the remarkable young woman she is. That she will know the same kind of love my dad gave me.

The taxi pulls up to a bungalow, and I am immediately struck by its charm. It's everything I imagined California to be. The one-story home is made of bright-white stucco and topped with a terra-cotta tile roof. The well-trimmed lawn boasts a perimeter of flower beds, and I wonder which of the ladies in the *stew zoo* has a green thumb. I see lemon trees and orange trees such as I'd never seen in the cornfield country of Red Lion.

I think back to reading *The Secret Garden* with my mother when I was a child, and I imagine it would have looked something like this.

She would have loved to see me here.

I step out of the cab and pull the fare from my wallet. The driver watches me as I glance up.

"Those are eucalyptus," he says, following my gaze to the trees lining the street. The treetops look like they would graze the roof of a four-story building, and they cast a pattern of shadows onto the pavement.

"You'll see them all over this area," he continues. "They were brought over from Australia."

"Did they send koalas with them?" I ask. The clean air is strengthening me even to the point of being able to joke.

He scratches his beard and shakes his head. "The wildest animal you'll find around here is the occasional bobcat. And maybe an opossum once in a while."

I think back to my day at Villa Vizcaya with Joe and the feral iguanas we saw roaming around. It takes very little, I've discovered, for my thoughts to go to him. Even with something as unrelated as a koala and an iguana, my mind seems inclined to make any connection it can.

I try to shake it from my head. Joe is an entire continent away.

And I am still married.

"Let me help you," the driver offers. It takes him six trips between the front door and the cab to fully unload all of Beverly's boxes. I look under the welcome mat for the key that was promised, and there it is.

He insists on helping me inside, and it's only after I've tipped him generously for the unexpected assistance that I get a chance to look around.

The boxes form a perfect throne, so I sit down to catch my breath. The living room is just as charming as the outside, and though I quite like the turn toward modern decor that I see in magazine advertisements, this cottage woos me with her arched doorways, nicked wood floors, and colorful tile fireplace. It sparks my imagination and makes me wonder about all the people who might have lived here before me.

What were their stories?

What will mine be?

Already, I like that this chapter of my story is beginning in California. The very air feels fresh in my lungs.

It is then that I notice the sound of a radio coming from a door down the hall. Ricky Nelson singing "Travelin' Man."

"Hello?" I ask into the emptiness, loud enough—maybe—to be heard over the music.

The radio turns off.

"Who's there?"

A woman comes out of a bathroom brandishing an electric curling iron as if it were a weapon. Half of her long blond hair is straight as a pin and the other half cascades down her shoulders in spirals.

I put my hands up. "It's me. Judy Goodman. I'm renting a room here with Beverly Caldwell. Is this the right address, 9812 Clarendon Road?"

"Oh!" She puts the curling iron down on the counter behind her and takes wide strides over to me.

"Pinky Martin. I'm sorry—we weren't expecting you for a few more days."

"Didn't Beverly start our lease for today?"

Pinky grins, and I take the moment to look her over. She's wearing a pink housecoat and fuzzy pink slippers. A nickname, perhaps?

"No, tomorrow! But it's not a problem! We were just planning to scrub everything nice and shiny for y'all and have some champagne ready to welcome you. Now you're stuck with just me, a few dust mites, and half a carton of milk."

"And a hot curling iron?"

"Oh!" she says, looking behind her and picking the device up by its handle. "I wasn't thinking. I was just startled to hear someone come in."

I smile at the whole scene. She has no idea how dreamy this is to me. The girls in school never liked me since my father wasn't from Red Lion. This kind of camaraderie was something I wished to have my whole life.

My mother would console me, holding my head against her shoulder and stroking my hair, promising me that these silly high school hurts were not what friendships were based on. Someday, I would have more friends than I could count. I was only now beginning to believe it.

"So how about it?" Pinky asks. "Ice water or milk? Don't let it be said that I'm not a generous hostess."

Her grin reveals blindingly white teeth. All straight, no gaps.

"I like milk," I offer.

"Perfect. And now that I think of it, I'll warm some over the stove, add some Swiss Miss, and we'll have ourselves a party!"

That sounds incredible. But I'm sorry to have intruded. "You look like you're getting ready to go somewhere," I offer as an invitation for her to recant.

Pinky shakes her head, and I find it amusing how differently each side of her hair reacts. One side flat, one side bouncy. "Just practicing with that thing." She points to the curling iron. "I got it on a layover in Paris last month, only to realize that our electrical voltages don't match up with Europe's. So an electrician finally came in today and jerry-rigged something for me, and now I'm getting to test it out before a date I have on Saturday night."

"You're a stewardess too?" I had thought she would be based on what Beverly said, but it was good for conversation anyway.

"Mm-hmm. All of us are. The Blue Meatball girls of Pan American Airlines."

It's my turn to grin. I've heard the nickname of the Pan Am logo, and I love that these girls adopted it so cheerfully.

I'm thinking about a statement she made a few moments ago. "There's a flight from San Francisco to Paris?"

We'd had to memorize all the routes that Pan Am flies before our final exam, and I didn't recall that one.

"Oh, honey," she says, stepping closer to me. From here, I can see that she's chewing gum. Pink, of course. "There's what you learn and there's what you *learn*. Dear old San Francisco might be your home base, but when you really get adept at the bid system, you can route yourself all over the world as long as you manage your minimum of sixty-seven hours a month and don't go over the maximum. That's not to even mention what you can do with standby. You can fly anywhere that Pan Am flies at no cost to you as long as you have space in your schedule and a flexible personality. *And*"—she takes a breath—"if you watch for it, you can catch a ferry flight between here and the East Coast. Sometimes, you have the whole plane to yourself—just you and the pilots."

I knew this in theory. It had been covered in class, but only briefly. Now that I'm meeting someone who actually knows how to navigate the complicated system of route bids and standbys and empty planes being ferried coast to coast, I can taste the very real possibility that I might, in fact, see all those places that Frank Sinatra sang about on that album.

Just think—Judy Hall Goodman of Pennsylvania, tacking pins into her childhood map and dotting the world with her adventures!

Not for the first time, I am struck that this endeavor was about far, far more than escaping *from* something. It is heading *toward* my new life.

Pinky snaps her bubble gum with such polished perfection that it reminds me of Beverly. Beverly, who is hopefully sipping tropical drinks on Waikiki Beach right about now.

"You girls lucked out. The room that Marsha had was the biggest one. Picture windows right in the front of the house, lots of light. Two beds. But that broad could afford to pay for both beds, and she liked her privacy."

"Where did Marsha go?"

"Married! Can't have a husband while working at Pan Am, but you sure can meet one!"

So I've heard.

Pinky shows me to the space I'll share with Beverly. Right off the living room, so I won't have far to move all these boxes. She wasn't exaggerating. The sun sits high and bathes the room with light. I step into one of the largest beams, and the heat is as satisfying as taking a long bubble bath.

But blessedly much less intense than Miami.

As soon as Pinky leaves the room, I open my hands at my sides, close my eyes, and tilt my head upward.

This. Is. Glorious.

I feel like I've been born into a new skin.

One bed is closer to the window than the other, and I want to let Beverly have it, especially after her efforts to get us this place. So I walk toward the one by the closet and fall forward, muffling a scream of delight into the quilted mattress. I kick my legs up and down.

I can't remember the last time I was this happy.

I wake up from having apparently napped in that silly position, sprawled across the bed with one leg hanging over the edge. I'm feeling better than I have in days, though I rub the base of my spine to work out the kinks that formed while I was sleeping.

The house is quiet, and I find a note attached to the refrigerator with a flimsy magnet that has a tiger on it and says BANGKOK.

> *Sorry you didn't have the welcoming committee we'd anticipated. But everyone will be here tomorrow night, so don't make plans! In the meantime, we're just a few blocks from Burlingame Avenue, where you'll find most everything you need to settle in. Take a left as you leave the house, and then your first left at the corner. In six blocks, you'll cross the tracks and be at the start of*

the avenue. Alpha Beta is on that end. I'd start there. And if you haven't been to one, be prepared to be surprised.

Pinky

P.S. You fell asleep before I could even make the hot chocolate. Rain check!

I sling my macramé bag over my shoulder and head out, thankful for her anticipating what I'd need to know. The sun is setting, but just barely, so I should have enough time to get to the store and back before it's dark.

I arrive at Alpha Beta, and as soon as I enter, I see what Pinky meant. This is not your average grocery store. I have never seen anything like this in Red Lion or Miami.

Within their categories, everything is alphabetical. Anise next to apples next to asparagus. This makes some sense in the perishable sections of the store, but down the aisles, it is quite different.

Cheerios next to Cocoa Krispies. Chicken noodle next to cream of tomato soup.

And farther down: Skippy peanut butter, Spam, Starkist tuna.

California is surely a different world.

Though I have to admit, it makes everything easy to find.

I pick up what I think I can easily carry back and walk up to the register.

Large tote bags are nice in theory, but now that I need to dig around for my wallet, I find it cumbersome. My hand moves past a tin of peppermints and a wool sanitary pad and brushes up against a package that I don't remember putting in there. I ignore that and finally find my wallet, paying the $4.35 in exact change.

It's not until I'm back in my bedroom that I empty the contents of my purse onto the bed. There *is* a package. I hadn't imagined it. I open the brown-paper wrapping and find a purple leather notebook. And a letter. A letter from Joe.

CHAPTER NINETEEN

Beverly

I lead the way to a grass-roofed shack on Waikiki Beach and slap a five-dollar bill on the counter. Hard enough to turn my hand red. Good thing I have the night ahead of me. We can't drink eight hours before a flight. But tonight, I'm free to do what I like.

"Two pineapple rum drinks," I say, having glanced only cursorily at the menu. I will have plenty of trips to Honolulu to discover what my favorite tropical drink will end up being. But today, I don't want to give a man a chance to order for me or pay for me or have any sense of ownership over me. I had enough of that in New York. So I'm turning the tables. My tiny rebellion.

I feel power swoosh through my veins, pulsing with more vigor than I imagine a kiss ever would.

"I could have gotten those," Mark says as I turn around. I can't tell if he looks wounded or impressed behind those sunglasses.

I suppose eyes really are the windows to your soul.

But if I had to choose based on his tone, I'd say it was the former.

"I have no doubt that you could have gotten them," I answer. "But this is about what *I* can do."

Maybe that was said a little too emphatically. Maybe it was *all* a little too emphatic. But New Beverly is still new to me. Like the pair of Pan Am heels that I'm still nursing blisters from, I have to break this version of me in.

He smiles at this, at least. And it seems genuine. Another point to him for not being scared off. The egos of most men in New York seem as solid as bedrock but are actually built on nothing more than quicksand.

"At least let me secure the chairs."

"I—" I begin to protest, but this time I stop myself.

"Somebody has to wait for the drinks," he says, pointing to the bar. He leans in as he says it, managing to put a seductive inflection on completely ordinary words. Or am I just imagining that? A chill runs down to my toes even as my neck feels hot where his words have landed.

"Thank you," I acquiesce. And he walks off to take care of what will not be an easy task by the looks of the busy, bustling beach.

I bite my lower lip to keep from smiling as wide as I want to. Because as much as I hate to admit it, there is something nice about being taken care of as well.

Being a woman is full of contradictions. Can I not encompass it all?

The bartender slides the two pineapple rums, complete with paper umbrellas—aha!—across the heavily lacquered counter. I pick them up, their ice-cold glasses cooling me down on what is still a very warm afternoon. I rub one across my forehead for relief.

I see Mark standing by two chairs with pink fringe, waving to get my attention, and I head his way. So he's had success. Another point for him, and just a few minutes in.

Maybe I should stop keeping a tally.

Maybe he really is just a good guy.

He has already taken his shirt off and is wearing only swim trunks. If my feet were not bound by shoes, I would curl my toes into the sand to keep from stumbling at the sight. He looks like he's just walked out of a magazine advertisement. The kind where they find a nearly perfect model and then brush away his imperfections in order to leave the impression that perfection exists.

But he is the *after*. Mark Oakley, my 15A passenger, is a living, breathing embodiment of a photograph that has already had its touch-ups.

Of course, I saw his photo in *LIFE*. But jeez Louise, the man in person is an Adonis.

Thank goodness for the coolness of these drinks. I feel my temperature rising.

Look at me, setting the women's movement back a notch. All this talk about not *needing* a man.

But what do they say about *wanting* one?

I raise the glasses in acknowledgment and walk over to him.

"The attendant is bringing an umbrella shortly. The *real* kind. Not the drink kind," he says, tapping the wooden top of the garnish. "I noticed that you don't have a hat."

"You don't have a hat," I retort.

Damn. I should have prefaced that with *thank you*. If Sister Mary Clare could hear me, she would beat my wrists with a ruler.

"I'm not the one who needs to preserve her porcelain skin."

"Please don't tell me that all the girls fall for lines like that."

He takes his sunglasses off, and I am surprised by his expression. I expected one of flirtatious confidence, but instead, he looks confused.

I swallow. Hot dog. That wasn't a line. It was a compliment.

I squeeze my eyes shut, concealed, thankfully, by my own sunglasses. In that second of darkness, I decide to start over. Not just this conversation, but this racecourse I've seemed to set myself on, so determined to exert my independence that I have forgotten that the very essence of humanity, of man and woman, is give and take.

"Here is your drink," I say handing the one in my right hand to him and hoping to quickly move past my gaffe.

He waits for me to sit before he joins me.

"Cheers," he says. The ice in our glasses sounds like little bells as we tap our drinks against each other. I can't help but be distracted by his golden, muscular legs as he stretches them out in the sand.

"Here's to the first of many trips to Honolulu," I stumble out.

"Here's to *moving* to Honolulu," he answers.

I tilt my head. "You're moving here?"

Mark takes a sip, and a look of bliss comes over his face. He props his elbow up on the side of the chair, and I can't help but lean toward him. Something about him draws me in.

I never felt that way for poor Frederick.

"For the next two years, at least."

"Does this have anything to do with the article in *LIFE*?"

I'd hoped to find a copy at the airport newsstand before getting into the taxi to the hotel, but as the plebe of the group I didn't want to be the person who delayed them.

Mark's cheeks redden at its mention, and I am struck by how attractive the characteristic of humility can be. It's not a common one where I come from. I would do well to take notes.

"Yes." He looks down before meeting my eyes again. "I'm a swimmer."

"So I gathered from the headline. But there are lots of swimmers in the world, as you know, and not all of them get featured in a major magazine. Spill the beans, 15A."

He takes a breath, and though I can hear the buzz of people all around us on Waikiki, they fade into the distance as I give him my full attention.

"I was in a car accident when I was a kid. Broke both of my legs, and I couldn't put weight on them for weeks. But there was a public swimming pool near my house, and my uncle took me there after my casts were off so that I could get used to movement again. I fell in love with the water and went on to join my high school swim team, lifeguarded in the summer, and then got a scholarship to Columbia to be on their team. I won gold at a national tournament this year, and now I'm training for the Olympics in Tokyo."

I am stunned for a moment and pause before I speak. "That may be the most impressive short biography I've ever heard."

He blushes again and shrugs his shoulders. "It's the only one I've got."

So for the past few years, Mark Oakley lived just miles away from me in Manhattan, and I was too busy hobnobbing with the Park Avenue and Wall Street sets to realize that men like him existed. Well, that just beats all.

"What did you study at Columbia?"

"Business," he says with a tone of nonchalance. It surprises me—Mr. Wall Street's devotees would have led with that rather than wait to be asked. It's their greatest badge of honor, and they are certain that everyone else will think so too.

"Did you have any interest in pursuing that as a career?"

He shrugs. "I found the classes interesting, but I didn't care for the people."

It's an interesting admission. "What do you mean by that?"

"I did a few internships. And I liked the work. But honestly, the people were ruthless. Everyone trying to get ahead, no matter who got in their way. No, thank you."

"Where did you intern?" If it was in New York—which I assume it was—I've probably heard of all the places.

"Blakesworth for trading. Caldwell Corp. for banking."

I hope he doesn't notice me flinch when he mentions the last one.

But he does. "It sounds like you know it."

I am speechless at first, stunned to be having this strange conversation on the sands of Waikiki. That it took flying all the way here to meet someone who'd been in the same orbit with me all along. Why, we might have even been at some of the same parties and not even known it.

"Caldwell. That's my family," I say at last. My father and my grandfather. Their scowling portraits adorn the lobby. Mark probably walked by them every day.

He smiles. "I saw your last name on your name tag. For about a half a second, I wondered if you might be related. But then I thought that if you were *that* Caldwell, you probably wouldn't be—"

"A stewardess," I finish for him.

"Well, to be honest, working at all. I'd have thought they'd have you practically betrothed to some vice president of some department. Isn't that how it normally goes for the daughter of a modern knickerbocker?"

It's a term that gets thrown around a lot in New York society, referencing the old money of the Roosevelts, Schuylers, Kings, and their ilk. The Caldwells do not date back quite that far. But yes, if those families were still at the top today, my father would be right alongside them.

So his comment was well aimed.

He speaks up when I have remained in stunned silence. "Sounds like we both felt the need to escape that particular method of a slow, painful death."

I couldn't have said it better myself.

I take a sip of my pineapple rum to wet my throat, as it's gone dry. I cough a little, having swallowed too quickly. But manage to say, "And you gave all that up?"

I'd done the very same thing, but I'd never considered that a man might.

He rolls his eyes. "Without a second thought. In fact, it just made me prefer swimming all the more—I compete against my own best time. If I'm faster than someone else, great. If not, it's not the end of my world."

"Those sound like passive words for an Olympic competitor."

"My goal isn't to beat anyone else. Only to leave the water knowing that I have given it everything I've got."

They don't make men like Mark Oakley in New York. Still, I feel like I have to ask.

"Are you from Manhattan originally?"

He throws his head back and laughs.

"Definitely not," he says. "This is going to sound like a cliché, but I'm a country boy who moved to the big city. I'm from Nacogdoches, Texas."

"Naca—" I try to repeat.

"Na-ca-doh-chis," he says, emphasizing a drawl. "I'll make you a deal. If you can spell it correctly, the next round is on me."

"And if I don't?"

"Next round is still on me."

I pull my sunglasses down and squint at him, relieved that we have left the conversation about New York behind us for the time being.

"So they grow gentlemen in your part of the world."

He holds up his hands in defense. "I have all the respect in the world for the modern woman, and having two sisters taught me that women are far tougher than men. But you can't squeeze the Texas out of me all at once."

"You haven't really left me a choice, have you?"

He grins. "Call it pure selfishness. I always enjoy seeing people attempt this."

I purse my lips. I like a challenge.

"Okay," I ponder. "It must not be spelled like it sounds or otherwise it wouldn't be such a game to you."

I stare at him and he stares back, the intensity of the challenge making my heart beat faster. Or maybe it's him. But I am a competitive sort, so who knows.

"K-N-O-C-A—"

"Nope. There's no *K*."

"You can't cut me off midspell."

"Midspell? Is that a word?"

"I'm making it a word."

"Regardless, I'm trying to spare you the embarrassment."

I roll my eyes and start again.

"N-A-C-A— "

"Beep! Thank you for playing, Miss Caldwell. Ladies and gentlemen, tune in tomorrow for another episode of *Spell. That. Name.*"

I punch him lightly in the arm and am surprised by how easily we've settled into this rapport.

"That's not fair. I would have gotten it eventually."

"*Eventually.* Maybe. But you just worked a long flight, and I have to meet my new trainer at Sunset Beach bright and early. Neither of us has all night for you to work it out."

Just the mere mention of the evening coming to an end deflates me. The sun is slowly waning and the bright-blue sky that greeted me upon our arrival has mellowed into a lavender unlike any I've ever seen.

"All right, 15A. Here are three words you are never, ever going to hear me say again. Ever. *I. Give. Up.*"

Mark leans toward me, and this time, there is no doubt that his intention is very much of the flirtatious kind. My breaths become shallow and short.

"Remember, I compete for a living. I may well accept that challenge you've just thrown down."

I match his posture, coming closer almost to the point where our foreheads are touching. "You're on."

We're staring at each other once again, under the pretext of this game we've fallen into, but almost as soon as it starts, a gravity washes over me that tells me that I am standing at the precipice of something I didn't expect. Suddenly, I don't want to get on that plane tomorrow. Not if it means leaving him behind when all I can think about is wanting to talk to him for longer.

I break the silence, but neither of us move.

"You still haven't spelled it for me."

"N-A-C," he begins. Slowly. Lingering over every letter, each one rolling off his tongue as if he's tasting it, and though I never would have

thought of spelling as *seductive*, it is perhaps the most romantic thing I have ever heard.

"O-G-D," he continues.

My eyes soften. We still haven't looked away from each other, and his words are nothing but an alphabetic jumble, but they serve as the reason, the glue, that we are studying each other, gazes telling us something that words are not.

"O-C-H-E-S."

"Wait a minute." I pull back, the spell broken. "That's not so hard. I would have guessed that."

Mark sits up straight. "Eventually."

"Eventually? Back to that word? I would have gotten it in four tries. Five, tops."

He throws his head back and laughs heartily. "But would it have been as much fun as this was?"

I stop talking. I don't want to tell him he's right.

But he's right.

I take the easy way out and change the subject.

"So where's Sunset Beach?"

Mark shakes a finger at me. "I see what you did there, and I'm going to be nice and let you get away with it. But to answer your question, Sunset Beach is on the other side of the island, over an hour away. I'm going to do my Olympic training there."

"Why at the beach? And why that particular one?"

"Because it has monster waves. Especially in winter. It's considered downright dangerous to anyone but the most experienced surfers and swimmers."

I sense that he is telling me because it is a fact, not because he is bragging.

"Well, I suppose already having a gold medal makes you pretty experienced."

He shrugs. "I can't take that for granted, though. This is my chance to get better."

"This is your chance to win at the Olympics."

Mark takes his sunglasses off and looks out at the water, but I see moisture gather in his eyes.

"I'm sorry," I say, placing a hand on his arm. I don't know what I said, but it clearly hit a nerve.

"My parents died in that car accident I was in. And my little brother. If I didn't have photographs, I wouldn't even remember their faces anymore. But I do remember a few things. The way my mom made shrimp linguini with those tiny shrimp that would often go on sale at the supermarket. How my dad and brother and I used to go fishing at Bayou La Nana. And how we'd always, always listen to the Olympic broadcasts on the radio."

I swallow hard, the traces of pineapple rum turning bitter with the acrid taste of regret that wells up in me in sympathy with him. It's moments like this where I remember how very fortunate I am, much as I am quick to complain. Mr. Wall Street might not be Mr. Fuzzy as a father, but my goodness, at least he is still alive. And I know he loves me in his own way, even if I've often had to excavate to find it.

But I equally regret, if I'm honest, that despite how tragically Mark's family was taken from him, they had happy memories that I can't relate to.

It is one more unexpected piece in this puzzle of New Beverly that I'm seeking—I want a family. A real family. A close-knit family. Why can't I hope for that? Aren't women being told that we can have it all?

The feelings, the alcohol, the warm beach air overwhelm me, and I cover a yawn that I cannot hold back.

Mark notices, even though I'd hoped he wouldn't.

"Look at the time," he says.

Why do I feel that he really said this for my sake? That if I hadn't revealed my exhaustion, we might have stayed here longer? Might have had that dinner he originally offered?

"And I have a flight to prepare for."

I know it's the smart thing to do. For a lot of reasons.

We both grow silent for a moment. I've kept my sunglasses on and realize that they are actually my shield. My protection from more than the sun. In such a short time, we have laughed and nearly cried, and I can't remember a time when I felt so immediately at ease with someone.

And so confused about what I'd seemed so certain about.

Mark sets his hand on the armrest of my chair. Inches, then centimeters, then millimeters away from my own. I feel my heartbeat in my fingers, but I'm scared by what this means.

"I'm glad I met you, Beverly Caldwell."

A beat. And then I say, "I'm glad I met you, 15A."

It's a nickname. A term of intimacy. But equally impersonal, keeping him at a distance.

Whichever way I want it.

Which way do I want it?

"The next round of drinks is on me," he says as a reminder.

"But you said—"

"Not tonight. Next time."

I feel a flush through my body at the very thought of a next time.

He wants to see me again as much as I want to see him, and the recognition of my part in that frightens and thrills me.

It has indeed been a day of contradictions.

Of tightrope walking.

"Next time," I agree.

The sun has descended farther, and people on the beach are atwitter about the *green flash.* So we turn our heads to the western horizon in time to see the actual rotation of the earth visible with the sun as the focal point. And, indeed, when it has just disappeared from view, there is a greenish spark. A cheer rises from the crowd, and it seems like the best opportunity for a goodbye.

It is only after I've sent Rachel's dress to the laundry, and I'm in my hotel bed, insomnia coming over me as I review all that happened, that

I realize that I ran off before we could exchange the information that might help us find each other again. He only knows that my Pan Am flights will take me here occasionally.

And I only know that he will be moving across the island to a dangerous shore called Sunset Beach.

Mo'orea, French Polynesia
Today

A cruise ship passes across my view. It is heading away from the island, and I am relieved for the return of solitude. I arrived this morning on a ferry that was littered with chicken droppings, and I much prefer the authenticity of that to the artificial world that a city-on-the-sea creates.

The enormous white behemoth had been docked next to the ferry, dwarfing our little vessel into near invisibility.

I have cruised once before—I think it is almost a requirement as soon as your hair has fully turned gray and plucking the first hints of them is a distant and futile memory. My husband wanted to go on one, and I could never deny him anything.

I understand why someone might like to see points across the world with the ease of unpacking one time and having excellent cuisine available at all hours of the clock. And though it felt unnatural to see Broadway-quality dancers steady themselves onstage as twenty-five-foot swells tossed the ship back and forth, it was not the reason that it was both my first and last time.

It was the people that got under my skin. The ones who rose before the sun and attached parrot-shaped clips to the backs of the prime swimming-pool chairs, staking their claim with plastic and terry cloth while galivanting off for hours before returning. All the while rendering them unusable to the rest of us. Or the ones who muscled into the buffet lines to gorge themselves on food that is seemingly limitless. God forbid someone else get to it five seconds before.

Ah! How it made me miss the golden years of air travel when people treated the privilege that it was with the sophistication and appreciation that it deserved. They call those days the Jet Set age now with a nostalgia that makes me feel every bit as old as I am.

That is not to say that we did not have our challenges with passengers. Human nature is unchanging, and some of the more colorful stories from our days in the air have become legends among us alumnae. But there was always a sense, at least, that it was a special and hallowed thing to cross the ocean.

I digress. But it has me thinking of you, especially today. There is some small comfort I take in your premature departure—you never had to encounter the many obstacles that we survivors do as we age. Cruise passengers aside, I could do without stiffening joints and backaches that make it an impossible feat just to get out of bed. If I were more religious, I might find some satisfaction in the eternal merit of those sufferings. But as it is, they only make me count the days until I, too, am at rest. With you and with my dear husband.

If I were more religious, I might also hesitate to scatter your ashes in these waters, as I've been told that at the end of the world we will be reunited with our bodies, something that cannot be done if we've been reduced so microscopically and thrown to the whims of the wind.

Goodness, I am in a strange mood. Another consequence of age, I've discovered. When time is running out, impatience settles in, and though I do try my best to remain youthful, there are limitations to being an octogenarian that even the most ardent Pollyanna can't overcome.

I wonder if anyone today even knows who Pollyanna is.

But never mind that. I have returned to this glorious island at last, and I shall not waste another minute with anything that does not include soaking up the beauty and reminiscing with you.

CHAPTER TWENTY

Judy

I am awake long before my alarm clock goes off, and I stare at the swirls of the plaster in the ceiling above.

The sun rises in the east and sets in the west.

There are four time zones in the continental United States: eastern, central, mountain, and Pacific.

My first thoughts are rather unexpected, though maybe they were influenced by my dreams—flashes of sitting at a metal desk in grade school, dust falling from the chalk as the teacher writes geographic facts on the board.

Things that I learned long ago but are only now taking shape since their relevance has seeped into my life. Growing up, geography meant maps to me—particularly the one hanging on my wall with all my colored pins. But the nuances—*The sun rises in the east and sets in the west*—bore little meaning until now.

What else had I learned that might emerge from long-dusty corners of my mind? And what was ahead of me to still discover?

Everything.

I had taken for granted in Miami that a morning bus ride to the beach could result in a most spectacular sunrise. But here, dawn is a mere glow, and it is the sunset over the water that would inspire poems if I were gifted with words.

East and west are more than points on a compass. They shape the day depending on where you are in the world.

But I don't spend long pondering all the ways I will discover the nuances of geography in the weeks to come. Because Joe's letter and the leather journal he gave me are sitting on my nightstand and I have thought of little else since setting them there. I have nearly memorized his letter, having read and reread and reread it. It has an anchoring effect on me. This tactile connection between us is more comforting than I might have imagined. It's not the words themselves that give me solace, as they are merely a rundown of all his favorite hidden places from his world travels. It's the consideration he put into writing it at all and in giving me the means to write my own down in the journal.

Not since my father has a man shown such regard for me.

Joe's suggestions are some I will take to heart as I explore. The high tea in the crooked hotel in Blenheim, England. The butter curry at the stall run by a blind man in a New Delhi market. The restaurant in Rome built over the ruins where Julius Caesar was murdered. These are just some of the things I have to look forward to.

For now, I'm looking forward to breakfast.

My stomach is roaring with hunger—it's nine o'clock in the morning in Pennsylvania and Florida. It's only six here. But I don't want to disturb my housemates by rummaging through the refrigerator.

I feel around for a pack of saltines in my purse, left over from Beverly's care for me while I recovered. They're mostly crumbs—dust, really. But I'll take anything, so I open the corner of the plastic wrapping and tilt my head back, letting the tiny pieces cascade into my mouth.

I stifle a cough as the crumbs get caught in my throat.

Other than a raging return of my appetite, I am feeling fine today. Better than I can recall in a long time. Today will be my first flight working as a Pan American stewardess. And tonight, I will sleep in Honolulu. Honolulu! I can hardly believe it.

The check-in process is intimidating, to say the least.

The city bus pulls up to the departure terminal at San Francisco, or SFO as my code memorization reminds me. Only half an hour into wearing this uniform in public for the first time, I am already aware of the power it seems to command. I'd captured the eyes of most of the passengers on the ride over, drawn to me as if I was Jayne Mansfield herself. I'm not as blond nor as buxom as she, but the Pan Am uniform—or maybe that of any stewardess—seems to have the same effect on the males of the species.

As I descend the steps, the bus driver leaps out of his seat to carry my bag down for me, though I would have been quite capable of doing it myself. It's not as if he can walk all the way through the terminal in escort. Still, I appreciate the gesture. Though not the catcall whistle that follows. Maybe from him, maybe from one of the passengers. The whir of the airport deflects sound, so I can't be certain.

It's something to get used to, I suppose. If I had Beverly's cool confidence, I might have turned around, thrust a hip, and flashed a smile. But I have been too scared for the past few years to even make eye contact with another man, lest Henry accuse me of coming on to him and my skin paying the price back at home. I think that particular feminine wile has shriveled.

Though Joe Clayton has begun to resuscitate it.

I realize the irony. The miles and miles that happily separate me from Henry are the same ones that make it impossible for me to imagine a future with Joe.

I grip my bag and walk up to a ticket counter. I dial the extension that has been written in my instructions.

"Pan American offices," says a voice that is weary enough that I can assume she is probably near the end of her shift.

"This is Stewardess Judy Goodman reporting for flight four twenty-five to Honolulu."

"Come on back, Miss Goodman."

Miss. Not Mrs. How refreshing it is to hear that.

I'm not going to correct her.

I can't wait for it to be true.

I walk through a door behind the ticket counter that I know leads to the offices, because this, too, is in the set of instructions provided in a manual printed especially for the SFO staff.

I pull my white headscarf off, its gauzy sheerness briefly casting the room in a haze. The wind in Burlingame was rather gusty when I'd left, and as I'd had my hair cut and set the day before, I didn't want to disturb it. Now, with just the blue cap on top, I catch my reflection in a nearby window and notice that my head is the perfect oval shape, apparently the goal of the overall look. My skirt is the regulation one inch below the knee. My eyes are brushed with regulation blue eye shadow, but light enough that it could still be considered *natural.*

The office is abuzz with thirty or so girls, a sea of cornflower-blue uniforms that make one indistinguishable from the next. We are all an average of five foot five with only a couple of inches more or less between us. Chin-length hair like mine, matching lipstick, heeled shoes. Sporting the oval-head look with their caps on.

We all look like Jackie Kennedy.

And our skin—all white, just like our gloves.

I think of Ronelle. How I wish such an opportunity was open to her. But there is hope. I read the newspapers and follow the stories of desegregation, and I cheer on the Freedom Riders in their quest for civil rights.

As backward as little Red Lion can sometimes be, it is still twelve miles above the Mason–Dixon Line dividing the North and the South. Twelve miles on the side of right.

We'd learned, as Ronelle helped me study for the Pan Am interview, that a black woman had been hired four years ago by Mohawk Airlines, a mid-Atlantic regional company, and several smaller ones had followed suit. The major companies can't be far behind, and I hope that Pan Am will be the first.

"You look lost."

I turn, startled out of my musings.

"Rosamaria!"

"You remember!" She spreads her arms and wraps me in a hug that I needed more than I realized I did.

"It was only a few days ago. I may be overwhelmed, but give me *some* credit."

Rosamaria pulls back and laughs, and I am more grateful for a familiar face than I want to let on.

"First check-in?"

"Is it that obvious?" I clench my jaw, worried that I'm somehow broadcasting my inexperience.

"Only because I'm sure I had the same expression on my face three years ago."

"Three years! So you've outlasted the typical eighteen months."

"Not for long." She holds up her left hand and flashes the enormous sparkling diamond on her ring finger.

"A passenger?" I ask.

"Yes." She grins. "Sometimes clichés exist for a reason."

"Won't you miss all this?"

"Desperately! Though I won't have to watch my candy intake and worry about weigh-ins. And good thing—my fiancé's family owns a chocolate factory."

"Well, doesn't that sound dreamy? I'm so happy for you."

Rosamaria rubs my arm. "Don't worry. You'll have your turn. Single, successful businessmen know that there's no better place to meet a beautiful, intelligent, and worldly woman than right here on a Pan American aircraft. Why, some of them take trips just in the hopes of meeting their Mrs.!"

I didn't think of myself as beautiful, intelligent, or worldly. But it occurs to me again that my view of myself has been molded by my husband. Who had nothing to gain, as he saw it, in a wife who had any confidence in herself. I want to believe Rosamaria. And shouldn't the fact that Pan Am chose me out of so many applicants underscore it?

Wouldn't the catcalls suggest that?

That might not be the most edifying way to restore my image of myself, but it's a wound that may take many varieties of remedies to heal.

"Anyway," Rosamaria continues. "There's no need to rush into that. Fill up your passport, love. See the world. There's plenty of time to settle down and make your babies. Maybe your daughters and mine won't have to make the choice between the two."

"My hus—" I begin. But I stop myself from finishing that sentence.

My husband didn't want children, I had nearly said. *My husband thought children would distract me from him.*

A voice comes over the loudspeaker, saving me from trying to cover up that slip. My heart pounds in relief. I can't lose this job before I've even started it.

"Flight number four twenty-five, please come to the check-in desk."

"That's me," Rosamaria and I say at the same time.

My spirits lift. What a relief that someone familiar will be on my first flight!

"Round the world," she whispers. "My final hurrah. How far are you going?"

I have the itinerary memorized. "Honolulu, Guam, Hong Kong, Tokyo, Bangkok. And then back."

Her eyebrows raise. "Wow, they're throwing you right into the fire the first time out. But I hear they're doing that more often—better to test your stamina early on and weed out any underperforming recruits before they're in it too long."

I feel a look of terror come over my face, and she notices. "But not you, Judy-girl. I'm your crew chief for every one of those legs, and I'll make sure you dazzle."

"Captain Boyce wants to see you." Rosamaria taps my shoulder while I'm in the galley washing coffee cups. "It's time for your baptism."

"My baptism?" I ask. Something is up. For the entirety of this flight to Hong Kong, I have seen the stewardesses wear bemused looks on their faces when they glance at me, but no one would spill the beans.

Rosamaria just smiles. "You'll be fine."

I trust her. I do. But still, I feel nervous as I set my drying towel down and make my way up the aisle. I pass first class, wishing I could take a swig from a bottle of Dom Perignon to steady my nerves.

I knock on the cockpit door and turn the handle.

"Ah, Miss Goodman. You're just in time." Captain Kenneth Boyce greets me warmly with a wide smile and perfectly straight teeth. "Have a seat."

He points to the seat behind his, and I buckle up. The copilot tips his hat to me.

"Have you heard of the checkerboard landing?" Boyce asks. His voice is naturally loud, maybe a symptom of his twenty years as a pilot, attuned to the volume required to speak over the sound of the jet.

I shake my head.

"This is your baptism, then," he says. "Every stewardess gets to sit up here for her first descent into Hong Kong."

That doesn't sound so bad. But why would it be noteworthy?

"You see," he begins. I'm sure he's given this speech many times, but he has a paternal way about him that makes me feel like it's just for me. "The Kai Tak Airport is sandwiched between the mountains and at the edge of the city. You'll see it all in about ten minutes as we approach. Usually, our instruments prepare us for a straight shot on a runway, but the mountains and the city don't allow for that in Hong Kong. So it will look for a while like we are heading straight toward the mountain." He pauses for dramatic effect. "Because we are."

Before he can elaborate, someone from the control tower speaks over the radio, and he turns his attention toward preparing the 707 for landing. I watch Captain Boyce and his copilot flip various levers and turn on buttons. In no time, I see the mountains in the distance, just as he had indicated. It is a beautiful sight—land rising out of water. And as we get closer, I can make out the ripples of the peaks and even see the tips of the high-rise buildings.

It is an incredible city from the air. But before I can linger on its charms, I feel us lose altitude as the mountains grow closer and closer.

And closer and closer. We *are* heading straight toward them.

I cling to the armrest of my seat, my hand turning white from the strength of my grip. Lower and lower we go, the mountains right in front of us. It seems as if we will crash, and my new life will be over before it's begun.

I begin to see details—trees, windows, cars below us. The mountain is dead ahead. And then—I see an enormous red-and-white checkerboard built into its side. All of a sudden, the plane takes a sharp turn to the right, veering us away from our obstacle and straight into the city. I am still holding on to the armrests, afraid that I will fall out of my seat, despite the restraints. Left and right, I can see the buildings—even the people in the buildings. Even people hanging out their laundry. Our wingspan seems as if it will graze them, if not completely topple them. But Captain Boyce is calm. Not a glisten of sweat on his balding head.

They are not worried even as I am terrified. Their calm is the only thing that gives me comfort.

Lower and lower we go. I can see cars, buses, dogs.

And then—just ahead, a clearing out of nowhere. Lights on either side of it.

The runway!

The nose of the plane is still elevated even as I feel the wheels in the rear bounce on the pavement. A sense of relief washes over me, and yet I feel the residual blood rush from the ordeal. We level out, and the pilots deftly slow the 707 to a crawl. We taxi toward the terminal, and I sit in stunned silence.

"Sorry about that," Captain Boyce says as he takes off his headphones. "I wanted to prepare you better, but I called you up a little late, and we needed to focus on what the control tower was telling us."

"It's like this every time?"

"Every time." He grins. "A welcome unique to Hong Kong."

I have, indeed, been baptized.

Hong Kong is already my favorite layover, and I've only had two before that.

Just like Beverly and I had heard, the stewardesses are greeted at the terminal by a small Chinese man with a green measuring tape strung around his neck.

His English is quite good and spoken with a British accent, something that surprises me until I learn that the city, in fact, is under British rule until its lease reverts to China at the end of this century.

It isn't only the man's English that impresses. As various stewardesses say hello to the familiar face, he addresses them in their own languages.

"Bonjour, Antoinette," he says to a TWA girl, kissing either side of her cheek. "Veux-tu des vêtements?"

Would you like clothing?

And again, in what I assume is Norwegian, as one of our Pan Am crew approach him.

"Ah, Helene," he says as he bows. "Du ser vakker ut i dag."

Helene responds with rapid words that I do not understand, and by the looks of it, he doesn't either. Still, it's a good shtick—memorize simple greetings, get to know the stewardesses as they regularly pass through. And it clearly works. Each girl, in turn, switches to English and begins discussing the various stages of clothing they've commissioned from him.

Mr. Chan, as I overhear them calling him, nods to Helene, and begins to wrap the measuring tape around her—bust, waist, hips. Taking notes as he goes, ever nodding. Right here in the airport.

I have to hand it to him—Helene, more than any of us, is strikingly beautiful. More so than even Marilyn Monroe herself had been. Blond, curvy, exotic. But Mr. Chan handles himself with the utmost professionalism, which is more than I might be able to say for most men in his very fortunate circumstance.

So when he turns to me, I don't need Rosamaria's encouragement to give this a try, though she is eagerly forthcoming with it. It seems like a rite of passage for all stewardesses making their way through Hong Kong.

"You are new," he says, deducing that I speak English. Or perhaps that is his standard opening no matter what, since it's the universal language of the skies.

"Yes." I hope it's only obvious because he hasn't met me before and not because I'm wearing my inexperience on the sleeves of my uniform.

"I am Mr. Chan," he says, placing his right hand over his heart. "Will you do me the honor of letting me make you a silk dress?"

"I would love that."

He nods again. "For you, a big discount."

Rosamaria jumps in with her deep alto voice. "You say that to all the girls, Mr. Chan."

He laughs and then shrugs his shoulders. "Am I wrong? I have made six dresses for you already."

"You have the memory of an elephant, Mr. Chan," she admits, matching his good spirits. "And I'm here for another. A wedding dress. If you can fit me in."

"A wedding dress! For you, beautiful Rosamaria, anything." He takes her hand and kisses it, and there is a sincerity to it that I find endearing.

"But I'll need it in a hurry. This is my last trip here, and one of the girls is going to pick it up on her route in two weeks."

"It is not a problem," he assures her.

We follow him outside the airport after a brief stop at Customs and walk the four blocks to the bus stop. After a ten minute ride, we step off and into a busy, narrow street. My feet hurt in high heels that were not built for this terrain, and I stumble into Rosamaria as my ankle buckles.

Lucky for me, she is more experienced with this kind of footwear, so she is quick to catch my arm before I can come to any injury.

"We're almost there," she shouts above the cacophony.

I feel her grab my hand as we walk upstream against the flow of the crowd, and I'm reminded of the short walk in New York between Grand Central Terminal and the Pan Am offices just a few months ago. Buildings tall enough to pierce the sky. Black exhaust that sputters out of tailpipes. But also, I see rickshaws pulled by sweaty, often barefooted runners. Bicycles—so many bicycles—weaving through human and mechanical throngs with a fluidity and ease that is astonishing.

In the midst of this, mountains rise to my right, and water glistens to my left. Though even the water carries its own traffic jam of cargo ships and red-sailed junk boats. I've seen it all in photographs. None do it justice.

I am out of my small-town element. But this is what I signed up for. This is the living, breathing *world* that my hope-filled pushpins marked on a drugstore map. As intimidating as it is, it is also electrifying.

Alive. Alive. Alive. My heart beats to the rhythm of this city, and I don't know if I've ever felt so alive.

We take a sudden left and duck into a narrow storefront, flanked by other shops not much wider than their own doorways. I smell something delicious wafting through the walls next door, and my stomach growls. I was too occupied on the flight over to eat as much as I should have. Or maybe too nervous. But the feast in front of me now is not of the tasting variety. It is instead a wonder for the eyes.

Mr. Chan's shop is covered with shimmering fabric. Floor to ceiling, wall to wall. Yellow silks with red embroidery. Blue silks with silvery borders. Golden silks the color of the sun, radiant on their own without any additional embellishments. Behind the walls, invisible machines whir with activity.

Rosamaria takes my hand and leads me to a rack of ready-made dresses. They are more billowy than I can imagine wearing. She must see the surprise on my face.

"These are just the samples," she explains. "You try them on, and Mr. Chan cinches them with pins. Not everyone who comes to Hong Kong has to weigh in before flights like we stewardesses do, so the samples have to accommodate a variety of bodies."

Mesmerized, my hand caresses one particular offering. Four dresses back, I've seen a bit of purple peek out.

Henry hates purple. For no discernible reason, he has a visceral reaction to it, just as some do to bow ties or long beards. So I never wore it, even though it's a color I've loved ever since I was a child. My parents even painted my bedroom a soft lavender at my request. But after marrying him, I never brought anything purple into the house.

It's a small thing. An act of rebellion that would be indistinguishable to anyone witnessing it. But to me, the drive to purchase it feels like I have been infused with power. I don't need anyone's permission to buy this. It's just for me. For my own sheer pleasure.

"I'll take this one," I declare. I am surprised by my own determination.

Rosamaria laughs as I hold out the tip of it just far enough to get a better look.

"You haven't even pulled it off its hanger, Judy. Mr. Chan has a process. You pick several selections. Try them on. See how you like the style. Tell him where you want its length to fall, how deep the neckline should go. What kind of embroidery you'd like as embellishment."

I know she's right. And I don't want to cause a stir. But I've already attached myself to the purple one emotionally as one might a scraggly puppy in a pound. I try to tell myself that I'm rescuing this dress, wrinkled and forgotten as it's squeezed between so many others. And when I pull it out, maybe it will be the ugliest cut imaginable, but I won't care. I tell her I'm sure.

I want *this* one.

Mr. Chan shuffles over and pushes the glasses atop his head down onto his nose.

"The lady says this is the one," Rosamaria says on my behalf.

Mr. Chan nods and doesn't challenge my strange request. Maybe he just wants the sale. Or maybe he knows enough about the human soul to recognize one that is wounded. I sense that he has the same intuitive qualities that bartenders and hairdressers have when working with their patrons.

He pulls it out, and I close my eyes for a moment, afraid that I've made a mistake. I'd be too embarrassed to admit it. But when I open my eyes, Mr. Chan has draped it over both of his arms, holding it tenderly as if it were a priceless Ming dynasty vase.

My breath catches at the sight. I love it. I *love* it. It's already cut smaller than some of the others. Still too big for me, but shapely enough that I can envision how a tailored version of it will fit on me.

Mr. Chan beckons me to follow him to a trifold mirror on the corner, and I stand on a carpeted riser. He holds the dress up against my body.

Rosamaria has followed us, and her eyes grow big.

"It's gorgeous, Judy. I've never seen anyone find *the one* on their first try."

Even though I'm already convinced, it's reassuring to hear her enthusiasm. Approval is not a sensation that I am used to.

"Now—try it on, and then we'll pin it," Mr. Chan directs.

He points to a curtained room, and I follow his instructions. I turn my back to the mirror—it's full length and makes me shudder. I haven't seen myself head to toe in a mirror since leaving Pennsylvania. Beverly was right that I've become skin and bones.

I hear Rosamaria and Mr. Chan talking beyond the curtain, and she's commenting on the softness of one of the fabrics he's showing her. I can't stay behind this curtain forever.

I slip the dress over my head, and the silk flutters over my skin like a butterfly's caress.

An image of Joe comes to me. His hands soft as the silk. His hands touching me in all the same places. My skin flushes, and I feel dizzy.

Where did that come from?

I haven't thought of Joe in days. Much.

If you didn't count the dreams I'd had about him.

Almost every night.

"Judy? You okay, girl? Did you drown in purple silk?"

I take a deep breath before answering, steadying my voice.

"The zipper was stuck. But I have it now. I'll be right out."

It's only as I open the curtain that I realize that this dress does not have a zipper. I hope they don't notice.

Rosamaria and Mr. Chan turn at the same time as they hear me step out onto the parquet floor.

Their eyes widen at the same time, in the same way.

"Judy Goodman, you are a stunner!"

Rosamaria steps forward to take my hand and leads me toward the trifold mirror.

And she's right. Wow, is she right. The shade of purple looks as if it was specially spun by angels with my skin tone in mind. I turn right and left, and the dress swishes with me, casting out nearly every doubt about myself that I'd ever invited in.

Who knew that clothes could do that?

Mr. Chan doesn't speak, but that's understandable. He has a dozen pins wedged between his lips.

He gets to work. I feel him pinning the dress to knee length, pulling at the shoulders. His hand flits across my chest. Quickly, like the wings of a hummingbird. And not in a leeching way, but with the professional approach one might experience at a doctor's office.

I keep my eyes looking straight, using the mirror to see the shop behind me instead of looking down. I don't want to see the results of his handiwork just yet. I want to save the surprise of what Mr. Chan is doing when I can see it all at once. Through the reflection, I'm able to watch a few more women come through the door in their TWA uniforms. I wonder which stage of this process they're in. Are they here to select fabric? Try on the work-in-progress and adjust the measurements? Pick up the final dress? They look like they've been here before. Like they've already tasted the elixir of Hong Kong that I am just an hour into discovering.

"Aha!" Mr. Chan speaks at last, and I allow myself to lower my eyes to look.

I'm speechless. It is perfection. My thin frame looks curvy. It is tight on the top, a slit down the middle stopping just short of scandalous. And cinched at the waistline, a feat I wouldn't have thought possible with mere pins.

But I guess that's why all the girls come to see Mr. Chan. And come back. And come back. I'm already thinking about the next one I'll want.

"I'll take it!" I exclaim, meriting a twinkly laugh from Rosamaria.

Mr. Chan writes some notes on a pad of paper, and Rosamaria follows me back into the makeshift dressing room, insisting that taking it off once it's fitted requires some assistance. Unless I prefer getting poked with pins. Her hands move expertly—she's done this before—and before I know it, I'm putting the Pan Am uniform back on and waiting while Rosamaria makes her own selection. White silk with ivory embroidery. It will be a beautiful gown.

The shopgirl writes up our receipts and takes our deposits in dollars. I follow Rosamaria out, and she hails a taxi and gives instructions to bring us to the Hong Kong Hilton. I learned in Honolulu that Pan Am keeps blocks of rooms so that the crew can return to a familiar place as they travel from port to port. In Honolulu, it's the Royal Hawaiian Hotel on Waikiki Beach. The Hong Kong Hilton when making this first stop in Asia. Then Hotel Okura in Tokyo. Hotel Siam in Bangkok.

And so on. Five stars, all. Luxury at every turn.

It is a way to make it feel like home and to keep variation to a minimum since each passenger manifest brings enough variety to keep anyone occupied for a long time.

Juan Trippe isn't satisfied with that, though. I heard from the other girls that he is going to build a hotel chain—the InterContinental—so that all the airline's and passengers' money stays under a Pan Am roof rather than in Conrad Hilton's coffers.

When we arrive at the registration desk, I see that our bags have been sent ahead and are waiting on a bellhop cart. I smile at this efficiency.

But there, on the desk, I notice something that steals the smile from my face.

Days old, a *New York Times* headline screams danger:

Drive In Vietnam Wins Wide Gains

Conflict between the countries seems inevitable and I feel it more acutely being on this side of the world. And reminds me more than ever of the mission that was spoken of in training—that Pan Am stewardesses are ambassadors of the United States. The glamour of what I am embarking on is tempered, for the moment, by this solemn charge.

CHAPTER TWENTY-ONE

Beverly

On my second flight to Honolulu, I hand out one junior-captain wing to a little boy and two junior-stewardess pins to little girls. As well as a bassinet for a baby seated behind the bulkhead. I brace myself for whines and cries that never come. The girls of Marymount had nothing on their deportment.

As I walk up and down the aisles, I can't help but glance at seat 15A. I knew, of course, that the passenger would not be Mark Oakley, but my heart flutters at the memory of our first meeting. And our drinks on Waikiki.

The crew is atwitter, though, because Montgomery Clift sits in that place, nine years removed from that time my mother rented out an entire movie theater on Lexington Avenue for my twelfth birthday, and my friends and I squealed when he graced the screen in *From Here to Eternity*.

He is still a looker, in the words of my fellow stewardesses, flecks of gray distinguishing his black hair, the embodiment of the disparity between men and women as they pass each successive birthday.

He garners a good bit of whispers in the galley and in the jump seats, even though there are plenty of stories to go around about much bigger stars who have sat in the seats of the illustrious Pan American fleet. I note that he is here in coach. Not first class. Probably an indication of how much a studio believes an actor to be worth. How long it's been since he's had a hit.

I thought I would be more excited to see my first celebrity on one of my flights.

I might have been. If he had not been seated in 15A.

And I might have forgotten about Mark Oakley, or at least tried to, if, upon my return to SFO, an elaborate bouquet of pink roses had not been waiting at the offices at San Francisco with my name on them.

With a note that revealed his address in Sunset Beach, Oahu. And a plea to come visit next time I was on the island.

"I accept, Operator."

I'm happier than I'd anticipated when I hear my mother's voice as she approves the charges for the collect call. She'd insisted that I save the money I am earning at Pan Am—I am still paying off the uniform and absorbing the expense of living in California—and this is the first time I am taking her up on her offer.

I've refused her attempts, however, to wire funds to me behind my father's back. If Mr. Wall Street doesn't want me, I don't want his money.

"Beverly!" she says, nearly shouting. I can hear her excitement. I have a tinge of regret that we spent my entire childhood misunderstanding each other so thoroughly. Now that we are treading upon the first bits of a real relationship, I miss her. I honest to God miss her. When for all those years, I couldn't get away fast enough.

Maybe that is merely the natural devolvement of every mother and daughter during those challenging last years at home, but I doubt it.

If movies are to be believed, it can be a contentious time. But Upper East Side culture allows cordiality and propriety to conceal emotional distance, emotional rifts, and it is only now that she and I are letting our vulnerabilities seep out. It's only now that we are relating to each other in a way that I find genuine.

"Where are you now, my dear? What time is it?"

I look out the window of my balcony room. I'm on a high enough floor that the Waikiki sunbathers look like colorful little specks dotting the sand. Just as before, there is a spectacular view of Diamond Head to my left. Pan Am spares no expense for my comfort. And this layover will be two whole days.

Rachel is my roommate once again, though just like last time, she refreshed her lipstick and headed out.

"I'm in Honolulu, Mom. And it's just after noon here."

That means it is three o'clock in California. I am overdue for lunch, and my stomach is letting me know. But I didn't want to call too late in New York.

"Isn't that a funny thing?" my mother ponders. "You're just beginning your afternoon, and I'm putting my pearls on for dinner with your father and one of his clients."

"Where are you going?"

"Delmonico's."

"I might have guessed."

"It's near his office, and it always impresses."

"No doubt you'll be having the filet mignon, burned to a crisp, with blue-cheese crumbles and rosemary potatoes on the side. And you'll take the blue-cheese crumbles off at the last minute, deciding that the calories aren't worth it."

She laughs. "Am I such a creature of habit?"

I could set my clock by my mother's predictability. That's why our bimonthly jaunts to get our hair done at Sami's had been so special. A break in our daily routine.

"Let's see. Tomorrow is Friday, so you'll be playing bridge at Molly Ashby's penthouse and stopping into Saks afterward because they will have just put their new shipment of shoes on display."

She laughs again. I am enjoying this relaxed side of my mother.

"I can't deny it. And you've made your point. Though you're wrong about the potatoes. Your father commented that I've put a few pounds on, so it's salad for me, no dressing."

I ignore this comment. Our relationship will have to mature quite a bit more before I can pontificate on how she shouldn't let a man's opinion of her body take such root. Especially when I know her to be so slim that you can't see her if she turns sideways.

I stretch the telephone cord past the balcony door and sit on the chair, kicking my shoes off as I set my feet up on the ottoman. The sky is cloudless, the temperature perfect. I don't miss the New York pace that was all I ever knew.

"You should come see me," I suggest, surprising myself.

"In Honolulu?"

I shrug, which seems a silly gesture, as she can't see it. "Sure. Honolulu. San Francisco. Hong Kong. Wherever. Get out of New York. Especially with all that troubling business brewing with Cuba. Missiles can't make it to the west as far as I know."

I'd read that schoolchildren were doing drills in expectation of a showdown with the Communist nation. Anyone within missile range of Cuba was on alert. Including New York.

I'm more worried than I let on. I think about Miami and everyone we met there. It's spitting distance from the island nation.

Although with what seems to be brewing in Vietnam, it makes me wonder if anywhere is safe.

Perhaps tens of thousands of feet in the air, far above the conflicts on Earth, is the very best place to be.

My mother never has followed the headlines. "I wish I could, but I can't do that, Beverly. You know your father expects me to be at these client dinners. And they seem to be happening even more frequently. Life goes on for us."

I used to love that my parents were away for so many evenings. Not that I was one to sneak boys in or pinch money from their wallets. But the air of our rooftop apartment felt a little less stale, a little less stifling when they weren't in it.

Yet now that I'm here, seeing the world and chasing my dreams, it occurs to me that my mother is a prisoner of sorts. Of my father's expectations. Of her rigid schedule. Of the life she'd crafted for herself.

Who is my mother? Do I really know her?

Does she really know herself?

"Think, though, Mom," I say, finding newfound ease with the more casual moniker. "Which of Dad's clients would up and leave the firm if you weren't there? I'm not minimizing your importance—goodness knows that if I were a client, I wouldn't want to be trapped at a dinner table with him alone for hours either. But what is the price of that? When do you get to just be Diana Caldwell rather than Mrs. Wall Street?"

"You know I don't care for that nickname, Beverly." I wince at her half-hearted reproach, but I don't give in.

"Well, it's the natural one when you're married to *Mr.* Wall Street, isn't it?"

"Your father provided very well for you because of how much he works."

I feel my blood warming, the direction of the conversation bringing up old sentiments that I'd prefer not to revisit.

But distance has emboldened me.

"Wonderful. Because I was so much better off living on the penthouse floor of the building instead of the third floor along with regular people, even though it meant that my father was at work before I went to school and came home after I'd already gone to bed. Do you realize that six whole days went by before I realized that he'd shaved his beard?"

That had happened just a few months ago and had been an ill-advised decision on his part, a poorly aimed attempt to look younger. Mr. Wall Street's face was definitely better off hidden behind well-maintained facial hair. When that escapade didn't work, he swelled his ego by purchasing a Shelby Cobra, forest green with white stripes across the front, a flashy new roadster that sat unused in the garage except for its placement in the photo spread that *Business Week* did on him.

Not once had he taken it out for a weekend cruise into Connecticut as he'd planned. So it remained an expensive monument to his useless effort to remain young and virile.

Or rather, to appear so.

My mother lets out a breath. "I'm sorry, Beverly. There I go again, a creature of habit. You don't know what it's like to come from nothing and to work hard to hold on to everything."

"I hear that, Mom. But it doesn't have to be so extreme, does it? Dad's good at what he does. You don't think he could have provided you all the security you needed *and* still been home for dinner?"

I can imagine her dabbing a tissue to her nose and wished there was some way that telephones and televisions could be one and the same so that I could see her.

"Yes. Yes, you're right. But I've lived this way so long that I haven't considered a notion like that in, well, as long as I can remember."

"So let me help you consider other notions," I suggest, using her own words in order to open her up to the point I want to make.

"Like what?"

"What were your dreams before you met him?"

My father is older than my mother by fifteen years. She'd been his secretary, fresh from typing classes at Katharine Gibbs's Secretarial School. I long suspected that she had not been the first secretary he'd dallied with, nor the last. But she is the one who had gotten pregnant, winning the sperm lottery as I liked to irreverently think of it, so she was the one who was awarded the wedding ring.

Not that it was ever discussed, but mathematics are not so challenging that I can't count backward from nine months. My existence predates their wedding anniversary.

"I dreamed of not being poor," she answers me at last.

"But there must have been something more than that."

Shame on me, I think, as soon as those words leave my lips. Do I really understand what she went through? Or am I only looking at it through my own comfortable perspective?

She sighs. "Beverly, I grew up during the Great Depression. And you've heard my story. Having a dream beyond mere survival was an unimaginable luxury. Too impossible to even entertain a hope."

This hits me hard. It takes me a moment to even form a response.

"You're right. I'm sorry that I didn't sound very sympathetic."

I hear her chuckle, and I'm grateful for the levity. "I've done all I've done so that you wouldn't have to experience what that's like. Apparently I've done my job very well."

Too well, I think. So well that I've had to run away to find out what it means to live in the real world.

I wonder what would have happened if she hadn't married him. If she'd lived with Sami and had me out of wedlock. She might have cut hair for a living, and I might have made pennies sweeping up the discarded locks.

For a moment, it seems idyllic.

Simple, unrestrained.

But more likely, she would have been ostracized. Even now, whispers abound when a woman has a baby and there's no ring on her finger. The man, however, escapes unscathed.

I can see that she didn't have any other choice. She did it for me. And I've indeed lived a life most can never imagine. I swallow hard, and the lump in my throat feels akin to the sharp pain of strep.

"You've done many things very well, Mom."

I can feel her smiling on the other end. So I continue.

"Let's start from scratch, though. Your job with me is done. Dad's position is amply secure. What are your dreams *now*?"

The silence goes on for so long that I fear we've been disconnected.

"I don't know," she finally says. Finally admits.

I want to press further, but I sense that I've been hard enough on her. We can continue this line of conversation another time.

"How is Sami?" I say instead. I put lots of sunniness in my voice to counteract the somber turn we'd taken. And I hear the relief in her voice.

"Good. Much better, Beverly. Much. She'll be so excited to hear that you're in Honolulu."

"Has she told you more about her family?"

My family, I think. But it still feels foreign to think it.

"She has. She wrote some cousins in the Philippines while she was recovering at the Waldorf, and she just received an answer. She has the address of some nieces of hers and asked me to pass it along to you."

I write down what she tells me. I'll have to ask the front desk where it is. Oahu is a big island, and I know nothing of its geography.

Except that Waikiki is as far from Sunset Beach as you can get.

That one, I'd looked up.

"What will I even say?" I ask. "Isn't she estranged from them?"

"Family is now and forever, Beverly. She's already written ahead asking them to welcome you. You might be the catalyst for a reconciliation."

"That's a lot of responsibility to place on my shoulders. I'm still learning how to make a decent dirty martini while I'm thirty thousand feet up in the air. And without spilling it on a passenger."

Her voice gets soft. "It's not a responsibility, dear. It's an invitation. Neither Sami nor I have any expectations. Only a hope that I can give you back what I took from you—a sense of family."

I look down at the note I've written and run my finger over the ink. Aluahaina Street. Wherever that is, I'm going to find them.

I'll send a postcard from the hotel before I fly out telling them when I'll next have a layover in Oahu. Asking to come see them.

But that's something for tomorrow. Tonight, I'm going to see Mark Oakley.

I see him from afar, relieved that he has come. I'd sent him a letter and invited him to meet me in the lobby of the Reef Hotel in Waikiki at this date and time. In New York, everyone I know has a telephone, but I've come to learn that elsewhere—hello, budget—there are more often party lines. And as Mark hadn't left a number for an exchange, I assumed he was altogether without one.

So there was a healthy likelihood that he wouldn't show. Or didn't get my message.

Or didn't want to come.

After all, the girls here are beautiful and exotic. Perhaps our flirtation has been no more than that. The very idea deflates me.

But there he is. Goodness, I'm feeling my bones turn to lava just at the sight.

I stand, steady my legs, and walk over to him.

His eyes light up when they see me, and I am more relieved than I want to admit. He is here. He's all I've been thinking about since that last evening on Waikiki.

"Hello." He smiles, taking my hands in his and giving me a polite kiss on the cheek. My skin burns in that spot, and my thoughts dance to imagining more.

"Pan American isn't putting you up at the Royal Hawaiian this time?"

"They are. But—"

"There are too many eyes," he finishes. I am surprised that he had the same thought I did. I wanted to go somewhere away from the crew, the pilots, even the staff who would come to know me on my many visits there. As much as my blood feels fiery around Mark Oakley, I do not want to open up the gossip channels when I don't yet know if there is something worth gossiping over.

I'm sure he doesn't need that kind of attention either.

"Too many eyes," I agree. "So thank you for meeting here. I heard about a show that the Reef Hotel has on Monday nights. I thought we could stop in. A Night in the Philippines."

I'd seen a brochure in one of those tacky tourist shops along the beach last time I was here. My eyes were drawn to it because it mentioned the birth country of Sami—the cradle of my heritage that was still a stranger to me.

"I've heard of it," he says. "But I've been training too much to take in the sights. Good thing I have you for that."

He grins and I am again molten.

I check my watch. The show starts at seven, only five minutes from now. Pan Am has trained us to be vigorously punctual, and it has become a part of my very fabric.

I lead him to the hotel's ballroom, and we are ushered to a tiny cocktail table with two seats. Mark holds mine out for me, and I take it, pleased with his gentlemanly ways. The tightrope returns—I am an independent woman who likes a man to show her this kind of regard.

Maybe that sets the women's movement back a bit, but right now, I don't care.

We are served some kind of tropical drinks. Guava, perhaps. I love it.

The show begins with six young women entering the stage, wearing matching plaid dresses of orange, gold, and brown hues. On their heads, they wear conical black hats, topped with matching plaid fabric. The program indicates that they are doing the Itik-Itik Dance, also known as the Duck Dance.

Indeed they do look rather avian as they wave their arms over their heads and step around the imaginary rice paddies that the program describes. I wonder if Sami knows this dance, if her mother might have taught it to her. If I would have these steps memorized if my mother had not married Mr. Wall Street and instead raised me south of Houston Street.

But if she had, I wouldn't be here. Right now. In magical Hawaii with this dreamy man by my side.

All in all, a good trade.

As the women exit the stage, six men take their places. Each is shirtless, drawing a comparison to my memories of Mark on the beach, none measuring up to his picture-perfect physique.

"I think you might need to add coconut shells to your swimming attire," I say, flashing a grin at him and referencing costumes of the men onstage. I'm used to seeing pictures of hula girls with coconut brassieres, but this is entirely different. The men each have ten shells on their bodies—two on their shoulder blades, two on their pecs, two on their hips, two on their thighs, and two in their hands.

Mark grins back and leans in just as the music starts. "I think they'd look better on you."

I feel a shiver run through me at the suggestiveness of his tone. And though he has pulled out my chair, and though I'm certain that he won't let me pay for our drinks, I don't mind making the first move. I slide my hand over to his. The warmth of his hand in mine floods me with a sense of security. I expected, frankly, something more carnal in nature given the heat that clearly races between us. But in this simple gesture, I feel like I am home.

That's crazy. Right? I know so little about him, and yet that's the word that comes to mind.

I wonder what to make of that.

The Maglalatik Dance begins, and I try to refocus on the performances. The music is rhythmic and goes up and down in a simple, folksy way. But what surprises me is that the coconut shells are not just for decoration—they become instruments themselves. The men clap the shells together, and it sounds like tap dancing. But in this case it's not coming from their feet, it's choreographed so that the clicks happen over their own bodies—and even each other's. With perfect coordination, they leap around the stage, garnering applause even before it's finished.

I look over, and Mark is equally fascinated. I am bemused that both of us are swaying to the beat.

I can't see dear old Freddie back in New York doing this. I can't imagine anyone I know back home doing this. And yet here is this amazing, surprising man losing himself in the music as much as I am.

The show takes us on a musical journey through the Philippines, a piece of the Polynesian puzzle that makes up Hawaii. In another circumstance, I might be keener to pay attention, but I am blissfully distracted by the presence of my companion.

The show ends with the Dance of the Maiden in the Moonlight, but well before its first notes resonate, Mark and I are ready to leave. The Reef Hotel had offered an unexpected glimpse into my alternate past—what I'd come on this adventure to find. But time is precious, and my brief layover is a potent reminder that I very much want my present to be filled with getting to know Mark Oakley better.

We glance at each other, already wordlessly speaking the same language, and we slip out before the final measures.

A sign in the lobby points the way to the beach.

The night sky is dark, illuminated only by a full moon that casts rippled strands of light over the Pacific. Ukuleles play in the distance, and romance permeates the air as honeymooners and lovers stroll with dreamlike strides.

"I love that sound," Mark says, breathing in the fresh air. "The ocean waves breaking against the shore. I sleep with my windows open at night and listen to them until I fall asleep under their spell."

"I would like to hear that." I realize after I say it that it sounded like I want to lie in his bed with him. It's not what I mean.

Or maybe it is.

This island makes me feel like I am walking in a dream. Like I am an uninhibited version of myself.

I slip my sandals off, and Mark does the same, taking both pairs in his right hand as he holds my hand with his other one. We leave the vast lanai of the hotel and step onto the sand, our feet sinking into its softness. I assume we are going to walk the length of Waikiki—or at least back to the Royal Hawaiian. But Mark leads me to the water's edge.

He drops our shoes to the ground and pulls me close to him. The moonlight frames us as if it were a spotlight, but I give it no more attention than that because all my senses are overwhelmed by his nearness. Only my thin gauzy dress and his light linen shirt are between us, and as I press my hands against his chest, I can fully appreciate his well-toned swimmer's body. I shiver even though the night air is warm.

I move my hands to his neck, look up at him, and invite him—dare him—with my eyes to kiss me.

I've never been kissed. I've only read about it. But I'm certain that if—when—Mark Oakley kisses me, it will be better than in any novel.

He leans in, eyes open, intensity stirring feelings in me that I don't have names for. Then he closes them and places his lips on mine.

I'm glad he's holding me because I want to collapse at his touch. My head feels dizzy, and all I can think of is . . . more. More of this. Forever.

And yet, it is gentle. I want to be engulfed in this, and I can feel the tension in his neck as he holds himself back. The restrained discipline of an athlete. I want to bless and curse it all at the same time.

Mark pulls back, leaving me aching where he has awakened me.

"Beverly," he whispers. He tucks a strand of hair behind my ear. "You are so unexpected."

He doesn't have to explain. I know what he means. Neither of us came to Honolulu for this.

And yet we found it.

CHAPTER TWENTY-TWO

Judy

Joe is coming to San Francisco.

Joe is coming to San Francisco.

I still can't believe it.

I don't know if I want him to.

Of course I want him to.

I'll put my hair up.

I'll put my hair down.

There is only one thing of which I'm certain: I know what I'll wear.

It took me only one additional flight to Hong Kong for Mr. Chan to have my purple dress ready. Usually it takes three trips to complete one of his masterpieces. Or so I've been told, but I had been so enamored with the sample on the rack that he'd agreed to tailor that very one rather than create my dress from scratch.

I suspect Rosamaria had slipped him a little money to make it so. You didn't have to be in Hong Kong for very long to discover that its lifeblood is tips and bribes and under-the-table transactions.

However it happened, my beautiful silk dress is hanging in the closet I share with Beverly, and its inaugural appearance will be tonight.

When Joe takes me out to dinner.

It's only been three weeks since I've seen him. But it feels like so much more. The contrast between training in Miami and actually working the flights is vastly different. So much so that training is a distant memory, as if it happened to someone else. I've grown up in this short span of time.

I already know that I love the coffee that comes from Kona when I'm in nearby Honolulu and that my favorite version of it is served at the counter at Tops. And though I've graced its vinyl stools four times now, I still thrill at the fact that the opening scene of Elvis's *Blue Hawaii* was filmed there.

I've already ordered two more dresses from Mr. Chan. One for Ronelle—who deserves a thousand of them. And another for me—this time made from a gorgeous golden silk with red butterflies embroidered on its hemline. Red being the Chinese color for good luck.

In this short time, I've also discovered that the soldiers stationed at another Pacific stop—Wake Island—will gather in the dance hall near the airport when a weekly flight deposits pretty stewardesses, the boys dousing themselves in cologne to cover up the sweat that permeates their uniforms after a long day in the tropical heat.

I can only imagine the education another few weeks will bring.

But in all that time, through all those adventures, Joe has not been far from my mind.

The doorbell rings at six sharp, and I recall that Joe Clayborn is punctual. Beverly says that timeliness was drilled into us so thoroughly during training that we wouldn't recognize our former selves. Maybe the same is true for Joe. Are any of us the same as who we were before becoming part of this company?

Lorna, another of our housemates, offers to get the door while I pause in front of the mirror and dab at a stray smear of lipstick. She's just finished the latest *Andy Griffith* episode, a show that fascinates her endlessly because its depiction of small-town American life is so different from what she knew in her hometown of Munich. I'd been listening from my room. In tonight's show, Barney tries to set Andy up with a girl after he has an argument with Peggy.

Even in Mayberry, love is a frequent topic.

"Judy!" Lorna calls. "There is a man here for you."

The truth is, she knows all about Joe. As do all the girls living in this house on Clarendon. Beverly had dished about it a little more than I would have on my own, egged on by a bottle of champagne that a male passenger had bought for her. But in the end, I was grateful for their counsel. I hadn't listened to my mother's concerns about Henry, so the advice of such worldly women was welcome.

Of course, I hadn't told them that I was married. And that, at least, Beverly kept secret.

The consensus among the girls: go for it.

After all, Pan Am had been the catalyst for many inner-airline romances. Why not mine?

"Hi," I say as I step into the living room.

I didn't know how much I missed him until this moment, when he is standing right in front of me. My heart seems to still and race at the same time. And the room empties itself of all its oxygen.

"Hi," he says in return.

Lorna looks at both of us and rolls her eyes. "Well. As scintillating as this conversation is, I have to pull myself away. I have the early flight to Tokyo to prepare for."

I smell Chanel N°5 on her as she walks past me, the same scent that Beverly wore until we went to the Woolworth counter, and I insisted she find a perfume that she could be happy with for less cost. She settled on Revlon Aquamarine, marveling that she could buy their whole line—milk bath, bar soap, powder, and eau de toilette—for less than the price of one bottle of Chanel at Bergdorf's.

Lorna turns around and places her hand on the doorframe. "Gute Nacht, you crazy kids. Don't do anything I wouldn't."

Then she winks. "Which leaves you with *plenty* of options."

The taxi pulls up to Tosca Cafe in the city. In my short time living in California, I had not yet set foot in San Francisco itself, having spent the few days that I wasn't crossing the Pacific getting to know the charming little town of Burlingame. So as we drive, I am torn between looking at the city by the bay through the window on my right and the wonder that Joe is sitting to my left.

But I am spared having to jump right into conversation—the driver keeps the radio so loud that talking is impossible, music in a language I don't recognize permeating every inch of the car. Instead, Joe and I exchange smiles.

His nearness is putting every nerve I have on alert, and it is all I can do to keep my smile from reaching ear to ear.

The taxi comes to a halt, and I instinctively reach my hand out to grip the headrest to keep from slamming into it. Joe hands a few dollars to the driver and, in no time, comes around to hold the door open for me. My Hong Kong dress is clingy, which is excellent for turning heads but is like a straitjacket when moving in it. I swing my legs sideways over the seat, grateful that the butterfly dress I've ordered from Mr. Chan is a bit more loose fitting.

But I can accept my lack of movement because Joe hasn't taken his eyes off me since we left the bungalow. They remind me of the exaggerated way a character's eyes pop out in a cartoon, and I am aware that Joe is trying to control his reactions as much as I am.

My cheeks burn at the realization.

I take his hand, comfort and energy pulsing in it. As soon as we reach the sidewalk, he shifts to pressing gently at the lower part of my back, guiding me through the crowd.

Tosca Cafe is abuzz with activity—fitting for how I am feeling right now. There is a line of fifteen people or so waiting to get in. But Joe walks right up to the hostess.

"Clayton, party of two."

Of course he would have made a reservation in advance. How dependable of him.

The leggy girl is wearing a skirt whose hemline sits just below what might be considered legal, but Joe doesn't seem to notice, even when she bends over to pick up two menus.

"Right this way, Mr. Clayton."

She leads us to a booth in the back corner, and I slide onto the red-vinyl seating, thankful that the slippery texture is a good match for silk. Better than in the taxi. Joe makes sure I have the side from which I can see the whole restaurant, whereas his view is the wall. Well, more than just a wall. I noticed an enormous framed mural of Venice as we walked this way.

Venice. I wonder if that's a place I'll ever see during my time at Pan Am. I wonder if Joe has ever been. He hadn't made a mention of it in the letter that came with the journal.

"I see you've paid a visit to our Mr. Chan," Joe says, hands folded on the table. Strange first words given the weeks apart, but I kind of like how he eased right into talking as if we had just spoken yesterday.

"I should have realized that you would know all about him."

He tugs at his shirt collar. "This is the best linen I've ever worn with the best tailoring known to man."

I laugh. "Yes. Then you know him well. Though I have to say, you didn't choose the most exciting of his fabrics." Now that I think of it, I don't know if I've ever seen Joe branch out beyond a basic white or brown shirt. Except for the time he went crazy and wore pale yellow at Villa Vizcaya.

Joe takes a sip of the ice water that the waitress set on our table and grins. "I'll leave the fancy stuff to the ladies. I'm plain old Joe, and I'm happy that way."

"That's a departure from the animal kingdom, then," I say. "Mr. Chan's shop is like a candy shop for colorful peacocks, and you dress like a peahen."

As soon as I say it, a burning sense of embarrassment washes over me. I'm afraid I've missed the mark. It was meant to be a humorous observation, not a slight. Actually, I like *plain old Joe*. A lot. I prefer his simple mannerisms to Henry, who took every opportunity to flex his imagined superiority. It was exhausting to keep up with such an ego.

Thankfully, Joe looks unruffled. I'm out of practice. I haven't been out on a date in several years.

If this is a date.

I hope it's a date.

"So what brings you to San Francisco?" I ask, eager to change the subject and leave my misguided statement behind us.

"You do."

Every part of me freezes. I'd hoped as much, but it was another thing entirely to have him admit it.

"Me?" I grip my water glass. My hands need to do something.

Joe leans in, but his hands remain folded in front of him. "What you see is what you get with me, Judy. I felt a spark between us in Miami. I'd like to see what that might mean. And we happen to be lucky enough to have jobs where we can hop on a plane and find out."

"How long will you be staying?"

It's not the best response, but it's the first one that comes to mind.

"My flight back is tomorrow at two o'clock."

My heart is sitting on a seesaw right now. He's here. Then he'll be gone.

But he's here *for me*. That's what matters.

"So you took a ferry flight all the way from Miami just to take me to dinner."

"Yes." He unfolds his hands and sets them just a bit closer to me, though he never breaks his gaze. He lowers his voice and there is a hint of vulnerability in it. "Am I imagining the spark I mentioned?"

I shake my head. I am not one to believe in love at first sight—and I'm not even saying that's what I feel for Joe. Any notion of love I've ever entertained was tarnished and it will take some time to polish. But I did fall for that purple silk dress back in Hong Kong the moment I saw it, and it gives me hope that my instincts might not be irretrievably gone.

That it's not too late to make up for old mistakes.

Life is too short to live it in the past.

"No," I answer. I feel as resolute as my one-syllable answer sounds. For the first time, I reach out to him. I take his hands in mine, the boldness of it intoxicating me before we even order our drinks. So it can't be mistaken for liquid courage. This is one hundred percent me. Judy Goodman. "You are not imagining the spark."

I feel my breathing become heavy and my chest tighten as the implications of his trip hit me.

"Judy, are you all right?"

Joe slides his hand across the table and holds mine.

"I'm fine," I say, clipped. "Why do you ask?"

"Because you look like you're going to be sick. And your foot is restless under the table like you're doing a tap dance. Did I—is my flight out here moving too fast for you?"

He noticed. Either I'm not hiding my nerves as well as I thought, or he is a particularly perceptive man.

I have to tell him about Henry.

But if I tell him, he may have to report it to Pan Am.

I could be fired.

And worse, I realize.

I could lose him.

I pull my hand from his and wrap my own together. I am tempted to look at the table—it's easier than meeting his eyes. But he deserves better than that.

"No," I assure him. "Not too fast at all. This is—I am."

I let out a big sigh before continuing. Here we go. "Joe, I'm married."

Joe sits up as if an electric volt has gone through him. The look on his face is difficult to read—is he angry? Or merely surprised?

It feels like an hour passes between us, but according to the clock on the wall, it's mere seconds.

"But—your application. It said you were single."

My lip quivers, and it takes everything in me not to cry. "I lied."

No mistake this time. He doesn't mask his look of betrayal.

"Wait, though," I hurry, suddenly feeling words coming faster than I can say them. "It's not what you think."

I begin to tell him the story. More than he probably wants to know and with a rapidity that would rival a speeding train. About meeting Henry at the Lancaster market. About how he dazzled me, about losing my mom, and then being swallowed into a world of his creation until I was lost as well.

About Ronelle, who helped me escape into the welcoming arms of Pan American.

And about Beverly's plan for me to go to Mexico to dissolve this horror once and for all.

The waiter approaches, pad in hand, ready to take our orders, but I see him assess our body language, and he wisely turns around and walks away.

When I am done, I dab the cloth napkin to my nose, quietly apologetic to whoever has to wash these, for that is not their intended use.

Joe is quiet, arms folded.

I feel like the balance of the whole world is teetering on this axis.

Then he speaks.

"I am so sorry," he says. He releases his arms and puts them back on the table, leaning in.

"For flying out here?" I whisper.

My heart is racing to the point of being painful.

But a smile begins to spread across his face, and his eyes soften into sympathy.

"No. No, dear Judy. Never sorry about that. Glad as hell, to tell you the truth. I thought there was something about *me* that was holding you back. I'm *sorry* that you have been holding on to this. And especially that you had to go through it in the first place."

These were not the words I expected. My hands fly to my face, and the tears come. My shoulders are heaving, and I can't control any of it. It is as if everything I've endured for the last few years is ready to be released.

Joe comes around and slides into my side of the booth, enveloping me in his arms. The wool tweed on his jacket itches my face, but it is the most glorious sensation because it tells me that I am *alive* when I have felt numb, dead all this time.

He strokes my hair, and I feel people around us looking at me. But Joe seems oblivious to everything except us.

This is what it should feel like to be in a man's arms.

I pull back at last, and I can feel how the makeup I'm wearing has melted on my face. I even see the faint curve of my mascara has landed on his white collar.

"I'm sorry," I say this time. But despite my apology for this spectacle, I feel amazing. Light. Released and new. I'm reveling in it and all it could mean.

Joe takes the napkin I've been holding and dips it into my water glass, wiping it gently across my face. "You have nothing to be sorry for. You're a brave woman, Judy Goodman, to do all you've done."

"You—you won't have to tell Pan Am? They're your employer."

He straightens up and exaggerates a professorial tone to his voice. "It is an indisputable fact that the stewardesses who represent Pan American Airlines must exhibit, above all things, grace under fire, and be ready for everything that is thrown their way. It is my professional opinion that Judy Goodman has demonstrated this skill in abundance and shall remain employed by the company for as long as she cares to."

I smile. I can't help it. This is a cute look on him.

"Besides"—he shrugs—"I'm not your manager. And thank goodness for that. You don't come under my authority, and I feel no obligation to bring it to their attention."

I grab his hand and feel myself squeezing it tight enough to cut off his circulation. But he doesn't flinch.

"I'm going to fix this," I promise. "I want a fresh start."

"I want that for you too. And if you need me to back away for a while so that you can do that, I will."

"No, Joe. Dear, dear Joe." I stroke his face and like the feel of his gentle stubble against my fingers. "You are the very best part about starting over."

If Beverly asks me later what we ate, what we drank, I won't remember. Because for the remainder of the evening, Tosca Cafe becomes a blur while Joe is in full focus to me. An observer might find our conversation trivial as Joe steers me away from heavier subjects, sensing my need for levity.

It is not until after his taxi pulls away from my doorstep, after he has walked me to the stoop illuminated by a flickering bulb, after he has drawn me into his arms and kissed me with both delicacy and desire that sets my toes aflame, that I notice a car parked across the street.

The window is rolled down, and cigarette smoke spirals upward, and I see a man in the shadow and haze watching me as I unlock the door.

My stomach tightens in panic even as my head tells me that I'm imagining things.

But the man looks a whole lot like Henry.

CHAPTER TWENTY-THREE

Beverly

The plane hits an air pocket, and my stomach lurches into my throat. I've flown often enough to recognize that this kind will be sustained, so it does not surprise me when Captain Davis calls me up to the cockpit and tells me to make the announcement that everyone needs to buckle up, including the stewardesses.

You know it's serious when the stewardesses have to go sit in the jump seats.

It's just as well—I burned myself on a casserole an hour ago and haven't been able to tend to it yet. My first injury of what will certainly be many. Like rings on a tree, you can tell a stewardess's time in the air based on the number of burns on her arm.

Whereas my skin is red, Judy's skin looks green from the rough air. But stalwart girl that she is, she makes her way down the coach aisle confirming that all the passengers are buckled and secure. I see her grip the backs of the seats to keep her balance, and when we both arrive at the rear of the plane, we collapse into our seats and keep silent until we're certain that we won't lose our lunches.

In moments like these, I rue the circumstances of geography that place our country squarely between two oceans. To travel to either Europe or Asia, one has to cross a vast span of water. And though we studied the mechanics of the airplanes in Miami, and I know there is little to fear, it is still my instinct to wonder if this kind of turbulence will send us down into the belly of the Pacific.

So much for the Pan American advertisement that shows two people in first class and boasts, "So smooth, so free of vibration, chessmen won't move until you move them."

Well, maybe in comparison to the old prop planes, as far as I'm told. But that does nothing for my anxiety at this moment.

"Distract me," Judy screeches as she places both of her palms on her stomach.

"I heard that Joe Clayton kissed you, and don't go denying it."

It was exactly the right thing to say. At the mention of Joe's name, Judy's face relaxes, and she actually smiles.

"He did," she answers coyly.

"*He did*? Two words? That's all you're going to give me?"

"It's not ladylike to kiss and tell."

I roll my eyes. "Fine then. Tell me this much. Was it a *ladylike* kiss?"

Her green hue turns pink as she blushes. Mind over matter.

"Mostly."

"*Mostly. He did.* My, aren't we loquacious? Three whole words. After all I've done to get you two together."

She folds her arms, and her grin grows wider. "Fine. It was proper enough that it wouldn't have garnered any attention if we'd been out in public. But—"

"Oh yes. There has to be a 'but.'"

"Buuuut," she draws out. "I could tell that it has the potential to be so much more."

I nod. Though that was a mistake. My stomach didn't like that. I need to keep still. "I see. So it was a smolder. Calm on the outside but fiery underneath."

"Yes." She leans in. "A *lot* of fire underneath."

"Interesting. Interesting." I stroke my chin in an exaggerated motion. "So what we have here is a smolder that's covering a fire that's really an *inferno*."

This time, she rolls her eyes. "And now this conversation is officially getting out of hand."

"Those are my favorite kinds, of course." I love to goad her.

"And what about you and Mark Oakley?" she asks. "Smolder or inferno?"

I smile. I've told her a little about my two-day layover last time. The Reef Hotel. The sail the next day on the Ali'i Kai catamaran. The evening movie at the Waialae Drive-In.

The kissing? I haven't spilled those beans yet.

But definitely inferno.

Drive-ins are rather ideal places for that. The confinement of the car. The concealment of the dark.

The details I'll keep to myself. Most people have good imaginations.

"I'll say this. The ones who seem all calm and respectable on the outside are often boiling cauldrons inside."

I look at Judy and see the frozen look of shock on her face. I can tell I've struck a nerve, and I realize that my flirtatious statement could be understood to have a whole different meaning. Henry. She'd married someone who presented himself as one thing only to be another after the wedding. And not in the Casanova way I'd been teasing at.

"Oh, Jude, I'm so sorry. I wasn't thinking." I lay my head against hers and squeeze her arm. Mercifully, the plane stops rocking in that moment.

"Don't worry. I know what you meant. It's just raw for me because I thought—I thought I saw him the other day."

"You *what*?" I sit up straight so quickly that the buckle around my waist tightens in protest.

She hangs her head and picks at her nails. "Just as Joe left the house in Burlingame. There was a man outside in a car. In the dark, he looked like Henry. It gave me an awful fright."

"But it wasn't him?"

I never had told Judy that Henry came searching for her in Miami. I'd hoped that the wild-goose chase I'd led him on had given him the hint to stay away. I was going to protect this girl, whatever it took. I was relieved that we had this flight together. Maybe we could finagle it to have more of our routes coincide or talk to our other housemates to make sure that someone was always scheduled to be at our home base of SFO whenever Judy was.

Even as it crossed my mind, I realized that it was too complicated to work.

"It wasn't him, though," she says with relief. "He was waiting for a neighbor who came out of a house a couple of doors down not long after I noticed him. He had been looking at me—which I did find unsettling—but he might as easily have been peering at our house number to see if he was in the right place."

"What would you have done if it had been Henry?"

Judy squirms in her seat, but I can see that she understands the merit of my question.

"I don't know, to be honest. Run inside and lock the door?"

"That's not a plan, Jude. You need a plan."

Now I'm really regretting that I didn't tell her about his Miami trip. What if he doesn't take that hint? What if he comes looking for her again?

I realize that there's no reason I can't tell her now. She has to be alert. She has to know that he could come back.

"Judy," I begin.

But before we can continue, the pilot announces that we have clear air and that drink service is ready to begin.

"You have to book a flight to Mexico."

Judy and I are not assigned a room together at the Royal Hawaiian, so we'll have to talk about this later. She is clearly exhausted and gives me a quick kiss on the cheek after receiving her key at the front desk. She says that she is going to take a nap before watching the sunset on the beach later. That's how I'd like to spend this evening in Honolulu. Ideally on Sunset Beach with Mark. He told me how beautiful it is, and goodness knows I could stand to kiss him again. But today, I have a different agenda. To meet my family.

When I wrote him, he understood. Besides, I'll see him sooner than later. Judy and I are both on the Honolulu to Wake Island to Tahiti to Hong Kong route, which reverses itself before returning home.

I can wait the ten days. I hope.

I take the elevator up to the fourth floor and turn the key on room four-eleven. I never tire of walking into a hotel room. The scent of freshly washed cotton sheets is a heady delight, mixed as it is with the smell of salt water. The balcony door is open to let in the breeze, and the room this time is low enough that I can hear the waves like they're thunder. As much as I want the bed by the window, I'm rooming with Rosamaria tonight, and she's planning to stay in.

I drop my Pan Am–issued blue vinyl bag on the opposite bed and eye those soft-looking pillows. Turning around, I walk toward the bathroom sink and turn the faucet on to its coldest setting, splashing the refreshing water on my face. I scrub the thick foundation off my skin, trusting that bleach will restore the towels to their brilliant-white color. Mascara comes off in curved streaks as I avoid the delicate area under my eyes lest I wrinkle before I should. I dab on some moisturizer and consider what I'm going to wear. I run my hand down the emerald-green dress that Mr. Chan finished for me on my last trip to Hong Kong. And then I consider the sundress I packed for time at the beach.

That's one thing I've learned about Hawaii. The less, the better. Less cosmetics. Less fuss about my hair. Less clothing. Life is simple here.

But the green silk dress wins out. After all, I'm meeting some of my family for the first time and representing my mother. I have to look my best.

A line of taxis waits at the edge of the hotel's portico, and I rattle off the address on Aluahaina Street. The driver takes up the entire seat in both width and height, his straw-hatted head hitting the top of the car. He wears a bright-green Hawaiian shirt with yellow plumeria blossoms all over it and it makes me think of Mr. Chan's shop.

It occurs to me that Honolulu and Hong Kong both fall near the Tropic of Cancer, facing each other as if they were sister cities. I send a mental wave to the place across the other half of the Pacific and think about how, in just a few days, I'll be back in the shop picking up the red bolero that I've commissioned for my mother.

Isn't it marvelous to live in a century where this is possible?

Fifteen minutes into our ride, the driver utters his first words.

"See our new memorial? Over there," he says, pointing out the left-side window.

He is thickly accented, though I do not know the island's history well enough to identify it. He could be Samoan, Tongan, or hailing from a myriad of other Polynesian islands. I want to ask him but don't know the local customs enough to understand if that would be considered rude. I detest when people make assumptions about New Yorkers that are far from correct, and I'm determined not to do the same thing.

I have so much to learn.

I look to where he is indicating, and far out on the bay, I see the rectangular white building sitting in the middle of the water. It's the USS *Arizona* Memorial, commemorating the attack on Pearl Harbor. I'd read about it back in May, shortly before leaving for Miami. It had just opened and I'd looked forward to seeing it ever since.

Has Mark been there yet? Maybe it's something we could do together on a future trip.

The driver takes a right, slow and easy, unlike New York taxi drivers who sometimes make you feel as if you want to get your life right with

Jesus before entering one. Not here. I'd recently heard the phrase *island time*, and this is a good example of it.

I kind of like it.

He pulls up to a house—a duplex, as I look closer—and I hand him three dollars for the two-fifty fare.

Here we go. I'm buzzing with anticipation. My cousins had written back to my address in Burlingame agreeing to meet me on this layover. Their enthusiasm was palpable both in their words and in miniature watercolor scenes of Hawaii that one of them had decorated the stationery with.

You don't go to all that trouble if you're holding a grudge.

Besides, the family troubles happened long before any of us were born, so there seems no point in perpetuating it.

I like them already.

There are two front doors to the left of the carport, but I don't have to wait to figure out which is the correct one. The one right in front of me swings open.

"Cousin!"

This is shouted in my ear as I find myself enveloped in a tangle of arms before I can even see what is happening. As I step back, I see two girls near my age and nearly identical to each other.

Karina and Ann. Despite their beautiful letter, I would not have guessed I'd receive this kind of reception. Their brand of exuberance is certainly not how we greet each other in New York. There, it's a polite kiss-kiss on the cheek, like the chic in France.

"Come in, come in."

I couldn't tell which one said it.

I follow them up a straight and narrow staircase, expecting their home to be similarly cramped, but I am surprised to find that it is quite spacious and even modern. The ceiling is peaked and made of painted-white driftwood. The living room, kitchen, and dining room are all one open space and completely casual in comparison to the ornate formal rooms of most Park Avenue homes. It evokes that *island time* I was just thinking of. And as if to punctuate that, the floor-to-ceiling windows reveal a thin line of blue that would be enough to advertise it as having a water view.

"Take your shoes off," says one of the girls. "No one wears high heels in Hawaii."

I notice that her long black hair lays at her waist while her sister's stops midback. Perhaps the only way I'll be able to tell them apart. Once I know who is who.

I am immediately aware of how spectacularly I have overdressed. They both have loose-fitting floral dresses on, and their feet are bare. Their skin is a coffee-colored shade of brown, and I wonder how much of it is heredity and how much is sun exposure. I am more curious than I would normally be because of our shared blood.

"I'm Karina," the longer-haired one announces, answering a question I have not yet asked.

"I'm Beverly." They know that. But it is all I can think of to say. Because I'm looking at Karina's eyes and I see my own. And my mother's. And Sami's.

Remarkable. It's like a puzzle piece. It all fits. I feel giddy, like an explorer at the dawn of the discovery he's hoped to find.

I feel like I *belong*. What a strange thing to experience so immediately and in such unfamiliar surroundings.

"And I'm Ann." The other girl laughs and takes my hand, pulling me over to the table that sits next to the kitchen. She sets a cutting board in front of me.

"We're putting you to work. This is your initiation to Hawaii."

Karina comes from behind her and places a long knife and an enormous pineapple on the board.

"I've known you for two whole minutes, and you're putting me to work?" I grin as I say it, surprising myself with both my words and my ease.

"Wait! Don't cut it yet!" Ann runs off and comes back with a fitted bedsheet. She wraps it around me as if I'm in a hair salon, evoking images of Sami, and ties it in an awkward knot around my neck. "We wouldn't want you to get your pretty dress dirty."

"Maybe this was a bad idea, A," Karina says, putting her hand on her hip. "We didn't realize you'd be so—dolled up."

I feel every bit of my misstep. Nothing about these girls is fancy. And yet they exude natural elegance with their shiny hair, flawless skin, and lithe bodies that suggest a great deal of time spent outdoors. There are no debutantes here. Except for me. And I am already finding that lifestyle far less attractive than the one I'm immersed in at the moment.

Karina starts to pull the sheet away, but I place my hand at the back of my neck to stop her. "No—I'll cut it. I want to cut the pineapple."

She looks at me askance, and I recognize the expression as one I've seen on Sami before. Especially the time when I suggested an unusual haircut before she talked me out of it.

I assure Karina that I'm up to the task. If I stain the dress despite the precaution, so be it. I'm sure Mr. Chan could take the remaining fabric and fashion something else wonderful out of it.

I would give everything I've ever had to permanently feel the camaraderie that I am feeling right now. A dress is nothing in comparison.

Something delicious is wafting from the kitchen. Ann is stirring a pot, and I ask her what she's making.

"Adobo chicken," she says as she sprinkles some pepper into it. "To serve on top of poi."

The only word I recognize is *chicken*.

"The adobo is Filipino, and the poi is Hawaiian," she explains. "The perfect welcome for our dear cousin."

Karina pulls out a chair and sits next to me. She doesn't seem to have a role in the preparation of the dinner, but I'm glad as I have so many questions, and she's undistracted as I talk.

"Tell me all about New York," she says, putting her elbows on the table and resting her chin on her palms.

I don't want to talk about New York. I want to hear all about them. About the family I didn't know I had. But Marymount taught me to be a gracious guest as much as a gracious host.

I slice into the pineapple as I talk, and I see them get most excited by the more glamorous things I describe. So I emphasize the fancier part of my life in the city, careful to hold some things back so as not to appear to be bragging.

This was not so tricky when all my friends came from my social circle. But I've been putting restraint into practice as I've met some of the girls on Pan Am. And now, my cousins.

By the time they've had their fill of tea at the Plaza Hotel, carriage rides in Central Park, and shows on Broadway, Ann has finished cooking and tasted the dish and declared it ready. She sets an array of beautiful ceramic dishes on the table. And I have muddled my way through my task. The cubes are not perfectly square, but Karina says brashly that "it's not going to matter as you digest them."

I smile to myself. I can't imagine such a thing being said at the tables I've sat at with my mother. "Kar, we've been pestering Beverly long enough with our questions," Ann says to my great relief. "It's your turn now, cousin. Do you have any questions for us?"

I scoot my chair in, catching the corner of the sheet on the leg of it. But I don't dare take it off, despite looking like a deflated hot-air balloon. The adobo chicken is bathed in a red sauce that would be murder on silk.

"Yes," I answer. "Please tell me everything. From the beginning. About the family."

The sisters look at each other and then back at me, and I smile at the way their expressions are identical to each other. Right eyebrows raised, lips pursed as they ponder the request.

Karina takes a deep breath and begins. "You know about the rift, of course. Our mutual great-grandmother was beside herself when our auntie Sami and her sister left for the United States. And the *eastern* part of the country, no less. She knew when she said goodbye that she would never see them again. And that letters might take weeks and weeks to get back and forth. They say she died of a broken heart."

I nod. This is as much as my mother told me.

"So what is your part of the story, then?" I ask. "If the family was so upset about them leaving, how did you all end up here?"

Ann takes over and gives me a chance to take my first bite of the adobo. It is *amazing*. Like nothing I have ever had. And—criminy, as it sits on my tongue, it is *blazing hot*.

I take a drink of water as discreetly as I can, though it might take the entire Pacific to quench it. But I want to hear every word that Ann has to say. My ears steam as my mouth stays shut.

"After her death, the family split further. There were four siblings. Sami; your grandmother, Gloria; our grandmother, Diwa; and a sister named Tala. Sami and Gloria went to New York. Tala stayed back, as she felt an obligation to keep up the family's small restaurant in Manila. But Diwa missed her sisters. And as soon as she was old enough and had saved for the ship fare, she followed them to the United States. But the little money she had was stolen while she was on the ship, so when she arrived in Honolulu, she had nothing. Nowhere to stay. And definitely no money to continue on to New York."

I sit back and cross my arms, taking this in. I'd met a Gloria when I was quite little. The first time my mother took me to Sami's for a haircut. I must have been four or five. She smelled of gardenia perfume. Too much of it. But I didn't mind because she gave me a big hug and slipped me some candy when we arrived. That happened a few times and was indelible on me because I never received such warm embraces at home. And because I loved the candy.

On one visit, she wasn't there. I remember asking Sami where she was. And she answered that Gloria had left to live with God. I didn't understand what that meant, and I didn't ask any more. Because a look passed between my mother and Sami that seemed sad.

A chill runs through me at the memory. So Gloria had been my grandmother. No wonder I'd taken such a liking to her. Not just the hug, not just the candy. But maybe there was some subtle connection we had by way of our shared blood, and I sensed it without knowing what it was.

I remember it feeling like what I felt now. The instant liking of my cousins.

That puzzle piece fit.

"And my grandfather? Do you know what happened to him?"

I remember my mother saying that he'd been American. A teacher. But I didn't know his name and had not yet been able to ask this question.

Ann shrugged. "I don't know a lot. Just that he died only a few years after they'd moved to New York. Maybe the Spanish flu? I feel like that's what I heard at one point."

Wow. To move all that way for love. To have given up so much. Only to lose him. I wonder if Gloria had thought it had been worth it.

"And what about Diwa?" I persist. "Did she ever see her sisters again?"

Ann crosses her arms and rests them on the table. She hangs her head as she answers.

"Sadly, no. It wasn't just expensive to travel, but it would have taken her away from work for too long. Hairdressing doesn't make millionaires."

"Wait—Diwa cut hair too?"

"Yes—apparently they used to practice on each other growing up. It was a skill they could use since they didn't have much formal education. Diwa—our grandma, our lola—worked at the salon here at Hickam Air Force Base until she died. Our mom took her place and still runs it."

Karina speaks up. "High and tights. Over and over. Both famous for a perfect fade." She smoothed her hair with an exaggerated stroke.

Ann continues. "She wanted to be here to meet you today, but she and our dad already had tickets for their annual trip to Las Vegas." She laughs. "If you spend enough time in Hawaii, you'll learn that Vegas is the most popular flight out of here."

Even more family to meet. I am insatiable for it.

I pick up a pineapple chunk with my fingers and pop it in my mouth. As the sweet juice spills out over my tongue, it occurs to me that until recently, I would have been appalled at my own lack of manners. In New York, a regular dinner had a minimum of seven utensils, and never, ever were our fingers used. I'd not ever been allowed to order a hot dog from a street vendor for that very reason.

But here—here I am abandoning over two decades of polish for this casual comfort.

With a big sheet surrounding me like a tent.

I've had enough of that, at least.

I stand up, remove the sheet, and bring my plate to the sink.

"No, we can do that! You'll ruin your dress." Karina hops up and tries to take the plate from me, but I don't let her.

"I don't care about the dress. I'll wear something else next time. If you'll both let there be a next time."

"Are you kidding?" Ann asks. "Consider this home. We'll even get you your own mattress if there is any chance of tearing you away from your digs at the Royal Hawaiian." She puts her nose up in the air in an exaggerated expression of affluence. But I know she's only teasing.

Funny, but staying here with my cousins holds more appeal than any of the fancy hotels I've stayed in so far. I look at my wristwatch. It's still early. I don't have to head back yet.

Karina must be thinking the same thing. "For dessert, how about we pop some corn and watch *The Beverly Hillbillies*?"

Ann grins. "Hey—Beverly! Life imitating art. Here you are, our own princess from New York, hanging out here in little old Oahu." I land a light punch on her arm, surprised that I feel such familiarity so quickly.

"I can't remember when I've had so much fun," I admit. "So if that's life imitating art, I'm all in."

Ann tosses her head back and laughs. "This is your idea of fun? Oh, cousin, you haven't seen anything yet!"

We turn on the television. As one show turns into another, we make more popcorn until I am full. Full in heart and in stomach. Hours pass and no one really pays attention to what is airing. Our chatter never has a lull and everything changes only once a yawn escapes me.

I try to cover it up before they can see, but I'm not quick enough.

"Kar, we've kept her too long. She had that long flight, and then we've gone and monopolized her evening."

"Yes. Gosh, we could go on all night. I'm sorry, Bev. Can we drive you back to make up for it?"

I don't want to leave. Don't want to make that early flight. But the offer to drive to the hotel and spend even a few more minutes with these cousins who have welcomed me so immediately is a small consolation.

As I lay my head on the pillow that night, I smile dreamily, pleased that this went better than I could have imagined.

I can't wait to tell my mother.

Mo'orea, French Polynesia
Today

I told myself I wouldn't cry. I've had a lifetime to prepare for this moment. So I supposed that imagining it might take the sting out of the reality. But it's only served to enhance it.

Before we graduated in Miami, Pan Am had us fill out all our proper legal paperwork. Wills, medical directives, funeral plans. I didn't want to think about any of those things. It felt like we were tempting fate. But they would not let us graduate without it, and you calmed my nerves, assuring me that it was a gift to our families to communicate our wishes so that they didn't have to guess at what we would have wanted. You surprised me by choosing to have your remains stored in an urn rather than buried underground. I'd never known anyone who made that choice.

But you, Beverly, always made decisions that went against the grain, and I loved you for it. Your life was too brief, but it was fuller than anyone I'd met before and since, and it has influenced me in a thousand different ways as I got to live all the years that you didn't.

I open my bag and pull out the alabaster vase you bought on our jaunt to Cairo. It seemed the appropriate choice. You haggled for it in a dusty roadside market as if your very life depended on getting a deal. Not because it was expensive or because you couldn't afford it, but because you craved the challenge. And after you'd won the back-and-forth, the gleam in your eye mellowed, and you gave the man his original asking price after all.

It's one of my favorite memories of you, and one that I told at your funeral. Because it described you precisely: competitive and compassionate.

They are not mutually exclusive traits. As you proved again and again.

I remove the silicone wrap that I'd put on the top of the vase. As unceremonious as it is practical. A breeze blows by, swishing the palm leaves that are shading me. I quickly put my hand on top of the vase so that the wind doesn't take you before I'm ready.

But I'll never be ready. It's the one thing I've procrastinated about in a lifetime where I've been known as punctual and efficient.

It's now or never.

I sprinkle a few of your ashes into my tremoring hand.

"You were gone just as you were starting your new life."

I blow the ashes onto the sand as if they were the white fluff of a wishing flower.

I sprinkle more. There is less of a tremor.

"You left behind a family who loved you. Who was just getting to know you."

This time, I aim for the water.

I pour the remaining bits into my palm and set the vase down near a coconut. I bring my other hand to join the first, cradling you.

I hang my head and feel the cry start in the pit of my stomach, crawling up my chest, making my shoulders quake, and letting out a sob that sends a group of birds flying off in fear.

Sometimes the most painful memories feel like they'd happened only yesterday.

CHAPTER TWENTY-FOUR

Judy

"I've got Rothmans King Size and Pall Mall."

"But I smoke Newport."

"I'm sorry, sir, we don't have that brand."

It takes effort to smile as widely as I am. My jaw is stretched to its maximum. To the point of throbbing.

"And you think that's what I've paid a small fortune for? To have you tell me that you don't have what I want?"

Here's what I want. I want to tell him that although Pan Am strives to make every customer happy, there is the small problem of practicality. We're limited as to what we can store in an aircraft. If only he could see how I can whip up an omelet or a beef Wellington in a galley kitchen that is half the size of an average elevator. Or how luggage is stored in the cargo below in a dazzling display of geometry. There are many feats of genius on this jet craft, but having the variety of a tobacco shop is not one of them.

I also want to show him where the exit door is, thirty thousand feet above the ground.

But I can't do that either.

"On behalf of Pan Am, we are so very glad that you have chosen us for your traveling needs. As we are landing in Papeete soon, I can recommend a small shop called Pickle's just a short walk from the airport where they sell locally made cigarettes, and I've been told more than once that after you've had them, you'll never want to return to your old brands."

This is an exaggeration. I have been in that shop once before. To buy tissues when the dryness of the cabin air caused me to have a nosebleed. I saw cigarettes there out of the corner of my eye, but whether they were international brands or local ones, I couldn't say.

I continue to smile at him, a frozen expression that feels like it would look cartoonish, but he doesn't notice.

"Be a good girl, then, and pour me a whiskey. Straight up. Jameson."

I am about to tell him that we've already poured our last of it, and I could bring him some Jim Beam instead. But just then, I feel his hand slide across my rear end as if it's his to possess. Then, a squeeze.

"Right away, sir." I turn sharply and walk to the back of the plane, feeling the burn of anger in my cheeks. While Pan Am does not condone such behavior in passengers, neither do they encourage us to make a scene.

The greater good here is to ignore it, even if it's not my own greater good.

"You look like you've had an encounter with Mr. King up in first class." Lyla Murphy, a stewardess who hails from Ireland, pulls me into a hug.

"It shows?"

"Unfortunately. It's a rite of passage for anyone on this route. Mr. King travels the full Asian itinerary every three months for business. You'll learn how to lean away from him and still do your job."

I let out a sigh of frustration. "People like him shouldn't be allowed on flights."

She shrugs. "I wish I could say that was the worst of it, but if you're here long enough, you'll find that a number of the men think that they can take liberties with us."

Lyla looks left and right and then giggles. "Here's a small consolation. Mr. King isn't his real name. That's just what he has us call him. It's actually Jed Beerwinkle. Check out the manifest." She slides her perfectly manicured finger down the sheet hanging in the back, and there, indeed, is seat 2A. Definitely not a Mr. "King."

I want to share in her laughter, but the sting of a man putting his hands on me uninvited hits too close to home. It might seem like it did no lasting harm, but I've just left two years of marriage to a man who believed that the wedding ring he put on my finger gave him the right to put his hands—his *fists*—wherever he liked.

Small allowances make way for bigger ones.

Beverly comes to the back near the end of the exchange, hands on her hips.

"Don't worry, Jude. I'll take first class if the crew chief will let us switch. And I'll spit in his whiskey straight up before serving it to him."

"How did you know that's what he ordered?"

She shrugs. "I know the type. There were plenty of men like him in my father's circles. And they all drink the same thing."

For two seconds, I consider it. But I'm not going to let a man intimidate me again.

"Thanks, but no thanks. I can't let you fight my battles."

Ronelle had done more than enough of that. I didn't need to have more friendships based on their defense of me.

"Atta girl."

I pour some Jim Beam out for our Mr. *Beerwinkle* and resist the urge to spit in it, as Beverly had suggested. I won't let him reduce me to something less than I am.

But it does encourage me to do something I've been frightened of doing—when we get back to San Francisco, I'll see when I can schedule a block of days to fly south and get my Mexican divorce.

"Happy New Year, Judy!"

"Happy New Year, Beverly."

"Welcome to 1963. This is going to be the best year of our lives."

"Cheers to that."

We're sitting on the balcony of a local hotel that has been fully rented by Pan Am. Tahiti will be a future site for Trippe's InterContinental brand, but the future Hotel Taharaa here in Papeete is still at the drawing stage. I know this because when we arrived and punched our time cards at the Pan Am airport offices, we saw the artist's renditions, and it looks like it will be as incredible as I've come to expect. Built into the side of a mountain with an enormous thatched roof and tiki statues dotting the grounds. It won't be complete for several years, and I think about what my life will look like then. Where Beverly will be. Will it find us still working as stewardesses?

I can't help but think of Joe as I imagine the future. What's left of my paycheck after rent and expenses goes to long-distance phone calls, as do his. Not when I'm flying—the international rates would render both of us broke. But most nights back home in Burlingame involve long conversations until he starts yawning. An indication of the three hour time difference, not of his boredom. And when my stops home fall on weekends, he tries to catch a deadhead flight to see me.

I may be the only woman in the world for whom a man flies six hours there and back just to have dinner.

I breathe in the tropical air and pinch myself that I am here in French Polynesia, almost as far away as I can get from the person I'd run away from. And as far away from the person I most want to run to.

I'm missing Joe, wishing he could be there to see this. And yet I'm relishing this opportunity to go to a place where so few can even dream to travel.

I'll send Joe a postcard, as I do from every layover, and then put thoughts of him to rest. Because as much as I love him—yes, I've admitted that I love him!—I especially appreciate that he encourages me, in every single conversation, to put myself first. And that means basking in every moment, every destination, for myself. Not merely in relation to how someone else may like it.

"There will be time enough for all the other things," he assured me the last time we talked.

And time, today, is on my side. Because we've just been told that a mechanical issue is grounding our plane and a new one may not be available for a week.

Beverly and I are going to have a vacation.

We slip out early the next morning, before the sun has even risen. Beverly got a tip from the front-desk clerk that the fishing vessels leave the island much earlier than the tourist boats, and that for a couple of American dollars, one should be willing to take two ladies who are trying to evade the passengers lodged at the same hotel.

Everyone is being put up at the hotel on Pan Am's dime since the delay is the responsibility of the airline. And though there is no expectation that we have to work or to entertain anyone, a lobby full of passengers creates too many opportunities to let those instincts kick in. Our copilot, First Officer Touka, was actually the one who suggested we leave. Word of Mr. King's roving hands had reached his ears, and as a father of three daughters at his home base in Japan, he felt particularly protective of us.

We consider going to Bora Bora, but it's much farther out, so we decide upon the nearby island of Mo'orea. It's only an hour's boat ride from Papeete, so we won't be far away if we get word that a replacement plane has gotten here sooner. Because then we would have to scrap our plans. Not checking into a flight is an offense for which we'd be fired immediately. An inability to be reached would not be an excuse.

Lyla has offered to send for us if she hears anything as long as we promise to stay close to the dock and remain easy to find.

The fishing boat has just pulled around a hill that has been our only view of Mo'orea ever since leaving Papeete, and it reminds me of Dorothy stepping into the colorful world of Oz.

"Heavens to Betsy, Judy. Have you ever seen anything like this?" Beverly's big eyes widen even farther as she takes it all in.

"C'est beau, n'est-ce pas??" says the fisherman as we stare, jaws agape.

"Yes, so beautiful," I answer in French.

But the word is not adequate in any language. Especially in English with all of its limitations.

Jagged spires of mountains pierce the sky like castle ruins covered in moss. The water is turquoise, blue, indigo. Enough shades that no thesaurus could conceive of. And it is so clear that we can see down to the ocean bed. Fish in every color of the rainbow swim underneath, and blackbirds fly overhead, singing their song and spreading their wings in a gentle glide. The sun has risen to just above the tallest peak in the east, and it sits like a golden crown on top of it.

"La Baie de Cook," the fisherman says as he points to the bay on our left. "Mais nous naviguons vers la Baie d'Opunohu."

I'd seen a map of the island back at our hotel. It looked like the footprint of a dinosaur or a bear, the two bays jutting into the land with slender spaces between. I know that the main dock is at the next bay, so we are bypassing this one named for Captain Cook after he came to the island to study the movement of Venus.

Venus, goddess of love.

I think of Joe again.

I know he wouldn't have come here on any of his flights because the route has only just been opened. But maybe he can still go someday.

Maybe he can go with me.

It is a place designed by nature for *amour*.

Beverly leans over the front of the boat and spreads her arms out wide, making it appear that she is collecting the breeze in an invisible net. She looks so carefree and almost childlike. I snap a photo with the camera I've finally bought and I'm pleased that I haven't distracted her by doing so. I return it to my bag and take small steps to join her, careful to keep my balance as the waves gently rock the boat the closer we get to the shore. Her eyes are closed, and she is frozen in the pose.

I do the same.

I feel the wind on my cheeks, and I throw my arms out so wide that they're nearly behind me. The muscles in my shoulders protest, aching from the movements in the cramped airplane cabin that I'm still not entirely used to.

But I banish the thought as soon as it enters my head because this moment is about freedom, not work.

The boat lurches forward, and my eyes fly open. I grip the deck rail and look to my right to see Beverly. The jolt made her fall to the ground, but before I can ask if she's hurt she lets out a most marvelous laugh.

"This is better than a ride at Coney Island," she yells with a smile. "Or what I imagine a ride at Coney Island to be like."

She doesn't get up and instead grabs my hand to pull me down with her. We lay back on the deck, not caring that our backsides are getting wet from the splashes that have come overboard. Instead, we move our arms and legs back and forth like we're making snow angels and giggling just loud enough to hear each other over the shouts of the fisherman as they start making their preparations to dock.

We probably look ridiculous. And I love it.

One more jolt. The boat has arrived at the dock, and we sit up to see the fishermen throwing ropes overboard to secure the vessel. A couple of them glance our way and snicker at these two crazy American women.

I stand up first and hold a hand out to Beverly, who grabs it and pulls herself up.

"That might have been the best experience of my life," she says as she smooths her hair back with her hands.

"Really? Not Paris or London or any of the other fabulous places you've been?"

"Better. I promise you. Because even there, there is a way to act, a list of things to see. *This*, Judy, this is nothing but pure *li-ber-a-tion*. And how often can you say that you ever get to truly feel like that?"

I can't disagree.

As we step onto the dock, we grip each other to steady ourselves, our equilibrium off-kilter from the boat ride. Sea legs setting in. Beverly tips the fisherman and thanks him for the ride.

"Le plaisir était pour moi," he answers. *It was my pleasure.* He wipes his right hand on his pants and puts it out for us to shake. I take it, and my small one sinks into his large, cushy palm. If a handshake were a hug, this is what it would feel like. He goes on to tell me that there is a tourist boat every evening after sunset that returns to Papeete. Kind information, but it is our hope to stay for a few days.

"Àquelle heure est le coucher du soleil?" I ask just in case.

What time is sunset?

He shrugs his shoulder and grins. "Il n'y a pas de temps a Mo'orea. Regarde le soleil."

There is no time in Mo'orea. Watch the sun.

There is no time in Mo'orea. I feel that. The rest of the world just celebrated the turning of the new year with fireworks and fanfare, but I sense that here on this little island, it's merely a day like every other.

Paradise.

The fisherman turns around to remove the ropes, ready to set into deep waters for the day's catch. I'm glad we didn't take the tourist boat to get here. We have a few hours' head start and can find an ideal spot before the day-trippers arrive.

"Let's go over there," Beverly says. "I see breakfast."

A woman wrapped in a red sarong is setting up a fruit stand underneath a grass-topped roof, and I imagine it will provide perfect shade as the sun continues to rise. At her feet, two toddlers draw rudimentary figures in the sand while another woman sits on a nearby rock wall and nurses an infant. She is bare chested and thoroughly unfazed by our presence. I am moved that this culture can see something like this for the natural beauty that it is. A woman could never get away with that in Pennsylvania.

Chickens peck at invisible crumbs around our feet. Roosters strut about, shouting their cock-a-doodle-dos.

Beverly, however, is focused on the fruit.

"Bonjour," she says to the fruit seller. The woman smiles in return and bows her head slightly. "Deux avocats, deux papayes, deux bananes."

Two avocados, two papayas, two bananas. A truly tropical breakfast.

But then, I see her wipe her eyes with the back of her hand, and she points to a pile of spiky red balls. "Dix," she whispers.

Ten. Either Beverly doesn't know the name of the odd fruit or she doesn't know it in French.

Or she can't speak at all. I see that she is overcome for a reason I can't determine.

The woman puts everything into a wrinkled brown bag and exchanges it for the coins that Beverly holds out.

She walks toward the beach, and I follow, sensing that she needs quiet in this moment.

We walk and walk, and I pause only to take my sandals off. They have hard soles, and I'm finding their inflexibility difficult on the sand. The ground is strewn with coconuts, fallen palm branches, and seashells, and I am careful not to step on anything that could cut my feet. But I wouldn't trade it for the sensations I feel as we continue.

"Here," Beverly says at last. I look back, and the fruit stand is barely a pinprick, but I think we are still close enough that Lyla could send someone to find us if she gets word that a replacement plane is arriving sooner than we expect.

Beverly's chosen our spot well. We're shaded by a canopy of palm trees, and the sound of the breeze as their branches sway reminds me of the wooden maracas that were a staple in my grade-school music classes.

"They're rambutans," she says. And I understand without her demonstrating that she is talking about the spiky red fruit. "I've never seen one in person. Only as a flavor in candy. Filipino candy from my aunt's salon in New York."

She goes on to tell me more than she has ever revealed. About her parents, her life in New York, and then Sami, Karina, Ann.

"I always wanted a sibling," she confides as she stares out at the water. "A sister, specifically. A brother might have been too much like Mr. Wall Street, and I might have suffocated in a household saturated in testosterone. But a sister would have been a confidante. A partner in crime. A best friend."

I want to tell her that I understand what she means. That I, too, was an only child, and though I was close to my parents, it was not a replacement for the instant playmate that a sister could have been. I want to tell her that I was ostracized in Red Lion for having a French-speaking father. That I knew many people who wouldn't leave the county out of superstition. Even a man who didn't travel to the next county, Lancaster, for his own father's funeral. So a man from another whole *country* was eyed with suspicion. And I was the unhappy recipient of that brand of mistrust.

So I well understand the feeling of loneliness.

But I don't tell her this. Because this is her moment, and mine will come in due time.

Like the fisherman said, there is no time in Mo'orea. I do not need to hurry. Our stories can unravel at their own pace.

"I didn't expect this, you know," Beverly says. She turns her eyes from the water and toward me.

"Expect what?" I ask.

"That sisters can be chosen. You're like a sister to me, Judy. I know I've been brash and opinionated, and I'm beginning to think that it's just my way of keeping people at arm's length. Because I've never been in an environment that felt real. And I was craving it. I was *craving* it, Judy. I thought it was just a drive to have a different environment and that Pan Am would give that to me. But I've found more than just pretty places. I've found people who even in this short time will no doubt be a part of my life forever."

I reach into the bag and pick out a papaya, enjoying this discovery that Beverly is making for herself. It's not often that you're given a front-row seat to someone's metamorphosis. The papaya peels easily and its juice runs down my fingers, leaving them sticky. Its black seeds spill onto the sand and onto my bare feet. But I don't care. I take a bite—equally messy—and it is an explosion of flavor unlike any I've ever known.

By the time most tropical fruit is put out in the grocery-store aisle in my town, it's traveled thousands of miles and is nearly tasteless. And that's *if* the stores are even stocked with such exotic varieties.

In Red Lion, different fruits, like different people, are met with suspicion.

This papaya, though, tastes like God personally came down and touched it with his finger. The world is missing out.

Beverly sees my enjoyment of this and picks hers out of the bag too. I use the silence as an opportunity to respond to her.

"I feel the same way, you know. Ronelle showed me that. And then you. Sometimes family is who you choose, not just who you share blood with."

I pick at a blade of wild grass and get a soothing satisfaction out of tearing it down the middle into two symmetrical pieces. It elicits such a peaceful feeling.

"Don't you think it's ironic," Beverly says, "that I had to run away to Pan Am to grow closer to my mother?"

"Closer?" I ask. I sweep my arm parallel to the horizon. "We're in French Polynesia, if you haven't noticed. We're about as far away as we can get from everyone we know."

She pulls a rambutan from the paper bag and throws it at me. "You know what I mean!"

And before we know it, we're engaged in a heated rambutan fight, each of us scrambling to grab more, aiming for the other, crossing our arms to shield us from the deluge. It's the perfect fruit for it—their red spiky shells are too soft to damage our skin, too thick to be damaged by our shenanigans. Still entirely edible.

When we've worn ourselves out, we pause and notice three small children standing on the beach and staring at us. Their skin is brown from a lifetime of sun living, their feet bare, their hair tangled from what is no doubt days and days spent near the glistening water. I can't tell who is a boy, who is a girl, as none have shirts and all have long hair.

One of many cultural nuances I've enjoyed since working for this airline.

I'm envious of their carefree lives.

Or maybe they only look that way. I'm learning more and more not to make assumptions.

Beverly grabs the bananas and holds them out, but the children scamper off. She hands one to me instead, and peels one for herself. She takes a bite, and a look of utter bliss washes over her face.

"I'm telling you, Judy. When I die, I want my ashes to be spread right here on this beach. Then I'll never have to leave it."

"That sounds perfect."

"I'm serious," she says. And she looks at me then, her bliss turning to something that sends a shiver through me that I can't comprehend.

"Promise me," she whispers.

"I promise."

CHAPTER TWENTY-FIVE

Beverly

"As I live and breathe, it is Mark Oakley in the flesh. On my doorstep."

My own Olympian is standing under the portico of our Burlingame bungalow, and I feel a tingle run through me that cannot be attributed to the mist that is blowing over from where a hose attachment is watering our lawn.

"Geography can't stop what we have." He grins, and I know that he intends to be corny. I roll my eyes.

Then I step forward and grip the collar of his Hawaiian shirt with both hands, pulling him toward me and pressing my mouth against his with all the ferocity that months of imagination could conjure. He lifts me up with seemingly no effort and wraps my long legs around his waist. He sets my back against the door and presses into me. Mouth, torso, hands.

It's the drive-in all over again.

Hallelujah, I have missed this!

"People might see us," I whisper when I can catch a breath.

"People can leave a quarter on my suitcase for the show," he says.

We stop just at the point where we might cross a line, and I slide my legs back down to the herringbone brick on the porch. They nearly buckle, and I turn around to grip the doorknob for fear of falling. As I do so, I catch my reflection in the glass. My hair is matted, and my lipstick has smeared.

Mark takes my hand and pulls me toward him again, this time with gentleness. He presses his forehead against mine. "Best kiss ever." He sighs.

No one could argue that.

"What are you doing here?" I ask once we are sitting down at the dinette in our kitchen. I've moved his suitcase to the bedroom I share with Judy. But not because he'll be staying. We have a house rule that there will be no overnight visitors of the male variety. We've all spent enough time in hotel rooms as we travel that we cherish any night in which we can sleep in our own beds. And no one wants to come out in their nightgown and curlers to find a stranger.

"I got a last-minute offer for a Coca-Cola photo shoot, and I'm flying to Los Angeles tomorrow. But I couldn't come to California without seeing you. So I booked myself through San Francisco first."

"My, my, how about that!" I marvel. "Will we see you grace more magazine pages, then?"

He doesn't answer. Instead, he runs a finger down my arm, leaving a trail of goose bumps.

"How did you know I'd be here?" I ask. There's no way he would have known my flight schedule. And there was every chance I'd be somewhere in Asia.

"I didn't. I just hoped."

"You are crazy, 15A."

"I would be crazier not to give it a try."

He stands up and towers over me, wrapping his arm around my waist and planting another kiss on me, this time a deep one that thoroughly defines the term *swoon*.

"I'll bet you say that to all the girls." I stand up to take the whistling teakettle off the stove, but he stops me, wrapping his other arm around me in protest.

"I don't have any other girls," he says. Each word enunciated, slowly and deliberately.

Leaving no doubt that he means it.

I meet his gaze, soft but intense, and I feel like I'm standing on a cliff questioning whether or not I should jump.

"We barely know each other, Mark."

"Exactly," he says. He stands up, and I admire how he is a full head taller than me. I'm so used to being the strongest, boldest person in a room, but with Mark, I feel delicate. Like my femininity is getting a chance to emerge because I don't have to prove myself to anyone. Like I don't have to fight for myself all the time. "Because you have to be one special girl for me to be ready to forsake all others based on a couple of visits and a handful of letters."

"That's—"

"That's crazy." He nods. "I know. You already said that. But I've already been going crazy in Sunset Beach thinking about you the way I do." He runs a finger through a strand of my hair. "I can't wait for you to see it."

I have a heightened baloney meter, well honed in New York City. And Mark's words are not registering on it. After all, once I'd finally had a chance to read that *LIFE* article, I saw how it had practically knighted him, explaining how he volunteered teaching handicapped children how to swim.

Surely he has flaws. No human being escapes that sad fact, myself included. But Mark Oakley seems like the sort of man whose foundation is so solid that none of the typical cracks can topple it.

I am nervous. Meeting a man this early on had not been a part of my plan. But then the best things in life are often the unexpected ones.

"Crazy can be good," I finally acknowledge.

"How about we retire that word?" He doesn't let me respond, though, because he is placing feather-like kisses around the perimeter of my mouth. The heat from his breath shoots lightning down to my toes.

The front door opens, and I leap back. Judy comes in, shopping bags on her arms, mail and magazines in her hands.

She flips through the letters. "We have a past-due notice for our water bill. Vanya must have forgotten to pay it again. And there's a letter from your mother. And—well, that's strange. A special-delivery letter for me from Pan Am. Registered mail."

Only then does she look up.

"Oh! Hello." The bags start to slide down her arms as she stares at Mark in surprise.

Before I can introduce him, he walks over in four long strides and takes the bags from her, setting them on the couch. Then he puts out his hand with all the assertiveness of the Texan that he is.

"Mark Oakley. You must be Judy."

"Mark Oakley," she says slowly as she takes his hand. She catches my eye, and we know each other well enough by now that her expression asks me if she should act like she's never heard of him when, in fact, I've shown her every letter he's ever written. Even the ones of a romantic nature.

"I'm a friend of Beverly's," he says.

"Yes. I see that. How nice to meet you." The stilted tone of their conversation makes me want to laugh, but I keep my composure.

"Here, let me help you with that," I say, reaching into the bags. Judy and I both just completed the long Asian segment, and our refrigerator is bare. I pull out eggs and milk and red wine. And before I can carry any more, Mark joins me and puts items away in the refrigerator and pantry.

"Was there a sale on tuna tins?" I count eight cans. It would take me a year to go through that much tuna, and I'd have to have a knife held to my throat to do it. A lifetime of Alaskan salmon at Delmonico's can make a seafood snob out of a girl.

"No, but my monthly weigh-in is next week. One of the girls on my last flight told me that's her secret to staying slim."

"That's the secret to getting mercury poisoning," I retort. "Besides, Judy, remember that I've seen you in your skivvies. You're still too thin, if you ask me."

I'm sorry that I'm having this conversation in front of Mark, but the unusual purchase took me aback, and I've been meaning to talk to Judy about my concerns anyway.

"I can't risk Pan Am firing me, Bev. You know what's on the line for me."

I sigh. She's right. But I hate to see the pressure she puts on herself. Even more than the airline does.

I stack the tins in a cabinet. "Did they not have any dented ones?"

Judy has continued what she calls Beverly's Budget Basics class with me, never missing an opportunity to teach me about day-old bread, damaged cans, and off-season sales. It was my first instinct to turn my nose up at these things. But then she got me right where she knew I could be convinced. "Think of it as a competition," she'd said. "You against the other customers, you against the store. The lower the price, the greater your victory."

I know that's not how she views it—for Judy, it is an ingrained survival skill. But the beauty of letting someone in enough to know you—really know you—is that they know what hits your buttons.

I smile wanly at her, protective of this friend I've grown to love so much.

"Put your feet up, Judy. Mark and I will finish putting things away," I shout to her over my shoulder, and I'm pleased to see that she agrees, if reluctantly. She collapses onto the couch and throws her feet over the arm of it.

"Oh, I forgot to tell you," I say again from the kitchen. "Joe called. There's a ferry flight from Miami to San Francisco this weekend, so he wants to come out and see you."

"What did you tell him?"

"I told him yes, you dummy. Would you really have wanted me to check with you first? I know your calendar as well as my own."

"Oh my goodness!" she cries suddenly, shooting straight up. And I can tell it's not a reaction to what I just said.

Mark pauses just as he's putting a bag of rice away, and I turn my head at the alarm in her words.

"What's wrong?" I ask.

She is holding a letter from the mail pile. The certified one from Pan Am.

"I'm being grounded. They found out that I'm—"

She looks at Mark and then at me. The desolation in her eyes is heartbreaking.

"They found out about Henry."

CHAPTER TWENTY-SIX

Judy

Joe cancels his ferry flight and insists on meeting me in New York instead. He arrives an hour before I do and meets me at my gate at Idlewild. He wraps his arms under mine and lifts me up, gently rocking me as I bury my face into his neck.

"You're not battling this alone," he whispers.

At the Pan Am building on East 45th, Joe stops me at the door of the typing pool.

The clack-clack-clack of the typewriters compounds an already pulsing headache, which compounds the knot that has taken residence in my stomach ever since I received that letter from Pan American.

> To: Judy Goodman
> From: Arthur Ledbetter, Director of Personnel for Pan American Airlines
>
> Re: Employment Review
>
> Mrs. Goodman: It has come to the attention of Pan American Airlines that your marital status is in question. A man claiming to be your husband

> contacted us with a marriage certificate. Please report to the corporate headquarters in New York on June 11 at 2:00 p.m. for a review of this matter. If it is found that your application for employment was not accurate, you will be immediately terminated.

"I know Arthur," Joe says. "He's the one who recommended me for the training position in Miami. Why don't I talk to him first?"

I feel my bottom lip quivering, and I am conflicted.

A Pan American stewardess takes on the world. She speaks multiple languages, walks with poise, handles emergencies as if they are child's play. I'd tackled all of those things, but this makes me feel utterly reduced. It has been a fantasy to think that distance would sever the hold that my marriage has on me.

"Judy," Joe says, taking my hand and rubbing it with his thumb. "I'm not insisting. This is your decision. But if you want any chance of staying on with Pan American, I may be your best shot."

I nod, too spent with worry to advocate for myself. I haven't slept since the letter came, fretting about what will happen if they fire me. Where will I go? How will I be safe from Henry?

Joe places a kiss on my forehead and walks me over to a leather couch in the hallway.

"One way or another, this will all be over soon."

An hour later, Joe and I are sitting on the same side of a diner booth. The dizzying black-and-white checkerboard floor keeps me awake, as does the mug of strong but stale black coffee that I've been sipping for what seems like an eternity.

Despite the reason, it is exciting to be back here again. There is a buzz to New York that makes me feel like the world still turns and that my problems are less significant than I know them to be. For a moment, it is comforting.

"So what happened?" All I know is that Joe winked at me when he came out of Arthur Ledbetter's office, but he didn't want to talk in the elevator in case anyone overheard. I have been out of my mind wondering.

He looks at me with a hesitant expression, as if he doesn't know if he's delivering good news or bad.

"You're getting a six-month suspension, unpaid."

My hand flies to my mouth as I stifle a cry. A *good* cry. This is definitely better than I'd hoped for and more than my infraction deserves.

"Six months?" It seems like a lifetime. And yet, it's better than the alternative.

"Yes."

"But I thought—I thought they were going to fire me."

He sips his coffee and nods.

"Yes. That's the rule. I asked them to find a compromise. I tried for three months and they stretched it to six."

Almost to Christmas. I'd have to find another job to keep up with the rent and groceries. Not what I imagined, but certainly not impossible. I knew I should consider myself lucky. They had every right to fire me.

"Why would they do even that?" I wondered.

Joe doesn't look at me and instead hangs his head.

"Why do you think, Judy?" he mumbles.

I don't understand at first, but then the realization washes over me.

"You told them about Henry, didn't you? I mean, *all* about Henry."

He nods again, words failing. When he looks up, his eyes are bloodshot. This has been an ordeal for him too. I hadn't even considered that.

"Only enough to convince them. It—it wasn't going in your favor, no matter what I said. I'm sorry. You and I hadn't discussed it, and I should have asked. But it's the only card I had."

I fold my arms on the table and let this sink in. I should be angry. The details of my marriage had not been something that had been easy to tell even Beverly or Joe, but to have them exposed to a stranger makes my chest pound and my breath heavy.

I hang my head down, too, and it dawns on me that we must look like quite a pair. All around us, conversations prattle on. A child telling his mother about a project at school. An elderly couple ordering "the usual" to their waiter. A young couple in the new throes of love holding hands across their laminated menus and looking so innocent of the challenges that the world holds.

In contrast, I have a decision in front of me.

I can be angry at Joe for sharing something so secret, so sensitive.

Or, I can listen to the tug in my heart. Which tells me that I want to be the googly-eyed couple talking about trivial things with Joe. I want to be the mother, someday sitting across from Joe's child—*our* child—talking about his teachers. I want to be that elderly couple, still together years later, so comfortable with each other that conversation isn't even necessary. Memories, struggles, joys, losses etched on their skin through wrinkles.

I can retreat in bitterness. Or I can forgive.

If it even requires that. I know he was just trying to protect me.

"I understand," I say at last, looking up again. "I know why you felt like you had to do it. And it sounds like it made a difference."

Joe grabs my hand, obviously grateful for the olive branch.

"It did, Judy. It did. It gave them just the room they needed to declare it a special circumstance and give them a reason to settle at a suspension."

Six months. It dawns on me that they probably hope I'll quit in that time and remove myself from being an issue at all. But I can't let that happen. I just got past my probationary period. There is still so much to see and do. I'll do whatever it takes to return. Find a simple job to pay the bills and count the days until I can get back up in the air.

The waiter sets down our plates—we'd each gotten bacon-and-tomato omelets.

I take my fork and pick at the meal. I am ravenous, but my hunger pangs are overshadowed by another sense of crossroads.

It is not lost on me that all that I am dealing with may be more than Joe bargained for. On one hand, it has shown me how dependable he is. But on the other hand, I need to do my part to get things in order, what I have been making excuses to avoid.

I make an important decision for the second time in almost as many minutes.

"Joe, did you watch the movie *Pollyanna* when it came out a few years ago?" Emboldened by my decision, I take a big, wonderful bite of the omelet. The tomatoes burst like fireworks in my mouth, fitting of a celebration.

"Sure," he says, cocking his head in confusion at the change of conversation. "On a layover in London. The whole crew went to a theater in Piccadilly. Great flick. Better than I was expecting. Why?"

"The Glad Game. I thought it was such hogwash for Pollyanna to try to find the good in every circumstance. That's not how real life works, and I was living proof of it. But I think I may be in a better position to understand it now."

"What do you mean?"

"Well, I'm obviously going to miss the work and the paychecks for the next six months. But if I apply her philosophy, I can say that I am *glad* that the deck is cleared to do some things I should have done a long time ago. First things first. I'm going to Mexico to get my divorce."

All that budgeting I'd done with Beverly was going to pay off. I'd been particularly frugal because of the example I was trying to set for her. So I had just enough in savings to make those things happen.

Joe smiles. "I think that's an excellent plan. And I might be able to improve upon it."

"What do you mean?"

"I negotiated with them to let you keep your flying privileges during your suspension."

The man can read my mind.

CHAPTER TWENTY-SEVEN

Beverly

It had taken more than a month to plan this. Between my flight schedule and Judy's temporary job at Alpha Beta, this Mexican divorce thing was taking longer than we both wanted. But we were here at last. Juàrez, Mexico. We'd heard it was faster and less busy than Tijuana.

Well, *that* was a laugh. Too late to change plans now.

"Now I know what it feels like to be a sardine," I tell Judy.

"I'm sorry I asked you to come. I had no idea it would be like this."

"Hold still, Judy. I'm going to swat a fly that's caught in your hair."

I flick the pesky little bug off Judy's coif. I'd insisted on letting me do her hair for such an important event, but little did I know that half of the East Coast would be in Juárez, Mexico, looking to break the ties of holy matrimony.

"Joe had been willing to come," she says in an apologetic tone.

I would put my hands on my hips, but there is no room given the smash of people in this basement hallway at the Municipal Palace of Juárez. We'd flown to El Paso on American Airlines and bused across the border. Like everyone else here. Looking to cut out years of red tape in the US.

I shake my head. "No. Absolutely not. Joe's a peach, no doubt about it. But there are just some things—messy things—that you should simply not expose your lover to."

"He's not my lover," Judy protests.

"Not *yet*. That's why we're here. To clear the way for the unspeakable bliss that awaits you two."

Judy rolls her eyes. She doesn't let me get away with laying things on too thick.

"All the same," I continue. "Why do you think they don't let men in the delivery room when a woman is having a baby? Because he *does not need to see* what goes on down there. Or he may never want to, you know, revisit that area again."

"Beverly! I think we have strayed from the point of this conversation."

"Not in the least. It just *proves* my point. You and Joe are in the *wooing* phase of your relationship. Don't let him see the mess of you getting a divorce in a swampy hall in Mexico."

"And don't you think, assuming our relationship lasts for a very long time, that there will be plenty of mess? Isn't sticking around for that what love is all about?"

"Sure it is. But at least get a ring on that unpolished finger of yours before making him think that you're more trouble than it's worth."

"Beverly!" she says again, and I fear that I've hurt her feelings. But one glance tells me that she is more than used to putting up with my candor.

"I didn't say you're *personally* not worth it, Judy. I'd say the same to any woman. Don't worry. You're a peach too. You and Joe. Two peachy peaches. Going to make cute peachy peach babies someday."

She rolls her eyes for the second time in as many minutes. "You're ridiculous."

"I'm honest."

"You know, you use that excuse a lot."

"Mark says the same thing about me."

"Well, now I like him even better."

I shrug. But she's right. Judy and Mark share the annoying habit of letting me go just so far with my pontifications before reeling me in.

But they're good for me, and I know it.

"Número cuarenta y siete," shouts a man at the counter.

"If only they spoke French in Mexico," I complain.

"He said *number forty-seven*."

"Thank you," says Judy, turning to the stranger who helped us out. A woman with dark circles under her eyes. Everyone here has a story, and she seems to be no exception. Judy glances down at our paper ticket. "Ten more to go until us."

I wipe some sweat from my forehead. "Speaking of Mark, I finally saw his place in Sunset Beach." I wish I could have gotten there sooner. But between short layovers, visits to my cousins, and some routes that didn't take me to Oahu at all, I'd only recently been able to make it to the far side of the island. Content to visit with Mark whenever he could make it to the Honolulu side.

Judy smiles. I know that she is eager to talk about anything other than why we are here today.

"Swanky, I'm sure."

"Surprisingly not. In fact, not at all."

"Do tell."

As ticket numbers are called, one by one, we step forward in line while I tell her the story of my most recent trip to Hawaii.

"My girl is here at last!" I begin, telling her the first words out of Mark's mouth.

Our flight had been delayed by six hours. First, a thunderstorm had grounded our aircraft that was supposed to come in from London to San Francisco. They were able to ferry a flight from Los Angeles only to learn that upon landing, a gear got damaged. By the time that was sorted, the original flight had come in. Though stewardesses are only paid from takeoff to touchdown, we'd been allowed to punch in and help the overwhelmed gate attendants keep the restless passengers happy during their terminal wait. Most travelers were appreciative of the lengths we went to—pulling Maxim's trays from storage, warming them up in a borrowed airport lounge kitchen. Fetching water and ice from the employee offices.

Others were indignant, demanding refunds and threatening to *call the company president*. As if Juan Trippe could control the weather or magically make repairs from his office in New York.

I wanted to shout, "You are about to fly to *paradise*, you dirtbags! Shut your trap and show a little gratitude."

But I didn't. And I was rather proud of myself for that restraint.

So by the time I arrived at Mark's—an hour's taxi ride from the airport—I'd missed the sunset. But I was mollified with the thought that I could relax in a steaming-hot bathtub and wash the travel and inevitable galley spills off me.

It wasn't to be so.

After Mark swept me into his arms and twirled me around, I smoothed my hair and took a good look at my surroundings.

There wasn't much to see.

Behind me I could hear the ocean roar, just as he'd described. But in front of me was a diminutive building. Practically a shed. A lone light bulb hung from a porch with barely enough room for the two chairs positioned on it. And beyond that, a door stood open to reveal—a room.

One solitary room.

Mark kissed me then, swallowing my disappointment without even realizing it was there. I lost all sense of time, space, sense when his lips moved away from mine. Slowly, slowly down my neck. He hooked one finger around the starched white collar of my uniform and breathed onto my exposed collarbone, sending chills down my skin.

"Welcome to my 'ohana," he said. I was confused—*'ohana* was the Hawaiian word for family, as far as I knew, but then I remembered that Karina and Ann had mentioned once on a subsequent visit that it was also the name for a small house on the property of a larger one. As I looked up, I indeed saw a larger house very far off in the distance.

But my original interpretation of the word—family—had struck a nerve.

Family was a notion that up until recently had evoked resentment. But the discovery of my relation to Sami, the growing warmth with my mother, the cheery companionship of my newfound cousins, was replacing it with something that bordered happiness.

I liked the word *'ohana* coming from Mark's beautiful lips. Family.

This 'ohana—this shack—however, left much to be desired.

Mark lifted me up and carried me over the threshold as if I was his bride, and he set me down on the threadbare couch that faced a thirteen-inch television. The antennae stretched almost to the top of the low ceiling. As did Mark.

A quick look at my surroundings revealed the rest. A corner kitchen, a twin bed covered with a native-made quilt. A dinette with two chairs, one of which had a foot-high pile of books.

"Is there—is there a toilet?"

It had been a long flight. A long taxi ride. This was an essential question.

"Yes." He grinned like an excited little boy. "Wait until you see it!"

He took my hand and led me through a door I initially didn't see. But rather than take me to anything that resembled what one might call a lavatory, it revealed only a tall fence with the darkening sky for a ceiling. The toilet was roughly installed, sans seat, on one end of the semi-enclosure and a showerhead protruded from the wall on the other.

I looked at Mark. He clearly loved it.

The Ritz Paris, it was not.

"I—" I started. Not even knowing what would come out of my mouth next.

"I'll give you your privacy," he said.

He stepped back inside, and I looked around me to make sure that no one could see in. But the fence was in surprisingly good shape. No knotholes through which anyone could peek in. No buildings around us that could look down on me.

Not that any people or buildings were anywhere close by.

I unzipped my skirt and hovered over the bowl so I wouldn't fall in and focused on the showerhead, wondering what it might be like to shower outside. I'd never been camping—the thought appalled me. But somehow . . . somehow I was intrigued. Mark was so happy here. I had to give it a chance.

I flushed, relieved that there was at least attached plumbing. So it wasn't totally irredeemable. I let my skirt fall to the tiled floor. Then I unbuttoned my jacket and blouse and all my undergarments until I stood, fully naked, under the evening sky. I stepped forward and jiggled the handles until cold water spurted out of the overhead faucet. I flinched at first, and shivered until it warmed to a manageable temperature. I let the water fall over me as I stretched my arms over my head. I was exhausted and exhilarated all at the same time, and it was a marvelous feeling. I looked up—the sky was nearing blackness, and I stopped counting at forty stars with many to go.

I heard a little knock, and I covered myself with my hands. A fruitless gesture, but an instinctive one. Mark's arm shot out, but I could see that his face was turned away.

"I heard the water start. Tempting, wasn't it? The outdoor shower. Here's some soap. And I'm putting a clean towel on the hook by the toilet."

I hadn't noticed the hook. I would have hung my uniform if I'd seen it. At least Pan Am will pay for my laundry at the Royal Hawaiian.

Mark's nearness made me feel the tingle of anticipation that I always felt around him. But I was impressed at his discretion. And a little disappointed, if I was honest.

I was tempted to invite him to come in.

The stars had clearly bewitched me.

But as the water ran cold again, the spell was broken, and I turned the faucet off. I toweled myself dry, gave a quick rub to my hair, and picked my uniform up off the floor.

I thought about putting it back on, but it had gotten wet. And it was quite dirty after the extra-long shift.

I wrapped the towel around myself, barely covering all my girlish parts. I stuck my head inside the door expecting to see Mark, but the room was empty. At the foot of the bed, he'd laid out some thermal pants and a matching top. And a silver-wrapped Hershey's Kiss. I put everything on and slipped the candy into my pocket.

Stewardesses weren't supposed to spend the night away from the designated hotel without permission, but the long delay had us all out of sorts, and I was going to hedge my bets that I wouldn't be missed. Besides, it wasn't as if I had planned on staying out here. But it was so late, and Honolulu was so far, and our already short time had been rendered even shorter.

It wasn't as if I'd never bent a rule before. Just not with Pan Am.

Mark Oakley was the kind of man I wanted to break rules with.

I stretched my arms again and closed my eyes as I heard the ocean waves even from inside the shack. I opened the front door to find Mark sitting in the chair, legs swung over the railing.

He jumped up as soon as he saw me, and his eyes grew wide. I saw his hands clench at his sides.

"I think—" He stopped and cleared his throat. "I think that you wearing my pajamas is the most gorgeous sight I've ever seen."

"Then you haven't gotten around much," I teased.

I put my hands on my hips, and he slipped his arms right through them as if they'd been invited. Instead of kissing me, he bent down and nuzzled my neck.

"Mmm," he said. "My favorite coconut soap. My favorite thermals. My favorite girl."

My eyes welled up with tears at the perfection of the moment, but I willed them away by the time he pulled back and looked at me.

"And did you see the chocolate? My little attempt at a turndown service."

I slipped my hand into my pocket and nodded. I unwrapped the foil and placed the chocolate between my teeth, leaving it there and looking at Mark with all the intensity that I felt.

His eyes grew wide again, and before I knew it, his lips were back on mine, the chocolate between us, until it had melted all away.

I could get into so much trouble for this.

"Don't tell me the rest," Judy says, holding up a hand. "I can well imagine."

I look around and realize that in getting lost in the story, I've gained an audience in the people around me.

I've never felt so awkward, telling this tale of my budding affair among a crowd of people who are dissolving their own. I put a hand over my mouth and whisper, "I'm sorry" so quietly that no one can actually hear it.

Judy speaks in a lowered tone. "Not that it matters, but with his Coca-Cola advertisement and his swimming accolades, I would have thought he could afford something more."

"That's the thing," I say. "The remarkable thing, really. Mark can easily afford more. But he doesn't want it. He wants the freedom of walking out and swimming in the ocean every morning. He wants the richness that a blanket of stars provides. And I—I'm surprised to say this, but I may be starting to want the same thing."

Mr. Wall Street would be appalled. But I think it is an excellent trade.

Just then, the man at the counter shouts, "Cincuenta y siete." Judy waves her ticket, and we step forward.

Judy

Mo'orea, French Polynesia
Today

As your ashes scatter over the water, my guilt is replaced by a lightness of heart that I did not expect. You are where you wanted to be forever, and I have, many decades late, fulfilled my promise. I hope that you have not been stuck in some purgatory state because of it, but even if so, you are released now, my dear friend.

I stand here in my bare, wrinkled feet, thinking of all that you missed. But rather than consider how you never bore children or got to know mine, the big things are erased by a small memory that winds its way to the top.

We'd sat here on these sands singing "Love Me Do," the ditty that became all the rage not long after we'd become stewardesses. A song by four boys from Liverpool oddly called the Beatles. That feels like yesterday. Which, ironically, became another of their hits. You would have loved it.

Would you believe, Beverly, that they became quite an international sensation not long after we lost you, and that their images still grace silly things like lunch boxes and drinking glasses? My grandchildren like them and cannot believe that I was working the flight that took those boys from London to New York for their debut on Ed Sullivan. *Joe, God rest his soul, pulled some strings to get me assigned to that flight.*

It was to be my last because he and I were married the week after that. Valentine's Day. It was a fitting way to say goodbye to you. That final flight.

The last time I donned the fitted blue suit. Or so I thought it would be at the time. I felt you there with me, serving champagne and strawberries to those long-haired youths.

And I smiled. Because in spite of knowing you on this earth for such a short time, you became an indelible part of my soul. Forever.

CHAPTER TWENTY-EIGHT

Judy

Beverly and I return to the El Paso airport. Our bus of new divorcées soars through the border patrol, who are accustomed to this trek by Americans.

I look around and see a spectrum of emotions on people's faces, ranging from quiet relief to outright exhilaration. I'm not sure I fit in with that.

I am numb. I feel like stone. Beverly, who has once again given me a seat by a window, takes my hand and squeezes it. Even that, I barely feel. I know it is meant as reassurance. But I sit in a kind of stupor.

It is done.

The Mexican government will send the paperwork to the state of Pennsylvania, and it will record this dissolution. Two names printed in black on white paper. It will be stamped, recorded, filed away. A mere number to them. But to me, that piece of paper is the end of a dream. The dream I had of having a marriage as happy as my parents had. The dream of the man I believed Henry to be.

I have gained something today.

Freedom.

But I have also lost something.

Innocence.

The girl from Red Lion is a distant memory, and in her place is a woman who has been through battle and bears its invisible scars.

I feel Beverly's grip loosen, and I look to my side and see that she has fallen asleep, her head tilted back and her mouth slightly open. Even in her awkward position, she is beautiful. That is part of her specialness. Beverly makes everything brighter, and I couldn't have done this without her. Since I can't dig myself out of my melancholy, though, I imagine what she would say to me.

"You have only to look to the future now, Judy."

My imaginary Beverly starts counting one finger at a time.

"Joe. Pan Am. Tahitian breezes. Croissants and brie under the Eiffel Tower."

I know she's right, or would be if she was actually saying it.

But in the moment, all I want to do is lay my head against the window and lose myself to the sweet oblivion of sleep.

The El Paso airport is bustling. An early season hurricane is swirling off the Maryland coast, and although the eye has not made landfall, all airports within a hundred miles of Washington, DC, are reporting delays due to heavy wind and rain. El Paso's skies are cloudless. But I know from learning about routes and airline schedules that there is often a domino effect in place when one part of the country is affected.

Beverly, perky after her brief catnap, leads the way to the Continental ticket counter. We hadn't bought our return tickets in advance since we didn't know for sure how long Juárez would take.

"And where are you flying off to today?" says the agent. A rare male in a typically female role. He straightens his tie as he speaks, and I can see how nervous he is in front of Beverly. Most men are like that. And the Beverly I'd first met would have played right into his attraction. But not since meeting Mark. I love this change in her. It's as if she'd found her center of gravity.

"San Francisco. Do you have any flights today?"

The man at the counter runs a slightly chewed fingernail down a list on a clipboard, and I keep the thought to myself that Pan American wouldn't tolerate anything less than a perfectly manicured hand.

"You're in luck. The four o'clock has been rescheduled to eight fifteen due to the East Coast weather. But it has a connection in Los Angeles. Would you like me to book two?"

Beverly sighs. It's an inconvenience, but we've certainly experienced worse.

"Please," she says.

"Wait." I lay a hand on the counter. An idea has just occurred to me. "What about Miami? Do you have any flights there tonight?"

Beverly grins. "Rapunzel has escaped from the prison tower of her marriage and is going to fly off to see Prince Charming?"

I raise an eyebrow at her. "You're mixing your fairy tales."

"My parents didn't read them to me when I was a kid, so I stole my nanny's romance novels and read them under the covers at night. I'm trying to speak goody-goody to you. Would you rather I make a reference to how your hero will rip off your bodice when he sees you? I'm far more familiar with those kinds of stories."

I resist an eye roll. I know she does this just to needle me.

"How about no fictions? I would just like to see Joe. I feel like our relationship had too serious a start, and since I have all this time off, maybe we can spend some of it together."

"Having fun?" Beverly asks. And I know from her expression that she means it literally, not suggestively. She always tells me I'm too serious. But now that I'm free, things are going to change.

"Sure," I promise her.

"*Fun* is my favorite word. You have my blessing." Beverly lays a hand on my head as a priest might.

"Excuse me," the counter agent interjects. "But yes. There is one seat on a flight to Miami tonight." He has been watching our exchange with fascination. But the line behind us is growing, and we shouldn't delay anyone more than they already are.

"I'll take it," I say. No matter what time it arrives, I'm eager to get to Miami.

I'm eager for this next part of my life to begin.

Joe's house is a little cottage in Coconut Grove, an area just southwest of the heart of Miami. The town is as charming as the name sounds, and although I have now visited some of the world's major cities—or at least those in Asia—this may be my favorite place of all of them. It reminds me of our bungalow in Burlingame, but with a distinctly Floridian flavor. The front porch is screened to keep away the bugs, the exterior is painted light blue to match the ocean, and the roof is metal to deter the weathering that the blistering Florida sun can unleash.

But where Burlingame is lined with eucalyptus trees, Coconut Grove is saturated, not surprisingly, with palm trees. Their trunks bear marks similar to those I've seen in Honolulu—holes bored by cleats as intrepid yardmen climb them to hack away at mature coconuts lest they fall on unsuspecting passersby.

I am struck that all these miles away, there are similarities. And though I know that the cold scientific explanation is that they straddle either side of the Tropic of Cancer, I prefer the more magical explanation that we are all tied to each other even across the globe.

Maybe that's what latitude and longitude are. Not merely measurements, but invisible strings that remind us of our connection.

"I took a guess. Cream and two sugars."

Joe finds me on the front porch, where I've adjusted the chair to take full advantage of the way the sunbeams are piercing through the screen.

"That's perfect. Thank you."

I do not tell him that I learned to like my coffee bitter and black because I tucked away a dollar of the grocery money that Henry gave me on the first of every month. Henry never knew any differently because he drank his *like a man* and without embellishment.

But that is the end. No more comparisons.

Joe sets a tray on the small round table between us, and I notice the light-caramel color of his own brew.

I take a sip, and though my tongue recoils at its sweetness, I look at Joe, settled into the other chair, and I suddenly cannot imagine anything being better than this.

You can have Honolulu's sunsets and Hong Kong's silks and Tokyo's cherry blossoms. My paradise is right here.

"How did you sleep?" he asks.

"It might have been the best sleep of my life."

Joe smiles. "I'm glad. I bought that mattress with my Christmas bonus. Down filled."

"You didn't have to give up your bedroom for me. I could have slept in the guest room instead."

He shakes his head. "It's quieter. Away from the street. I thought you could use the rest. You've—it's been a rough time for you."

If I'd needed any more reasons to thoroughly fall in love with Joe Clayton, it would be about what he hadn't done, more than all he had. He hadn't expected any more from me when I arrived than taking me into his arms, kissing my forehead, and setting my suitcase in the room that faced a small but lush backyard.

He hadn't expected me to talk about it all.

Beverly sent me off on that plane in El Paso with a wink when I told her I'd called Joe and would be staying at his house that night. But as much as I am aware of her opinion that going to bed with Joe would be the perfect way to erase Henry from my life, the opposite is true. And Joe senses it. I need some time to feel cherished above all else. I'd had to fend for myself after my parents died. Fend for myself in my marriage. Fend for myself in my budding career. It is bolstering to know what I am capable of.

But it was—is—exhausting as well. To sink into the gift of Joe's nurturing character is maybe the very sexiest thing he could have done.

"You can have your bed back tonight, though," I offer, returning my thoughts to the bliss of this morning on the porch.

"No. It's yours as long as you need it."

I know there are many meanings behind that.

It's mine as long as I need a place to stay.

It's mine as long as I need it to feel safe.

It's mine until I'm ready to make it ours.

These things, these important things, I know about Joe. And yet it is only now that I am learning little things like how he takes his coffee.

"I found out for you why they call Miami the Magic City," he offers.

I remember our evening at the Dominican restaurant when he first mentioned those words, and the memory of it fills me with warmth. It was beyond my hopes that it could lead to sitting right here, today.

"Why is that?" I ask.

"It's from a speech that an old Miami mayor gave in the thirties. Something like how when people arrive here ragged, they go through a magical transformation into happiness and contentment."

I let those words sit between us, and I close my eyes to imagine them. How right they are. The magic of this city has worked its way to my heart.

Although I think it's really Joe. I would feel this way wherever he lived.

I stand up and place my now-empty cup on the tray. We did all this relationship stuff in reverse. We've weathered serious things between us—work, distance, divorce—but we haven't had much experience having *fun* in each other's company. Beverly was right.

"Why don't you take the day off and we go exploring?" I suggest.

"I can't do that."

"Why not?" I don't like the pout in my voice, but suddenly the only thing I want to do is spend the whole day with him.

He grins. "Because it's Saturday. I already have the day off."

I raise my hand to punch him in the arm, but he's quick on his feet and catches my arm with his own, wrapping it around his waist and drawing me toward him. My head fits perfectly into his shoulder. He bends his head, and his lips brush the place where my collarbone meets my neck, and I feel a shiver run through me. He places a gentle kiss there. And then another just upward. And another upward of that until I can feel his breath in my ear. I want to melt, and if he keeps it up, this delicate motion, I may abandon everything else I thought and tell him that I need him. In every way.

"How do you feel about . . ." He lets the question linger unfinished, and both of my hands squeeze his sides.

Maybe I am ready to say yes.

"Monkeys?" he says at last.

I release my grip and step back.

"Monkeys?"

Joe is smiling, clearly amused. He has no idea how close I came to—well, not monkeys.

"What on earth are you talking about?"

He draws me back to him, and my body is still flush from what he made me feel. Although it was so gentle that even if a nosy neighbor had peered at us through her blinds, she would not have been scandalized.

Joe pushes a strand of hair behind my ear. "I've already taken you to the most beautiful spot in Miami."

"Villa Vizcaya," I murmur.

"Mm-hmm. I thought maybe I'd take you to the craziest."

I meet his gaze, and our eyes are locked on each other.

"I'll go anywhere you want to go, Joe."

He pauses and I feel a rush of warmth from the way he looks at me. "I may have been wrong just now," he says.

"What do you mean?"

His voice lowers, and he speaks slowly. "About the most beautiful spot in Miami. I'm looking at it."

We stand there for a half second that feels like an eternity before I push up on my toes and press my lips against his. Kissing him in a way that might scandalize an onlooker after all.

An hour later, Joe pulls up into a half-full parking lot. My hair is still wet from the quick shower I took. A proverbial cold one to shock me out of the heat of that kiss—that magnificent kiss on the front porch. I had been both relieved and disappointed when Joe had pulled away, breathless, and said, "We should get going."

But the magnetic pull that had begun made every part of me aware of his closeness. It was torture not to hold his hand as he drove south down the highway.

Now that he's turned off the ignition, though, Joe comes around to my side of the car and helps me out. A gesture I appreciate even if I don't need it. I can balance a tray of six hot coffees and a silver carafe of steaming water with one hand during turbulence thirty-five thousand feet in the air. I can step out of his lime-green VW Beetle on my own.

It occurs to me that 1963 is a strange time to be a woman. Our capabilities are being recognized in new ways every day, but we are surrounded by chivalrous norms that I don't want to have disappear.

Maybe the sweet spot is to be found in the balance of it all. I know that Joe respects what I do. All while loving me and wanting to care for me. I think I like being cared for.

"I've been saving this one for when you came for a visit," he says, taking my hand as we make our way to the ticket booth. "I picked up a brochure for it at the airport and thought it was something you'd like."

"I was already planning to take a week off soon and fly to Miami. I guess my forced sabbatical just made this happen, well, even sooner."

Joe plans a quick kiss on my temple as he pulls out his wallet. "I'm sorry about how it happened. But I am not sorry that you're here."

I squeeze his hand. "I'm not sorry I'm here either."

As we walk toward the entrance, I laugh at the sign:

Monkey Jungle, Where humans are caged and monkeys run wild.

An acne-faced teenager takes Joe's money. I remember those days of such youthful challenges and how my dad assured me through my tears that I was beautiful.

Joe makes me feel beautiful. It occurs to me that my parents would have liked him. And he would have liked my parents.

"Here's a map," the teenager says with a shortage of enthusiasm. "The rainforest is off to your right and the amphitheater is down the path on the left. Don't miss the chimp show at the top of every hour. We have over five hundred monkeys from six continents."

It sounds like nothing I've ever heard of. I'm already glad Joe brought me here.

Joe checks his watch. "It's almost eleven. Should we start with a show?"

"You read my mind."

We veer to the left until we see the small seating area that has already drawn a crowd. At eleven on the nose, two chimps, Kimbo and Billy, come out from backstage and entertain us with antics from riding go-carts to playing the guitar.

"Why is it that we find it hilarious when animals do human things?" Joe leans over and whispers to me just as Kimbo is donning an astronaut's helmet and stepping into a toy space capsule.

"I don't know. You think we'd be shocked to realize we're not as superior as we think we are."

"Maybe. But it's quite a stretch between strumming some chords and building an aircraft. I think humanity is safe for the time being."

"Did you ever have any animals as passengers?" I ask.

"More than I would have liked. I ran several routes from South America to Miami that would take on monkeys and parrots before loading them onto train cars. And once, I worked a charter flight that flew a full cargo of cattle to Colorado."

"I thought Pan Am only did international routes."

"For people passengers, yes. The charters are another story. Try catching a ferry flight sometime and sharing it with a barnyard."

"I can't imagine the cleanup," I say.

"And you don't want to imagine the smell."

Billy puts on a showgirl wig and starts strutting around the stage. More laughter. I can't help but giggle at that one, and I see that Joe's eyes are twinkling.

When the show is over, we head to the enclosure for Bulu, the six-hundred-pound gorilla.

"Wow. Imagine him in first class," I say.

"You'd have to shove out the Maxim's to make room for the bananas."

I look Bulu in the eyes, and something about the intelligence behind them tells me that there is more to him than we might ever know.

"I don't know," I answer. "I think he might like Maxim's."

"Aren't they herbivores?"

I shrug. "I think Maxim's chicken cordon bleu would make a meat lover out of anyone."

"You're right about that."

We continue on, pausing at an aquarium into which the Javanese monkeys are diving, and comment on how much they would like the waters of Honolulu.

Our discussions are silly and simple, and I love every minute of it. This is just the levity we needed.

We end our adventure at the rainforest, and it is easily my favorite part. We walk on a narrow pathway through an Amazonian jungle. On our sides and above us is wire mesh that gives us a remarkable view of the surrounding environment. We can barely hear ourselves talk because one loud family of monkeys—I don't know which kind—is sitting right on top of where we're standing, and their furry behinds are smushed into the mesh. The mother holds on to a baby while a small one climbs all over her. The father comes over and sits down, back turned to them all, and the mother picks a few bugs off his fur.

"Would you look at that," I say over their cacophony. "Looks like he's not the type to bring her coffee on the front porch in the morning."

But right after I say that, the father sweeps the small monkey into his arms and hoists it on his back. He swings from branch to branch until they are both settled on the one above our heads. The mother continues to hold the baby in peace.

"I stand corrected. He probably does."

Joe puts his arm around me and we continue on.

As we head toward the exit, we notice a gift shop. We enter through its stone arch, and my eye rests on the postcard stand. I have to get one for Ronelle. I've sent her a postcard from every one of my trips. This one will beat all. I look through a few of the choices and spy Joe putting a package under his arm and taking it to the counter.

It's not until the next morning that I learn what it is. I am again sitting on the porch when Joe brings out the tray of coffee. His is in a plain white mug, so very typical of him. But mine is in a china cup with a saucer—and the Monkey Jungle logo emblazoned across both of them.

It becomes our habit every day, earlier on the weekdays when he has to go into the office. The monkeys are replaced one morning by a more elegant duo. A china cup and saucer with delicate bird-of-paradise flowers hand painted on them.

"From Vizcaya," Joe says as he stirs sugar into his own white mug. "Now you have one from each place we've been to here."

We add to the collection over time. Joe comes to see me in Burlingame for the first weekend of every month, and I fly out two weeks later for a couple of days. He is always ready with a new place to show me—the Coral Castle, the Everglades—and each time, he finds a cup and saucer that reminds him of that place.

Each time, he gives me his bedroom, his down mattress.

One October morning, Joe goes out for a run after our coffee. I wash and dry the newest set, putting it on a shelf next to its neighbors. I look at the original two—monkeys and flowers—and smile. I love the sweet life we're taking slow steps to build. I sense that we have many mornings like it ahead of us.

The phone rings, awakening me from the little daydream I've been having about our future.

"Hello?" I answer, hoping that he wouldn't mind me picking up his phone.

"Judy! I'm so glad it's you."

"Ronelle!" I clasp my hand to my mouth in disbelief. Though we've exchanged letters all this time, it's been far too long since I've heard her voice. "Is everything okay?" We never call. Long distance was expensive for both of us. But I'd always made sure she knew how to get in touch with me. Just in case. She has the Burlingame house line. And Joe's.

This couldn't be a casual call.

"It is and it isn't. And so you don't worry, I'm calling from a pay phone so that no one can listen on the party line. I wanted to let you know that Henry must have finally gotten the copy of your divorce papers from Mexico. We could hear quite a racket all the way at our house last night. And this morning, there was a bunch of your stuff at the curb waiting for trash pickup. I waited for him to leave, and I went over to check it out. There were piles of your clothes. Torn. Some scorched with cigarette burns. Your suitcase was busted open, and he'd shredded that map you love so much."

I feel rigid. I imagine what it must have been like for her to discover all that. But my concern is over Ronelle, not over the loss of things that I said goodbye to over a year ago. That was my old life. I've made a new one.

"There is some good news among that, though. I found your Sinatra album in the pile. *Come Fly with Me.*" She lets out a small laugh. "I think Henry must have already thought it was done for because he left that alone. It was just sitting on top of everything."

"No wonder." I laugh with her. "I'd worn that thing out on my own."

"I saved it for you."

"Ronelle. Thank you."

I feel tears well up in me. That little connection to my dad. That part of my life I never want to let go of.

"Thank you," I say again.

"Anyway," she says. "I doubt he has any idea where you are. But you can never be too careful. I know you're on a leave of absence, but can you get yourself out of the country for a while?"

My mind goes through the possibilities. I have six weeks left until they reinstate me. Although my flights would be covered, my hotels wouldn't be. So leaving would be expensive. Joe doesn't have any vacation time left. But then I think of Beverly. She has already been talking about taking some time off to meet her mother in Europe. Maybe she won't mind if I tagged along. Not when she knows why.

"Yes. I think I can work that out. I wish you could come with me, Ronelle. I miss you."

"I miss you too," she says. "Hold on, Judy."

She sets the phone down, and I press my receiver closer to my ear. In the background, it sounds like she is getting sick.

She returns. "Sorry about that. I really should go."

"Are you okay? It sounded like you're unwell."

I can feel her smile across the phone line.

"I'm doing as well as I can be for someone having a baby."

"A baby! Ronelle!"

I slide down to the floor. Life is such a spinning wheel of joys and sorrows.

"Yeah. We're adding another Rorbaugh to the world."

"And Richard and his family?"

"Are over the moon," she finishes for me. "I just need the rest of the world to catch up."

Oh, how I hope it does.

CHAPTER TWENTY-NINE

Beverly

"This is going on Mother's room charge, so please don't skimp, Judy."

My word, it feels glorious to be sitting in the dining room of George V. It's been far too long since I've been to Paris. And since Judy came along—an addition we were more than happy to have—my mom splurged on a suite of rooms in our favorite hotel near the Champs-Élysées.

The city of light has not lost its magic. It's as wonderous as the first time I went and all the times since.

I've surprised myself, though. Last time I was here, I never thought I could be happy in anything less luxurious. High-thread-count sheets and room service at the tip of my finger. Now my favorite days are my Honolulu layovers with Ann and Karina in their duplex, or with Mark in his rustic ʻohana.

I can hear a phantom of my father telling me, "How the mighty have fallen."

But I don't feel fallen.

I feel found.

"I don't want to take advantage of this, Bev," Judy pleads. I am torn from my thoughts by the sincerity of her words. "I'm perfectly happy with water and a croissant."

I shake my head. "Well, they even charge you for water here, so you might as well order champagne. And yes—the croissants are out of this world. But you need some meat. And eggs. And butter on everything."

"Surely that's not how the French eat. Look at the women. They're thin as rails. And—we can't gain so much that our weigh-ins are problematic."

"Fine," I concede as I wave a hand to the waiter and point to a bottle of champagne at the next table. "Let's compromise. One week of unbridled indulgence while we're in Paris. That will give us four weeks to taper off, and we'll be in flying shape just in time to return to work."

"Fine," she agrees. "But I still feel like I'm taking advantage of your mother's offer to pay for all this."

"Oh, please. Look. She's never going to leave Mr. Wall Street. Her set doesn't divorce. And Sami would put her head on a platter and spritz her hair in holy water if she did. She found religion after her ordeal last year. But there are better ways to get revenge. Like running up some credit-card bills. And whom has she enlisted to help her? You and me, baby. Cheers. We've earned it."

The waiter comes by just in time to make our *cheers* a reality. I clink the crystal glass against Judy's, and it makes the satisfying sound of a bell.

Judy must think the same. "That reminds me. I would love to see Notre-Dame while we're here. My mother always wanted to go, and my father promised he'd take her to Paris on their twenty-fifth anniversary."

I know that anniversary never happened. That she lost them both before they made it that far.

"Of course. You cannot come to Paris and not see Notre-Dame. But other than that, let's leave the week open to where the *brise* takes us. Because if you arrive in gay Paree with an itinerary, you have missed the whole point."

Judy sips the champagne and wrinkles her nose. The bubbles must have tickled her.

"Pan American has taught me a lot," she says. "But among the most important is that not everything has to happen now. I have to believe that if there is a place I want to return to, I will. Look at us—how many times have you and I now been to Asia? Two women who had never been before. So, Beverly, I will do Paris your way. See where those breezes take us. Because I will return."

"*We* will return," I correct. "I declare that you and I should spend the rest of our lives planning one trip a year. Girls only. Husbands and babies are all well and good, but there is nothing that replaces the unique comfort that is found in the company of a friend."

I am saying this as much for myself as her. If not more. Now that we're here, now that we've had the extraordinary experiences that we've had, I want to ensure that we will hold on to that long after we've left the airline behind.

"Is your mother joining us today?" she asks.

"Not until dinner. She has fittings scheduled at Burberry and Chanel today for her winter wardrobe. But she made reservations at a little place right near Notre-Dame, in fact. Au Vieux Paris. It's been around since the sixteenth century. You'll love it."

Judy sits back in her chair, and her eyes glaze over. I can tell she likes the champagne. And I'm getting a kick out of indulging her like this. It reminds me of those tequila shots we had in Miami. It seems like it was so long ago. We were different girls then than the women we are now.

"Wow. The sixteenth century. It's hard to even imagine. I think the oldest thing near Red Lion is a little colonial building in York. And even that is a re-creation of the building that was originally there."

"Yeah. There's something about being in such ancient surroundings that puts a lot of things in perspective. No matter my problems, these places were here long before us and will be here long after we've met the angels."

"I like that. Met the angels."

"I did that for your sake, Judy. You know my mouth. I can come up with all sorts of euphemisms. My favorites would make you blush."

She puts up a hand, but does it in the lazy manner of someone touched by intoxication. "I can imagine. That's all I need."

I drink the last of my bubbles in one fell swoop and motion to the waiter for another.

"If you think this is all old, though, Judy, wait until you see Rome."

"I can't wait. And where should we go after that?"

I shrug my shoulders. "That's as far as I planned. We don't need to be back in Burlingame until mid-December. I've bid a route that will put me in Honolulu over Christmas. I know that you'll want to spend time with Joe before we head back, though. So that gives us a few weeks. Where would you like to go?"

Judy pulls out her wallet and unfolds a piece of paper that is so worn it's almost falling apart. I recognize it immediately. It's not that old—just over a year—but it's clearly something she has clung to. She hands it to me, and I read them off.

"Hawaii. New York. Paris. Capri. London. Vermont. Brazil. Mandalay. Chicago. It's our list, Judy. From that day in the training hangar."

She nods. "Mm-hmm. The places Frank Sinatra sang about on the *Come Fly with Me* album."

I put an elbow on the table—Mother isn't here to fuss about my lack of etiquette—and I lean in. "We can cross a few of these off. Hawaii. New York. And here we are in Paris. Not bad for only a year into the goal. And we can surely hit a few more of these before we return to California." I fold it in half and look up at the gilded ceiling of the hotel before handing it back to her. "Okay. This is exactly what I'm talking about. Once a year, we resolve to see at least one of these places together."

I see her eyes light up. "I'm in."

"And we'll have to add to it. We're going to be friends for much longer than these will take."

This time, her eyes get watery, and she slips her hand across the table to hold mine.

"Much longer."

On our last evening in Paris, Judy insists that I spend time alone with my mother. I resist at first, not wanting to leave my friend alone in the city, but she tells me that she'd like to take a walk along the Seine and find some flowers to leave in the water for her parents. I realize that I don't need to be so protective. Judy's cheeks are rosy, and her steps are light. Mother treated us to a shopping trip to her favorite stores, and despite Judy's protests, we managed to rack up some hefty bills for Mr. Wall Street at Hermès and Caron. I selected a burgundy scarf that looked stunning on Judy and exchanged a large bottle of En Avion for the small one she'd brought to the Parfum Caron counter. Named for the first female pilots, the perfume felt like an appropriate homage to our sisters in flight. And it smelled sensational with its notes of carnation, orange, and sandalwood.

Tonight, my mother has hinted at a surprise for me, and indeed, I do not expect the path we take. A taxi drops us off at the base of the Rue Foyatier in Montmartre. It is past dinnertime, and the streets are drowsy with flickering streetlights that are reflected in puddles. In all our times traveling to this city together, we have not come to this part of town, and the venture reminds me of our trips to Sami's in SoHo. There is something clandestine about it.

As we ascend each step of the steep path that takes us deeper into the heart of Montmartre, I see the brilliant-white church of Sacré-Cœur reveal itself. If the Eiffel Tower is the heart of Paris, Sacré-Cœur—despite its name actually meaning *sacred heart*—is the city's crown. I've seen it at a distance from many vantage points, but never this close.

It is remarkable.

"Are you sure you can walk well in those shoes?" I ask her, looking down at her slim heels. "Maybe we should go back down and take a taxi to wherever we're going."

She smiles, and I wonder why I ever doubted her. My mother can carry off effortless elegance as well as any Parisian native. "If my feet form blisters, I will consider it my penance."

I don't understand what she means, but I don't press it. Instead, I distract both of us with chatter about Ann and Karina and their parents and a recent trip where I met them in Las Vegas. I know my mother is excited that we have connected and that I've finally found the piece of myself that was missing. She mentions wanting to come out to Honolulu with me, and I assure her that they will welcome her as warmly as they have me.

At last we reach the top, and despite how many hours I spend on my feet as a stewardess, I am breathless from the effort. I look back and marvel at how far we came. Easily over two hundred steps.

"It's beautiful, isn't it?" my mother says. The lights illuminating the church send a sparkle to her eyes as she gazes at it. There is a look on her face that I have not seen before. I might call it—reverence?

"It is," I say slowly. The church revealed its magnificence bit by bit with each approaching step, but here, up close, it boasts a splendor that defies words.

I am still trying to figure out why this is our destination.

"I have always avoided coming here because it's overrun by crowds," she whispers. "Or so I've heard. But my priest told me about a beautiful way to see it away from people. It's why I wanted to come on this trip. And I've wanted to see it with you."

I hear all the words, but the only one that stands out to me is *priest*. Since when did my mother become religious? But I like it on her. Something that is separate from my father. Something that can be her own.

I wonder if this is Sami's doing?

She pulls a piece of paper from the pocket of her mink coat and reads the directions that are printed on it. She takes my hand as if I'm a child, and I find myself liking the feeling that it evokes. I wouldn't have known that such a simple gesture could carry several meanings. I recall her holding my hand when I was an actual child and something about it felt like I was being corralled. This time it feels—it feels loving.

I let myself be led. Every step that we take toward the church, and then around to its side, feels full of purpose.

At last, we come upon a wooden door. We are so close to the church that in looking up it seems like it pierces the sky, which is brightly lit by the overhead moon. It must be ten o'clock, if not later.

My mother knocks and the door opens. Standing in the doorway is a small nun, clothed head to toe in a white habit topped with a black veil. It is striking in its contrast, but not only the colors. I am flooded with a sense of contrast to the world itself. The nun's face is radiant and peaceful even as she herself is simple. Behind her, there is a white room, sparsely adorned, but quite welcoming. It is nothing like the opulent Paris that I am used to. And her look of contentment is one we used to spend countless hours and dollars chasing in Fifth Avenue stores.

The nun has been expecting us.

"Good evening, Mrs. Caldwell," she says in French.

"Good evening, Sister Catherine. Thank you for having us."

I follow them both into the room. It is a warm haven when the night outside is so cold.

"As we discussed in our correspondence, it is typical for our pilgrims to stay overnight at our guesthouse. But I appreciate that you are in Paris with your daughter and that it is her friend's first time in the city. I can well understand why you would want to be closer to the center of the city. We'll ring a taxi for you when you're ready to go back. I do hope you will consider staying on a future trip, though."

"I would love to," my mother responds. And I can tell that she means it. All my life, I have been able to detect the tone in her voice that says just what the listener expects to hear. But this is not one of those times.

We follow Sister Catherine down the hallway and pass several other sisters identically dressed. Two are wiping down dining tables. Four are gathered in prayer in a small chapel.

I am reminded of our Pan Am uniforms. Our version of habits, but with shorter skirts and fitted blazers. But a symbol that announces that we are a team. We are family. I can see that these nuns are similarly fulfilled in their cozy austerity.

The whiteness of the convent rooms gives way to a gray-stone hallway that looks far older than the rest of it. And beyond that sit two wooden doors that frame an elaborate stained-glass scene.

Sister Catherine folds her hands, and they disappear under the billowing fabric of her habit. She nods her head and says, "I will leave you here so that you can contemplate in privacy." She turns and leaves. Her footfalls on the stone floor are so silent that I could almost believe she is a ghost.

My mother opens the door and lets me go in before her.

Suddenly, we are transported into what feels like another world. It matches the opulence of the city, but in this case, the eye is directed upward rather than outward. We are inside the colossal basilica and we are alone. Alone, save for statues and candles and two people praying in the pew closest to the altar. Above us, we are surrounded by mosaics and at their peak, a dome. The one that seemed to pierce the sky in the moonlight does the same by candlelight.

My mother links my arm with hers, and we stroll around the perimeter of the nave. She takes slow, deliberate steps, and I suspect she is trying to avoid the sound of her heels echoing in the vast space. Perhaps she needs—or is seeking—a dose of that serenity that made the nun's gait silent.

I inhale the scent of incense, candle smoke, and history. It is an intoxicating blend.

My mother whispers, but even then, her words echo into the nearby side chapels. "The irony is not lost on me that it took you going away for us to become close."

I nod. These sentiments are many years late. But I find myself void of resentment. As if regret cannot exist in this hallowed space.

"I've made mistakes, Beverly. I've chosen security over love, comfort over relationships. But I'd like to believe it's not too late for me to rectify that."

"You already have, Mom," I say. "Look at us." I glance down at our intertwined arms.

"I spent several nights at Sami's bedside when she was in the hospital. And more at the Waldorf while she recovered. Being with her—made me feel like my old self again."

"Are you going to leave Father?"

My mind races with the implications. It would certainly make headlines, to say the least.

She shakes her head. "No. Nothing like that. I made a vow and I take that seriously. He's not a bad man, Beverly. He is a driven one. Maybe that's my mission in this stage of my life. To help him discover what I'm relearning. The beauty of slowing down. Of appreciating the little joys in life rather than missing them while achieving more."

"Stop-and-smell-the-roses kind of stuff?"

We pause, and I look up at a statue whose shadow is elongated by the candlelight. The tarnished brass plaque reads Saint Francis of Assisi. I think I remember reading about him. A rich Italian boy who gave up everything—even the literal clothes on his back—to serve the poor.

"Something like that. I've realized that riches are their own kind of poverty. Certainly, material needs are met with an ease that others struggle for. But inside—in the soul—there is a restlessness for more that can never be achieved because it is impossible to ever have it all. There is always more to acquire. Something newer. Someone with an even grander fortune."

"I don't know, Mom. You have me worried that you're going to fling off those Christian Dior heels and don a veil to live with the nuns here."

She laughs and again it echoes, this time enough that the couple of worshippers in the front pews look back at us.

"Maybe in another life I would have. But no, this is the life I shaped for myself. And it's had beautiful moments. The best of those being with you, even if I didn't show it well. Now it's time to soak it in rather than miss it."

I think about Mark and his little 'ohana on Sunset Beach. The happiest days of my life have been spent there with him, even though there have been too few of them. But they've made me care little that my father cut me off from my accounts. And they've even tamed the wild independent streak that jetted me off quite literally into Pan Am's open arms. Maybe my mother and I are coming to the same conclusions at the same time, though I have a head start of a couple of decades in life.

The truth is, if Mark Oakley proposes to me, I will be quite happy to become Mrs. Oakley. Cheering him on from the stands at championships. Lobbying Pan Am to change their policy on married stewardesses by demonstrating that women can, in fact, give quality attention to both.

Interestingly, by expanding my world, I've come to appreciate the small spaces in it.

As if reading my mind, she says, "I feel the need to give you the motherly advice to pursue love over money, but I have a feeling that you have already set yourself on that path."

I have told her little bits on the phone about Mark, but have hesitated in giving more because the telephone lacks the intimacy that such conversation needs. But this—this beautiful church—evokes the gravity and comfort that makes it feel like the perfect setting.

Our stroll has taken us to the back of the church, so I lead my mother to the last pew, and we sit down.

"You're right," I say. "I'll tell you more about Mark."

CHAPTER THIRTY

Judy

It is just after ten in the evening, and in Rome, the night is just getting started.

Beverly and I are sipping a cappuccino at an outdoor table in the Piazza Navona in Rome, reminiscing about the adventures we've had these past few weeks. Jet setting and zigzagging whenever and wherever seats became available. We've crossed a few off our Sinatra list, and added ones he didn't sing about.

Now, our adventure is nearing its close. One more stop after Rome. We have just finished a shared plate of bucatini alla carbonara after the soup course, the fish course, and the cheese course.

No one eats like the Italians.

Beverly leans back in her chair and rubs her stomach in the most inelegant fashion I've ever witnessed with her. "I never thought I'd eat again after Cairo. I will forever treasure seeing the pyramids, but the mummy's revenge is a very real thing."

"I think it's called Montezuma's revenge," I correct.

"Can't be. Montezuma was Aztec. Not Egyptian."

"The where doesn't matter. The how is the thing. The guidebook said not to drink the water. And even to brush your teeth with Coca-Cola."

"But I didn't drink the water," Beverly bellows.

"I know, I know. But you drank the hibiscus juice at the perfume shop."

Beverly throws her hands up, almost looking like the Italians have rubbed off on her. "When they offered it, I didn't want to be rude. And I wasn't thinking about how water is the base for juice. I was going for the cultural experience. That's the Pan American way."

"Good thing one of us was thinking. I've never played nursemaid to one quite so—indisposed." Goodness, she'd been a mess.

Beverly rolls her eyes, a gesture that is usually my territory. "If we weren't already friends, that would have cinched it."

"And you did buy me a beautiful alabaster vase afterward."

"A small token of gratitude," she acknowledges.

"One I will always treasure."

We've declined the salad course and the cannoli that the waiter tries to offer. After a meal such as what we've just had, the cappuccinos are all we can fit in.

Besides, we have one more stop on our grand overseas adventure and then it's back to Pan Am regulations. The end of my suspension is almost here, and I'll be back to rolling carts down slim aisles in no time.

I haven't yet told Beverly that I'm going to put in for a transfer to Miami. I have missed Joe terribly these last few weeks. I've sent postcards to him and to Ronelle, but neither could respond as we never knew where we'd be staying.

One expensive phone call during a layover in Athens was all we needed to acknowledge that being a country apart was not a very good plan for our future.

If we marry, I'll have to give up being a stewardess. But I'll stay long enough to at least meet the eighteen-month average of a career like this.

Beverly leans forward. "Why do I get the feeling that everything is about to change?"

I don't know if she's picked up on my musings or if she's having some of her own.

"Because it is."

She folds her arms. "You're going to move to Miami, aren't you?" She must have seen the startled look on my face. "Don't act all surprised. You wear your heart on your sleeve. You and Joe are going to go off and make babies and live happily ever after."

I nod. "Yes. Probably. Eventually."

"Yes. Definitely," she corrects. "Just don't forget your old friend Beverly."

"As if I could."

"Yeah. I'm like that. Unforgettable."

"It's not as if you don't have your own plans."

She shrugs. "You're right. We haven't talked about it, but gosh, I miss Mark. And I'm pretty sure it's mutual."

"Of course it is." Beverly doesn't know that I'd met up with Mark on a Honolulu layover and he'd taken me shopping to get my opinion on an engagement ring. When I'd first encountered Beverly at the interviews in New York, I would have said that she was a woman who expected something opulent. The kind of ring you could see from the moon. But the Beverly I'd come to know had grown up. I had a feeling that she would appreciate something that was elegant in its simplicity.

"So London will be our last hurrah for now. But at least when everything changes we'll have our annual girls' trip," she prods. I get the impression that she's afraid we won't really do it. It's not often that Beverly seems insecure.

"Whatever happens, wherever we each live, we will make that happen. You will always be an important part of my life." I feel my eyes getting teary as I say it. The love of a good man is a sacred thing. But the love of a good friend may be even more so.

"I have an idea." Beverly sits up rashly enough to scoot the chair back.

"I'm bracing myself."

"Hear me out. London is our last *girls'* trip for a while. But what if we cap this off with a trip with the boys when we get back? They've never met, and I'm sure they'd get along like cheese and crackers."

"I like it. But where?"

Beverly drums her fingers on the table. "Somewhere none of us has been."

That could be a tall order. But I'm game.

"It would have to be pretty close to Miami," I say. "Joe used up all his vacation time coming to see me in Burlingame, so it would have to be over a weekend."

"Perfect. Mark has a swim meet in Atlanta the first week of December, so that puts him in the same corner of the world."

She thinks. "Key West?"

I shake my head. "Joe has been. The Virgin Islands?"

"I went in high school over a summer break."

We are both silent for a moment. Then Beverly has another idea. "Puerto Rico."

I think of beaches and palm trees. Similar to our love of Honolulu and Tahiti, but with its own unique culture.

"I like that idea."

"Me too. Let's send a telegram to the boys and stop into a travel office when we're in London to see if they have some brochures."

I sip at the foam of my cappuccino, well aware that it will keep me from sleeping tonight. But it's all worth it.

Our discussion is interrupted when the tone in the restaurant changes. A buzz makes its way around the room. Conversation shifts from person to person, stranger to stranger. It's like the childhood game of telephone, though with Italians, it's accompanied by the flailing of arms and the rapidity of speaking that we've come to appreciate in our short time here. Some women pull handkerchiefs from their pockets and dab their eyes.

"Mamma mia," we hear. Several people cross themselves. "No, no, no!"

"Whatever could have happened?" I ask Beverly. The steam from my cappuccino has disappeared, and my drink cools as I watch this strange occurrence.

Our waiter hurries over to us. His eyes are red and puffy.

"You are Americano, no?" he says.

"Yes. We're Americans," Beverly reassures him. I can see the confusion in the wrinkle of her eyebrows.

"Mi dispiace. Mi dispiace per il tuo presidente."

Presidente. That's not a hard one to translate. But why was he saying it?

We learn soon enough. John F. Kennedy has been killed. Shot in Dallas today while parading in the presidential limousine through the downtown area.

For the next few days, everywhere we go, we hear, "We are sorry about your president." It is as if this one tragedy has united the world in collective concern for our well-being over such a senseless event.

Even our beds in our simple hotel room are adorned with fresh flowers and a note from the hotel manager expressing his sorrow for his "American friends."

I am actually relieved to be here across the pond during this unusual time. While thoughtful in their words of sympathy, the Europeans are nonetheless getting on with their lives. But to read the American newspapers that made their way here, it is all anyone at home can talk about.

I don't think I would want to be saturated in it. It is too much to bear.

Beverly and I had one good cry about it together and then resolved not to let it ruin the remainder of our trip. "If anything," she'd said, "it's a reminder that life is short and you should enjoy every minute of it. Which I think we've been doing."

So it is with this renewed fervor to give life everything we have that Beverly finally lets me in on a secret. A surprise in London.

Our trip to Paris had been funded by Beverly's very generous mother, and the stay at George V was like something out of the movies.

But we'd spent the following weeks in hostels and small hotels to save money and ate two meals a day rather than three.

London was to be indulgent like Paris.

"This was Mother's idea. I promise," Beverly says when we have left Italy behind and pulled up to our hotel in London. "She set us up at the Savoy. Not only because it's her favorite place to stay or because the cocktails at the American Bar are like nothing else anywhere, but because of its proximity."

"Its proximity to what?"

She lets the black cab pull away, then points across the River Thames.

"To that bridge. The Waterloo Bridge. And on the other side of that, the Royal Festival Hall."

None of these words mean anything to me. And she knows that. She is just ratcheting up the dramatic revelation. I let her have her fun and play along.

"And what is showing at the Royal Festival Hall?"

She grins wide enough to power all of London.

"Frank."

My heart stops. I fall back onto my bed before sitting back up. Then, my heart starts to race.

"Frank?"

"Sinatra, baby!"

I think I fainted after that.

Judy

Mo'orea, French Polynesia
Today

I stay on the beach until well after the sun fades away. At this time of year, it is winter in the northern hemisphere, but summer in the south. My old bones are appreciating that. By living in Miami, I've gone as far south as I can tolerate. But this heat envelops me in a comforting way. I feel it like it's a hug from you.

I look up and see the stars twinkling in unparalleled brilliance. I think about that last night in London. How you and your mother conspired to create what became a night I'll never forget.

You took me to Harrods, and we each picked out a dress. And we learned that your father, softening somewhat now that you'd really and truly been out on your own, insisted that we put them on his account. Clearly, your mother was making some headway in helping him appreciate the more important parts of life.

I chose a formfitting burgundy dress that had golden threads that glistened in the light. A fancy nod to the pink-and-yellow sweater from my mom.

You picked a dress of emerald-green velvet, off the shoulders, and utterly gorgeous. Utterly you.

The Sinatra concert was pure magic.

Our seats were on the right side of the theater in a little box that gave us a terrific view of the stage—and of the other patrons. You told me that it was a special concert for dignitaries.

And though we were no one special, you said that there were perks to being Mr. Wall Street's daughter now and then.

You pointed out Princess Margaret to me, and she was even more beautiful than in photographs.

The best moment for most people was when Frank sent the band away and sang, accompanied only by piano, "One for My Baby." Despite the vastness of the venue, he shrunk it at that moment to a small-town barroom and made every person in the room feel that he was singing only to them.

But you knew my best moment as soon as it happened. The one that made me cry. The one that prompted you to take my hand and squeeze it. Because "Come Fly with Me" was not just a song to me. It was my parents. It was the renewal of something that I let go of after they died. And it was my salvation when I was hired by Pan Am and could fulfill the promises that I made to myself to go everywhere he sang about.

That was supposed to be our plan. Yours and mine. We wrote down those locales and dreamed our big dreams. We did make it to Paris and London and Cairo and Hawaii together. And Joe, ever considerate, made sure that over the years, we made it to the rest of them. Every single one of them. That was no easy feat when children came along as well as their expenses. But he made sure it happened for me. And for you—at each place, I left a pinch of your ashes. So you were with me, dearest friend. Always.

Although you and I know they weren't and aren't your real ashes. There was nothing to gather. No body to bury. But I visited the site. With your parents. Grief stricken, all of us. We scooped up earth from where we'd lost you, and we let our hands sift it into jars—one for them, one for me. I'd like to think that even a bit of you was there. It's what I told myself at each place I traveled.

It's what I tell myself today.

CHAPTER THIRTY-ONE

Beverly

"Mark!"

I see my sun-kissed man waving to me from the airport window as soon as I step onto the landing of the stairs that are pushed up to the plane. I know he can't hear me, but he waves back, and I'm sure he can feel my excitement at seeing him.

San Juan, Puerto Rico, is a warm relief after the chilly winter feel of London. Our flight to Miami was almost canceled due to an expected snowfall in England, but we took off before the cancellations started rolling in.

Joe had joined us in Miami and then he, Judy, and I caught a short hopper to the island.

I know they are somewhere behind me, but I'm eager to leave that gooey-eyed twosome behind.

"There's my girl," Mark says as soon as I am within arm's reach. He wraps his arms around my waist and twirls me enough times that I have to hold my pillbox hat down before it flies off.

Hat be damned. He dips me, movie-like, right there in the terminal, and kisses me with matinee-idol smoothness.

Whether or not he wins the Olympics, the man is a gold-medal kisser. And this is just the variety that is here in public. What he's like behind closed doors is a toe curler.

"Don't you want to wait for your friends?" he says.

"We've got dinner reservations together. It's been weeks and weeks since we've seen each other, and I want you all for myself right now."

Mark hails a cab, and we're off to our hotel. The travel agent in London recommended one in Old San Juan that is also by the beach, so we don't have to choose between historical sights and tropical bliss. Though if I'd had to, it would be the latter, no doubt. There is something about the mix of Mark Oakley and sand in my toes that makes my heart palpitate.

"How was the meet?" I ask.

"Great. The boys did so well."

This is what I love about this man. He would fly across an ocean and across a continent just to support boys like the one he'd been photographed with in *LIFE* magazine. There had been a national tournament for handicapped swimmers, and a call went out for coaches and mentors. So naturally, Mark responded.

"I think this is what I want to do full-time, Bev," he says. "When my career as a swimmer is over. I want to be a coach. To children like this."

I squeeze his hand as we whiz by the whitecaps on our right. "I think that would make you very happy."

"But would it make you happy? I don't know where we would have to move or how much it would pay."

"I'm happy if I'm with you, Mark." Lordy, two years ago, I would have spat such sweetness out of my mouth. But now, it was simply the truth.

"It won't be Park Avenue."

"I left Park Avenue. Voluntarily. Remember?" Mark had been unfazed when I told him about the life I'd had up until now. He may have worn a pin-striped suit on that flight where I met him, but he was not one to be buttoned up in one every day.

"Okay. I just don't want you to wake up and be forty years old and have regrets."

"Don't age me just yet, Mark Oakley. I have seventeen more years before I reach that ghastly age."

He looks at me and laughs. "You're going to be fun to grow old with."

"You're going to sleep alone if you use the word *old* where I'm concerned again."

"Aye, aye, Captain."

But I smile. I would happily—well, almost happily—grow old with him.

We check in, and I immediately go to the balcony, just like I do every time I'm in Honolulu. I breathe in those ocean scents and feel a sense of home.

And nausea.

I sit down in the lounge chair.

Mark comes to join me, but then grows concerned.

"You look a little green, my love. Are you feeling okay?"

I shake my head. The mummy's revenge, as I still prefer to call it, was only the beginning. Once that had subsided, I still felt sick to my stomach. All through London. I just never let on to Judy.

"What's wrong? Should I call up a doctor?"

"No. There aren't any medicines that will help me."

"Why would you say that?"

"Because I don't think I'm sick, Mark. I think I'm going to have a baby."

At dinner, Mark watches over me like I'm a delicate porcelain vase. Another thing I would have winced at a couple of years ago. But I find it reassuring now. Our little secret.

I won't tell Judy until I've confirmed it with a doctor. And until she's put in for her transfer to Miami. I don't want her to change her plans for me.

And her plans definitely include Joe Clayton. I look at them across the table, and she is radiating with happiness. I'm happy for her. That mess with her ex-husband was more than any woman should have to deal with.

"How is your room?" I ask them. "Did you get an ocean view?"

Joe clears his throat. "Rooms," he corrects.

I raise an eyebrow. "Even now? It's 1963, you kids."

Look at me. I'm knocked up.

Judy blushes. "After we're married. And Joe agrees."

I shrug my shoulders. "I guess the world still needs some old-fashioned people. Balances everything out."

Judy knows that I just enjoy razzing her. I think the world needs many more Judys and Joes. Which is why I wish they'd hurry up and reproduce. But I know they will soon enough. As soon as that wedding ring hits her finger, they're not going to be able to keep their hands off each other. You can see the steam just brewing between them.

"So what's the plan? After Puerto Rico?" I ask.

Judy looks at Joe and then at me.

"Well, my reinstatement date is official. Joe has the paperwork. So I'll pick up some routes while I wait for the transfer to happen. Hopefully a few more to Hong Kong so I can get some dresses from Mr. Chan. And then some South American or European routes until—until we get married and I can't work for Pan Am any longer."

"Yeah," I respond. "I'm going to call the SFO office tomorrow and get put back on the schedule. As many as they'll give me to replenish all we spent on the trip. Mr. Wall Street might be thawing, according to my mom. But even so, I don't want his money."

Mark steps in and holds up a glass of champagne. We all do the same. "I think the only plans we should be making are to talk about what we're going to do tomorrow."

"Here's to that," says Joe.

We clink our glasses and take sips of the bubbly sweetness.

Joe pulls out a brochure. "I've been looking these over. What do you think?"

After the trip, Joe had to get back to work. Mark was flying up to New York to shoot a shaving-cream commercial. I think his endorsements as an Olympian were going to take better care of us financially than he realized. The man was positively chiseled and looked smashing in a photo. On film? Hot tamale, he'd probably melt the screen.

But our two days in Puerto Rico were ones for the books. Snorkeling, hiking in a rainforest, watching the sunrise on the beach. My nausea stayed at bay after Mark bought me some peppermints. What I really wanted was a cigarette, but I'd read in *Reader's Digest* that smoking might actually be *bad* for you instead of the health stick it had always been purported to be. And I wasn't going to take any chances.

We saw the men off to their respective planes, goodbyes difficult even though we were orienting our lives to be with them. For now, Judy and I were flying from San Juan to Mexico City and on to San Francisco. We hoped there might be openings for some stewardesses. Then it wouldn't just be a free flight. We'd get paid.

The clerk in the Pan Am office looks at the roster and shakes her head. "We're all set for those routes. But we are short for the San Juan to Philadelphia route. Short by two, in fact. A couple of girls called in sick and have to stay in Puerto Rico for a few more days. If you can take that route, we should be able to get you comped on a domestic airline to San Francisco."

Judy and I look at each other. "I'm game," she says. "Then we won't have to go through customs with a Mexico City layover."

"I agree."

The clerk looks up. "The plane does make a quick stop in Baltimore to deboard some passengers. Is that still okay?"

"Baltimore to Philadelphia? That's a puddle jumper. No problem."

Judy gives it the thumbs-up. "How long is the layover in Baltimore?"

The clerk checks her records. "Almost an hour and a half. Looks like they'll also be doing a pilot swap."

"An hour and a half!" Judy says. "I could call Ronelle. It's not too far a drive from Red Lion. I'll bet she'd hop in the car to come see me. It's been so long."

"Aw, Judy, that would be wonderful for you. I'd love to meet her."

"If she's up for it. She's pregnant. Five months along."

"I can promise you," I tell her, "pregnancy would not keep a good friend from seeing you."

I don't tell her that I can say this from experience.

There isn't anything I wouldn't do for Judy.

CHAPTER THIRTY-TWO

Judy

I find a pay phone and call the number that I know by heart.

I don't worry about the party line. If Henry's work schedule is the same as it's always been, he won't be home to listen in.

A man answers. Richard.

"Richard! It's Judy Goodman."

I never did change my last name back to my maiden one. I'll be a Clayton soon enough.

"Judy!" he says. Richard has been a great conspirator in our plan to get me out of Henry's clutches. I don't know him well, but I appreciate him more than I can say.

"Is Ronelle at home? I don't have much time and need to speak with her."

"I'm sorry, Judy. She's at the grocery store. Would you like for me to pass on a message?"

"Yes. Please tell her that I'm going to be at the Baltimore airport for an hour-and-a-half layover before flying on to Philadelphia. We'll land at seven this evening. I know that's a huge inconvenience, especially in her condition. But I wanted her to know I'd be so close. In case there is any way she'd want to come for a visit."

Richard laughs. "I know my wife, Judy. Wild horses couldn't keep her away. And she is the most can-do pregnant lady I've ever known. Tell me your flight information, and I'll write everything down and pass it along to her. No promises. But I'm sure she'll want to."

"Tell her not to come if the roads are slick, though. I heard there might be some rain."

"Just a sprinkle. And we need it."

"Thank you. Thank you for everything, Richard." I'm sure he knows what I mean.

"Judy," he adds, "you did a good thing leaving."

"I know."

Beverly and I borrow uniforms from the office at San Juan, knowing that there are always some stashed for emergencies. Mine is a little loose, and Beverly's is a little snug, but we both pass inspection. I turn in the mirror. It feels good to be back in a Pan Am uniform after all these months away. Better than good.

"Are you going to miss this?" Beverly asks me as we comb our hair.

"Yes and no. I'm looking forward to married life. *Good* married life. But I'll miss the adventure."

"I'm sure Joe will give you plenty of adventure."

"I do hope you mean that in the travel sense, Beverly."

She doubles over and laughs. "I *did*, but you came up with that one all on your own. I'm proud of you, Judy. My work is done here."

I feel myself blushing. "Yes. *Travel-wise*, I'm sure that with Joe's continued employment at Pan Am, we will have all the perks of travel."

She rolls her eyes at me. I guess I've rubbed off on her too. "You're no fun."

"I am who I am."

"And I love you for it."

The flight is uneventful save for some turbulence upon landing. We can see storm clouds in the distance, and I find myself hoping that Ronelle stayed at home after all. This will be more than a sprinkle.

But I'm wrong.

"Ju-deeee!" I hear as I step into the terminal.

"Ronelle!" I run into the arms of my friend. Her bump is noticeable, but not yet large enough to triangulate our embrace. I hold on to her, me clutching her sweater, and her clutching my blazer as we stand like crying fools, passengers scattering around us.

"I've missed you," I say without pulling away.

"I have every one of your postcards hanging up." Ronelle steps back but keeps her hands on my shoulders. "At first, I taped them to the refrigerator, but I ran out of room. So now I string them up and hang them in my living room."

"Richard doesn't mind?"

"I think Richard loves them even more than I do, if that's possible." She laughs. "Every time one arrives, he pulls out the encyclopedia and reads all about the place. And then he makes notes in the book with a pencil about where he wants to take me."

"Aw, that's sweet."

A voice comes over the loudspeaker.

"Paging Miss Goodman. Miss Judy Goodman. Please come to a service counter."

Beverly walks up just then. "What's that about?"

"I don't know. I'll go see."

"Hi, I'm Beverly," I hear her say to Ronelle as I walk away. I like the idea of them knowing each other.

I approach the counter. "I'm Judy Goodman."

"There's a call for you, Miss Goodman. Here you go."

I pick up the receiver.

The caller is breathless. "Judy," he huffs. "It's Richard. I had to warn you. But since Ronelle had the car, I couldn't go myself."

"Warn me about what, Richard?"

"Henry knows. Henry knows where you are. And he's heading your way."

"What? How?"

"After Ronelle left, he rang my doorbell. He had a friend over whose car wouldn't start, and he needed to borrow some jumper cables. He followed me to the garage. And he saw the note. Ronelle had dropped it when she was getting into the car. He saw your name on it. And your flight information. And he ran for his car and took off. I'd bet anything he's heading to Baltimore."

"When was this?"

"Forty minutes ago. It took me that long to get through to the airport. And the way he was screeching out of here, he'll make good time."

I don't know what to say. I feel dizzy. I do not want to see Henry. But what can he do? We're here at an airport with people everywhere. I have to be rational about this.

"Judy?" says Richard.

"I'm here."

"Be careful. That man was angry."

CHAPTER THIRTY-THREE

Beverly

I spot that lowlife before Judy does. It's been over a year since he showed up at our motel in Miami, but his image is burned in my mind.

After she came and told us what Ronelle's husband had warned, we decided to stay in the employee lounge until our flight was boarding. And we sweet-talked—*I* sweet-talked—the male attendant into letting Ronelle come with us too. I left them alone to catch up, though I knew by the sheer paleness of Judy's skin and the tremor in her hands that this wasn't going to be some happy reunion. Ronelle would surely be calming her down. In the meantime, I'm on lookout duty.

I hear him before I see him. He is standing at the same service counter where Judy had taken Richard's call and is demanding to know where she is. I stay some distance behind him and shake my head at the agent. She catches my eye and nods so slightly that I do not think Henry picks up on it. She doesn't know the why. But I know I stand here with some believability in my Pan Am blue.

Henry walks off, clearly angry about not getting the information he wanted.

I follow him as he goes to another counter, and this time, I stand closer. I don't want him to turn around in case he recognizes me, but I do want to make sure that no one tries to help him find her.

Instead of being insistent, though, this time the voice that comes out of him is that of a lamb. Kind and accommodating.

"I'd like a seat on the flight from Baltimore to Philadelphia, please."

I seize up when I realize what he's trying to do. But I don't think he'd succeed. Pan Am only flies international routes. This Baltimore layover is merely a drop-off for passengers from San Juan and a place to switch pilots. It would go against policy to let him on for the short leg.

"I'm sorry, sir," the agent says confidently. "We cannot sell you a seat, as we are not allowed to book domestic routes. FCC rules."

I relax. A little.

"Aw, what a shame," he says docilely. "Look, I know you have to do your job. And you're clearly very good at it. But my mama in Philadelphia is real sick. The family is saying I need to get there fast. And driving might not be fast enough. I heard about this flight, and, gosh, it would mean so much if I can get on it. I can even pay double."

I want to shout *no!* But I don't have proof of anything. I can't keep a reasonable-sounding passenger from making his request. I try to will the agent to refuse him, but she does exactly what she should and says that she will call her supervisor.

I watch her blush as Henry talks to her, and I understand the charisma that initially attracted Judy. He can clearly turn on the charm when there is something he wants.

I hear thunder in the distance, even over the buzz around the airport. But the skies look clear even as dusk sets in. So there is probably no hope that the flight will be canceled.

That would have been the perfect solution. I could have gotten Judy out of the airport and driven somewhere—anywhere—until we could get her on a flight as far away from here as possible.

The clerk hangs up the telephone, and I wince as she says what I had expected. "I have good news for you, sir. Given your circumstance, we can accommodate you. You will just need to pay the rate as if you had flown from San Juan because I have to write up the paperwork that way."

"Thank you. What a relief. That sounds perfect."

He takes out a checkbook, and she prints up a ticket.

No, no, no, I think. I've got to do something.

"There you go. Flight two-one-four. It departs at eight twenty-four at gate seventeen and will start boarding shortly before that." She checks her wristwatch. "That's actually very soon. I would head to the gate now."

Boarding! I have to keep Judy from getting on the plane, but surely she is going to hear the announcement in the Pan Am offices to come to the gate since the stewardesses have to be on board before the passengers. This gives me ten minutes. At most.

I race back to the employee lounge. I try to get Judy's attention, but her back is to me. Maybe that's even better—I need an ally.

I wave instead to Ronelle, gesturing as well as I can that I need to speak to her without Judy knowing. She nods and says something to Judy.

Judy does not turn around.

Thank goodness.

When Ronelle approaches, I pull her behind a pillar out of anyone's view and catch her up.

"I don't think she should be on that airplane with him," I say after telling her what he's up to. "It's bad enough here in the airport, but in that confined space, who knows what he's capable of?"

"I agree," she says in a determined tone. Ready for action. "What do we do?"

No wonder Ronelle is so important to Judy. She's clearly fierce.

I tap my foot while I'm thinking and then come up with an answer. "Tell her that the flight is canceled due to the weather. And tell her quickly before they make the crew announcements. Tell her that I found out and ran ahead to secure a hotel reservation, and that I want her to meet me there."

"And if she asks about Henry?"

"Say that he won't know to look for her in the hotel and that it's her best chance to hide from him."

"So we'll see you at the hotel?"

I shake my head. "No. I'm getting on that flight."

"Why?" She puts her hand on my arm.

"Because I'm going to keep an eye on him. And I'll spend the flight thinking about what to tell him to get him to finally leave her alone. I don't know what yet."

"Are you sure?"

"Yes. Plus, we can't have two stewardesses missing. They'll have to cancel the flight for real. And that's not fair to all the people who are ticketed and need to get home."

"Won't Judy get in trouble for missing it?"

"I'll tell the office that she started vomiting and has a fever. They won't want her on the flight in that case. And that will protect her from any repercussions."

Ronelle puts her arms around her belly, a gesture I've noticed in expectant mothers. I think of my own little child, so very new. Maybe it's the instinct of a mother that is causing me to act so insistently. But I don't think so. I would have looked out for Judy regardless.

"You're a quick thinker, Beverly. I hope we'll get a chance to become friends after all this."

"Years of thwarting the nuns in school. I'm glad I can finally put it to some good use."

She runs back to the employee lounge, and my heart beats hard with every second that passes on my watch.

I hope she gets to her in time.

I hope Judy listens.

I close the cabin door as soon as the captain allows it, and I begin to relax. Ronelle must have been convincing. Judy didn't make it on the flight.

My heartbeat slows. I hadn't realized how much it had been racing.

I kept myself hidden from Henry as everyone boarded, busying myself with other passengers' luggage and comforts. He's seated in the rear of the plane, near the bathrooms. Fitting place for him. I watch him from behind a curtain. His head is popping up and down, swiveling back and forth as he tries to see where Judy is. Maybe he'll assume that she's working up here in first class. Maybe that will make it an uneventful flight as he resigns himself to seeing her when we land.

I hope and pray he doesn't try to cause a scene.

But then, that wouldn't be his way. He saved that for behind closed doors. Saved it for her.

The flight time will be only forty-five minutes. I don't get to go on many of these, but I love them when I do. You hit the cruising altitude and almost immediately begin the landing process.

I sink into my jump seat and close my eyes.

Lordy, I am tired. And not just from the baby. That little cherry is the cherry on top of several whirlwind weeks. Good weeks. But exhausting ones.

I feel the plane level out, and I'm glad that it's brief because this is the point where I'd usually have to begin beverage service. Until someone hits the call button, I can stay hidden in this seat behind the curtain and have a few minutes of peace.

Before long, I feel the slow pressure change that indicates we are going to start our descent. I am called into the cockpit.

"Yes, Captain?" I say. It's always strange to not know any of the flight crew. There's rarely a route in which I don't know at least one person working, but the East Coast is not my normal territory.

"Air traffic control is reporting a line of thunderstorms surrounding the airport. They've given us the choice to continue on but with almost certain turbulence. Or to stay in a holding pattern for half an hour. Five other planes in the area are choosing the holding pattern, so we're going to do the same. I'll make an announcement, but please inform the crew to be attentive to anything the passengers may need."

"I will, sir. Should we hand out snacks?"

"No. I don't want anyone out of their seats, flight crew included. We may still get some bumps."

"Okay. And may I get you anything?"

"Some coffee and some prayers."

"That bad, sir?"

"It's not pretty out there."

I head to the galley and pour the captain's coffee, but the plane lurches, and I spill it all over myself. I don't have a spare uniform, but I at least make him another cup. I lean against the counter to hold my balance and finally manage to pour enough to make it worth going back to the cockpit.

I pull the door open just in time to see an intense bolt of lightning not far in front of us.

My hands shake as I hand him the coffee, but both pilots are scrambling to steady the plane and pay no attention to me. I pull down the cockpit's jump seat and my hand shakes as I try unsuccessfully to buckle in.

The coffee spills again.

Just then, the captain shouts to the radio tower, "Mayday, Mayday, Mayday. Clipper two fourteen out of control. Here we go."

Everything is bright.

And then everything is dark.

A Pan American World Airways, Inc. Boeing 707-121, N709PA, Flight 214, crashed at 2059 e.s.t., December 8, 1963, near Elkton, Maryland.

Flight 214 was in a holding pattern awaiting an instrument approach to the Philadelphia International Airport when it was struck by lightning. Immediately thereafter, the aircraft was observed to be on fire. A large portion of the left wing separated in flight and the aircraft crashed in flames approximately ten nautical miles southwest of the New Castle, Delaware, VOR. All persons aboard, 73 passengers and eight crew members, perished in the crash and the aircraft was destroyed.

The Board determines the probable cause of this accident was lightning-induced ignition of the fuel/air mixture in the No. 1 reserve fuel tank with resultant explosive disintegration of the left outer wing and loss of control.

—Civil Aeronautics Board Aircraft Accident Report, February 25, 1965

Judy

Mo'orea, French Polynesia
Today

If I hadn't married Henry, you wouldn't have sacrificed yourself for me like that.

But Joe and Ronelle pointed out that if it wasn't for Henry, I would have been on that flight with you, as planned. And then we would have both been lost.

I didn't want to hear it from them then. Logic is not an effective cure for grief. But time did illuminate the truth of what they were saying.

When I married Joe a few months later, I knew that I wouldn't be there if it wasn't for you.

When I held our first child, and then our second, and then our third and fourth, I knew that they wouldn't exist if it wasn't for you.

And in each grandchild, I'd think the same. All of them are here because of you, and there is not a day that I don't remember it.

But there's more. Two years after we lost you, Pan American started flying troops and refugees out of Vietnam. We did not have any children yet, and I felt a strong pull toward serving.

We got a marriage waiver with the airline so that I could sign up for these hazard routes. The friends we made in Florida didn't want me to go—these were dangerous missions, and we were indeed shot at on many occasions. Nor could they understand why I was eager to get back in the air after what happened to you.

But Joe knew that I would not make peace with your loss until I could justify my own survival. Joe knew that a Pan American heart was one that did not cower behind fear.

Those flights saved lives—lives that would have been lost without Pan Am. And I wouldn't have been there to help if not for you.

There was other good to come from it. Your parents, for example. Some tragedies tear a couple apart. It brought your parents closer together. Joe and the children and I saw them frequently over the years. They often took cruises out of Fort Lauderdale, and we would drive up to meet them for dinner. Can you imagine that? Mr. Wall Street taking off for weeks at a time to spend it with his wife?

You did that.

Mark was bereft. There is no way around that. It threw him into training even more intensely. That's probably what earned him the silver medal in Tokyo. I watched on television as he took the stand. He kissed his medal and held it up to the sky. I'm sure that was for you. He did go on and help young swimmers as he'd planned. And years later, he married a sweet girl from Georgia who was a volunteer for the organization. It was clear that he cared for her. But she never replaced you.

No one ever could.

The world will never know what you and the other souls on board would have contributed had they not all been taken so soon. But I know, at least, what the world lost when we lost you.

When we're young, we cling so hard, my dearest, to this earth. With everything we've got. Because we think it's all we have. But loss gravitates us toward the eternal as it looks for meaning. You led a life with tremendous meaning. You left a legacy. And that's the best we can hope for during our brief time here, isn't it? I know this as my own bones fail me. I will soon be with the angels, as we would say. And with you. And my Joe. I have tried to live a life that honored what you did, and I think I have succeeded.

For that is what we should live for. That is what we die for.

Love.

And I have known it so very well.

AUTHOR'S NOTE

Many of my family members have been involved in aviation, and I love all things related to airplanes. One of my favorite places is San Diego because you can get so, so close to the runway. I get a thrill out of seeing the details of the landing gear as planes approach the runway. And my favorite sound is that of an afterburner at a military air show. I feel alive when the thundering sound reverberates in my heart. Aviation runs in my veins.

But I don't like to *actually* fly.

I'm a much better spectator.

So I have always been in awe of the men and women who do the important and risky work of serving as flight attendants. It takes a special kind of person who is both flexible and disciplined, adventurous and organized, fearless and safety conscious.

In the 1960s, the profession was almost all made up of women, and it was a glamorous alternative to the limited career choices at the time. Given that and my passion for travel (even if I have to fly to get there), this seemed a natural subject for me to explore.

I didn't realize as I embarked on it how very ambitious a task it would be. There were *so many* fascinating eras for Pan Am—from its start as a mail carrier in Key West to chartered flights to Mecca to Vietnam War troop carriers. I could have chosen from thousands and thousands of stories. Add to that the completely global nature of it—there was almost no corner of the world to which Pan Am didn't fly—I knew that I had to narrow the scope in both time and geography.

I always knew that the title would be *Come Fly with Me*. I'm a huge Frank Sinatra fan, and I imagined what it would feel like to be a young woman when his album came out and he sang about all sorts of exotic places I'd want to visit. That set the tone for the time period. Then, I had to pick a location. There is an abundance of historical fiction set in Europe, but much less in the Pacific islands. The first time I got to go to a beach, I was thirty years old. And it was in Maui. Quite a place to start! We've been there almost every year since visiting my husband's family and even recently took a monthlong cruise that expanded my horizons to the islands of Oahu, Kauai, the Big Island, Bora Bora, Tahiti, and Mo'orea. In fact, I wrote the very first words of this book—the first scene in Mo'orea—on that island. I was inspired, but paperless and penless. A kind stranger lent me a pen and I pulled my recently purchased bottle of lychee liquor from its paper bag and wrote that prologue on the spot.

I still have the bag.

Regarding research, a good deal of what I've written is an amalgamation of the experiences of flight attendants at the time. I read training manuals and menus and in-flight magazines and brochures. Occasionally, I had to fudge a route or a date or other detail to make it fit the story. For example, I set a 1962 scene at the Taj Mahal in Miami, even though it wasn't completed until 1963. And I set a route to Tahiti in 1963 even though it didn't start until 1964. Also worth noting is that Frank Sinatra's famous performance at the Royal Festival Hall happened in 1962, not 1963 as I have it set. Nor was *Come Fly with Me* on his set list. But, hey, I had to include it! Aside from those tweaks, everything at that event was as I described it.

Incidentally, the word *stewardess* has long been a retired one in favor of the more progressive *flight attendant*. However, as I like to be historically accurate, I have used *stewardess* throughout the book since that's what was most commonly said at the time. And I was told by most of the stewardesses whom I interviewed that it is their preferred title.

Something else that they appreciated is that I did not write a "mattress romp" because they felt that it wouldn't have accurately represented the classiness of Pan Am that they valued in their years there. This is not to say that there were not romances and intrigues between crew and pilots and passengers. But the women were unanimous in saying that the oft-married pilots were more father figures than bed partners. And that romances between flight attendants and passengers often ended in marriage.

This did change in later years, and the profession of stewardess became highly sexualized, especially with domestic airlines that did not need to worry about their international image. But for my time period, I relied on the accounts of the women I interviewed, all of whom held their excellent reputations—and that of their beloved airline—in high regard.

I would like to note that Beverly's illness in Egypt from drinking hibiscus juice at a perfume shop is straight out of my own experience when I was twenty years old. I was so eager for the cultural experience in Cairo that I dismissed all warnings and paid the price. Little did I know it would be good novel fodder decades later! I also spent the night at Sacré-Cœur in Paris and consider it one of the most amazing and peaceful experiences of my life.

Travel is a great educator. But more so are books. I'm thankful to the many historical-fiction authors who have transported me to other times and places all my life, and I am grateful for the opportunity to contribute to the genre.

And finally, if you are someone who reads the end before the beginning, please avert your eyes, because the next sentence is a spoiler.

The crash at the end of the book was a real one, and all details of it are true.

If you or someone you know is experiencing domestic violence, please contact the National Domestic Violence Hotline at 800-799-7233.

ACKNOWLEDGMENTS

This book has been in my heart for many years. But it didn't take flight (pun kind of intended!) until I connected with Nancy Gillespie of World Wings International. WWI is a philanthropic group of former Pan Am stewardesses and stewards who continue the globally minded mission of the airline to this day. Nancy was invaluable in making resources available to me, the most treasured of which were the conversations I got to have with women who had been Pan Am stewardesses in the era in which I was writing: Sue Swanson, Pat Smith, Barbara Sharfstein, Pam Taylor, Fleur Lawrence, and Susan Denness. Their stories were riveting, and many of them—especially my favorites—the galley details—made it into the book. But more than that, the women embodied the elegance and class that I wanted to bring forth in the book. What did not make it into the book were the many celebrity stories they told me. So I will keep those to myself to protect the innocent and not-so-innocent. But I sure had fun listening to them!

Thank you, too, to the many World Wings women who reached out to share their stories. It was a happy avalanche of information and generosity, and I'm sorry that I could not visit with each and every one of you.

I am also grateful to World Wings for awarding me with a grant with which I was able to visit the extensive Pan Am collection at the Richter Library at the University of Miami. It was a miracle to whittle the resources down to twenty-five boxes out of the thousands that they preserve. I enjoyed the archival research with my daughter Claire as we laser-focused on items and documents that were pertinent to the book's time period and locations. (How fun it would be to peruse the whole collection—I could write a whole series of books about this magnificent airline!) Big thanks to Jay Sylvestre, Nicole Hellman-McFarland, and Ivette Uria of Richter for all their help.

I also appreciate the assistance of Linda Reynolds at the Pan Am Museum Foundation who helped me with additional resources.

It was a joy to speak at the World Wings convention in Scottsdale and meet more of the Pan Am family, several of whom were particularly memorable to me: Wendy Knecht, Patty Boyce Iassogna, Kathy Boyce Johnson, Dian Groh, Phillip Keene, as well as Stacy Beck with Pan Am branding.

Danielle Marshall of Lake Union Publishing took a chance on me ten years ago, so it is fitting to return to the Lake Union family with *Come Fly with Me*. She has been a champion and a friend from the start, and she sacrificed a significant amount of sleep to meet me one Nashville morning to take this to the finish line. She is a mother hen in all the very best ways, and I'm happy to be one of her chicks. Thank you, too, to the many people at Lake Union who had a hand in this—copyeditors, proofreaders, the author team, etc.

I am beyond grateful to continue to work with my agent, Jill Marsal of Marsal Lyon Literary Agency. She gave me my start and has been an excellent mentor and sounding board ever since. I always appreciate her honesty and encouragement, and I can't think of a better person to have in my corner.

I am thankful to my editor of several previous books, Tiffany Yates Martin, for her early insights and enthusiasm. And it was such a gift to work with Jenna Free on the developmental edits. I do so hope we will work together on future books!

Not for the first time, beta readers Marisa Gothie and Nicholle Thery-Williams have bolstered me through my doubts and proven that real friendships can start on social media. They were major contributors to the book-club questions, and I am so grateful for their insights.

Speaking of friendships, there are so many to name, but a few in the book world have continued to be particularly vital and dear to me. So I thank you, ladies, for the generosity of your love: Rochelle Weinstein, Dete Meserve, Joy Jordan-Lake, Suzi Leopold, Heather Webb, Fiona Davis, Jen Sherman, and Angelique L'Amour.

Locally, I am so grateful to have a writing community that is new but mighty! Since my last book, I have come to know and treasure: Kelsey Zhang, Gabby Lynch, Lisa Granger, Janet Belvin, Brian Forrester, Molly Farinholt, Catherine White, ML Brei, Gina Donohue, Mary Clemens, Frankie Gorrell, and everyone in the Williamsburg Library Writer's Group. No matter where you are in your writing journey, we are in it together.

Dave and Heather Clemens are also treasures who have been a joy to work with.

My life has been tremendously enriched through ministry work the past few years with these amazing people whose dedication and support has meant more to me than perhaps anything else I've ever been a part of: Mary Clare Sabol, Karen Tompkins, Felicia Anderson, Karen Brown, Christine Koenig, Stephanie Forbes, Joy and Buddy Ellis, Sarah and Ben Knight, Erin and Michael Brooks, Lindsay Lilly, Nan and Jim Beckert, Rene Sykes, Marcia Nelson, Bobbi Metzgar, Michele Rauchwarg, Heidi Meadows, Sheila Lancour, Nicole Lancour, Fr. Anthony Ferguson, Les Kayanan, Bob and Norma Hover, Janet Dupont, Heather Walters, Beth Walton, and Regina Yitbarek.

I have also felt so loved and supported by these friends in such special ways: Susan Schlimme, Joyce Hoggard, Camille Malucci, Yvonne Fazzino, Heather Sowers, Frank and Lark Smith, Ken and Shirley Masoner, Valerie Jerome, Ashley Peebles, and Nicole La Pera.

I am thankful for my enthusiastic readers who patiently waited through various years of me sending teasers about *Come Fly with Me*. Several life storms collided and put my writing on hold for a while, and

I am grateful to be welcomed back with such open arms. My favorite thing about being a writer is knowing this beautiful community.

To my family: In this book and through previous ones, I think I have finally squeezed in the names of all of your pets. In *Come Fly with Me*, we met: Eve Kiwi, Touka, Vanya, Lyla, Murphy, and Pickle. You guys are killing me with these names. Please pick easier ones in the future! Mom—if you get another pet someday, you should name it Sinatra. I dare you.

My siblings had cameos too. My brother, Paul, got a mention as a pilot heading out on a date with a stewardess. Given that he is actually a really dedicated husband and father, this gave him a moment of alter ego. My sister, Catherine, got to be a nun. (Though she is also the real-life baby almost born at midnight Mass.) So—two cameos for you!

I was telling someone recently that I am close to all my children and I am well aware of what a tremendous gift this is. Along with my husband of twenty-seven years, I call them all my "five favorite people," and indeed they are. So—big love and appreciation for Rob, Claire, Gina, Teresa, and Vincent. I love you to the moon and back. You are very kind with giving me space and support to do this.

And last . . . but actually first . . . I am grateful to God for all His blessings, His lessons, and most of all, His love.

BOOK CLUB QUESTIONS

1. This book takes place in what is often called the Golden Age of Air Travel. How does the experience of air travel, as depicted in this novel, contrast with our own experiences of flying today?
2. From the novel: "We are still caught in the shackles of a culture that limits our choices to teachers, nurses, or mothers, though there are cracks in that thinking that widen every day." What differences did you notice in career or lifestyle expectations for a young woman then versus now?
3. All of us have or had a mother or a mother figure in our life, and some of us are mothers ourselves. How does the biological or social role of "mother" inhibit the child from ever seeing that mother or mother figure as a person with their own hopes, dreams, and experiences?
4. From the book, "East and west are more than points on a compass. They shape the day depending on where you are in the world." Sometimes there is a fine line between flying toward something or flying from something. Which characters do you think were flying toward something and which were flying from something?
5. How has this novel altered your view of the function of flight attendants?

6. Throughout this book there is the theme of friendship between women. Friendships in this story are formed from shared adversity and shared experiences. What role do these friendships play in the lives and choices of the characters as the book progresses?
7. Many people look to the past as "the good old days," but how "good" these days were often depends on your race, gender, or class. What echoes of the societal structures and assumptions depicted in this book are still with us, and which have been altered?
8. The past has often been called a foreign country, and this book takes place in the past. Thinking from our own time as readers, how is the era its own character in the book?
9. *Come Fly with Me* is both the title of the book and a song title. What influence does this title have on the story arc? Frank Sinatra lists these places in the song: Hawaii, New York, Paris, Capri, London, Vermont, Mandalay, and Chicago. Which places have you visited, or do you want to visit these places?
10. The novel speaks of the bruises and scars of life that are both visible and metaphoric. How does this concept of "covering up" affect the story arc?
11. The paternal relationships of the two main characters in the novel are vastly different. How do these relationships influence the paths of their lives?

ABOUT THE AUTHOR

Photo © 2015 Gina Di Maio

Camille Di Maio is the bestselling author of *Until We Meet*, *The First Emma*, *The Beautiful Strangers*, *The Way of Beauty*, *Before the Rain Falls*, and *The Memory of Us*. In addition to writing women's fiction, Camille buys too many baked goods at farmers markets, unashamedly belts out Broadway tunes when the mood strikes, and regularly faces her fear of flying to indulge in her passion for travel. She and her husband have worked in real estate for twenty-five years in both Texas and Virginia. Together, they have four children—almost all grown—as well as a large German shepherd who thinks she's a lapdog.

Made in the USA
Las Vegas, NV
03 March 2025